A Forgotten Promise

Merged Series

Maxine Henri

www.maxinehenri.com

Cover designed by Sweet 'N Spicy Designs

Edited by Indie Editing Chick

This book is a work of fiction. The characters, incidents and dialogue are drawn from the author's imagination and are not to be construed as real. Any resemblance to actual events or persons, living or dead is fictionalized or coincidental.

ISBN: 978-80-69048-05-8

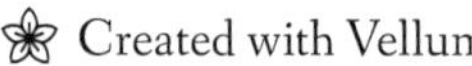

For all you, ladies, who might be lost at times.
Embrace your inner Goddess.

Prologue

Saar

Fifteen years old

"Saar, I heard Corm Quinn is going to ask you to the school dance," Arielle says.

Heat rises to my cheeks, and my pulse quickens.

"Don't be ridiculous," I pretend-scoff, while my entire body shakes with the possibility.

"You should let him know you're interested. Boys like him like confident girls," Arielle chirps as we walk across the schoolyard.

"I doubt he doesn't have a date yet." I act bored, uninterested. Like my eyes are *not* searching for him among the groups of students.

"But is his date as hot as you?" She pokes my ribs.

I stop. *Not this again.* "What are you talking about?"

She looks at me, deadpanned.

A few weeks back, a modeling scout gave me his business card when we wandered around a mall. The card has driven a wedge between us.

Arielle didn't even pretend to be happy for me, riddled with jealousy.

She's been teasing me about it relentlessly. And I didn't call the number because I didn't want her to feel less. To feel unseen. To feel not enough.

In a world where my parents either demand from me or forget I exist, and my brothers treat me like an annoying insect, my best friend has been my harbor, my reason, my home.

But the bitter aftertaste from the mall-outing afternoon has been lingering between us.

The bell interrupts our conversation, and we run to the class.

Corm Quinn? The 'most popular boy in my high school and three years my senior' Corm Quinn? A boy with dark blond hair and silver eyes who is so hot, all the girls fan themselves when he enters the room.

Me and him at the dance?

As unlikely as that is, Arielle has planted the seed.

For several days, the gullible me suddenly starts

noticing—or more like fantasizing about—his eyes holding mine a bit longer in the cafeteria.

Him hanging behind when his soccer game finished, right as my running practice was about to start. The almost-smile he sent in my direction when we ran into each other in front of the labs.

Only it wasn't me his eyes were searching for. It wasn't me the smile was for. It wasn't me he stayed behind for.

"I already have a date. Arielle asked me, but save me a dance." Corm winks at me before he joins his friends.

My stomach churns as I watch them leave. Before they turn the corner, he looks back and smiles. I desperately want to see regret on his gorgeous face, but he doesn't seem sorry, his smile a pure flirt.

Why would he be sorry, you idiot? He doesn't know he just crushed you and humiliated you. Because it wasn't really Corm who stabbed me in the back.

My best friend did.

The tiny blood droplets seep into the white rug. The glass shards reflect light in a kaleidoscope of colors, striking the mess on the floor, almost making it beautiful.

I stretch my limbs over the cold, hard tiles of my bathroom and clutch my cut hand to my chest.

The red sweats into my white T-shirt now. For such a minor cut, the blood loss should concern me.

But I'm not concerned about it. My heart aches with the betrayal. Arielle has been my friend since we were six years old.

She was. Until today.

I turn to my side. My bones meet with the unyielding firmness of the marble. The coldness wraps around me, penetrating.

I grip my wrist and run my thumb over the cut, the warmth of my blood almost comforting on the uncomfortable floor.

The cut is on the ball of my palm. Just above my wrist. Jesus, how would this look like if someone came in?

Perhaps they would think I tried... Would they, though? *Clumsy as usual...* I can almost hear my mother's voice in my head.

Fuck them. Fuck them all. Especially Arielle.

"Saar?"

My brother's voice startles me, but I don't move. It feels like an impossible mission. Lying here, away from the world, is uncomfortably comforting.

Being alone is what I know. It might not be

welcomed, but it's familiar. And now, with Arielle out of the picture, it's my destiny.

I trusted her.

I stupidly trusted her.

A knock on the door makes me turn my head. "Saar, are you there? Mom is pissed, and looking for you," Finn says.

Shit, I promised to accompany Mother to some fundraiser. Or rather, she ordered me to join her. I'm sure it's because one of her friend's daughters was coming. Nobody outshines Melody van den Linden.

Forgetting about the cut, I push up to sit and whimper.

"Saar? What's going on—" Finn barges in and freezes. "Fuck." He drops to his knees, grabbing my hand.

"Ouch." I pull it away from him.

"What have you done, Bambi?"

He looks from my hand to the shards, and I know what he must be thinking, but the lump in my throat is too thick to talk. I don't even berate him for the stupid nickname.

His eyes pierce through me. Questioning? Pitying? Worrying? Or all of the above, but for the first time in my life, it feels like he sees me. Like he sees my pain. Like he cares.

His attention coils around my ribs, squeezing at my

heart. The lump in my throat grows painfully. And in the absence of my best—former—friend, it sets me off, and I let out a sob.

Finn quickly inspects my hand and then the rest of my body. "What happened?"

No longer the accusatory *what have you done*, but rather a concerned *what happened*. Another sob shudders through me as he lifts me and sits me on the edge of the tub.

He rinses my hand and wraps it in a hand towel. He scoops me up again and carries me out.

"I'll take care of the mess," he says, his eyes darting to the no-longer-white rug. "Are you okay, Saar?"

And there it is again, a genuine concern. He even omits his stupid nickname and uses my real name—something he hasn't done in ages.

It all swirls inside me, and the dam breaks. I bawl, burying my head in the crook of his neck.

I try to talk, but among the sobs, I hardly make any sense. "A dance... I shouldn't have... I believed her... Corm... and now..." Even I don't understand my incoherent word vomit.

"Corm? Cormac Quinn? What the fuck did he do to you?"

That's what he got from it? I need to explain, but just the mere mention of Corm's name causes another wave of tears.

I let Finn carry me to my bed. He stays by my side until I fall asleep. And all the heartache and tears make me fall asleep before I explain it's not Corm who is the villain in this pathetic story.

* * *

"I think we should tell Dad," Cal whispers.

"Do you want them to lock her in some institution?" Finn argues.

That makes me snap my eyes open.

My brothers stand side by side, looking out of the window, their backs to me. Their legs apart, their hands in their pockets. They ooze confidence. Will I ever be like them?

They have been taking turns sitting by my side and plotting Corm Quinn's demise for two days.

I have never corrected Finn's assumptions. I haven't told him the glass broke because it slipped from my hand. I haven't told him Arielle is to blame for my pain.

I haven't corrected his assumptions because I'd lose their attention. The minute they would find out the truth, they would shake their heads and leave. And I really don't want to be alone.

Not yet.

The wound is still too raw. Not the one on my

palm that looks like an insignificant scratch now. The one in my heart, though?

Arielle told me to be brave, to be assertive, and ask for what I want. And I did. Confident like a Van den Linden. Like my brothers.

"Don't tell Dad." My voice is raspy.

My brothers turn in unison.

"Bambi, you're up. How are you feeling?" Finn comes over and ruffles my hair.

"I just want to be alone."

"What did that asshole do to you?" Cal snaps.

"Shut up," Finn berates him, but his eyes search mine, hoping for some answers. But he doesn't press. And I'm grateful for that.

"I don't want to talk about it."

It's true, I don't want to talk about it. I don't want to relive it. I know they would roll their eyes. I don't want to be the pathetic girl.

"Do you want to play GTA?" Cal asks.

My eyes widen. They have never let me play with them. "Really?"

"Only if you promise to go back to school on Monday. If you hide here any longer, Dad will find out," Finn says.

I nod, and Cal whisks me out of the bed, throwing me over his shoulder, drawing a laugh from me. It feels good to laugh.

* * *

I don't go to school for another week, faking sickness. I'm not ready to deal with Arielle. Or anyone else. Not that anyone else knows about her betrayal, but I feel like it's written all over my face.

Like it's commemorated by the faint scar on my palm.

I should have gone to school the day after Finn found me. It would have been easier. But with each passing day, my overreaction becomes more and more obvious to me.

Arielle must know she hurt me badly by now, and since I didn't face her right away, it's getting harder and harder now. How did I let things spiral like this?

At least my parents are too busy to notice. But that illusion tumbles when Mother floats into my room, her dress billowing behind her.

"We found you a perfect school in Switzerland." Her facial muscles are frozen, but I think there is a sparkle in her eyes.

She must have had her Botox injection earlier today. Are her eyes smiling?

Does sending me away bring her joy?

I swing my legs over the edge of my bed and sit up. "You want me to go to Switzerland?"

She huffs, hiking her shoulders, like explaining

herself is annoying. “Well, it would be best under the circumstances.”

“Under the circumstances?” I parrot.

She rolls her eyes, which looks scary and comedic, given the rest of her face isn’t moving.

“Saar, don’t you think for a moment that I don’t know what’s going on in this house. You’re clearly unstable.”

She shivers like the word caused her indigestion. Or maybe it’s the idea of a daughter who, instead of attending a fundraiser, cried in her room.

And if she, like my brothers, assumed the broken glass wasn’t an accident, why hasn’t she come to check on me?

Is sending me away from home her way of showing she cares?

I hate the tears that brim around the crevices of my eyes. Van den Lindens don’t show weakness. Perhaps that’s why she’s sending me away.

“Okay.” I swallow. “Do I finish the school year here?”

“Your father thinks it’s best you move now.” She turns on her heels but pauses at my door. “It’s for your own good.”

For my own good.

Her placating parting words shouldn’t make me feel better, but they do. Even though I know Melody van den Linden is only concerned about her reputation, somehow, I cling to those words, telling myself she cares about me.

And somehow, on the long flight to Switzerland, I make myself believe they sent me away for a better education, and I vow to never cry.

Not because of a backstabbing friend. Not for a boy who probably has no idea he hurt me. Not because I'm alone.

Somehow, I blend into a routine similar to the one I had back home. Somehow, it's easier to be this new, confident person around people who don't know me.

Somehow, I become the popular girl because my brothers come to visit me, and their brief presence on the campus draws all the girls into my orbit.

I ignore the fact they want me for my hot siblings. I don't want to get too close to them anyway.

But somehow, their friendly pretense helps me rebuild my confidence. Funny how people's attention, even under false motivation, can make you feel invincible.

Enough to finally call the modeling scout.

Chapter 1

Corm

"What else do I have today?" I throw my jacket on the bed and start undressing.

My assistant sighs and turns around. He's been complaining about the lack of boundaries. He hasn't been complaining about the paycheck. And since I sign the paycheck, I set the boundaries.

Sometimes, I just enjoy messing with him. It's not like I need to take a shower in the middle of the day.

"Saar van den Linden is coming," he says.

I pause. Maybe I need the shower after all. "What does she need again?"

He flips through his notebook. "She didn't want to say, but you agreed to meet her, regardless."

It's obvious he doesn't remember why she is coming, or he forgot to ask, but after spending my morning and early afternoon on conference calls, her visit might be fun.

The woman's face and body are on display on billboards and posters all around the world. She is stunning.

I'm intrigued by her interest in me. I'm prepared to return it tenfold if she grabs my interest.

Unfortunately, most women can't keep my interest for too long. When the initial physical attraction runs its course, it just becomes a dull transaction.

"Okay, I'll have a quick shower. She can wait a moment."

After I let the hot water beat down on my muscles, I wrap a fluffy white towel around me. I enjoy having a suite at the Aman Hotel. Their facilities and services are state-of-the-art.

Their business boardrooms are perfect for my needs, and having a bedroom a few floors above is a good perk. Sometimes, I don't even bother going down to the boardroom.

I purchased a house two months ago, but even at almost thirty, I'm not ready to leave this lifestyle yet. Perhaps ever.

I bought the house to appease my parents. To get Dad off my case.

Ever since his condition started deteriorating, he's been preaching about not wasting my life.

From my perspective, I'm living it to the fullest, not wasting time, because what his diagnosis taught me is that life is too short.

Maybe I'll rent the house. It's huge for one person, anyway. When I'm not out or traveling for business, even this room feels like the loneliest place in the world. I can't even imagine how a house would feel.

The movement behind the frosted glass of the double door suggests my visitor has already arrived.

Hastily, I open my wardrobe. I shouldn't keep her waiting. Why bother with clothes for this visit, anyway?

Sliding the door open, I drawl, "Saar van den Linden, what a pleasant surprise."

She whips around, smiling. It's a smile I know well. I won't pretend I didn't admire her pictures before. I mean, I'm just a man.

She takes me in, and her smile fades as she blinks. Fuck, she is more beautiful in real life.

Curls of dark blond hair frame her face. It's not the traditionally beautiful face. She has a sharp nose and cheekbones, almost masculine features. But somehow, they create an allure that draws me in.

Having dated models before, even famous ones, I shouldn't feel this impacted by her.

And yet, she has this contradictory energy around

her—confidence and vulnerability. She's holding her chin high, but she's fidgeting with her fingers.

And she is ogling me with wide eyes, raking her gaze down my torso. She seems half-surprised that I'm wearing only a towel, and half-attracted to what she sees.

I smirk, letting her admire until she catches herself, a pink hue rising to her cheeks. God, she's adorable.

"Why are you naked?" she blurts out, flustered.

"I was running late for our meeting, so I thought I'd better find out why you are here." I hold her gaze.

Her eyes twitch, and I can almost feel her need to look away. She fists her hands but perseveres, glowering.

"That doesn't explain your lack of clothes."

I keep her imprisoned in my gaze. I enjoy seeing her squirm, but I admire the fact that she doesn't surrender to the uncomfortable feeling.

Women don't even try to resist me—my charm or my demands. Not that I complain. But this woman is fighting with herself; I can see the war behind her eyes, and fuck, that's refreshing.

"I just thought that we might move to your reason for this visit rather fast, and then the clothes will come off anyway." I lean against the door frame, crossing one ankle over the other.

Her eyes widen. "You think I'm your booty call?"

I keep holding her gaze, trying to read her. Her eyes narrow slightly, lips pressing together—she's clearly exasperated. But she's not walking away.

Even if she came for a completely different reason —and I can't fathom what that would be—she is still here. Raking her gaze over my pecs.

"Aren't you?"

"That's preposterous. Why would I call your office if I wanted to fuck you? Why did you agree to the meeting in the first place?"

Okay, I don't know what the game is, but I'm half-entertained and half-annoyed now. "Because you're very attractive." I smile, and she flinches. She fucking flinches.

"I told your assistant I want to talk about your Hudson River property." She throws her arms up.

I guess said assistant just lost his bonus.

"I'll be right back," I snap and return to the bedroom, shutting the doors with such force that they bounce back.

What the fuck? She wants to talk business? Why? What's the significance of the Hudson River property?

That building is prime real estate, but it cost me only a headache.

A headache that started when I lost the designer, courtesy of Finn van den Linden, Saar's brother. He threw a tantrum when I wanted to hire his girlfriend.

Whatever that was about, I don't know. Dude hates me for some reason. But how does it tie up with the supermodel in the next room?

I yank a shirt from a hanger, find my underwear, and almost grab my jeans. Fuck that, she came to talk business, she will get a businessman. Why am I even so upset about it?

I put on a three-piece suit with a tie and return to the room.

She hasn't moved from her spot by the window, and I'm struck for the second time by her presence.

Physical beauty aside, the air of fragility around her doesn't quite match the determination in her eyes.

A pretend determination. Based on her fist clenching, the sheen of perspiration around her hairline, and her labored breath—that she's trying to hide—she is even more nervous than before.

And for some outlandish reason, that intrigues me.

"Well, Saar, have a seat, and tell me, to what do I owe the pleasure?" I flick my wrist and glance at my watch. "You have five minutes."

Glaring, she takes a seat by the fireplace. The seat is softer than she expected—I've sunk there myself before—but she somehow manages to fold her legs with grace.

I don't sit. Instead, I put my hands into my pockets and glare at her down my nose.

She fidgets, adjusting her skirt.

"Anytime this century, Saar. Preferably in the next minute, though," I say, not trying to cover the impatience in my voice.

I'm growing not only impatient but also upset with myself. Or just annoyed because of the misunderstanding. The reason for her visit feels like a rejection. I'm not used to those.

"I'd like you to sell the building to my brother Finn," she blurts out in one breath, avoiding my eyes.

Her request takes me by surprise. I tilt my head, observing her with a mix of curiosity and irritation. Her brother sent her?

He might hate my guts, but he is a good businessman. Why would he send his little sister to close a deal like this?

"I thought you were a model," I muse.

She frowns, like she doesn't follow.

"What made you believe you can close a real estate deal?" I elaborate.

I'm being unfair. I know nothing about her, and for all I know—or rather don't know—she could be a real estate genius.

Judging by her anxiety, though, I doubt that. At the same time, I respect the shit out of her for showing up here, believing she can get me to sell that property.

Heat rises to her cheeks, and she stands up. Only her legs don't unfold fast enough, and she stumbles.

My legs move of their own accord, and I catch her by the elbow. The touch sends a jolt of electricity through my body.

"Models don't have brains?" she accuses, yanking her arm away from me.

The touch affected me more than I'd like to let on. She has looks, guts, and we have chemistry. It's a shame I don't mix business with pleasure.

I study her for a moment, trying to decide what her angle is. "What's your offer?"

She startles, visibly shaking at my question. Did she come here not believing she'd get this far? Fuck, this is more intriguing than it should be.

"Look, my brother is the one interested in buying it, but given your relationship, I'm assuming you won't sell it. I came here to see what it would take to motivate you."

I raise one eyebrow, smirking. Now we're talking.

"Not that," she blurts out.

I chuckle. She's like a spooked horse, but she's not giving up.

"That building is not for sale. It's enough that my plans with it got delayed because your brother threw a tantrum."

"Everything is for sale," she counters, and steps back when she realizes how her words sound.

I step closer, her perfume invading my nostrils. She swallows hard.

"Maybe I shouldn't have bothered with my clothes then."

Her gaze. Her scent. Her voice. For a brief moment, she owns me.

"That's harassment," she rasps.

I sneer. "I thought everything was for sale."

We stare at each other for what feels like a very long time, but the light outside hasn't changed, so it must be just a moment.

I'm transfixed by her whole being. No picture, no poster does her justice. She's just too imperfectly perfect.

"Why?" I ask, still crowding her.

She blinks, but to her credit, she doesn't move. I intimidate and people cower, but not Saar van den Linden.

"Why?" she repeats.

Okay, now she's dragging this out unnecessarily. I step back to regain control over my body, my cock twitching in my pants. Part of me immediately regrets the distance. I shove that part to the side.

"Jesus, woman, keep up. Why did your brother

send you? Especially since he wants the building, and clearly he didn't send you to seduce me to get it."

I adjust my cufflinks, the conflicting energy coursing through my veins.

"Finn doesn't know I'm here."

Few things surprise me, and yet here we are. "I don't understand."

Which is kind of refreshing because usually, I'm the one two steps ahead while the others can't catch up.

She frowns, scrunching her lips to the side, and seems to deliberate for a moment. "Finn wants the building, and I want him to be happy, so I thought... Well, I wasn't thinking." She groans, shaking her head.

Now, that raw honesty is a fucking turn-on. Besides her loyalty to her brother, I kind of wish we could start over, forget the building, and just get to know each other.

Not only between the sheets. The thought shocks me, and now I'm even more annoyed.

"You came to motivate me to do something that makes no business sense to help your brother behind his back?"

She nods, rolling her eyes. Not at me, more at the situation, I think. Fuck, she's adorable.

"That is the most preposterous thing I've heard, and I'm mostly surrounded by idiots."

"Are you calling me an idiot?"

Most certainly not. "'I've not decided yet."

She gives me a look that would kill. I feel its hatefulness down to my bones.

"You know what? Go fuck yourself. I don't need you to humiliate me. This was a mistake. Just forget I was ever here."

She pushes past me and marches to the door.

"Saar, wait—"

But she doesn't stop. That is most possibly the first time someone didn't obey me.

I hate it. I respect it. I hate that I respect it.

Rooted to the spot, I call my realtor. "Jack, find out discreetly if Finn van den Linden wants to buy the Hudson River property."

"Okay, why?"

"I want to sell it to him."

"To him in particular? And why are you selling it—?"

"Just fucking do it."

I hang up and stare at the space where I got the last glimpse of her.

I think I've just met my future wife.

Chapter 2

Saar

Two years later

"Hmmm..." It's all my manager says, and the sinking feeling that I'm disappointing him rolls around my stomach.

I'm used to disappointing my parents—it's their default setting, anyway. It cost me—both time and money in therapy—to accept that Charles and Melody van den Linden only love themselves.

Disappointing someone who became my proxy father when I made my foray into this business—that's a very different story.

Vito Conti has been with me since I started modeling at fifteen. Rationally, I know that my leaving the industry after twelve years isn't *that* unexpected, but it still feels like I'm betraying him.

Vito shovels four spoons of sugar into his cappuccino. The man, with his impeccably styled salt-and-pepper hair and thick-rimmed glasses that accentuate his sharp, intelligent eyes, is always charming and composed.

But when he's reaching for sugar, I know he's stressed. That's his only tell, and I might be one of only a few people who knows that about him.

"Saar, this is..." Vito smooths his silver scarf, which matches his silk pocket square, and licks his lips. "I should have known something was up when you were waiting here for me."

I frown, failing to connect the dots.

"You're always late, and here you were chewing on your lip when I arrived. I'm the one waiting for you all the time. And this place," he huffs. "This is—"

Patrons—mostly tourists—in this busy coffee shop near the Piazza del Duomo in Milan are loud and distracting. I chose the spot for that reason, specifically. Somehow, it's easier to deal with a difficult situation among chaos.

It's like the ambiance of chatter and laughter makes the heavy conversation at our table more palatable.

Vito hates it here, and I should have considered that before I lied that I have another meeting nearby and wouldn't make it anywhere else.

The racket might distract me, making the task

oddly easier, but it's annoying Vito. A fail on my part for sure.

"Vito, I'm exhausted, and I don't enjoy the work at all. I'm objectified and disrespected and dying from fatigue. I thought about it long and hard, and I'm done. I'm not going to sign any new contracts."

Why can't I look at him?

"Saar, principessa, you know you're my favorite client, and I get it." He sips from his cup, his gaze roaming the room with contempt before it lands on me and softens significantly. "Of course, I support your decision."

I open my mouth to argue, but his words sink in, and I blink. "You do?"

A sad smile ghosts his sophisticated features. "Only the best for you, but I'm afraid I have bad news that might force you to revisit your retirement dream."

Concern mars his forehead, his thick eyebrows pulled together behind his large glasses. He leans forward and takes my hand, holding it between both of his.

The warmth of his palms would be comforting, but I don't let that lull me. I was prepared for some sort of manipulation, but his grave tone settles eerily inside me.

"There is no easy way to say this." His Adam's apple bobs as he takes a pause. "And frankly, I wanted to spare you until I have more details, but in light of your decision..." He takes a deep breath and licks his lips.

"Jesus, Vito, spill it. Whatever it is, I can take it. When have you ever treated me like a porcelain doll?" I pull my hand from his and lean back, crossing my arms over my chest.

An unruly strand bounces off my messy hairdo, right across my eye. I blow it away, but it just springs back. Everything about today is annoying.

It took me a year to finally find the courage to take this step. To walk away from the lifestyle I've known since I was a teenager.

And it's not even the walking away part that prevented me from acting sooner. Or my body that has been screaming for a break after the abuse of fad diets, irregular meals, lack of sleep, and constant jetlag.

It's the next stage that kept me in the grind of late nights, early mornings, runways, cameras, airports, and fast clothing changes.

The next stage of my life.

When I turned twenty-five, I thought I would first figure out my future career and then I'd quit.

Two years later, I'm just exhausted. My brain is running on fumes, unable to focus or to access enough creativity to find my reinvention.

Vito clears his throat. "Okay, I'm not going to

sugarcoat it. It appears that your accountant has been embezzling money from you."

He pushes his unfinished cappuccino away. Like the cup is somehow associated with the bomb he's just dropped.

I stare at him for a moment, the offensive strand of hair no longer an issue. "Maria?" Like identifying the offender is what's important here.

Vito has been taking care of my finances, so I haven't met my European accountant many times. Yet the few times we met, she came across as a kind, competent woman, with pictures of her grandchildren on her desk.

Vito nods. "I don't know the extent, but there are irregularities I'm looking into. From what I uncovered so far, you need to pay taxes you owe for several years here in Italy, and potentially in the US. And with the penalties, I'm afraid you can't afford much at the moment. You certainly can't quit."

My body heats as if I was standing in front of the spotlights. In fact, the light here feels like a camera in burst mode with a flash on my face. It's just my blinking.

Vito takes off his glasses and wipes his forehead. I've never seen him this uncomfortable. "I'm sorry, principessa, it's all my fault. You trusted me with your money, and I failed you."

A shadow of regret flickers in his eyes. The larger than life man shrivels, his shoulders sagging with guilt.

"Oh my God, Vito, it's not your fault. Don't you dare take the responsibility. She fooled you. She fooled us both." My voice carries, and I feel more than see people turning their heads. I lower my voice. "We need to call the police."

He closes his eyes for a brief moment, sighing. "Saar, before we find out more—and rest assured, I have a private auditor on the case already—we need to keep it quiet. What if she covered her tracks and you're accused of tax evasion? You know how eager the authorities are to use those who are well-off as scapegoats. It's good PR for them."

"Tax evasion?" My hand flies to my mouth. Fuck. "When will you know more?"

"Hopefully by next week." He takes my shaking hands in his, and this time I welcome the comforting gesture. "Why don't you return to New York and take a week or two off? We'll talk once I know more."

* * *

The beat pulses through me. I shimmy with the other bodies, moving in sync. The volume of the music drowns my thoughts and worries. Every muscle and joint screams, begging me for a break.

I'm exhausted, but I don't let up. The bass thumps in my chest, my skin slick with the humidity of the club. Bodies move around me, their heat mixed with the scent of sweat and alcohol.

I don't care. Amid this chaos, I can pretend I'm having fun. I can touch the illusion of freedom. And I can be anonymous.

Besides, it's the only way to make sure I fall asleep at night. Funny how I thought that when I finally had time off, I'd sleep like a baby for a month.

Clearly, my body is so out of whack with any normal cycles that I've been unable to fall asleep. My current financial troubles haven't contributed to my peace of mind. And the uncertain future is surely keeping me up.

The idea of slaving on the runways and at photoshoots makes me want to cry, and I haven't cried since I was fifteen.

Instead, I've been going clubbing every night. A few drinks and hours of dancing are a highly effective avoidance tactic, but only if administered on a regular basis, with no time in between for grim reality to sink its teeth into my consciousness.

Someone's hard body presses into mine. I rock my hips in the rhythm. I lean into it. Him, by the feel of it.

It's a slower song. I hate the change of pace. I don't

want intimate, and I have enough melancholy taking up space in my head at the moment.

But I have to admit my body is ready to slow down. Closing my eyes, I let the stranger sway us. A smell of vodka and a way too strong aftershave tickles my nose.

I want to step forward, but it's like my body is so grateful for some reprieve, I'm unable to follow through on that need.

I might just fall asleep for a moment here on this unfamiliar chest.

Fuck, I should go home.

Home? As if.

When in New York, I used to stay at my parents' house. But since they stopped talking to us, I would usually crash at Finn's or Cal's.

My home this week has been an impersonal hotel room. My brothers are ridiculously happy with their new wives, and I didn't want to bother them with my moping. Especially since I'm not ready to share my failure with them.

A new song calms the rhythm even further, and I shiver as the dancefloor empties a bit. Only couples pressed tightly together remain moving around us.

Okay, I really should go home. But the smelly guy feels like a welcoming pillow. Maybe I can rest here for a moment longer. Only a moment, for my brain to make my legs walk.

Unfortunately, after a few beats, he dips his head and his mouth dusts my neck. I rock away from him.

Before I manage to leave, he stumbles and reaches for me. I shake off his arm, his touch snapping me out of my dance-induced stupor.

"I'm leaving." I raise my hand to stop him.

"Come on, don't be a bitch after you teased me with those moves." His hand grazes my waist again.

Fucking asshole. I'm not in the mood for this. I spin around to slap him, but my hand slashes through empty space, nothing but air rushing through my fingers.

I waver. I'm not even drunk, but the momentum and the missed target shifted my body. I blink, disoriented. Jesus, I should have left sooner.

A security guard is dragging Grabby Hands away, his face a blur in the flashing disco lights.

Fuck. A decent slap would have been cathartic. I fist my hand, but before I can turn to finally get to the exit, a bulky man steps in front of me.

Another security guy. "Are you okay?"

Wow, this place really takes women's safety seriously. I smile at him. "Yes, I'm fine."

What I want to do is to snarl that I can take care of myself. I don't. Even with my head buzzing with fatigue, I behave.

I'm skilled at keeping my feelings, commentary,

and needs in my head. That's the only way to survive in my industry. No, not mine anymore. Goddammit.

I'm about to turn, but I glimpse the security guy looking up and giving a slight nod. I follow his gaze and groan.

Of course, Cormac fucking Quinn is involved in this nightclub. I've purposely avoided all my usual hangouts. Mostly because my friends don't know I'm in New York.

I'm not ready to talk about my situation and deal with their sympathy or pity. I'm not even sure how to deal with it, and I don't want to get anyone involved. Especially since my best friend, Celeste, is now married to my brother.

The last thing I need is Finn and Cal snooping around and asking why I don't work. Or why I need money.

But as it turns out, the last thing I needed was Quinn saving me like I'm some sort of damsel in distress.

It's funny how our path keeps crossing. It's definitely not funny how I grew to hate his guts.

And now, he's Cal's business partner. Every time we run into each other, he attempts to flirt with me. More like taunting me to prove I'm just a pretty face with no substance.

His gaze meets mine—dark and... well, blank.

That's new. Usually, he rakes his eyes over me like I was his meal.

Perhaps he's high, but if I ever saw a look void of emotion, that's the one he's giving me right now.

He breaks our stare like he's bored with me already —asshole—and turns back to his companion, a woman with breasts so large I wonder how she keeps from tipping over.

Okay, another club to take off my list of places to get lost in. Does he really own most of them? Is this his pastime? Like that company he started with Cal doesn't make them busy or rich enough?

After a short cab ride, I arrive at my hotel. Fully awake. Fuck. I don't know if it's the Grabby Hands or Quinn's dead gaze that pumped enough adrenaline into my veins to wake up my brain.

Or I might have just done it myself by not leaving sooner. Now I'm probably so tired I won't be able to sleep.

I don't. I stare at the ceiling, trying to quiet my thoughts. The shadows change the white walls while I watch the night meet the dawn, and the streets awakening slowly.

At seven in the morning I take an hour-long hot bath, and finally feel my body and mind shutting down.

Wrapped in my towel, I shuffle toward the bed and

fluff the pillows. I drop the towel, enjoying the freedom of being bare, and with a sigh, I sink into the soft sheets. Only to groan right after because the house phone rings. What the fuck?

"Yes?" I snap.

"Ms. van den Linden, I'm sorry to bother you. I'm Roger, the day manager. I regret to inform you that your credit card charges have been declined. Do you happen to have another card we can use?"

"Come again?" I must be delirious with fatigue.

"I'm sorry to bother you. My name is Roger—" He takes my damn question literally.

"Okay, Roger, I haven't slept all night. It must be some sort of a mistake. Just try it again."

"We tried multiple times and contacted your bank before we bothered you. This card has been canceled. I'm really sorry, but I'll have to insist you get us another one."

"I'll come down." I hang up and stand.

The ground swirls, but I find purchase on the edge of the bed to steady myself. Shit, I stood up too fast. When was the last time I ate?

Clearly, years of modeling robbed me of basic habits. Fuck. Not bothering with the underwear, I slide into a T-shirt dress I find on the ground in the corner and grab my phone.

While I wait for the elevator, I dial my manager.

"Principessa, I was going to call you. How are you?"

"Vito, the hotel claims my credit card was canceled."

"But of course, I told you I'll be canceling it."

Did he? Fuck, what's wrong with me? I don't recall that conversation. "Why?"

"You can't incur more debt until we understand what's going on. Your checking account currently has five hundred euros."

The elevator door opens, and its current occupants stare at me, shuffling to make room, but I don't get in.

"What exactly are you saying, Vito?"

"Isn't it too early there? Why don't we talk after you have breakfast—"

"Stop babying me, Vito, what the fuck is going on?"

The heavy pause on the other side makes me want to throw the phone at the wall.

"Saar, it's worse than I thought. I'm working with the auditor to prepare the evidence to press charges, but it may take some time. You need to be patient."

"Patient? I'm staying at a hotel I can't pay for."

"Perhaps I can book a job for you while you're there?"

I shiver at the idea. I'd rather live with my parents. Another shiver tightens the knot in my stomach. Or be homeless.

"No, I'm getting my brother's jet to fly over there and deal with this shit."

"Saar, don't overreact. It's better I find out all your options first. I'm going to wire you two thousand dollars to settle your current bill."

"Vito, I can't take your money."

"Principessa, it's the least I can do for you. You're in this fucking situation because of me."

"Vito—" I sigh. "Okay, please settle the bill for me here, and I'm going to stay with my friend."

"Good call. I have business in the States in a few days, so we can sit down and review the situation."

The idea of having him here gives me an unreasonable jolt of happiness. Vito, with his kind eyes, always stirring me in the right direction, subbing for my father without even knowing it. "Thank you. What would I do without you?"

He sighs. "Saar, I'm going to sort this out. It's my fault I trusted that woman."

"Stop it. She fooled me as well. I better go and pack."

After a moment, he sighs again. "Saar?"

"Yes?"

"Maybe you need to look into accessing your trust fund?"

I can almost hear how much it pains him to even suggest that. He knows I want nothing to do with the van den Lindens' money. Nothing that came from my parents.

"I don't—"

"I know, I know how you feel about that. But it might be just a temporary solution, so you can settle."

"It's not that easy."

"Why not? Fuck them, they never showed you any affection, so at least now their money can help you when you need it the most."

"Even if I swallow my pride, Vito, I only get access to those funds once I'm married."

Chapter 3

Corm

An incoming video call vibrates my phone, and I groan. I'm of half a mind to let it ring out.

Taking out a cup, I fill it with coffee and swipe the green button. "Mom." I set the phone against a fruit bowl on my kitchen island.

She fidgets with the phone, and I wait while I first see a close-up of her finger, then a glimpse of her library, and then her nose. I take a sip, waiting, my lips quirking up.

Every single time she attempts a video call, we go through this.

Finally, she stretches her arm and angles the phone to show her face. Her blonde hair is styled in a low bun at her nape as usual, and she is wearing her reading glasses on a string around her neck. And a kind expression.

I miss her. Fuck.

She marches down the hallway of her home, a woman on a mission. One would think she is a professional influencer with a selfie stick despite the rocky start of every freaking call.

"Thank you for the flowers, Lovie."

God, I wish she would drop my childhood endearment.

My mother isn't the only woman who gets flowers from me, but she is the only woman who gets them truly from me. Not from my assistant, Larissa.

Lately, there have been too many bouquets arriving at her house instead of me. I can hear the sadness in her gratitude.

"Sorry, Mom, I couldn't make it for lunch today. I had work." I take a generous gulp of my coffee to hide the lie and almost burn my tongue.

"I know, I know. Declan mentioned you have something."

At least my brother didn't skip the family lunch. Thank God his little fiends make Mom happy.

When I say nothing, she adds, "When will I see you, Lovie?"

"I've been really busy."

And fucking upset with you for not telling me the truth. And then for telling me the truth.

I recognize the soft decor of her bedroom. A bedroom where I used to snuggle with my parents when I was a boy.

"I know we all grieve differently—"

"I'm not grieving, Mom. I'm upset. I'm angry. I'm disappointed. I'm..."

She sighs. "Look up grief online and confront your feelings, Corm." She sits at her vanity and positions the phone against something. "You can pretend you don't love him all you want." She takes off an earring. "You miss him. I miss him." She takes off the other earring. "Almost a year ago I lost my husband, but it feels like I lost my son as well."

She delivers the last words into the mirror, avoiding my eyes. This is not a guilt trip. My mom doesn't manipulate, but she is no pushover either. Always honest—bar one significant instance—always supportive, always patient.

I put down my mug and brace against the counter, bowing my head. Fuck. The cocktail of my emotions gets a new potent ingredient. Guilt.

"Why don't we have lunch this week? I'll have Larissa schedule something. She can get us a table at Casa Cassi."

I'm not ready to step into my childhood home. It's full of memories. Full of him. Full of the lies.

Casa Cassi is Mom's favorite restaurant, and getting a reservation might be impossible on such short notice, but I suggest it anyway. And ignore the edges of my consciousness that are already canceling that plan. The florist will make more money soon.

"That would be lovely. I love you, Cormac."

A lump swells in my throat at the genuine affection in those words. The remorse in her voice is like acid on a fresh wound.

Only the wound isn't fresh anymore. I should have been able to swallow the bitter pill and move on with my life.

And yet… the man I'd looked up to, the man I'd loved all my life, had brought me to my knees. From beyond his fucking grave.

"I love you, too, Mom."

"Be safe, Lovie."

I hang up, finish my coffee, and decide to hit the gym.

As soon as I rev up my Lambo, I amend the plan. After my workout, I'm keeping the car in the garage and going out.

As an owner of several clubs, I've never partied in them beyond the necessary schmoozing with VIP guests. That has changed in the last several months.

Clubbing is the only way to cope with his betrayal.

* * *

"What?" I bark into the phone, after I finally located it under my pillow and answered to stop the offensive ringing. Fuck. My head hurts.

"Good morning, sunshine," Roxy, my office manager, purrs.

The woman is the bane of my existence. Correction. Everything lately has been the bane of my existence.

Unfortunate. Uninspiring. Un-fucking-bearable.

"You better have a good reason for calling me," I snap, the words rolling from my tongue with unwarranted harshness.

Roxy chuckles. "Does saving your ass count as a good reason in your book, asshole? I mean, boss."

Fucking Roxy.

I turn to lie on my back and run my hand over my face as if that would wake me up. Or sober me up. I pull the phone away from my ear to check the time. Shit. I slept for two hours.

"What are you saving me from, Ro?"

She hates when people call her Ro. I hate to be rudely awakened. On a Saturday, no less. I guess we're even.

"Why do I even bother?" Her eye roll is obvious even through the line.

My silky sheets rustle, drawing my attention. My gaze lands on a pale ass. Fuck. The last thing I need is the whole dance of sending someone on their walk of shame.

Leaning forward slightly, I check my companion's hair color, hoping that would help me remember her name. It doesn't. The movement, however, sets off the agonizing pain in my temples.

I stumble from my bed and pad to my bathroom in search of a painkiller.

"Roxy, since you already inconvenienced yourself with this call, why don't you tell me the reason?"

I might be a dick to her, but I respect the shit out of this woman. She wouldn't have called unless it was pressing.

Roxy Moretti possesses the best combination of capable, professional, and just enough unhinged to enjoy working with four men—her bosses—who are demanding, selfish, and extremely busy.

And occasionally real assholes like me this morning.

If she ever tries to leave us, I'd pay her my salary and destroy the fucker who dared offer her another opportunity.

"Again, why do I even bother?" she quips.

"Hold on." I put the phone on the vanity, grab two Advils, and chase them down with water. I wince at my reflection. I aged ten years in the last few months. *Thank you very much, Dad.*

Returning to my room, I fall back into my bed and put the phone to my ear. The pills are not working yet, but the glass of water humanized me enough to deal with Roxy.

The woman in my bed groans and pulls the pillow over her head.

Roxy tuts. "Sorry to interrupt the main program, but you're to play golf with Donovan Hale in ninety minutes."

"Why the fuck didn't you call me sooner?" I bark, and hang up on the background of her laughter as she says 'you're welcome'.

I shake my head and playfully slap the woman beside me. She groans again.

"Sorry, sweetheart, but I have to go to work. Get moving." I jump out of the bed and pull the covers from her body.

"Hey." She peeks from under the pillow. "It's Saturday."

"Sorry." I shrug. "I'll call you tonight." My smile is more honest than my words. But the combo seems to appease her enough to rise.

"Can I at least shower?"

"No time for that. I'm really sorry. I'll have my driver drop you off and pick you up again tonight at seven."

She pouts, but starts collecting her clothes.

"I need to get ready. Just close the door on your way out."

She pouts even more, but I disappear to the bathroom.

I desperately need to shave and shower, but grooming doesn't seem as important as decreasing my rude lateness. I splash my face and brush my teeth before I dash to my closet.

My last-night companion intercepts me on her way out of my bedroom. At least she finally understands the urgency, and only sends me an air kiss. "See you tonight."

Fuck, I hope she won't steal anything on her way out. It would serve me right for bringing her here. What was I thinking?

I wasn't. I've been numbing the pain of my father's betrayal with copious amounts of alcohol, and some recreational drugs. The fucking numbing is fleeting. The consequences are lasting, and keep piling up.

I get dressed in record time, but a quick check of my Rolex makes me dial Roxy again.

"The helicopter will be there in five," Roxy says before I can speak.

I sigh, hanging my head. "Thank you."

"I expect a bonus with my next paycheck." This time, *she* hangs up.

I don't have time to contemplate her behavior, or mine, because the rhythmic thumping of the helicopter blades chopping through the air propels me to action.

During the hour-long flight to the Fishers Island Club, I text my assistant. Luckily, Roxy hired Larissa and trained her well, so I don't have to bother with explanations.

Send a gift to the same address my car drove this morning.

LARISSA

Flowers or jewelry?

Flowers only.

The card should apologize for not making it tonight.

You're a douchebag, Quinn. The thought surprises me, because when have I ever felt any remorse for my actions?

Be hard on the issue but soft on people, son. My father's words sneak up on me. *I've been hard on the issue all right, Dad. But I can't be soft on you. I can't forgive you.*

The now very familiar taste of his duplicity triggers my impulse to drown it, and I pull a flask from my jacket's inner pocket to medicate the feeling that has been eating me up.

I've been so fucking angry, I almost lost my company after I got arrested a few months back. Merged isn't my only venture, but it is the most important one.

It used to be.

And now… Fuck if I know.

Dad suggested the concept to me. Even though I already had a very healthy income from my silent partnerships in several nightclubs, a gold mine, a pleasure resort, and a healthy stock portfolio to grow my trust fund, my father felt I needed something to hone my talent for business.

He shared his vision, one that his disease stopped him from bringing to fruition, and like a good boy, I lapped it up and slaved to make it happen. For him.

And now? I wish I could drop it. Just sell it to someone he hated and laugh. But the old man knew me. He got me involved, and hooked.

And now I'm stuck between hating my firm because it was his idea, and loving it because it's my baby.

Merged might be my only legacy. The only company with my name attached to it.

The helicopter touches the ground, and I take another swig, regretting the late night.

"You're late," Donovan Hale huffs, patting his round stomach when I enter the club's restaurant.

"Don, nice to see you." I smile and shake his hand. "My apologies. The wind in Manhattan delayed my take off."

I pull the chair to sit, but the president of Atlas Ventures, a global investment firm and our biggest client, stands up and moves toward the exit.

My stomach churns at the sight of the breakfast spread. I could use some solids along with my liquid reinforcement. Salivating, I sigh and grab a bottle of water before I follow my client.

The longest fucking day of my life keeps stretching on. My mouth is dry, my stomach is protesting my poor lifestyle choices, and my head is throbbing.

The sun beats with unforgiving enthusiasm, especially for early April.

I curse whoever picked today for a game to appease the man whose current business interest would elevate Merged in the financial world. We would become the go-to firm for future high-profile deals in the technology sector.

It takes an inhuman amount of effort to maintain a smile as I use the last remnants of my charm to appease the douche who makes the decisions. It's good form to let him win, but the man is so bad at golf.

Even in my current state, swinging my club without aiming, we're at the last hole with the same handicap.

"You look like shit, and if I'm to be honest, the recent media coverage of your behavior..." Donovan glares at me, stroking his silver goatee.

My shoes sink into the soft, trimmed grass of the green. The end to this ordeal of the day is only one hole away.

Donovan closes one eye, measuring the angle of the possible trajectory of his ball. *It's ten inches away—just fucking sink it in.*

He turns this way and that way, like the task at hand requires real preparation. A blind person could get this hole. This is his best position yet.

"My personal life has nothing to do with my business."

Unfortunately, he straightens as if abandoning the task. He swings his club like a pendulum beside his leg. "Doesn't it? Look, we were all patient after your father passed, but it's been months... My board doesn't want to be associated with scandals."

The mere mention of my father's death in connection with my recent PR nightmare boils my blood. As if his death triggered my behavior. But, of course, everyone assumes that.

I don't know if that makes me a good son or an emotional loser in everyone's eyes. And frankly, I'm too tired to revisit that angle.

Ignoring the anger cruising through my veins, I smile at Donovan. "Your board will be kissing your ass once we help you sign the AetherTech merger."

"There, there, Corm…" Fuck, I hate his condescending tone.

Donovan Hale is closer in age to my father than to me, which makes his patronizing spiel worse in my eyes for some outlandish reason.

"While AetherTech is a cutting-edge tech company," he continues, "it's not one of those hipster startups. The company is controlled by people with more traditional values."

I smirk. "And they're still driven by profits."

He leans forward, tapping the ball gently with his club and, thank fucking God, doesn't miss. "All I'm saying is that while I appreciate you were the first to warm up the deal, there are others who can see it through."

The first, or the only? They were after AetherTech for months, and only got their first meeting thanks to me and my partner, Xander, and his connections.

Donovan fucking Hale dares to threaten to steal the negotiations away from my firm?

But I know when to choose my battles, so I miss the hole. Twice. Smiling, I shrug at my opponent. "Congratulations, Don. You play a mean game."

I extend my hand, and he shakes it.

"I promise to be on my best behavior." I wink at him.

"I don't trust you, Corm."

"But you need me to get significantly richer."

* * *

I doze off on the way back home, which makes me feel even shittier because a brief shut-eye only messes with my head and my body.

The helicopter drops me off on the roof of my house, and as much as I want to go straight to my bed, I need to eat something first.

I pull out one of the foil-covered dishes. My chef comes twice a week and leaves meals for me. I eat out so often that my housekeeper ends up feeding her family with most of them.

Without registering what I'm warming up, I shove the dish into the oven and pour myself a tall glass of water.

I consider getting a glass of whiskey but drop the

idea. I might have been reckless lately, but I'm not stupid.

Movement behind my window catches my attention. The oven dings, and my stomach growls. Chicken masala aromas permeate the air. Fuck, I'm hungry.

I sit on the kitchen island stool and don't bother serving myself a portion, but dig into the baking dish. I open my security app.

A few spoonfuls and clicks later, and I drop the cutlery and run outside.

"Motherfucker," I growl, opening the service door at the side of my house.

The man going through my garbage, a long lens hanging from his shoulder, startles and, unfortunately for him, freezes.

While the paps love my pictures when I'm out, my house has been spared. I hit my personal low when I brought a woman here last night. In fact, I vowed to clean my act because of that.

But seeing a stranger trying to make a quick buck trespassing on my property ignites the rage that has been simmering inside me all day. All month. Several months.

And I forget my vow to clean my act, or my promise to Donovan, and before I think better of it, my fist connects with the intruder's jaw.

* * *

"Are you fucking kidding me?" Xander storms into my office on Monday morning.

The youngest of the four partners at Merged, Xander is our Chief Strategy Officer. He is highly intelligent, and annoyingly passionate.

This is the problem with having partners. They fucking butt into your business. All. The. Time.

I open and close my sore fist, but I don't move otherwise. Seated at my desk, I let him have his tantrum.

He marches across my bright, large office toward my desk. "I called all the favors to get you a golfing Saturday with Hale, to make sure this goddamn deal is still ours, and you fucking hit the headlines as soon as you shelved the clubs."

He throws down printouts detailing and exaggerating the unfortunate events of Saturday evening. Was I right to break that asshole's nose? Of course. Should I have done it? Probably not.

Reckless billionaire CEO assaults an innocent citizen. An innocent citizen swiping through my garbage and trespassing to profit.

Money can buy everything: charges dropped after

Cormac Quinn assaults a journalist. Thank God for good lawyers. Not that I can digest that I had to pay off the loser. He was no journalist. He was a paparazzo.

Cormac Quinn leaves a high-end club with a stripper. Shit, that's who she was.

"I thought the idea of online media is to save paper." I toss the printouts across the desk, back to him.

"Are you fucking kidding me?" He throws his arms up in exasperation. "Hale called me—didn't even bother to call you—to say that they are pulling out."

"Bullshit."

My confident comeback is a feeble attempt to stay in control while my life is spiraling down.

I can't even blame this on my old man. He might have triggered me, but I've indulged in the anger like a spoiled brat. Goddammit.

"I don't know what the fuck is going on with you," Xander continues. "But I didn't sign up to have the CEO arrested a month after we founded this business, or have all our associates questioning his sanity every single day."

"My personal life is nobody's business." I stand up, my chair rolling and hitting the glass wall behind my desk with a thud.

"Screw your life, Corm. Your personal *image* is this

company's business. Fuck whoever you want, drink, party, get high, but do it discreetly."

It sucks to be scolded by a man who's four years younger than me. At twenty-seven, he already hit the 30 under 30 list twice, the fucker.

"It might be too late for that." Declan walks in, followed by Cal van den Linden who closes the door.

Well, look at the impromptu partners' meeting.

"I talked to three board members at Atlas Ventures, and they gave Hale an ultimatum: either you're out or he is. Guess which option he is rooting for?" Cal smirks and sits down on my white leather sofa on the other side of the room, casually, as if he is enjoying this. He probably is.

While we found some resemblance of decent professional behavior, there is no love lost between us.

I glare at the men in front of me, and for the first time in... well, ever, I don't have a quip on my tongue. While I don't give a shit about my personal reputation, I give a shit about losing money, or my business rep.

Fuck. I press the button of my internal line.

"Yes, Mr. Quinn," Larissa says in her soft Russian accent.

"Get me AetherTech on the phone." I rein in the poison in my voice.

While Larissa is more than capable of shaking off my verbal assaults and even returns them, I need to exude calm in front of the three people glowering at me right now.

My brother, Declan, knows nothing about the betrayal from the man we called Father. He has enough on his plate with two small children whose mother is MIA, and a major pain in his ass.

And who, unlike me, despite his personal turmoil, acts as our Chief Financial Officer with integrity and the utmost work ethic.

While I run to nightclubs to drown my issues, he escapes his at work.

Xander joined our quartet with enthusiasm and probably regretted it ever since. From what I know, his antics are probably even more scandalous than mine, but the fucker manages the discretion he's just demanded from me.

And then there is Cal, who is married and settled, and so fucking happy I want to claw his eyes out.

I am failing all of them, but I won't admit it.

"Mr. Cherynowski is on line one." Larissa's voice interrupts our silent glaring contest.

"Vladislav, how are you?" I pick up the receiver and widen my eyes, but none of my partners move to leave.

Fuck them. I reach for my chair and sit, turning it. The skyline of Manhattan spreads in front of me, giving me a false sense of privacy.

"Better than you, I guess," the AetherTech's CEO chuckles.

"Listen, you know how the media is. The fucker was going through my garbage," I admit.

I never comment on any of my recent indiscretions, but I did my homework, and I know Vladislav Cherynowski values his privacy above all.

"Fucking vultures," he murmurs.

"But I admit I acted on impulse." I take a bite from the humble pie and sigh. "Donovan Hale's board is not happy."

He remains silent, so I continue, "You know that we have the expertise in-house to help you with the best transition post-merger..." I launch into my pitch, knowing I haven't lost him yet since he took my call.

"Look, Cormac." He sighs when I'm done. "I know you'd be our best option to move forward, but you're not the only one. Atlas wants this merger; I want it, too. To be honest, it's taking too long to iron out all the details, and my time is too precious to brief and start over with another intermediary."

It's a weak endorsement, but beggars can't be choosers. "I appreciate that."

"Don't be cute with me. Your reputation is an ongoing concern. I'll not answer calls from Atlas unless you're at the table because you will get me a good deal. That being said, you have two months to clean up your act. That's how long I'm willing to stall them. One more media coverage—"

"There will be none. You have my word." I feel like a kid sent into detention, and I hate it. I loathe myself for this situation.

"Oh, you misunderstood. I want coverage portraying you as an upstanding citizen. A pillar of the community."

I snort. "In two months? No one will believe that."

"You better make it believable."

"Vladislav, you want me to stage PR photo ops in shelters?"

"That wouldn't hurt, but something more wholesome would sell your story of a tamed daredevil."

"I'm listening."

His next words shake the ground under me. Fuck. My. Life.

I turn slowly and hang up the receiver, before I lift my gaze to meet the expecting eyes of my partners.

"So?" Xander prompts.

"He is out of his fucking mind."

Chapter 4

Saar

CELESTE

I still don't understand why you wouldn't stay with us.

Because you lovebirds make me sick.

CELESTE

Cynical as ever. Caleb and I would love to host you.

CORA

What's wrong with my place?

CELESTE

That I'm not there.

You're pregnant and cranky.

CELESTE

(Eye-roll emoji) At least I have a reason to be cranky. What's your excuse?

I lived with my brother for half of my life. Now it's your turn. Enjoy him. (devil emoji)

LILY

I have a day off, let's have coffee. All four of us (smiley emoji).

Raincheck

"At one point, you'll have to see them." Cora looks at me, unimpressed.

While I wasn't ready to see my friends yet, I also couldn't stay alone in Cora's apartment. Alone with my thoughts, and her two adorably mean cats.

Finding a new purpose in life is a tough task. I wasn't expecting it to be easy. I was prepared for the darker moments and learning by failing.

What I wasn't ready for was the additional financial uncertainty on top of my existential crisis.

So here I am at my friend's bistro, sipping on a luxurious latte as if life was normal.

"I know, I know." My gaze follows the activity on the street, avoiding Cora's eyes.

"Well, if you need to talk, I'm here to listen," she says.

I bite my bottom lip and turn my head, smiling at her. "Thank you."

"In the meantime, let me cut you the biggest slice of apple pie." She winks.

Her ginger curls bounce as she disappears back to her kitchen.

Cora is almost ten years older than me. She left her corporate job to take care of her father's bistro.

She started anew. Perhaps she is the best person to talk to about my next steps.

I take a sip of my coffee. I really should stop drinking this shit. I haven't slept well in I don't know how long. It feels like ages. Since I was fifteen, probably.

A few patrons are enjoying an early lunch at the table beside mine, chatting happily. A mother is nursing a baby in the corner while taking forkfuls of her pie. A lanky young man reads a book in the corner.

Life seems to stop here, in this bistro, allowing people just to be for a few moments, enjoying themselves. Maybe that's my problem. I need to learn how to slow down. How to be without doing.

Who knew that relaxing is a skill one has to learn? Of course, I'd have a massage or some downtime in between gigs, but there was always the next job on the books.

I pull out my knitting from my bag and decide that just being is exactly what the doctor ordered.

I inspect the colorful pattern of my work. A blanket, I guess. Or it might end up being a shawl. Knitting became a meaningful way to spend time while waiting during the long days at work.

I learned it from a girl at a photoshoot in the Caribbean many years ago. We arrived at the island, and the weather turned to shit, which delayed the shoot.

She knitted to pass the time. I finished my book, and in the absence of anything else to do, she lent me needles and taught me the craft.

Far from being an expert, I love the mindfulness it brings, along with the relaxing and stress relief. It became essential for me in dealing with my demanding job. Perhaps now I could enjoy it for fun and creativity.

A man in a suit and the most ridiculous silver comb-over walks in, marching to the counter. The mother in the corner is now burping her baby. The group beside me is getting ready to leave.

The stillness has a different energy now, and while I enjoy my needlework, I'm still restless.

Sanjay, Cora's employee, is talking to the Suit, who seems agitated.

"Get me the manager right now," the Suit bellows.

"What's going on?" Cora emerges.

"Are you the manager?" he snaps, and Sanjay dashes away to wipe the empty tables.

"Yes." Cora wipes her forehead with her forearm to

tame her curls.

"Well, you're not very good at your job."

What the fuck? She asks him a question, but I don't hear it. She seems composed, trying to defuse the situation, but she blinks rapidly and takes a small step back.

"I want my order to be ready when I come to pick it up," the Suit yells.

"Could you please calm down? You ordered five minutes ago, and if you don't want raw chicken in your salad, you need to wait another five."

"I will get a ticket in the meantime. I'm double-parked."

Cora wipes her hands on her apron and blinks some more. Fuck it. What a bully. I make my way to the counter.

"What do you think you're doing?" I point my knitting needles at him.

He frowns at me, his face red like he's on the brink of a heart attack. "Mind your own business."

"Why don't you go mind your business back in your car, so you don't get a ticket."

"Who the fuck are you?" He turns to Cora. "And you, stop gaping; go finish my stupid salad."

Cora's eyes widen, before she looks at the reading guy and the mother, heat rising to her cheeks.

"How dare you speak to her like that?" This time I poke him with the needle. "Get the fuck out of here."

Now, his eyes widen. "Are you going to let her speak to me like that?" He looks at Cora. "What kind of establishment is this?"

What an asshole. How dare he speak to my friend like this, embarrassing her in front of other customers with his unreasonable demands?

I poke him with the knitting needle, the ball of yarn dropping to the floor. "Go get your salad somewhere else, and while you're at it, try to look for your manners."

He throws his arms in the air. "I'm going to give you zero stars." He marches out, spitting profanities.

I sigh. "Are you okay?"

Cora nods, and then chuckles nervously. "What a prick. He was so ridiculous, I didn't know what to say. How to respond to such absurd behavior. Shit. Thank you."

I lean down to pick up my yarn. "Can I have his salad now?" I smirk.

"Sure, babe. I didn't know you knit."

"I'm full of surprises." I snicker.

And of secrets, as of late.

"Saar, Saar, open your eyes."

Cora's voice penetrates my foggy mind. Fuck. It's

not just her voice; my body is shaking. I pry my eyes open. *She* is shaking my body.

"What are you doing? I was sleeping." I roll onto my back and cover my face with my forearm, darkness pulling me back.

"I saw that, and I also saw this. What the fuck?" She is louder than usual. Or it might just be my haziness.

I peek from under my arm. Beside my friend's feet in white sneakers, small white pills are strewn on her dark, hardwood floor.

I groan. "It's not what it looks like."

I sit up on the sofa that has been my home for the past week.

Cora lives in a small apartment in Brooklyn. To be honest, her entire place is smaller than some of the hotel rooms I've stayed in.

But it doesn't bother me. Beggars can't be choosers and all that. It's not like I had many other options. And I enjoy staying with Cora. She doesn't pry. She is almost never here.

The only downside is the sofa itself. That fucker is uncomfortable. It's like trying to rest on cactus needles. And I needed to sleep finally. So I took a sleeping pill, because I need my brain back.

Not that my latest situation suggests I ever had a brain to begin with.

"Saar, I tried to give you space. You're obviously going through something, and you're avoiding Celeste. I think it's time we talk." Cora sits in an armchair across from me.

A thick, black headband keeps her ginger curls from her makeup-less face, a frown splitting her forehead. She purses her lips into a straight line, and observes me with her hazel eyes like she truly cares.

I fidget and look away, because... Well, because I'm ashamed. Because I'm drowning in self-loathing.

I drop to my knees and sweep up the pills with my hand as if they represent all my problems. Only now they remain in my palm, their shiny coating melting into my sweaty skin. And I don't quite know what to do with them.

Just like I don't know what to do with my financial conundrum. Or with my life in general. Sighing, I sag onto my behind, leaning against the sofa.

"I haven't slept well for almost two weeks, so I took two of these. I probably didn't close the lid properly, and they tumbled to the floor."

This explains what plausibly happened. It doesn't explain why I'm avoiding Celeste, or why I'm crashing at my friend's.

There is a part of me that wants to tell her, but an equally eager part of me hopes she won't ask anything else.

"I hope my cats didn't eat any of them."

My eyes widen first, and then I drop my gaze to the mess in my hand. "I'm sorry, Cora. I'll move out—"

"Don't be ridiculous. Pitt and Clooney are okay." As if the two calicos waited to hear their name, they jump into Cora's lap and settle.

She cups their heads with one hand each and soothes them, moving each of her thumbs between their eyes from their little noses up to the crown of their heads. They close their eyes in bliss and start purring.

In the van den Linden household, pets were never allowed. Later, my jet-setting lifestyle didn't allow for one. I can see how these two are therapeutic.

"You don't have to move out until you sort out whatever is going on, but finding you spread on my sofa every night like you're waiting for something... I'm not sure I can help you, but I can sure as hell listen. Whatever it is, Saar, I won't judge."

She continues the thumb-petting motion, and somehow, it soothes me as well. One of the cats—I still can't tell them apart—stretches his leg languidly. Fuck, I want to be a cat in my next life.

"My accountant embezzled money from me. I found out too late, and I'm pretty much broke. And probably owing taxes in two countries."

I speak so fast, I almost trip over my own words.

Like I need to spit it all out before I chicken out and keep the reality hidden deep down where it's been eating me up.

Cora puffs out breath from her cheeks. "Fuck, Saar, I'm so sorry."

I play with the melting pills in my hand. "Don't be. I let other people deal with my finances, so I shouldn't be surprised. I deserved it probably."

"Stop it!" One cat jumps from her lap, probably disturbed by our conversation. *You and me, buddy, you and me.*

"Look, I don't even know how bad it is yet. My manager is investigating. He's coming to New York tomorrow, and I'll know more. In the meantime, I really appreciate you letting me stay here."

"Of course. I wish I had a guest room—"

"Now, you stop it! Don't you dare apologize for giving me a roof over my head." I smile. "I really appreciate it."

"You should probably get rid of those before they melt into your skin and you overdose." She gestures toward my palm.

"I'd love to sleep for a week, though." I push to stand and shuffle to the bathroom. After flushing the pills, I wash my hands.

"You don't want your brother to know." Cora leans against the door frame, her assumption about my reasons for avoiding Celeste right on the money.

I nod. "Celeste wouldn't be able to keep it from him. And I don't want her to be in that position. And I certainly don't want him to come to the rescue. I need to fix it myself."

"Why?"

Her question throws me off. Why?

I dry my hands, avoiding her gaze. Why?

Because I don't want Cal to judge me. I don't want to hear him sigh and go into rescue mode.

Because all my life, people have been taking care of my affairs. First, because I didn't have a choice—my parents, my brothers. Later, because it was just easier.

It's time I take care of myself. If only the task didn't feel so daunting.

"He would throw his money at the problem. I don't want that."

Cora huffs. "Can he throw his money at all my problems?"

She's been struggling to keep her father's bistro afloat. She's the most hardworking person I know, and yet she can't get ahead.

"Would you *really* accept that?"

She frowns.

"I'm serious, Cora; let's say it's not my brother, but someone else who would have the means and the will to help you out. Would you just accept their financial help?"

She stares at me, her jaw tense, and then she sighs.

"I thought so."

It might be pride, but accepting money doesn't come easy to a woman. Even if that woman is in a desperate situation. Fuck, most of us have a block to ask for any help, let alone financial.

I walk out of the bathroom. In the kitchen, I fill a glass with tap water and gulp it down. The two pills I took are still trying to claim my brain, the fog not yet lifted.

Putting the glass down, I turn and lean against the counter. Cora sits on one of the two chairs at her small dining table by the window.

She says nothing. It's like she knows I need to let it all out, but prompting me won't help.

"Perhaps my pride is misplaced in this case, but I can't help it. It's there. Besides, I quit my job, and I'm physically sick at the idea of returning to it. So everything in my life is in flux."

"You quit?" She stands and pulls two wineglasses from her cupboard. Retrieving a bottle of white wine from her fridge, she fills them to the brim. "We need this. What are you going to do?"

"I have no fucking idea." I accept the glass, and we both sit at her table.

The kitchen reminds me of the one I shared with other girls during my first year modeling in Milan. There were six of us sharing three bedrooms.

The kitchen only had a counter, with a fridge and a stove on one side of the narrow space and a table with two chairs on the other side. I used to sit on the counter when I ate from a takeout container.

After having lived in the van den Linden mansion, it was a shock to my system. I loved it.

"The timing sucks. Why would you quit if you're broke?" she asks with a genuine interest, and while I'm looking for signs of condemnation or judgment, there are none. And frankly, it's a valid question.

"I told my manager I'm quitting, and he told me he'd just found out. I know that the rational person would push through and work while the situation clears out. But I really can't, Cora. I can't explain it, but it really makes me physically sick."

"I get it. My corporate job used to suck the soul out of me. That's why I didn't hesitate to leave. And things have been hard and really tight, but I wouldn't be able to go back there." She takes a sip. "You really have no plans?"

I play with the stem of my glass and sigh. "I thought I'd take some time off and figure out what I want to do. But now, I might not have the luxury to take time off."

"I thought you had a trust fund."

"I do, but my grandfather didn't step into the twenty-first century, and the terms are as archaic as they come."

I don't tell her how I feel about using van den Linden's money.

Having spent a week here, I realized how privileged I am regardless of my current plight. I would normally meet Cora at her bistro, or we would go out somewhere. Confronted with her living conditions, I now realize how out of touch I've been, living in my own bubble.

"Archaic?" She picks up one of her cats.

"I have to be married to access that money." I roll my eyes.

She snorts. "That *is* as archaic as it gets. A convenient marriage seems to have worked for Celeste."

I persuaded my brother to marry Celeste when she was going to lose her visa. Now they are so in love, I hardly recognize my brother.

I look at her deadpan. "Will you marry me?"

She puts her hands on her heart in a dramatic gesture. "Why, I thought you'd never ask."

"It would show my grandfather."

"That is so fucked up."

I chuckle, but there is no humor in it. "You know what is the biggest irony? Those archaic clauses were put there because men used to believe women couldn't take care of their own money. Like we needed our fathers to hand the control to our husbands. That provision might be beneficial in my case."

"Saar." Cora sighs. "Don't blame yourself. You trusted someone who betrayed you, but that doesn't make you unable to control your own destiny, or your money for that matter."

But isn't that the story of my life?

"As soon as I left my childhood home, I handed the control to Vito, my manager. Not that any of this is his fault—"

"You see, if you don't find him responsible for what happened while he was in charge, why don't you extend the same grace to yourself? Saar, shit happens. Blame yourself; don't blame yourself. But you need to look forward and act. Fix what can be fixed. Take control. Move on."

It sounds so easy when she lays it out like that. "I don't have any experience other than smiling and being pretty. Do you know someone who is hiring for that?"

"You'll figure it out. You're a survivor."

"You think?" I hate the need in my voice.

As much as I hate the idea of modeling again, I can't deny I have been missing the spotlight. That sense of being seen, being accepted, being validated.

As false as those circumstances were, they supplied

me with confidence I might not possess when away from it all.

It's like I'd become invisible. Again.

"Everyone who grows up with a pair of evil parents like yours is a survivor." She raises her glass.

And I chuckle, toasting to that. The wine spreads to my legs, making me feel heavy and weightless at the same time. Shit, I probably shouldn't have drunk on those pills.

But the feeling is peaceful at the same time. The knot in my stomach has loosened a bit. My lungs stretch better on each inhalation, my mind floats on the cocktail of possibilities. Or more probably on the mix of sleeping pills with alcohol.

I scrunch my face up. "I'm worried I'll end up scavenging for discounts to have my lips enhanced or my forehead lifted, and I'll look like a wax figurine with a mouth like a duck." My tongue doesn't work properly.

Cora almost spits her wine, laughing. "Shit, Saar, I forgot you took those pills. Let's get you to bed."

She stands up, snakes her arm around me, and pulls me up.

"I don't even have a bed."

"You do tonight. We're sharing mine, you silly cow."

We stumble around the mirror, and I pout. "You

see. Look at me. I can't get discounted beauty procedures. I'd end up ugly."

"Okay, your future ugly lips are the least of your problems, but let's sleep on it." She drags me to her bedroom.

"I can't accept your bed," I protest as I fall into her sheets.

"Good night, Saar."

My body jerks as she pulls the duvet from under me, and I smile as the warmth and comfort envelope me.

Maybe I am a survivor.

"Jesus, Vito, when you said you had a solution, I didn't think you'd found me a husband." I shake my head, but the reality remains unchanged.

I'm still sitting across from my manager in an upscale restaurant on Madison Avenue. I'm still happy and relieved to see him after two weeks. I'm still avoiding the fact that I'm currently unable to pay the bill here.

I'm also shocked at his proposal to marry someone to access my trust fund.

"Principessa, I have four jobs lined up for you." He shrugs.

"I told you, I don't want to work. I can't, Vito," I say through my teeth. I'm fucking tired of repeating that to him.

He winces.

"I'm sorry." I sigh. "Four jobs wouldn't help me out of my debt, anyway."

My day started wonderfully. I woke up in Cora's bed rested. Like really, truly refreshed. Funny how sleep can shift one's mood. I decided to attack the day with renewed determination.

I called Cal and asked him to get me a contact for a good international lawyer. I might have suggested that it's for a friend of mine in Italy, but I really need to do this by myself, so it's a white lie only. How I'd pay the legal fees is a story for later.

I scheduled a meeting with Nora Flemming, a former model who is involved in charity now. Networking with someone who transitioned from the runway to a meaningful purpose and livelihood in her life might be a good first step.

After I took a short—mindful of Cora's utility bill—but invigorating shower, I pulled out my favorite dress. It's a simple, black, linen dress that is straight and roomy, covering my skinny torso but revealing my long legs.

It's like a formal version of a beach dress, and I felt better immediately after I put it on.

I breezed into this restaurant with a smile, and was so grateful to see Vito's kind face.

Before we even ordered, he explained what the auditor found out. And that's where the morning bliss came to a halt.

For parts of his speech, my mind went blank, but I got the gist. Vito is trying to sell my Milan and London apartments, but the market is down, so it might take some time. But the lovely Maria cleaned me out.

Vito is heartbroken, and he offered to pay for my expenses for the next few months. He filed the charges before he left Europe, but the case of a cheated foreigner would hardly be a priority.

It might take a very long time before I get my money back. If I get it back, because God knows where Maria hid it.

"But they would cover your day-to-day while you're trying to figure out what's next for you. I have some interest from brands looking for a spokesperson as well."

I perk up. "That might be more meaningful, and less draining. What brands?"

"A new line of tobacco vapes in Europe, and an energy drink here in the States." He looks at me from above the rim of his glasses.

My brief enthusiasm deflates. "I'll pass on both. If I'm to become an ambassador, I want a brand that is ethical, sustainable, or at least improves people's lives. One that has a positive story behind it."

He nods. "I'll keep looking. I'm sure something will come up over time."

"But I don't really have time," I mumble. "Who is the eager bachelor?"

"He's a businessman who needs to clean up his image. Remember how you helped that Norwegian prince a few years back?"

"Ansfrid? Of course I remember." I frown, not understanding how that is relevant.

Ansfrid is gay, and he needed his inheritance, but wouldn't get it on the grounds of his sexuality, so I posed as his girlfriend.

"It would be similar this time, only you'd benefit as well."

I cock my head, studying Vito. He's serious about this. And the idea isn't completely outlandish.

I would access my trust fund and get an annulment. Or a divorce, but at least I would be able to breathe.

"If I access my trust fund, wouldn't the authorities confiscate my money because of the owed taxes?"

Vito jerks his head, assessing me with unfiltered surprise. Yeah, I'm not just a pretty face. Another thing I did this morning was to read up on all the possible outcomes of Maria's actions.

"So you're considering it?"

That's what surprised him? Jesus, I need to stop assuming everyone thinks I'm incompetent and dumb. Vito has only ever supported me.

"Don't get excited yet. Regardless of what the police find out or not, I owe taxes, don't I?"

He soothes his dark green pocket square. "Yes, you do. But I'm sure your trust fund would cover that, and you still would have enough left. Besides, your future husband is rich." He hikes his shoulder casually.

I groan. "Is he old?" I guess I am considering this.

"Eighty. You might even inherit soon."

My eyes widen, and then I see his grin. "You asshole."

"Cazzo, wouldn't that be an excellent solution?" He chuckles, and I'm so grateful for his levity. I need every ounce of it.

"Okay, let's explore the option."

"Good, because his handler is here." Vito waves, and my gaze finds a woman in her fifties who smiles and saunters toward us.

Dressed in a navy pant suit, she walks with confidence, like she owns this place. My father walks like that. Like everyone can fuck themselves because he's above them all.

Finn and Cal walk like that, but without the attitude. They just naturally own the room the minute they step into it. I wish I was like that.

"Vito!" The woman air-kisses my manager while I glare at him for blindsiding me like this.

"I'm Betsy Ham. My jam is crisis and reputation management." She extends her hand, and I swallow a chuckle.

Her name doesn't match her aura. I mean, I don't know the woman, but I wouldn't expect a Betsy Ham to ooze so much testosterone.

"Saar van den Linden." I don't follow with a nice-to-meet-you because I don't want to lie.

She takes a seat.

"So where is the groom?" I ask, willing my lips to quirk up. Fuck, this is surreal.

Betsy snaps her fingers—she fucking snaps her fingers—at the waiter. "Can I have a glass of iced tea?"

My gaze turns to Vito, fully expecting him to be shocked, appalled, or just plain scandalized, but I find him staring at Betsy's cleavage. Gaping, in fact. Fucking men.

"Where were we?" Betsy brings her attention back to us after grilling the poor waiter, demanding flavors of iced tea that probably don't exist before she huffed and ordered a peach one.

"The groom?" I cock my head, not sure if I should laugh or run while I can.

"Oh yes. Sorry, he is late... Ah, here he is." She beams, raising her hand.

I lean sideways to get a better view of the entrance, but the man turns before I can catch his face.

Holding his hand on his hip, he seems to bark something into his phone, and then he listens, staring at the wallpapered wall in front of him.

Okay, he's tall and well-dressed. Like even from here, I can see his suit is tailored. I've been around fashion and clothes all my life, so I know how to spot quality.

His Ferragamo shoes are polished to the nines. When Vito said my potential husband was rich, he wasn't kidding.

But it's the way his jacket hugs his broad shoulders that steals my attention. It's like someone dressed a Greek god in expensive clothes.

And his ass. Well, from behind, it looks like it won't be such a hardship to spend my time by his side.

Turning, he puts his phone into his jacket, and I'm mesmerized by his fluid movement while adjusting his sleeves and cuffs. Such a simple, automatic motion, but he executes it with such grace.

Despite wanting to play aloof, the corners of my lips quirk up. And then my gaze lands on his face, and I freeze.

Over. My. Dead. Body.

Chapter 5

Corm

I put my phone into my pocket and fidget with my cuffs, briefly revisiting all my recent choices. Choices that got me into this fucked-up situation. One I really don't want to be in.

When Vladislav suggested I settle down—meaning, I marry and divert the media attention—I seriously considered giving up on the deal.

Do I need more money? Not really.

Do I want to fail at establishing the best financial group in the country? Fuck, no.

And if it should cost me my bachelor status for the time being, so be it. It's not such a steep price to pay.

According to my overpriced PR handler, Betsy Ham, I might get away with a fake engagement and a few staged photo ops in the next few months. With the right fiancée on my arm, she could get my image cleaned up pretty fast.

As soon as the deal between AetherTech and Atlas is signed, I'd break off the engagement and move on with my life, laughing at the fuckers with their archaic views and expectations.

I close my eyes briefly, reining in my irritation about the situation. Betsy promised I'd like the bride. And who knows, we might hit it off and enjoy the next four months.

My gaze follows the sound of Betsy's throaty laughter and lands on... Fuck. My. Life. What are the odds?

With her dark blonde hair styled in waves around her angelic face, Saar van den Linden looks like a supermodel. Obviously. No wonder fashion designers and brands pay to work with her. That face can sell air in a jar.

I came here with the let's-get-over-with-this-bullshit attitude. But seeing that Saar van den Linden is my potential bride just increased the value of this transaction.

The only woman who ever fascinated me enough to even consider having a wife.

I adjust my collar, ignoring the subtle jump in my heart rate. This is going to be fun. Or a complete disaster, if her glower is any predictor of the outcome.

When I saw her in one of my clubs recently, I didn't realize she was in town for longer than her usual day or two. Not that I've been keeping tabs on her.

Her nostrils flare, and she leans back in her chair, folding her arms across her chest. Her dark blue eyes shoot daggers in my direction.

She looks as fragile and even more defiant than when she came to see me two years ago. I tried to find out what was beyond that pretty face and fierce loyalty, but she's been immune to my charms.

But at least I sold that stupid building, and now she owes me; and I like my odds because, by the looks of it, she walked into this meeting blindsided.

Just like me.

I only have myself to blame for it, because I told Betsy I don't fucking care who my future fiancée is. I'm paying Betsy way too much for something I don't really want, so I expect her to deliver.

Well, deliver she did. This is a treat.

And a major complication. Saar's brother will never agree to this match. As much as I'd like her fine ass in my space. As much as this candidate has just enhanced the value of this fucked-up PR plot significantly.

Saar may intrigue me, but I'm not going to jeopardize my already shaken relationship with my partner, her brother. Especially since the reason I'm here is to protect the deal, not to break another one. Though I'm not above fucking with Cal.

Based on Saar's surprised scowl, the whole arrangement might be off the table already. But when have I ever given up this fast?

As I take my time walking across the restaurant, Saar moves her glower from me to the man by her side, and then to Betsy. She's ready to bolt and rip Betsy's head off. And probably mine.

"What a lovely surprise." I smile when I reach the table.

Saar stands up, her chair almost toppling over. "Book me those jobs, Vito." She storms away.

"Principessa." Vito, I assume, stands up. "Excuse me. We'll be right back." The pretentious prick pats the silky scarf inside his open collar.

I have no idea who he is, but I don't like the man. And why does he call her princess?

While he rushes away, I try not to follow to check if she's gone. Vito may irritate me at first sight, but I hope he gets her to come back.

"What were you thinking?" I accuse as soon as I take my seat, glaring at Betsy.

"I'm not sure what's going on." Her eyes dart between me and the exit, and I relish seeing her flustered.

"I guess you didn't do a very thorough background check." I enjoy not giving her more details.

"She's a supermodel, and will look great in pictures. She hasn't been associated with any scandals bar the falling out with her parents. And even that is more associated with her brothers. Besides, we could spin that as a found family, with a few pictures together with your mother."

She taps her long nails on the side plate and studies me for a beat before she continues, "Now, if there is a history between you and her..." She grimaces, like the mere idea is repulsive. "It might be the first and only instance where you were discreet and I didn't find out about it in my research. What's going on, Cormac?"

She sounds like my English teacher, patronizing and righteous.

"Betsy, in what universe did you assume that when Caleb van den Linden demanded I go through this sham to clean my image, he wanted his little sister to take any part in it?"

She opens her mouth, but I raise my finger to shut her up. While I was busy ogling Saar and reveling in this entertaining twist of fate, I completely forgot to consider one key element.

"Why does she need a fake husband?" I raise my eyebrow slightly, my face a stone otherwise.

I mastered that demanding look when I was a

teenager. My father used it effectively to get people to cater to him, expecting it, commanding it.

Betsy looks away for a moment. It may be imperceptible, but it gives her away. She's searching for an answer. Which can only mean one of two things.

She doesn't know—which would be a major oversight for someone as good at her job as she is. Or the truth needs to be sugarcoated.

I don't like any of those options.

"It's for financial reasons. She wants access to her trust fund. It's tied to her having a husband."

Betsy grimaces again, as if that would reinforce her stand on women's rights, and stop fuckers like old van den Linden from treating their daughters like property or business leverage.

Her or my opinions on the matter are irrelevant at the moment. What's more intriguing is why Saar van den Linden would need money.

"She must make a lot of money. Are you sure this wouldn't be another scandal in the making?" I force myself not to look toward the exit, where I more sense than see Saar arguing with that Vito guy.

Betsy straightens up, her cleavage practically covering the whole table, and looks at me like... well, like my English teacher again. Fuck this woman with her haughty attitude. "She wants to retire." She perks up.

"That's fine, but what happened? Did she spend all she earned?" I snort. "Well, I'll need a really good prenup," I say, unreasonably excited about the prospect of marrying Saar van den Linden.

But being the bastard that I am, I utter the words because I assume Betsy's brightening relates to Saar and Vito's return, which is immediately confirmed.

"An iron-clad prenup is one of my conditions as well." Saar sits down across from me, her features arranged in a stone-cold manner, a mixture of animosity and resignation.

And why does she look at me like her being here is my fault?

Those fucking blues. That's what always captivated my attention, her haunted gaze. I never allowed myself to investigate further what it is I see in her eyes.

Now, when she holds my gaze like it's a contest, something stirs in me. A weird, misplaced need to bring a spark to those eyes. To find out who or what made her so guarded. To protect her from it.

That is just a plain fucked-up sentiment on my part. Over the years, at every brief encounter, she made it abundantly clear she wants nothing to do with me.

And yet, she came back to this table.

"One of your conditions? There is more?" I smirk, leaning back in my chair.

"Before we move ahead," Betsy fucking dares to

interrupt. "Corm, this is Vito Conti. We have collaborated before. He's Saar's manager."

"Nice to meet you." Vito smiles at me like he is in any way relevant.

But he's relevant to Saar, because she smiles at him and he pats her hand. He returns her smile and nods. Reassuring her?

And why does a part of me want her to look at me with so much affection? Or why do I want to punch his face for touching her? Maybe pretending to marry a woman I have been mildly obsessed with isn't the best idea.

Betsy fidgets and clears her throat. "The two of you"—she points between me and Saar—"clearly don't need an introduction, but I hope your prior relationship won't be a problem here."

"There is no relationship." Saar looks offended by the mere suggestion.

Betsy gives her a professional, condescending smile. Why does she work with people if she doesn't like them? "What I meant is that from my client's perspective, your future relationship would require publicity. I would need you to not only pretend that you can stand each other, but actually pretend you are in love."

Saar snorts. "I have been photographed most of my life. I'm paid to look a certain way. I can look madly in love with him."

"Him" falls from her lips, flat and flavorless.

She leans forward, stretching her arm over the table. Placing her delicate hand on my chest, she looks at me through her lashes and smiles ever so lightly.

She licks her lips, and the gesture surges blood to my groin, my cock twitching. Her touch is light, but even through my shirt and my suit jacket, it burns me.

She dusts a nonexistent lint from the fabric. "You had something there, Cormy-bear," she breathes.

She doesn't fucking say, she breathes, and I inhale sharply like some teenager.

Leaning back, she winks and gives a blinding smile to Betsy, who is staring wide-eyed.

"Oh, was the pet name too much?" Saar blinks innocently. "Should I stick with a more traditional one and call him darling or honey?"

Fuck, she is selling the act well. Vito bows his head, hiding his smirk, pleased with himself like her performance was his achievement. Asshole.

What's more concerning, however, is my body's reaction to her fake display of affection.

Goose bumps, held breath, and a fucking semi in my pants. I better sign the deal between Vladislav and Donovan quickly. This is going to be a challenge.

My competitive nature kicks in fully, and damn me

if I don't see this through. She thinks she can rile me up; she's in for a surprise.

I lean back in my chair and crack my neck. Game on.

"Let's get this over with," I snap. "A prenup is essential. What other conditions do you possibly have?"

She bristles. "A prenup is essential for me too. Don't think for a second I need your money."

I chuckle, a low sound that seems to annoy her. "And yet, here you are."

She rolls her eyes. "No wonder you have to pay someone to pretend to like you. It's not just your reputation that is toxic; it's your personality."

"You need money, I need a wife. Let's not make this more complicated than it has to be."

"Again, I don't give a flying fuck about your money." Saar's voice is now laced with annoyance. "This is about what's mine. My trust fund is locked up because of a stupid clause. So, trust me, I'm not here for your millions, Quinn."

I push my chair out and cross one leg over the other, adjusting my cuffs. "Billions."

Saar huffs, exasperated. I should not enjoy this so much.

Betsy clears her throat, glaring at me. I guess if

someone captured the current mood on camera, we won't sell the happy story.

Well, Saar is not the only one capable of selling this. I stand up.

"Corm," Betsy warns.

I round the table, not leaving Saar's eyes for a moment. In one swift move, I grab her hand and pull her up. Fuck, she is really light.

The momentum and her surprise propel her forward, and she lands with her hands on my chest, her body flush against mine.

Before she can react, I snake my arm around her waist, pulling her even tighter to me.

She looks at me wide-eyed, and for a moment, she is just herself. A little bit vulnerable, and a hell-of-a-lot beautiful.

She wears no makeup, and for that beat of a moment, she isn't acting, posing, or pretending. She just is, taken aback, mask down. And for an equally brief moment, I find myself mesmerized, completely spellbound by her.

But she snaps out of it quickly and frowns. "What—"

"Make no mistake, The Morrigan..." I dip my head and whisper into her ear.

Her breath hitches, and I pretend the scent of her, the warmth of her, the feel of her, has no impact on me.

Plastered against me in my vice-like hold, she can certainly feel how 'not' impacted I am.

She shivers slightly. Good. I'm not the only one.

"I think there is a threat there somewhere you lost track of, Quinn." Her breath feathers the skin around my collar, and I take a deep breath to stop myself from bending her over my knee and teaching her a lesson.

But my unhinged thoughts aside, my lips quirk up. Fuck, she's refreshing.

"Make no mistake, The Morrigan," I repeat. "I have something to gain here, and I won't let your daddy issues fuck it up for me. You don't want to be on my bad side. Your teeth are not sharp enough for that. So let's keep this amicable before I put that mouth of yours to better use. You owe me a favor."

I didn't sell the Hudson River property to her brother to hold it over her head, but I'm not above doing it either.

Her chest rises and falls rapidly, her cheeks a beautiful pink color. "I don't owe you anything."

"We'll see about that." I smirk.

I lean back, not letting go of her yet. Gently, I tuck a strand behind her ear, and she shivers again, her lips trembling.

The heat in her eyes has a very different temperature than the angry glare she's been rewarding me with since I arrived.

There might not be media here yet, but I lower my lips to her hair, inhaling. Lavender and sin—I wish I could bottle her scent and take it with me.

I step back so suddenly she drops to her chair, her eyes searching for a target, avoiding mine.

"Okay, why don't we order lunch before we continue?" Vito suggests in his thick Italian accent.

"And copious amounts of alcohol," I quip, my gaze on Saar.

She bristles and opens her mouth, no doubt to retort. Instead, she sits back, eyes narrowing. "I have demands."

I don't flinch. "By all means. I'm curious to see how creative you can get."

"First, I want complete autonomy. My life, my schedule, my career—you don't get to control anything. You just smile pretty for the cameras and stay out of my way."

"Your career?" If retiring isn't her reason to be here, then what is?

She flinches. "Yes, my career," she snaps, and Vito reaches to touch the top of her hand. She glances at him before she straightens up, abandoning the topic. "No controlling me, no calling the shots."

I shrug. "Done."

She opens her mouth—and after my earlier macho move, I keep picturing those lips around my cock—but then jerks her head back and sags a bit, frowning. She didn't expect my cooperation.

"What?" I chuckle. "You're free to do whatever you like, as long as it doesn't embarrass me or affect the business. Anything else?"

"I want a separate residence. I don't care what the media thinks. I'm not living with you."

"I'm pretty sure you'd enjoy sharing a bed with me, but your loss." I shrug. "Deal."

I would certainly enjoy having her in my space. Taunting her. Breaking her. Claiming her.

"No deal," Betsy interjects.

Fuck, I almost forgot we are not alone. What the fuck is wrong with me? I'm always in control. In every fucking room. Every situation. And here I am, verbally and non-verbally sparing with this woman and forgetting about the real objective here.

"Miss van den Linden," Betsy doesn't sound like my English teacher anymore—more like a ruthless lawyer. Saar flinches. I rein in my irrational need to interfere.

"While I applaud your need for autonomy, this arrangement requires selling a fairy-tale love story. Mr. Quinn is under a tight schedule to improve his public image. And given the unfortunate current media attention, it won't be an easy task. I will need you to comply with a public appearances schedule. And you need to move in together."

I have to give it to Betsy, her tone doesn't leave much room for argument. Saar glances at Vito, and he gives her the compassionate look again.

First, why doesn't she search my eyes? It's me she will live with.

Second, compassion? Give me a break. I'm not a monster.

Some communication passes between Saar and her manager before she sighs. "Separate bedrooms."

Betsy gives us her insincere smile. "Wonderful. This arrangement will look great. You two look perfect together." Her eyes flick to Saar. "You're exactly the kind of woman we need to clean up Corm's image. Beautiful, sophisticated—"

"She is not a prop," I snap, cutting my PR handler off.

Saar's eyes widen, and she looks at me with... Curiosity? Surprise? Wonder? Gratitude?

"I understand I'm here to be arm candy." Saar's gaze on me turns harder.

I hold her gaze, unflinching, fighting the urge to send everyone away and spend time with her alone.

The silence stretches between us, thick and heavy. The tension rolls off her. Something shifted when I cut Betsy off, but I don't understand what.

Something about this woman is... She awakened the protector in me. A side I fucking didn't know I have.

She showed me her teeth. She doesn't need saving, and yet... It's concerning how much I want to unravel her. To understand what is under that carefully hidden persona she shows to the public.

Saar pushes her chair back suddenly, the screech of metal on tile echoing in the quiet room.

"This meeting's over," she says, standing abruptly. "You've got yourself a wife. Now let me know when you plan on parading me around."

Vito scrambles to follow her. *I guess you won't get that lunch, fucker.*

"Oh, one more thing, darling." She smiles at me, no longer selling anything besides animosity. "I want a big wedding. The biggest of the season."

She turns on her heel and strides out, her back straight, her head held high. She is so fucking attractive, my gaze remains glued to the exit long after she leaves.

Like her allure stays behind, demanding attention effortlessly. Stubbornly. Dangerously.

It should bother me. It doesn't.

Something about the way she stormed out sticks with me. That fire in her eyes. That intensity.

I laugh. This is not going to be easy. But it certainly

will be fun. Making Saar van den Linden mine suddenly feels as important as the Atlas/AetherTech merger.

"Fuck. As if I didn't have enough on my plate with you, now I have to tame a Bridezilla. Fucking Vito told me she was unproblematic." Betsy makes a derisive huff.

I turn to her. "Careful how you talk about my fiancée," I warn, and she laughs, but the sound dies on her lips when she meets my eyes.

I stand, buttoning my jacket. "Get her a wedding planner."

"I thought the plan was to stall and avoid the actual marriage." Betsy's expression tightens with frustration.

I smirk. "That's still the plan."

I think.

Chapter 6

Saar

"I want owls as ring bearers." I inspect my nails like my manicure is my only care.

The boardroom is bright with the sun coming in through the large skylights above us. Everything around us—the large conference table, the surrounding chairs, the low cabinets, and even the carafe with water—is sleek, luxurious, and designed to make you feel comfortable enough to spend more money.

I'm not spending my money, so I'm quite comfortable.

I have sat in similar offices many times. Ad agencies, creative boutiques, designer shops. This one isn't any different. But it is. It's all white and beige and pastel colors, and so sweet it's slightly sickening.

But I guess all wedding planner offices are like this one. And maybe if I was an actual bride I would appreciate the theme.

"Owls?" Cynthia, the senior consultant assigned to work with me, asks.

"Yes." I don't even look up.

I almost feel sorry for her, but I'm sure she is used to all sorts of brides. Blushing, excited, nervous, and demanding.

I'm demanding alright, but my demands have nothing to do with my dying desire to make my special day the best ever.

The petite brunette's smile is tight, but she writes my ridiculous demand down. "We'll look into it. We have reputable falconers in our database. I'm sure there are owls trained to deliver."

It takes a lot not to show my shock. Goddammit.

I didn't expect Betsy to set up this appointment. I guess Quinn is really in a hurry to get this done, and Betsy is set to deliver in style.

I'll give them style. I grab my phone and search for the most ridiculous wedding ideas.

I don't even know why I'm doing it. Like rebelling would get me to my financial freedom faster.

I still can't believe Vito talked me into this. I still wasn't completely on board with the idea of a fake marriage, let alone one with Cormac Quinn.

When he sauntered in with his light brown hairstyle in that sexy, effortless way, with his cocky smirk, and unfairly gorgeous face, it was satisfying to storm out of there. I didn't get far. Vito reminded me about my debt and the urgency of the situation. He listed the jobs he had lined up as my alternative.

And then he presented Corm as my fastest and least painful option, because where am I going to find a husband this fast?

"It really is a blessing, Principessa," he said, and I reluctantly returned to the table.

And I've been feeling like I lost ever since.

When I teased Corm to prove to Betsy I could deliver the illusion of a loving couple, my palm sensed the muscles under that suit, and something carnal awakened in me.

Stupid body completely betrayed my brain. And when he pulled me up and yanked me to him? Since when do I enjoy being manhandled like that? The dominance bleeds from his every move, every action, every word.

I love it.

I hate it.

I'm screwed.

I had to bail out of there, because being around him for an extended period is a hazard. And now I'll have to live with him.

The whole encounter felt like a loss, and I hate losing. Feeling desperate—and a bit confused, thanks to my body's reaction—I left with my head high, and with one last utterly stupid demand.

I don't want any wedding. Let alone the large, lavish wedding I pretend to plan here.

But here I am, abusing the woman across from me with nonsense, and she doesn't even flinch. Is my groom really willing to pay for all of this?

What a waste that would be. What exactly did Quinn tell her when he hired her? Will he even see these demands? God, the man infuriates me.

The Morrigan.

A goddess of unrest and war, she also foretells doom, death, or victory in battle. Well, I foretell that I'm going to win this one. Fuck him.

And why is *The Morrigan* the only word he says in the hottest Irish accent? His parents came from Ireland, but he grew up here. When he said it, I felt the lilting quality of the soft sound down to my core.

I groan.

"Are you okay?" Cynthia pours me a glass of water and smiles, tossing her shiny, high ponytail extension over her shoulder. "Planning a wedding is nerve-wracking, but rest assured, we will help to alleviate a lot of the stress for you."

"Will you get me another groom?" I blurt out, and she startles.

Shit. I guess she believes this is for real. I snatch the glass and gulp the water, emptying it.

She rushes around the table and sits beside me, tentatively patting my arm. "Tension between the couple is very common during the wedding planning. Do you want me to book you a session with our relationship coach?"

Jesus. Mary. Joseph. "Will Corm have to attend as well?" I bat my lashes.

"Ideally, yes. You're going through this together."

I bite my lip. Game on. "I'd very much like that. Will you make sure it gets scheduled as soon as possible?"

"Of course, Saar. Do you want to take a break?"

I wish I could be the fly on the wall when he finds out I booked this. He wouldn't say "deal" like he'd tossed around during our last meeting.

"No, let's continue. I'd like the groom's party to wear superhero costumes. Do you think Corm is an Ironman? Or a Hulk?" I scrunch my lips to the side, feigning that I'm thinking hard. "Green would suit him well."

Cynthia blinks a few times. "Let's park the attire ideas for our next session, once we confirm the colors. What about the menu? If we go with the best chefs in the country, or fly a Michelin-starred chef from Europe, we need to confirm as soon as possible."

"I want a fair. People expect gourmet meals. I want to surprise them." I really shouldn't have this much fun with this. I'll have to go through with this wedding after all. But it's not like he'd ever approve this. Would he?

Cynthia chuckles nervously. "You want carnival food at your wedding?"

"Isn't that a fabulous idea?" I shimmy my shoulders. Cynthia tries to hide her horror while I try to stay in character. "We could have a bouncy castle at the reception."

You got your goddess of war, asshole.

"A delivery? What is it?" I hold my phone to my ear, about to push the front door of Cora's bistro open.

New York seems to have remembered it was April, and the sun given way to the more familiar wind. I turn to protect myself, not wanting to enter the place while talking on the phone.

"I'm at the airport, principessa; just give me your address," Vito urges.

For some reason, I don't want him to know where I live. That I'm crashing at my friend's.

He knows of my desperate situation, but I told him I'm staying at my brother's. I don't want to explain why I lied. Mostly because I don't even know why.

"I'm not there, anyway. Have it delivered to Cora's bistro. I'll text you the address." And hopefully, the delivery will get lost. It's from Betsy's office, so it won't be anything I want.

"Okay, it should be there in an hour. I'll talk to you soon."

"Have a safe flight, Vito. I miss you already."

"I'll call you as soon as I talk to the lawyers. And Saar?"

"Hm?" I huddle closer to the entrance, like that could save me from the gusts of wind.

"Don't piss off the groom. You need him."

I roll my eyes. "I'll be on my best behavior."

"You'd better. Ciao."

"Finally," Celeste squeals as soon as I push the door and get inside.

She waves her arms like there are crowds between me and her table. Cora's bistro is actually quite empty. I glance at my watch and wave at Sanjay.

Sitting at our usual table, Celeste looks plump, glowing, a very pregnant and happy self. Always super elegant, her chestnut hair is blow-dried, falling in waves to her shoulders, and she's wearing a lovely green dress.

God, I missed her. My meeting with Cynthia invigorated me enough to finally agree to join my friends for our usual chat and coffee.

I rush over to hug her. "Don't stand up. You look..." I search for the right word, regretting that I started the sentence.

"Huge is the word you're looking for, *chérie*," Celeste says in her lovely French accent, laughing and perfectly comfortable.

"I thought you're not supposed to say that to a pregnant woman." I sit beside her.

I don't have one maternal bone in my body, but seeing Celeste with her swollen belly, and knowing this is my brother's baby too, I love the munchkin already.

I stare at her stomach. She married my brother out of necessity, and they still found their happily-ever-after. They hated each other at first. Like me and Corm.

A shiver runs through me. Was I really venturing into that territory? There is no me and Corm. I'm not looking for romance, let alone with him. And yet... he snakes his arm around me once—to deliver a threat!—and my mind wanders?

"Why are you glaring at your future niece or nephew?" Celeste puts her hands on her stomach.

Shit. "Sorry, babe, I got lost in my thoughts. Are

you sick of people wanting to touch it?"

"Do you want to touch my belly?" She tilts her head, her eyes narrowed.

I want to refuse, but reach my hand out regardless. Celeste smiles, that content smile that makes her glow even more, and places my hand over her stomach.

And nothing.

My hand is on my friend's stomach. Should I feel something? I swallow. This is awkward.

Celeste laughs. "The baby isn't moving right now. The only thing you might feel is my gas."

"Ew." I snatch my hand back, but we both laugh. "Why do people want to touch it anyway?"

"I don't know. The weirdest thing is, strangers ask to do it. The other day, I had to tell a woman she could touch my belly if I could touch her boobs."

I snort. "Did she take you up on that offer?"

Celeste waves her hand, grinning. "Enough about me being a beached whale. How are you?"

Yeah, being high on my wedding planning sabotage got me to meet my friends, but am I ready to tell them what a failure I am?

"I'm good. Where are Lily and Cora?" I deflect.

But Celeste knows me, and she draws her eyebrows together, pursing her lips. She studies me for a moment, but then decides not to pry. Thank God.

"Cora is in the back for a delivery, and strangely, Lily is late."

"But that has always been my superpower."

"I wouldn't call your tardiness a superpower." Celeste cackles, but before I retort, Lily enters.

She adjusts her hideous glasses and rushes over to us. "I'm sorry I'm late. I overslept. How are you?"

I wish there was a simple answer to that simple question.

"Here you are." Cora emerges from behind the counter and sits down. "It feels like we haven't seen each other for ages."

"It's nice to hang out together finally," Lily says.

She joined our little group only last year, when she first worked for Cora. And proved to be absolutely useless as a waitress, but quite loyal and fun as a friend. Cora had to fire her, but she didn't let her disappear from our lives.

"How long have you been in New York now?" I ask Lily.

"For about a year, why?"

"You still didn't find a good hairdresser?" I tease.

Seriously, the woman is beautiful, but she wears grandma glasses, and her pixie cut looks like she chopped it with a pair of blunt scissors.

"Saar," Celeste reprimands.

"What?" I shrug. "We're friends, someone needs to

tell her that hiding her beauty behind those glasses and that cut is a travesty."

Lily lowers her gaze, wringing her hands. Cora and Celeste are glaring at me. Fuck. I'm so worried about becoming the topic of this conversation that I offend to avoid playing defense.

I sigh. "I'm sorry, Lils, that was—"

"I'm okay with the way I look. Not everyone is a model." Lily shrugs and turns to get Sanjay's attention.

"I didn't mean—"

"I know." She winks, smiling.

Sanjay comes with a tray full of coffees and treats. "I took the liberty of preparing your usuals, ladies."

"He's a godsend." Cora sighs blissfully and takes her cup of Americano.

"What's going on, Saar?" Celeste asks, leaving no room for deflection. "You've been avoiding us, and you're clearly in your I-don't-care-about-anyone phase that flares up when you're struggling with something."

"Thank you for your unsolicited psych analysis," I grumble, sagging in my chair.

"Case in point," Cora deadpans.

I shake my head. I shouldn't have come here. "I can't talk about it. I was right staying alone until I figure it out."

"Or maybe you don't have to hide and let us help,"

Lily suggests, making me feel even worse for teasing her.

"Okay, spill it." Celeste pokes me with her elbow, always ready to offer some tough love. "You will feel better."

"We won't judge you," Cora reminds me.

I know they won't, but that doesn't make it easier to accept the current mess of my life. I cradle my cup of latte, staring at the white foam for a few moments.

"Fuck it. My accountant..." I look at Celeste. "You can't tell any of this to Cal."

Her face softens with compassion. She was my friend before she married my brother. Why do I keep forgetting that? I can trust her. I can trust these women.

I still can't face them, so I look down at my untouched cup. "My accountant embezzled from me; I'm broke. To access my trust fund, I have to be married. My manager found me a groom." I finally lift my gaze. "I'm getting married. Ta-da." I raise my arms above my head.

I giggle nervously, bracing for their contempt, judgment, or disappointment.

"Fuck," Lily says, shaking her head.

"When did the marriage part happen?" Cora asks.

"What do you mean? You knew about the rest?" Celeste's eyes dart between us.

"I knew about the money, and that she worries she will have duck lips." Give it to Cora to help smooth the edges of a difficult topic. Or just bring some levity.

Lily snorts, spitting out some of her beverage. She pounds her fist on her chest. "What are duck lips?"

"What you get when you go to those discount places in the malls to inject you with collagen," I explain.

Around the table, my friends' features are wary from being shocked, surprised, compassionate, and perhaps indignant on my behalf. I don't quite understand why I feel so uncomfortable sharing with them.

I grew up in a house where my father would punish me for showing any weakness or making a mistake. He would ridicule me, berate me, or ignore me for weeks if he was displeased with me.

I worked for years in an environment where my needs and ideas were not relevant. Where my willingness to follow simple orders was rewarded. Where I was more a prop than a person.

She's not a prop.

Corm's indignation on my behalf, his defense shocked me. Nobody. Nobody ever stood up for me like that.

Vito might have sometimes, but he mostly tried to rebuild my dignity after work. My manager helped me grow a thicker skin. Perhaps become too indifferent. I guess I'm a survivor after all.

But Corm, whom I've never even tried to be nice to, stood up for me. And I don't know what to do with that. I didn't need a knight to save me, but when one showed up, it formed a crack in my cynical wall.

So I responded the only way I could: I rebelled. I don't want to be grateful to him. I don't want to be impressed by his actions. I don't want to be thinking about him. Period.

"Okay, let's back up here." Celeste turns to me, her chair squeaking as she tries to maneuver her body to angle it properly. She looks at me with so much love I almost recoil. "Thank you for trusting us, and sharing with us."

I swallow around the lump in my throat and nod, unable to find my voice.

"Let's unravel this one bomb at a time though. And Cal will not find out until you're ready to tell him," Celeste reassures me. "Merde, I wish I could drink. How bad is the money situation?"

I sum up the bleak situation and even bleaker prognosis. As I talk, I wonder how I let things get this far. "I've been stupid really—"

"Don't you dare blame yourself," Celeste interrupts. "Can we help?"

"No, it's okay. I don't need your money."

"Yes, you do," Cora says. "But I guess that leads us to bomb number two."

"Who is the lucky man?" Lily asks.

I finally take a sip from my now cold coffee. "Cormac Quinn."

"Merde," Celeste swears again. She had her own grievances with Cal's business partner.

"But you hate each other." Lily gasps.

I fidget. "Hate is a strong word." I didn't realize my animosity toward him was public knowledge. I mean, Lily met him once, I think.

"I saw you two at Celeste's vow renewal. You didn't speak, just glared at each other," Lily says.

"I disagree. I think Quinn was looking at Saar like she was his meal." Cora chuckles.

"Wasn't he?" Celeste perks up.

"Oh, for fuck's sake. Have you seen the media coverage? Every woman is a potential meal for him. Nevertheless, us not liking each other is a good prerequisite for a successful arrangement."

Celeste raises her eyebrows, tilting her head like I'm full of bullshit.

I huff with exasperation. "I'm not going to fall in love with him like you did with Cal."

"So what's his angle?" Celeste asks.

"He needs his image repaired with a docile, smiling wife on his side." I nip a piece from Celeste's croissant.

She swats at my hand. "Hey, I'm eating for two. And Cal doesn't know you're the bride?"

Yeah, that's a bridge I'm not too keen to cross. "I hope he'll take it as well as you."

"He works with Corm, and he doesn't know yet?" Celeste gasps.

"Nobody knows yet."

Celeste sighs, and I whip my head to her. "Don't you cave. I need to tell him myself."

"Of course, but don't take too long, because that's a hard one to keep to myself." Celeste takes a generous bite of her pastry.

We sit in silence. My friends probably absorbing the news. Me? I guess I'm also absorbing.

The enormity of it. The absurdity of it. The finality of it all.

I lost my freedom in the last few weeks.

Moneyless. Jobless. Simply less. That's who I am at the moment.

"Isn't it weird this group doesn't seem to believe in marrying for love?" Lily breaks the silence.

"No complaints here," Celeste murmurs.

Cora chuckles. "Celeste married to get her visa. You to get your trust fund. Perhaps I should marry to make this business profitable?"

"You can make this business profitable without a man," I retort, annoyed by her summary.

Celeste might have married to gain something, but what she ended up gaining was love.

I may just gain ulcers from the stress of being around the man. *Your teeth are not sharp enough, The Morrigan.*

How does he deliver a threat, an insult, and stand up for me, all in one meeting? Asshole.

A gust of wind swooshes through the restaurant, and a delivery man looks around and heads to the counter.

Sanjay immediately points to our table. I completely forgot about my call with Vito.

"Saar van den Linden?" The man asks.

"That's me."

He leaves as soon as I sign for a small cube-shaped box.

My friends crane their heads. It's not from Betsy. It's from Cormac. I rip off the tape and pull out a small black box. A ring-bearing jewelry box.

Of course, he takes any opportunity to remind me this is just business.

I shake my head and snap it open. Glancing down at the solitaire, my stomach turns. It's absurd. No, it's obscene.

The diamond is the size of a small country. It catches the light in every direction, sparkling like it's trying to outshine the sun itself, as if this entire charade could be masked by the brilliance of one ridiculous rock.

I take it out of the box. Fuck, it's heavy. Just like everything about this transaction. For some outlandish reason, I slide it on my finger. The delicate platinum band wraps around my finger like a trap, cold and hard.

I could probably buy a house with this thing—or a small island, maybe. He could've gone for something understated, something that wouldn't scream fake from a mile away. But of course, he wouldn't do anything subtle.

It's like he wants everyone to know exactly how much power he has, how much control. However fake our relationship is, this ring isn't a symbol of commitment—it's a symbol of ownership.

And it's glaring at me from my hand like a taunt. Is this his response to my ridiculous wedding plans?

"Well, a romantic he is not." Celeste snorts. "And kind of careless to just send it over. You might need a bodyguard to wear that thing."

"That thing is going to break your finger." Lily leans across the table to have a better look. "It must be at least ten carats."

"How would you know?" Cora peeks at my hand. "It's blinding."

I yank the ring off my finger and return it to the

box. I'm not sure what he was trying to prove, but I'm sure I don't like it.

Again, I feel like he won a round. And where does that leave me?

Moneyless. Jobless. Simply less. Cormac Quinn's fake fiancée.

Chapter 7

Corm

"Here you go, sir. Enjoy your evening; your server will be with you in a moment." The hostess smiles and leaves.

My eyes clash with The Morrigan's, and by the looks of it, she's not thrilled about my lateness. Or about my existence in general.

I almost sit down, but then I remember Betsy has *accidental* bystanders spread around here to take secret footage of our date, so I step closer and lean in, bracing my arm on her backrest.

My lips graze Saar's ear. "I'm sorry I'm late."

I linger for a moment, telling myself it's for the purposes of leaking the news of our rendezvous.

But I can't ignore the lavender perfume, and the warmth of her skin so close to mine. It's almost unfortunate she hates me, because we could certainly enjoy this arrangement a lot more.

Keep your dick in your pants, you idiot. That thought flits through my mind, immediately followed by another one. *I will make her mine.*

She remains completely still, like she isn't even breathing. I don't move either. For anyone watching, I'm whispering something in her ear.

In reality, I breathe in her captivating scent and enjoy her discomfort. "You should relax, The Morrigan; people are watching."

She sucks in air and grabs my biceps, her nails digging in deep. If I wasn't wearing my suit jacket, she may have drawn blood.

"I'll relax as soon as you step back," she says through her teeth.

I chuckle and finally take the seat across from her. "What is it? Am I making you uncomfortable?"

She takes her Martini glass and smiles at me seductively. "It must be your charming personality."

I adjust my cuffs. "So you *are* uncomfortable."

She flinches. "I'm uncomfortable with this arrangement. Of course I am."

"I thought you needed your trust fund." I open the menu casually without looking at it. "There is nothing wrong with taking what's yours."

She snaps her eyes to me and blinks a few times,

like the concept is foreign to her. An interesting slip of her mask?

She doesn't believe she can take what's hers? Or is she surprised I said something normal, not motivated by my insatiable need to taunt her?

Our waiter shows up and startles when I glare at him.

"Just get us today's special and give us some privacy," I snarl.

I'm being an asshole here, but he interrupted a rare moment of honesty in Saar's eyes. Goddammit. The moment is gone.

"What a gentleman." Saar snorts. "A woman choosing her meal is too progressive for you?" She is spitting the words while maintaining a perfectly pleasant face.

"It's uncanny how good you are at this pretense. Some show you put on." I chuckle.

"Don't forget I've done this for years."

I raise my eyebrows but keep my grin. "Fake relationships?"

She rolls her eyes, but covers the gesture with quite believable fake laughter like I said something funny. "Play a role. Model. Be what others want me to be." She winces at her last sentence.

And suddenly, I'm interested in all her secret parts.

And there are many. She tries to hide them from me, but that makes her even more intriguing.

And why is my grin genuine?

"So smile, pose, repeat?" I tease.

She studies me for a long moment. "Yes, exactly, just a prop."

I lean forward. I shouldn't care about her feelings. And yet… "You were there when I told Betsy not to ever treat you like that. You were there, so don't you fucking dare to accept that label."

She may not like me, but I hate it when people accept a story about themselves that makes them feel less. Not that I've subscribed to this belief about myself lately.

"Aren't you using me as one?" She smiles sweetly.

I snort. I didn't force her to accept this deal. "This is mutually beneficial, but feel free to walk away."

"You would love to win, wouldn't you?" Her saccharine smile may give me diabetes.

And still, this is the face that sold shitloads of brands. Having spent almost no time with her, I already see how fake it is. How it looks colder up close and personal.

"Win? I didn't realize we're competing."

She laughs. "Of course you didn't." She rolls her eyes again.

"Why do you hate me so much?"

I reach across the table and grab her hand. She flinches and tries to recoil, but I squeeze.

I have yet to meet a woman who is uncomfortable with my touch. I guess today is the day.

She looks away for a moment, and then raises her chin high. "Not everyone is thrilled about pretending to love a man who has the emotional depth of a spreadsheet."

That rips an unexpected laugh out of me. I release her hand. "So I'm just a shallow man; that's your main objection?"

"You humiliated me two years ago. Now you need me to save your man-whore image. That doesn't make you a candidate for my best friend." She takes the silver linen napkin and places it on her lap gracefully, smoothing it with her hand.

"I'd argue you humiliated yourself back then. And you need me to get your money, so that doesn't give you the moral high ground here." I pause and take her hand again, this time bringing it to my lips.

Staring into her cold eyes, I whisper against the soft skin of her delicate palm. "You're contractually obliged to pretend to like me, The Morrigan. I suggest you try harder, because Daddy Dearest might never release the fund to you."

She blanches, but forces a smile. I kiss her knuckles, and try to ignore the shitty feeling my words stirred in me. Or the electricity surging through me when my lips connect with her hand.

I keep patronizing, humiliating, and threatening this woman, while insisting she's not a prop. Saar van den Linden certainly draws the *best* out of me.

I don't let go, my lips just lightly dusting her hand. She holds my gaze, and I wish I could read her train of thought.

She is probably considering if the trust fund is worth this whole charade.

I, on the other hand, am wondering if I can sneak in a clause about a shared bedroom into our agreement.

Someone clears their throat, and we both jump apart.

"Excuse me, your first course." A different waiter approaches. "A chestnut bisque with golden shavings. Enjoy." He places the plates in front of us and rushes away.

"Where is your ring?"

I didn't expect her to wear it. To be honest, I got that right out of spite. Just to mess with everyone, because this situation feels too much out of my control.

Spending millions on a ring for a fake engagement isn't reckless; it's unhinged. What point did I make? That I'm a rich bastard who clings to control like a child to his security blanket? Fuck.

"We're not yet engaged, but I appreciate the thoughtful and romantic gesture."

"If you wanted romance, sweetheart, you shouldn't be marrying for money." I pick up my spoon.

"Not your money." Her tone is terse, her countenance beaming. Fuck, she really can sell this well.

"The point remains." I take a spoonful.

"If you think I'd ever wear that ring, you're out of your mind. You. Don't. Own. Me."

"Saar," I say, an apology for I don't even know what on my tongue.

She blinks. "Betsy sent me the briefing." She dips her spoon in the soup and brings it to her mouth. "I think the love story they fabricated is reasonable."

The draft of our engagement announcement outlines how we ran into each other last year in Monaco and started seeing each other long distance. Saar decided to move back to New York to help me cope with my father's death.

I hate that angle, but I have business partners to think about, so I agreed.

"I wanted to ask you to give me one more week before we announce it and I move in with you."

"We both want this to be over as soon as possible. Why delay?"

She makes a frustrated sound somewhere between

a sigh and a groan. "I need a week of freedom to get used to the idea of a jail."

"I can guarantee that living with me is no hardship." The soup is surprisingly good. "Fine. As long as you don't go clubbing and get your pics all over the media."

"Of course, sir. Is this how you won't control me?"

"Mine and your public images are the reason for this deal, Saar."

She sighs. "I won't go clubbing. I need time to tell my brothers. I want them to find out from me."

"Why do they hate me, anyway?"

She puts the spoon down and covers her face. When she looks at me, there is resolution in her eyes.

"They misinterpreted something in high school. Unfortunately, unlike my parents, Finn and Cal are overprotective, and they blame you for something..." She lets out a long breath through pursed lips, like this is causing her stress. "Something you didn't do."

"High school?" I snort. "Why didn't you tell them I'm innocent?"

"Because they saw me for the first time..." Her eyes widen, and then she drops her gaze and picks up her spoon, dedicated to her soup.

When she looks up again, her eyes are pleading.

To let go of the topic? To not tease her? Again,

there is a vulnerable moment she shared—definitely a slip—and I itch to comfort her and find out more.

Neither of those is my right or privilege. And why does it bother me? I don't need drama in my life.

I decide to skip to the next topic. "Okay, I'll tell Betsy to announce our engagement next week."

She exhales visibly. "Thank you."

"I got an email from the wedding planner."

A smile ghosts her face.

"Real classy," I deadpan. "But whatever my bride wants."

She opens her mouth, and then closes it. Her jaw tightens, and she sags into her chair. I guess she was expecting I'd argue with her. I don't need to bother; it's not like *that* wedding is happening.

She gives me another magazine smile. "I'm glad you approve."

"You think I'm a Hulk? Are you having superhero fantasies about me, Saar?"

Her cheeks flush with a warm shade of pink. "You wish."

"I actually do, The Morrigan."

Her eyes flare with something, and while I don't know her enough to identify it, I'm sure it's not disdain or anger. It's something more simple, primal.

She gives me a fake chuckle—I suppose for the

onlookers. "You know what they say, darling, careful what you wish for."

I guess this arrangement is going to be full of threats.

* * *

"What the fuck?" Cal comes from somewhere and barrels into me as I speak to Larissa.

My assistant moves the chair like he could hurt her through the heightened counter of her desk. Or she just wants a better view of the drama. Knowing her, it's the latter.

I step away from my seething partner and lean against the counter. "What do you need, Caleb?"

"You went out with Saar," he barks, and grabs my lapels. "I swear to God—"

"Get your hands off me. Your sister is a grownup. She can spend her time however she wants."

After the semi-uncomfortable dinner last night, I drove her home in silence, and she fell asleep in the car. Like an open mouth, full-on drooling, out-of-it kind of a snooze.

I parked in front of the building where she currently lives with her friend for another forty minutes before I woke her up.

She looked like she needed the rest. Even with her jaw slack, she was beautiful. It was probably my only chance to see her like that. And I enjoyed seeing her so peaceful.

What I don't like is her neighborhood. To her protest and chagrin, I walked her to the door of her apartment. It's a small shoebox of a place, barely big enough for one person, let alone two.

I need to investigate just how dire her financial situation is. Something doesn't add up here.

"Haven't you hurt her enough?" Cal's nostrils flare, spitting the words into my face.

I remain calm. Unmoved. At least, physically. I want to punch his face for daring to attack me in the middle of our office. I want to push him away, but I also know that leaning into his wrath would only make him feel justified.

"I'd never hurt her," I enunciate into his face. "Unless she asks for it," I add, only because I'm an asshole. And I've been having a shitty year, and I want to spread the feeling. I'm that generous.

"My sister is off limits." He drops my lapels and shakes his shoulders, his hateful gaze boring into me.

"Again, van den Linden, she's an adult with a functioning brain. I didn't force her to dine with me. I did, however, enjoy it. And she did, too. Especially the dessert." Yes, I'm definitely an asshole.

The only thing either of us enjoyed was verbal

sparring—I know I did—and the proximity to the end of the evening. The sooner, the better.

The comment sets him off again. "Don't you fucking..." He clenches his fist, his knuckles whitening before he draws his arm back.

A mess of dreadlocks flashes behind him, and Roxy grabs his arm. She practically hangs from his biceps with her two hands before she pushes us to my office.

Banging the door closed, she puts her hands on her hips. "What is wrong with the two of you?" To say she looks pissed would be a gross understatement.

I put my hands into my pockets and glare at Cal. "You were all for my fake marriage." I shrug, and Roxy gasps.

Caleb lurches forward, and this time, the fucker punches me. I stagger backward, the metallic taste of blood spurring me into action.

"Idiots," Roxy shrieks as I return the punch, the shock of contact with his jaw reverberating down my arm.

Fuck, that hurts. And it feels good. I guess I can add brawling to my current list of unreasonable behavior.

Cal swears and launches at me, but strong arms jerk me away from him. I pant like I've just finished a 10K run, and it takes me a moment to recognize

Xander is holding Cal. I try to shake off the hands holding me back.

"Stop it, you eejit." Declan's words penetrate through my adrenaline-infused mind.

My brother lets go, but steps in front of me. He glares at me while I try to figure out how to get out of this like a winner.

Or at least not like a complete *eejit.* That word pulled me out of the fog. My father used it a lot.

Declan raises his eyebrows, unimpressed. That's the problem with older brothers. Especially the ones you respect. They can put you in your place without a word.

But there is another problem with older brothers. Especially the overbearing ones who try to steal their sister's autonomy.

"Are you out of your fucking mind?" Roxy hisses, keeping her voice down like we could leave this office and pretend in front of our employees that nothing happened.

The room descends into a beat of silence, filled with anger, panting, and if I was willing to look, a lot of judgment from those not involved in the fight.

Have I just fought because of a girl? A woman? Well, that's a first. Especially since the woman in question would probably side with her brother and add another punch.

Roxy shoves my shoulder. "With his sister?"

"Don't get involved, Roxy," I warn.

"I wouldn't if you took your schoolyard behavior outside of this office." She bows her head and takes a deep breath, and then turns to Caleb. "While I understand your motivation, next time punch him somewhere that is not here."

"Of course, it's all my fault." I snort. "Get out of my office. All of you." I wipe the blood from the corner of my mouth, my bottom lip already swelling.

"She doesn't deserve any of this. And certainly not you. Stay away from my sister." Caleb rakes his fingers through his hair, pacing in front of my desk like a caged lion.

If I'm honest with myself—which I haven't been much lately—I see his point. If I had a sister, I wouldn't want her anywhere near me. Especially not me as of late.

I raise my arms in mock surrender. "As you wish. She will probably be devastated, seeing as she is really interested."

He spins to probably launch at me again, but Xander blocks his attack. "Bullshit," Cal barks.

I crack my neck and walk around to sit behind my desk. "Why don't you ask her?" I regret saying it as soon as the words leave my mouth.

I promised her a week.

Here I was thinking I've sunken as deep as possible, but there is always room to improve. Or to fuck up more, in my case. If I give my word, I keep it. Apparently not anymore.

But it's not like I really broke the promise. Why neither of us thought about her brothers seeing the photos from our date is beyond me.

I suspect all my partners have a news alert set up with my name. Especially since my image is what can make or break this firm.

I guess Saar's week of freedom just shrank to minutes. But the cat is out, and at least we can move forward faster.

"Are you seriously considering dragging Caleb's sister into your image-recovery scheme?" Declan shakes his head.

"She came to me." I shrug.

"No fucking way." Cal snarls, and Xander puts his hand on his shoulder.

"As I said, ask her. For all intents and purposes, we've been dating long-distance for a year. You'd better get the story from Betsy, so you are prepared to sing about me being madly in love."

"No way Saar would agree to that. Why? What do you have on her? Have you blackmailed her?" Cal yells.

"Caleb, keep your voice down," Roxy warns, but

like all the others in the room, she is looking at me with expectation.

"I don't need to blackmail people, especially not women." I lean back in my chair.

"That's not my experience," Cal retorts.

Fair enough. I did motivate him to join this company in a not-very-ethical way when I announced his involvement before he signed up.

He got an additional ten percent of the company out of that stunt, so he should be pleased.

"I never blackmailed you. I helped you with your slow decision-making, and made you richer in the process."

"There is no way she's willing to do this. Not for you." Caleb shakes his head.

"Obviously," I deadpan.

"Why then?" Xander asks.

"For herself. As I said already. She's a grown-up woman, with her own brain and independence." I put my hands behind my head and look at Cal. "She will tell you when she wants."

"I'm not allowing that," Caleb says through his teeth, the anger radiating from him.

Xander pats his back. "I don't think it's your decision, dude."

Cal gives him a look that could kill, but Xander only shrugs.

"Okay, I suggest everyone cools off in their respective offices, and the two of you"—Roxy looks at me, and then at Cal—"will have coffee together in the staff cafeteria, laughing at each other's jokes, as soon as you can swear not to get physical."

"Anytime. I have nothing against my future brother-in-law." I wink.

"Fuck you." Cal turns to leave, but Roxy blocks the door.

"Fuck you all. I thought you both wanted that deal. I thought we're all on board with helping to prove to the world Cormac is an upstanding citizen. And we can all agree that is quite a task. Can't we?" She glares at Cal.

"Hey," I protest, while all my partners nod.

She looks at me, daggers shooting from her eyes, but then she focuses her exasperation on Cal. "I'll now remind all the employees of their NDAs, and let's hope nobody uploaded a video of your altercation already."

"Yeah, great for our image." Xander groans.

"This testosterone-filled environment is way above my paygrade." Roxy spins on her heels, rolling her eyes, and walks out.

My partners file after her, Cal followed by Xander, who is still patting his back like he's a puppy that needs training.

"You need to get your shit together." Declan shakes his head.

"She came to me," I defend myself, but even to my ears I sound like a douche.

"Since when is Cal's sister the only woman in the world?" He continues shaking his head, disappointment rolling off his shoulders as he leaves my office, closing the door behind him.

Fuck them. Fuck them all. With their righteous attitude. With their honest opinions and concerns.

Fuck them for calling me on my bullshit.

But my indignation is short-lived, because I may be reckless, but I'm not senseless. Somebody ought to call me on my bullshit since I haven't been able to.

The dose of candor sobers me up. And pisses me off. I can do what I want. It's not like I've been forcing her. But fuck, the sooner I close that deal, the better.

I fish my phone from my pocket and dial Betsy while I walk to my office bathroom to assess my swollen lip.

"Corm, the date night photos are trending well. Good job. I have some ideas—"

"Announce the engagement." I don't let her finish. Why does this woman always think she is in charge? I called her, for fuck's sake. This is my conversation.

"We will next week."

"Now," I growl, putting the phone on speaker and laying it on the vanity.

"Based on last night's success, and the media speculation about your relationship with Saar—by the way, people love her; we couldn't have picked a better—"

"Betsy," I warn.

"I recommend we plan some sort of a public declaration? A romantic proposal?"

I snort, turning the faucet and wetting a towel to wash the blood off my face. "Are you high? That's tacky. Just fucking announce it and move her in. I'm away for four days, but I'll leave instructions with my housekeeper."

"Okay, but a romantic proposal might be a good photo op."

"Fuck romance. Just get it done."

Chapter 8

Saar

CELESTE

Merde. I thought you were announcing next week.

LILY

Congratulations, I guess (wink emoji)

CORA

What did I miss?

LILY

Saar is officially engaged.

CORA

How did your brothers take it?

I smile and stretch my arms above my head, and Pitt and Clooney jump from my legs, disturbed by the sudden movement.

I swear that after two weeks here, I can understand their mewing. Right now, they both told me to go fuck myself for interrupting their slumber. Grumpy cats.

But I smile away. Because I slept. I slept. I slept for... I search for my phone, padding the floor beside Cora's sofa.

Five p.m.?

Jesus, I was so lulled by the drive from the restaurant that I fell asleep the minute Corm left. And a bit in his car.

Why did he need to accompany me to the door? That man is so annoying. I could practically smell his judgment of Cora's place.

Asshole.

Are you having a superhero fantasy about me, Saar?

You wish.

I actually do, The Morrigan.

That charged exchange turned my blood to molten honey. God, I hate the impact he has on me. When he leaned in to whisper in my ear after his late arrival at the restaurant, my mind went blank, completely overwhelmed by the tingling of my skin and the fluttering in my stomach.

Also, why was he late? That's my thing. Not that that is anything to be proud of, but still. It's freaking annoying to be on the other side of that particular bad habit.

The good mood from my needed sleep evaporates as I replay our date. I wish he wasn't so... so... him.

There were moments when I forgot my mask, and he latched onto those moments with his gaze, making me want to share with him. When his smirks disappear, it's like his gaze alone turns the temperature in the room up by several degrees.

I clutch the phone to my chest and enjoy the bliss of rested body and mind, minus the thoughts wandering to last night. Hopefully, I broke the weird insomnia cycle.

My phone vibrates in my hand, and I check the screen. Finn.

"What's up?" I sit up, smiling. I'm met with silence, and my heart rate spikes immediately. Shit, did something bad happen? "Finn? Is everything okay?"

He sighs, and I hear Paris whispering something. "Is it true?"

I saunter to the kitchen in search of coffee. "Is what true?"

Finn growls. "What the fuck, Bambi? Cormac fucking Quinn?"

I freeze. What does he know? What is he talking about?

When I say nothing, Finn snorts. "I guess congratulations are in order, but somehow I can't fucking find the joy in the announcement."

The morning—afternoon—bliss fades as quickly as a trending post on social media. How does Finn know? I don't want to disappoint my brother, but I guess it's too late for that.

"Are you mad?" My voice comes out hoarse. Shit, this is not the right question to ask.

Finn utters another heavy sigh. This one stretches over the phone line and falls right into my stomach like a lead ball.

"I'm shocked, I guess. Has he bullied you again somehow? Saar, you don't have to do this. How did it even—"

"It's not real," I blurt out.

"I would hope so," he snaps.

"Finn." I hear Paris's voice. She must be standing beside him, calming him, and probably worried about my sanity. Shit.

"Can we talk about this in person?" I hate how small my voice sounds.

"Where are you? I didn't even know you were in New York. What's going on, Saar?" There is concern in his voice.

A genuine concern.

For a teenage girl whom he found bleeding on the floor in the bathroom. A girl who grew up into a woman who still craves his attention. Who still craves to be seen.

For a woman who is an adult now and should stand up for herself.

"Look, Finn, I'm okay. Everything is fine. Why don't we have dinner together, perhaps with Cal as well, so I don't have to explain twice?"

'Not that I owe you an explanation' is on my tongue, but I swallow the words, because I don't really have the moral ground to suggest that. He assumed something all those years ago, and I never corrected him.

My lie impacted his life two years ago when he acted on his misplaced hatred, and it almost cost him his wife, so I owe him an explanation at least.

"Where are you?" he growls again.

"I'm staying at my friend Cora's before I move in with Corm." I shiver at the idea.

How did I end up here? Damn Maria for stealing from me. And my grandfather for setting up a trust fund like it was the eighteenth century.

Finn sighs. Again. How much of his disappointment can I take? "But you're okay? Safe?"

"Yes, Finn, I'm okay. I'm sorry you found out... How did you find out?"

I put him on speaker so I can make my coffee. But I change my mind and open the fridge and take out a bottle of Chardonnay instead. It's 5 p.m. already, after all.

"What do you mean, how did I find out? You and your *fiancé* issued a statement." The word fiancé probably triggered his gag reflex.

I pour myself a generous glass. Fucking Quinn. He promised me a week. To adjust. To tell my brothers.

Why did I tell Celeste the real reason for the marriage? If I pretended the engagement story was real, I wouldn't need to explain the money to my brothers. But with everything going on and with my insomniac brain, I didn't think this through.

"I didn't realize we were announcing today. I've been jetlagged, and I just... I finally slept well. I wanted to tell you first, but..."

"It's okay, Bambi." Another heavy sigh. "As long as you're safe."

I swallow around the lump in my throat. "I'm safe, Finn." Moneyless. Jobless. And broken, but I think I am safe.

"I'll talk to Cal, and we'll have dinner this week. Sooner rather than later. And come visit your nephew."

After we hang up I sit, staring at Cora's black-and-white-checkered backsplash for I don't know how long.

He promised me one week.

I check my phone and read through messages. Cal called me ten times. Jesus. Fucking Quinn. He promised me a week.

But what was I thinking? Trusting him? Asshole.

My watch says it's almost six. I hope my fiancé is a workaholic, because I have no idea where he lives, but I know where he works. And I need to kill him.

* * *

"Excuse me, sir." I smile at a young man who just left the coffee shop in the corner of the office building where Merged is located.

On his way to the turnstile, he turns and raises his eyebrows. "I know you..." He searches to connect the face with the name.

I giggle. "I get that a lot, but I'm not her." I lie.

I don't have an inflated ego to assume he knows who I am. I've just lived with my face plastered all over the world for twelve years.

He frowns and smiles. "You're right. You look much better than that model. What's her name?"

"Who cares?" I shrug. "I work upstairs, and I left my key card at my desk. I've been calling my colleagues, but everyone is gone. I need to be here tomorrow at six in the morning to prepare a boardroom, so I really need to recover my card." I bat my eyelashes at him.

"They can help you at the front desk." He beckons his head toward the long counter under the shiny sign listing all the companies in the building.

"I know, but they would also call my boss. I just started working here this week, and he'd get upset. He yelled at me three times today already. I can't lose my job."

Compassion covers his face. I knew we could bond over an asshole boss. He leans in and whispers, "Let me smuggle you in." He winks. "We wouldn't want you to lose the job."

"Thank you."

After he gets me a visitor's pass, we enter the elevator together. As soon as the door closes, I step to the farthest corner. Shit, why are we the only two people in here?

He smiles at me through his eyelashes and doesn't say anything while we ascend. He's kind of cute. And normal. Just a normal guy who looks at me like I'm a normal girl.

I wonder what it would be like if I had a chance to even try something normal with someone normal. Will

I ever? If I don't work for a year or two, will people forget about me?

The idea grips my stomach in a vice-like hold. I'm so used to my own publicity that normal scares me. Why am I even thinking about it? Normal is not for me. Not for the next few months, anyway.

"I hope to see you around." He holds the door when we arrive at my floor.

I smile at him and rush outside.

I step into the sleek reception area. The counter is shiny white and unoccupied. Fuck. I hope he's here, because yelling at him over the phone would be highly anticlimactic.

There is a corridor to my left and one to my right. Should I just walk around and call his name? I chuckle at the idea.

"Saar?" Roxy, holding several folders to her chest, appears.

I met her once, at Caleb's Christmas vow renewal, and I liked her instantly. She's a no-nonsense woman who puts her bosses in line without a worry in the world.

"Roxy, hi."

She marches to me, frowning. "Do I want to know how you got up here?"

I bite my bottom lip. "No."

"Are you here for Cal?"

My eyes widen. "Shit. Is he here?"

She giggles. "I think so. Are you here for the Asshole?"

My eyes widen even more. Is she calling her boss an asshole openly? "Yes?"

"Does he know you're here?"

I want to lie, just like I lied downstairs, but something tells me Roxy's bullshit radar is precisely calibrated on account of working for the Merged founders.

"No, he doesn't. I wanted to surprise him." I don't know if she knows her boss's engagement is a sham.

Her grin is naughty. She probably knows more rather than less. "Let me show you his office, and no worries, Cal's is on the opposite side of this floor. And they are both in a timeout, so I doubt you'd run into him."

"A timeout?" I follow her fast steps down the corridor lined with glass-wall offices and cubicles.

"Your brother cracked your fiancé's lip. The latter reciprocated with a bruised chin." The condemnation is palpable in her tone. "What can I tell you, good times."

"Shit," I mutter.

"Larissa, is Corm available?" Roxy asks a middle-aged woman behind another white, sleek desk. I guess that's Corm's assistant.

"Is he ever?" Larissa rolls her eyes. I like her.

"This is his fiancée, Saar. You should give her your number, so she can organize her future husband's agenda. I'm sure he'd love that." Roxy leans against the counter.

Larissa chuckles. "Nice to meet you, Saar. Don't listen to this crazy woman. She is pissed at him, but I know my place. I'm here to protect his agenda."

Roxy snorts. "Well, Saar, this is as far as I could get you. See you later."

I stare at the solid wooden door in front of me.

"He's on a call." Larissa stands up, eyeing me like I just delivered anthrax to her boss. He'd deserve it.

"Is he?" I tilt my head, challenging her.

"You're welcome to wait, but it might take an hour. He just started." Larissa points to a single chair by the door and sits back behind her desk.

The chair looks lonely and pathetic. Just looking at it, I feel like Corm is winning. Larissa's fingers run over her keyboard expertly while I hover beside her desk, filled with indecision.

I look around, but there is no other seat. "Look, Larissa, clearly you're great at your job, but I need five minutes with Corm."

"If he wants those five minutes with you, he'll let me know."

I jerk my head back. "He knows I'm here?"

She continues typing, giving me only a slight nod.

Before I can ask her more, Corm's office door swings open, and he gestures me in.

I have a hard time containing my smile when I see his swollen lips. I don't condone violence, but seeing this man in a state that is less than perfect is satisfying.

"What is the projection?" he barks, still on his call.

As I pass him, he moves, and my arm brushes his chest, or just his jacket, but regardless, an electric current runs down my spine. I snap my head to the side, shocked by my unwelcome reaction. Our gazes collide, and we remain frozen for a beat.

His expression isn't friendly, but it's not calculating and cold as usual. He holds my gaze like he did two years ago in his ridiculous hotel suite office. Like he can't decide if I'm good or bad news, and it pisses him that he wants to find out.

Or I'm just projecting shit because I'm starving for attention. Fuck.

I want to step away, but it's like my body craves the tingling in his presence that his slightest brush with my skin caused. I feel it all the way to my core. The unacceptable attraction scares me.

It takes all my strength to hold his gaze. I'm only marginally aware that Larissa is probably watching our weird stand-off.

Corm stares back at me. It's unnerving. And

somehow rewarding. What is it about his gaze that just takes me as a prisoner?

For a brief moment, or an equally brief conjecture of my imagination, I almost believe he enjoys having me in his orbit. Which also freaks me out.

A voice is droning on in his ear, but I don't know if he's listening. A small bruise colors his chin slightly around his swollen lip. I've never realized how well-defined his jaw is. God, the man is annoyingly handsome. My fingers itch to trace the wound.

Or to squeeze some lemon into it.

He raises his eyebrow impatiently, and I remember why I marched into his office.

After he closes the door, he gestures to a sofa in the corner and shoots a rapid fire of questions at the person on the other end of the line.

I ignore the offered seat. Instead, I look around trying to shake off my body's reaction to his accidental proximity.

I don't know what I expected, but I didn't expect his office to be so bright. It's modern and full of white and beige accents, with a spectacular view of Manhattan.

It's also welcoming. Like his personality is the only offensive thing in this space. Like he landed in this office by accident and didn't bother to redecorate it into the dark colors of his soul.

Without thinking much about it, I move around the place. The shelves to my left house books, binders, and two lonely photographs in simple black frames.

One is of his brother, Declan, scowling in a family portrait with two small children. I recall his wife left him.

Well, if he was scowling like that and his personality is similar to his brother's, I don't blame her. But leaving behind two children? Not even my mother is capable of that.

The other picture is of an elegant woman. Based on her features, she must be Corm's mother. But there is no father. Were they divorced?

Corm's father passed away last year. According to our engagement statement, his recent public indiscretions are related to that loss.

But then why wouldn't he have a picture here? I turn to check his desk, and my gaze meets his. Cormac is scowling at me—and wow, he mastered that look way better than his brother.

"Are you looking for something?" he growls.

"A picture of your father," I answer honestly before I remember we're at war. Goddammit.

"Why are you here?" he snaps.

"What a warm welcome." I give him a saccharine smile.

He cracks his neck. "I had the day from Hell, and I don't need you adding to it."

What a prick. "Maybe if you kept your word and didn't behave like an asshole, your day would have been better."

"What do you want, Saar? I'm not interested in your attitude." He glares at me.

I've never realized how much tension radiates from his body. He may stand with his hands in his pockets, the picture of casual annoyance, but he's vibrating with energy that is about to explode.

Is it just today, or was I so concerned with my own reactions to him that I didn't notice before? And fuck, I hope I won't be around when the volcano erupts.

I fold my arms over my chest, and his eyes drop to my cleavage. For some stupid reason, it makes me feel self-conscious.

I move my arms behind me and shove my hands into my jeans' back pockets. And I hate him a bit more for making me cower like this.

"You jumped the gun, announcing the engagement, so don't blame me for having to deal with my brother."

He laughs humorlessly. "Believe me, sweetheart, your brother is the least of my problems, his little tantrum forgotten. I have a business to run here."

"I hope you're better at that than you are at the rest of humaning," I quip.

He eats the distance between us, and I hate that I back up. My back hits the bookcase behind me.

"I swear to God, Saar..."

He doesn't finish his threat, but his body crowds me in a way that is intimidating enough. Or it should be. Only I'm not scared. I'm so pissed at this man that no other emotion has room.

He smacks his hands on the shelf on each side of my head, caging me. He's only an inch from me, but my body rejoices with such a visceral reaction that I barely swallow a gasp.

His cologne of pure masculinity and assholeness hits my nose, and I almost lean in to get a lungful.

"Well, we both know your word is worth shit, so I'm not afraid of your empty threats." I'm tall, and yet I have to crane my neck.

"Pictures from our date are all over the internet. Cal saw them, so I only accelerated the process. I tried to call you, but you didn't bother answering, *sweetheart*."

He says the last word with so much disgust, I almost wish he drawled The Morrigan into my ear.

Wait? What? I don't wish that.

"Whatever," I snap, flustered. "You promised me

autonomy, and yet you lead the show and disregard my needs or opinions, blindsiding me."

"Again, it's not my fault the pics were already out." He growls, his breath fanning my skin.

Did he step closer? My breasts brush his chest with each breath. Or rather, each pant, because oxygen is in short supply, probably snatched by Quinn and his ego.

"Neither is it mine. It's your PR handler, not mine."

What is my point here? I can't think when he crowds me like this. So why am I not pushing him away?

"Fair enough, but let's be honest here. Neither of us thought about the staged photo op being a problem for your need to bend for your brothers."

"I don't bend for them," I breathe out, much weaker than I'd like to. Goddammit.

He chuckles and trails his thumb from my temple, down my cheek, to my lips. He runs it across my bottom one, his eyes burning.

I swallow, so my tongue doesn't dart out. My body got a free ticket today to defy my brain, apparently.

It's like he's a hunter and I'm his prey. He set his eyes on me, and I became a prisoner. There is heat in them, and also something ruthless and cold. But still captivating.

He leans in, his breath warm by my ear. "If history

shows us anything, you're not too keen to tell them the truth, so I'm sorry if I focus primarily on protecting my interests."

I shiver. Not because he's technically right, calling me out on my teenage failure. Or because he just confirmed he doesn't give a shit about my feelings.

I tremble because the combination of his breath, his scent, and his proximity short-circuits my brain, momentarily erasing my hatred and replacing it with raw need.

And if I'm not mistaken, he is as affected as me. Judging by his growing erection against my lower belly. Jesus.

I open my mouth, but no words come out. His face is only an inch from mine, and this close, his burning gaze renders me speechless.

Somewhere in the back of my mind, the logical corner offers words like "back off", "go to Hell," or "the deal is off".

In the reality of his office, his kingdom, his dominance, I'm not saying any of those thoughts.

And the sad part? It's not because I need this marriage probably more than him.

It's because his vicinity forges some incomprehensible intimacy. One that I apparently crave. We stand there in a silent duel, our chests heaving, my skin covered with goose bumps, my mind useless, and my core ignited.

I would be worried he could smell my inconvenient arousal, but judging by his boner, our bodies are not on board with our dislike for each other.

Hate sex?

His eyes sparkle with something dark. Can he read my mind? Did he really have the same idea as me?

We stare at each other, communicating with our blazing eyes only. I'm saying I wouldn't be opposed, but it would mean nothing. He's agreeing—well, in my mind he is.

I grab his lapels, not necessarily pulling him closer, just... I don't know what... giving him consent? Am I?

His sight drops to my lips. He's on board. Oh my God, we're going to fuck against this bookcase.

"Mr. Quinn, your seven o'clock with Japan is about to start." A female voice fills the room.

"Fuck," Corm mutters and steps away.

I almost collapse, because I didn't even realize how much was I leaning against him. I rush toward the door, not sparing him one look.

"Saar," he calls out.

I turn around slowly. Is he going to suggest we pick up where we left off? Is the moment gone? Shit. I can't decide.

"Yes." Goddammit with the breathy voice.

He's already behind his desk, typing on the keyboard, not even looking at me. "If you want your autonomy, don't fucking schedule a relationship counseling through your wedding planner. Don't control my time with your trivial mind games, and I will leave you alone."

Chapter 9

Saar

CELESTE

How is it @Saar?

CORA

Pitt and Clooney miss you.

CORA

Me too, strangely. (tongue out emoji)

(eye-roll emoji) This house is huge.

LILY

At least you can avoid your fiancé.

Silver lining (laughing emoji)

CORA

Housewarming party?

What a great idea! He's gone.

CELESTE

I wish I could drink. Merde.

"Thank you." I see the movers out and close the front door behind them.

Leaning against it, I sigh. So this is it. I'm officially living with my fiancé. Not that he bothered to show up and welcome me.

His housekeeper, Livia, gave me the keys and showed me my room.

"This is where Mr. Quinn wants you," she announced. "If you have any questions, I'll answer them tomorrow. I'm sorry, but my granddaughter has a play at school today, and Mr. Quinn allowed me to leave early."

She talks about him like he was an employer of the month. I can't possibly imagine Corm treating anyone with respect.

So here I am, all alone in my new home. I shiver at the idea. A bathroom here is probably the same size as Cora's entire apartment.

The place is massive—obnoxiously massive. The ceilings are so high, I swear you could fit a small plane in here, and judging by the heliport on the roof, it wouldn't surprise me if he did.

Why does he even need such an enormous place? Is it a status thing? The foyer is large, with a staircase on one side and a square archway across from it, leading to the dining room.

The floor is checkered black and white, and looks almost like a gigantic chessboard. As his future wife—fake wife—am I the queen or the pawn here? I'm pretty sure it's the latter.

Across from the front door is the entry into the corridor that leads to the living room, kitchen, and some other rooms.

In the middle of the rounded foyer is a large oval table with the most peculiar statue on it. The bronzed abstract monstrosity probably cost a fortune, and if its purpose is to scare away visitors, it does a pretty good job.

Behind the statue, a long corridor seems to end with glass doors leading to the backyard, I think. I'll explore that later.

Rounding the statue, I wander down the hallway to the living room. It's like walking into a high-end designer catalog.

The walls are soft gray, and everything is sleek and minimalist, but there's this strange warmth in the space. It's too clean, too curated, but still... comfortable.

It doesn't have that icy, sterile feel of my childhood home. No marble statues glaring down at me, no grand chandeliers flaunting our wealth to everyone. This place, for all its scale, feels more like a home than that mausoleum I grew up in ever did.

Jesus. What am I thinking? This is not my home.

It's just a temporary station, before I get my trust fund and finally stand on my own two feet.

I worked hard since I was fifteen not to depend on my father. And here I am, at twenty-seven, exactly in that situation.

The idea makes me want to cry. More so because I don't even know what to do with my life currently. I have no degree, no skills, no experience other than posing, smiling, walking, and being efficient at packing and navigating airports.

I have never written a resume or applied for a job. I worked hard for twelve years, and now I'm dependent, not on one man, but on two at the same time.

My father, who hasn't spoken to me in a year, and my *lovely* fiancé, who made it clear I shouldn't mess with him.

I haven't seen him for two days, and yet I'm still feeling the aftershocks of our last encounter. The way my body craved him. The way he crowded me. The way we parted.

Don't control my time with your trivial mind games, and I will leave you alone. Thank God Larissa interrupted us. Sex must be off the table. It's the last thing this hateful, temporary relationship needs.

I need to get laid. But I can't even go clubbing. Betsy sent me a list of events and commitments for the next two months, and I practically won't have time to sleep. Not that I've been sleeping much since the twelve-hour shuteye after our date.

I wander over to the dining room, my footsteps muffled by the thick, plush rug. Nestled in the middle of the large room, with floor-to-ceiling windows overseeing the manicured backyard lawn, is a long table, sleek and dark.

It's made for power dinners with CEOs and politicians, not for breakfast or genuine conversations.

I run my hand along the smooth surface, wondering if anyone's ever sat here long enough to spill coffee or laugh too loudly.

I'm irrationally upset he isn't here. Not that I need a welcoming committee, or to be in his presence, but somehow, being here alone makes me feel insignificant. Like he couldn't bother. Like I'm not important enough to put me on his agenda.

Don't be stupid, Saar. I'm not important. I'm just a means to an end. A photo op. Arm candy. He doesn't need to make an effort in the privacy of his home. Or anywhere behind the closed door.

Why the fuck am I so unsettled, blaming him for my lack of direction and purpose? Moneyless, jobless, without a plan, just... this. A fake marriage and a house so big I may actually get lost in it.

I grab a glass of water from the kitchen, take a long

sip, and set the glass down on the island, staring at the spotless counters.

Does anyone even live here? There's no sign of life, no clutter, no messy corners, no indication that anyone actually exists in this perfect, polished space.

I continue roaming the house aimlessly. I don't know what I'm looking for—some sign that Corm is human after all? A hidden room full of personality and warmth? Yeah, right.

Let's unpack. Something to be useful. It's going to be nice not to live from my suitcase for a change.

Taking two steps at a time, I go upstairs, and for a moment, I can't remember which way is my room. Jesus, this place is stupidly big.

When I finally find it, I open the window despite the cold weather. Cool air sprouts goose bumps on my skin. Anything to feel alive.

My room is huge. It has a small sitting corner and a king-sized bed. I open the double door to a walk-in closet and frown. Several designer evening gowns hang from the rod on the far wall.

Did he get gowns for me? Are they even for me? My eyes widen. Has another woman left them here?

I unpack, trying not to look at the dresses. Not until I know they are mine. It's not like I need beautiful dresses. Beautiful dresses feel like work.

But they keep taunting me. So I finally cross the

floor to look at them. There is a white card hanging on each of them.

What is that? It looks like a date and time. They are organized chronologically. The first date is in a week. Wait a minute.

I pull out my phone and check the schedule Betsy sent me. Sure enough, all the dates on the dresses correspond with an event I'm required to attend. Has Betsy's firm sent the clothes?

Are outfits for the same occasions prepared in Corm's closet? Is it Livia's job? Or is there someone else doing it? Fuck, this really is like being back at work.

And I'm so shocked, and entertained, by this glimpse into Corm's personal life that I wander off in search of his closet.

To my surprise, his bedroom is beside mine. I was expecting he'd relegate me to the farthest wing away from him. This mansion can house us both without us ever running into each other.

But of course, he needs to control this as well. Asshole.

His bedroom is simple, but like the rest of the house, annoyingly welcoming. The large king-sized bed has dark blue sheets and duvet. There is an armchair in the corner where a large window meets a balcony door.

The door to the bathroom is open, but I turn to open the other double door. Shit, his closet is large. Does he own a suit and a pair of shoes for each day of the year?

I spot the labeled outfits immediately. They are neatly suspended in the far section of this room—it can't be called a closet. There is a full L-shaped sofa in the middle, for fuck's sake.

Sure enough, the hangers sport labels similar to mine. There is golfing attire, tuxedos, casual wear. All marked with the date and time.

I lived around labeled clothes all my life, but someone using the runway system to organize their life is news to me.

I giggle, because somehow this little discovery makes him feel human. Like someone is dressing him because he can't do it himself. It's a stretch, but shit, I enjoy the revelation.

I really *am* bored.

And full of excellent ideas. Carefully, I take the hangers down and remove all the labels. I'm about to throw away the cards when I get a better idea.

I shuffle the cards and hang them back on the outfits randomly.

Satisfied, I leave Corm's bedroom and saunter to my en-suite bathroom. It's beautiful, with a vintage tub in an alcove and a lot of light streaming through a large window.

Turning on the faucet, I wait for the hot water. I strip and step in, slowly sinking my tired body into the steaming bath.

I stare at the high ceiling. So this is my life now? Stuck in a mansion, engaged to a man I can't stand, with no idea what to do next.

It's a beautiful prison, but a prison nonetheless. And here I am, stuck in it. Lost in this huge house like I'm lost in my life.

I roll my eyes at the dramatic thought. And then I get an idea. Maybe I can make this place more mine.

Or at least less his.

"I'm so glad you called." Nora Flemming is a beautiful woman.

It's not just her former model looks; there is a kindness and softness to her that just makes me feel comfortable.

The waiter comes to take our order, and I automatically order mixed salad without even looking at other sections of the menu, while she goes for pasta. I guess that's a new habit that will take a moment to form.

We're in a trendy bistro in Tribeca, and for the first time in my life I feel uncomfortable in a place like this.

Not because of the hidden and less hidden glances in our direction. That is something I'm used to. It's because I wonder how I am going to cover the bill.

"I hope I'm not bothering you—"

"Let me stop you right there," she interrupts with enthusiasm. "I was where you are right now. First, let me congratulate you on your decision. That business can be toxic, and even when we want to get out, once we take the leap, it still feels weird. I'm glad I can help."

"Thank you. That's exactly how I feel. I was looking forward to quitting, and now I'm just lost."

I look away quickly, because I feel like I'm lying to her. I'm not going to burden her with my financial issues. Even though those are contributing to my current state.

She reaches over our table and squeezes my hand, probably misinterpreting my hesitation. "Nothing to feel bad about. It's normal. From what you told me about your decision to quit, you're quite probably experiencing burnout. Get a therapist, and start eating and sleeping normally. It takes time to decompress from your now-former lifestyle. Speaking from experience."

I let out the air through my cheeks. "It's hard. I need money." Shit, it comes out before I realize.

To her credit, she doesn't question the premise. "Okay, well, if you think you're ready to try something new." She cleverly avoids my money slip, taking a sip of her wine. "I saw you talking at the Alzheimer's gala in London last year. You chaired the event."

Whiplash anyone? I guess she abandoned the topic altogether.

"Yes, it was a privilege to be involved. Frankly, those kinds of events were a great mental break from the everyday grind."

"You could have chosen to party or to sleep during your time off. Like some of your colleagues."

"And who could blame them?" I chuckle. "But I always enjoyed lending my name to a worthy cause."

"It was obvious at that gala. You were there, truly present, informed, a genuine ambassador. Your speech was so authentic, I wonder if you wrote it yourself."

Something warm spreads through my chest, and I smile, feeling an inch taller. "Thank you. Yes, I did."

"I'm sorry to pry, but do you have someone with Alzheimer's in your life?" she asks, just as the waiter brings our dishes.

"No, I don't, but as I said, I like to lend my name to a good cause. My job requires me—required me—to show up, shut up, and look pretty. I didn't want to do the same when I volunteered my time."

She beams at me with... I think it's a pride. In the

absence of any praise from my own parents, I'm craving her honest compliments.

She takes a spoonful of pasta and chews for a moment. "My husband purchased a media network, and we're looking at restructuring and landing voices to causes and topics that get overlooked or sidetracked by the mainstream channels because there is no money behind them.

"We will have several podcasts and a streaming service and some other outlets. I think you'd be perfect to host one of our podcasts."

My fork drops. I take the napkin and wipe the corners of my lips. I take a sip of water. None of the automated actions provide any clarity. "I have no experience."

"My vision is to talk about issues impacting young people—solo episodes as well as interviews. Nothing is set in stone, so you can input and create the final format."

"I have no experience," I repeat, unable to process why she would think I'm a good candidate.

"You researched and talked about Alzheimer's without any experience, and you did a damn good job. I go to these events all the time, and I tune out of most of the speeches. You gripped me from the first sentence."

Her enthusiasm is contagious. Almost. Because a

voice, quite a loud voice in my head, keeps saying I'd make a fool of myself.

"Thank you, Nora. I think I need to take your first advice and rest, and figure out what I want to do."

She gives me another smile, this one not reaching her eyes, and shrugs. "It's a shame this doesn't excite you. You would be great."

"Oh, it's not that. It sounds appealing... and scary." Mostly appealing, I think, if I tuned out the little devil on my shoulders.

"You know what? There is no rush. Why don't you think about it? Take a few weeks. If you want to talk about it more, call me anytime. But don't doubt yourself, Saar. You'd be perfect."

"You're too generous." I pick up my fork again.

"Let's be honest, I have an ulterior motive; your name would bring in listeners."

And the devil on my shoulder rejoices. Of course, it's not about my abilities. It's about my name. At least this gig wouldn't be about being pretty.

We finish our lunch talking about different topics, gossiping a bit about people from our industry, and without me realizing, brainstorming the show I told her I don't want to do.

The woman is a subtle manipulator, but I have a great time with her.

When we leave the restaurant, cameras accost us. Goddammit.

"Saar, where is your engagement ring?"

"When is the wedding?"

"Have you moved in together?"

"Why are you not wearing your ring?"

'Stupid ring would break my finger,' I want to snap, but I just look down and rush forward, my heart pounding in my temples while I shake with anxiety.

Luckily, Nora has bodyguards waiting outside, and they help us into her car.

"Sorry about that." I sigh when we pull away.

"Not your fault. I didn't realize you got engaged. I'm avoiding gossip sites at all costs. Congratulations."

"Thank you." My stomach churns as I muster my work-perfect smile.

"So where is your ring?" She chuckles.

A lump grows in my throat. It's not *my* ring. "Are you planning to sell the story?" I tease, acting more nonchalant than I feel.

She laughs and drops the topic. I laugh, and drop to another low point in my current life.

"Why wouldn't you come to us if you needed money?" Finn paces around Cal's large living room. He may get blisters if he continues.

I sigh and look at Celeste, who sits beside Cal on the sofa to my left. She may be the only reason why Cal is not pacing with Finn. Why he seems more on my side. Or at least, less vocal about his opinion on the matter.

Celeste gives me a sad smile.

"Because I don't need you fixing my problems." I try to stay calm.

Finn stops and looks at me, unimpressed. He doesn't have to say it, but I know what he thinks. He's been fixing my problems for a while—why stop now?

"Why do you need money?" Cal asks.

Both my brothers search my face like the answer is etched on my forehead. I stand up and walk to the wall of windows overlooking the city.

The night is still young, casting a veil of mystery over the skyline, softening its edges with the fading light of dusk before darkness fully descends.

I should just tell them the truth, but I'm even more embarrassed to confess to them than I was with my friends.

"I invested and lost," I say to the city, the lie bitter on my tongue. I guess, technically, I invested my trust in the wrong person.

Celeste sighs. Shit, now I'm putting her in a position where she'd have to lie to her husband.

Finn huffs. "If you wanted to invest, you should have asked us for advice. What were you thinking?"

Fuck. I spin around, fighting the tears of frustration. "I was thinking I can take care of myself. That I don't need my overbearing brothers to pamper me. That I can learn from my own mistakes like the rest of the world."

"Bambi." Finn sighs.

All the sighing and huffing and patronizing.

"I made a mistake. I'm correcting it."

"With Cormac fucking Quinn? You'd rather have him help you than us?" Cal raises his eyebrow.

"Oh, so it's your ego that is hurt? This is not about you. It's my life."

Both my brothers flinch. I feel like shit. They love me. They expect me to trust them with my problems.

Don't they get it, though? This is not about my relationship with them. This is about my relationship with me.

"It's a mutually beneficial arrangement. I thought you had something to gain as well," I accuse Cal.

He snorts. "There are plenty of women out there that could marry him."

"Well, it's me who got the honor. So back off. I'm sorry I didn't get the chance to tell you before the media circus started, but that's the only thing I'm sorry about."

"So what's the plan? You will just get your trust fund and divorce him?" Finn shakes his head.

"Yes, and I'd need you to pretend you're happy for me at the wedding, because this is a huge photo op for Corm." I fold my arms across my chest and look at Cal. "And for Merged."

"But he hurt you," Cal protests, practically jumping from his seat. Celeste puts her hand on his thigh. He glances at her, and his jaw relaxes.

"He didn't hurt me. And it doesn't matter. It happened years ago, and some teenage mistakes are completely irrelevant. In fact, the two of you are the only ones still feeding that history."

Suddenly, it feels completely irrelevant what happened back then. They try to control my life, motivated by care and love, but still. First my parents, then my brothers. And now... fuck, now my *dear* fiancé.

Finn bows his head, shaking it. "As long as you're happy."

I wouldn't go as far as being happy. "Everything is fine."

"I'm going to kill him if he hurts you." Cal stands and walks to a liquor cabinet hidden in his bookcase.

Not if I kill him first. "Thank you for your concern. I love you both, but I need you to let me fight my own battles."

"Fuck, Bambi, fight your own battles, but don't hesitate to ask for help."

Is that what I'm doing? Am I refusing the help foolishly? Believing it's a quest for independence?

* * *

I return to the empty house. Tired, but unable to sleep. Hungry, but not interested in eating. Bored, but unsure what to do.

I pour myself a glass of wine, and without bothering with the lights, I pad over to the living room.

Sitting on the bench in the window overlooking the garden, I pull my phone out. In the absence of my daily dose of attention from cameras, I decide to dive into the virtual world where I can pretend just like anybody else.

I miss living with Cora, and having a human conversation served with takeout.

Something prompts me to turn on the camera. The lighting is off. I look like I haven't slept in days and just argued with my brothers.

I look like me. I take a few pictures. No filter. No pretense.

Before I think about it, I open my feed. It would be the first honest picture on there once I post it.

I stare at the display, considering what hashtag I

should use, and before I realize, my fingers run across the screen.

My new home. From the outside, it looks like I've made it. It's all beautiful. And it's a lie.

All my life I've sold an illusion—the perfect face, the perfect body, the perfect life. The truth? For all the perfect I've lived, I have never felt more out of place than I do right now.

Am I the only one? We're constantly told we need to be something more, something better, something impossible.

I've spent years making myself smaller to fit the world's idea of beautiful, pushing myself to fit a mold. I'm exhausted. That kind of life is unattainable. And pretty damn lonely.

So this is me. No filter. No camera-ready look. Just me, sitting in a vast mansion, wondering what the hell I'm supposed to do next.

Do we all feel this lost when the facade falls away? Or is it just me?

Wow. It feels good to write freely what goes through my mind.

But it feels really vulnerable to share that with the world, so I save it in drafts and go to my bed where the sleep doesn't come.

Chapter 10

Corm

"We're trending well thus far. Saar is good for your image. The events I scheduled over the next two months will improve your reputation. And with her by your side, people might buy it." Betsy's voice drills into my brain. Fuck, I hate this spiel.

"Anything else?" I growl.

"As pleasant as ever. I spoke with Xander, and so far Atlas and AetherTech are reserving their judgment—"

"Betsy, mind your own business. I'm paying you to fix my image, not to plot with my partners or check on my deals."

"Oh, grow up. Your image is worth shit for you if those two don't buy it. Or rather sell it to their boards. I investigated both men, and I think the activities I planned might be right up their alley. You're now a huge supporter of an animal shelter, a cause close to Mrs. Hale. You're also attending several charity galas that Cherynovski supports."

Okay, maybe she knows what she's doing. I look out of my car's window. "Good job. I'm almost home, so if there isn't—"

"When are you introducing Saar to your mother? We should make that a public appearance."

Shit. My brother knows about the charade, and so does Saar's family, but the idea of telling my mom the truth doesn't sit well with me. Nor does the idea of lying to her.

Our relationship has been in limbo since the funeral, and I don't want to face her until I sort out my feelings.

I've been so angry, channeling my feelings into a party bender, and now replacing it with the borderline bullying of my colleagues and Saar. Fuck, I need to get my shit together. If only I could confront Dad.

But lying to my mom's face is not a bridge I'm ready to cross. "She hasn't been feeling well, but I'll schedule something."

"She must be better, because she was at a luncheon about renewable energy today."

I crack my neck. Fucking Betsy. Nothing happens

in this town without her knowing. And since when is Mom interested in renewable energy?

"I got to go." I hang up, done with the conversation. Before I introduce her to my mom, I need to make sure that Saar... What?

This shit is more complicated than I anticipated. On the one hand, she draws me with some invisible thread that attracts me to her. Makes her intriguing. Makes me want to peel off all her layers.

On the other hand, my future bride spits venom whenever in my vicinity. And I give her enough reasons; I'm not even sure why.

I thought playing with Saar van den Linden would be a great distraction from my recent problems. And there is the irrational but ever-so-present need to make her mine.

The challenge might not be worth it. The woman is attracted to me, and she hates me for it.

What was I thinking agreeing to this scheme? It's more a headache than a solution. Cal is right: I literally could have found a bride in no time. And yet I jumped at this opportunity.

Because she beguiled me two years ago, and when she finally fell into my lap, so to speak, I couldn't resist. And now, I don't know what I want anymore, and that's the feeling I hate the most. It's all her fault.

The car pulls through my gate and stops in front of my house. My phone rings.

Art Mathison?

That's fast. I briefed him only two days ago. The former hacker specializes in cybersecurity and surveillance.

"What did you find?" I don't bother with greetings. The man hates socializing. I admire him for that.

"I sent you an encrypted file."

"What's on it?"

He groans. "If you don't know how to read, use text-to-speech." He hangs up.

I push the front door open, and the smell of fresh paint assaults me immediately. I walk around my entry table, following the smell, but I stop.

A large flower arrangement reigns on the table instead of my hundred-thousand-dollar statue. I guess my blushing bride made herself at home. I can't say I mind this little touch. It's warmed up the large, cold foyer.

Let's hope the painting job—because the smell suggests she didn't stop with the flowers—is equally pleasant.

That hope dies a quick death when I step into the living room. Or at least what used to be my living room.

This room doesn't look like it. Unless someone ate

several kilos of Smarties and then vomited all over my walls.

And where the hell is my furniture? Is that a sex chair by the window? And a real-size stuffed giraffe? Right next to an antique-looking statue?

And what's with the fucking antlers on the wall? This is not a hunting cottage. Or a safari. Or a museum of design mistakes.

I cross the hallway to the dining room. Kill. Me. Now.

My solid-wood dining set, hand-fucking-made in Italy, is gone. Instead, there is a red faux-leather booth like this was some fucking diner. There is even a jukebox in the corner.

The Morrigan. I'm going to kill her.

I rush to the kitchen. Thank God it's unchanged. Livia steps from the pantry and smiles.

"Mr. Quinn, you're back. Should I warm up something for you to eat?" She puts down a basket with vegetables.

"I'm not hungry. Where is Saar?" I tap my fingers on the marble counter.

"I think she went upstairs. She must be tired, bossing around those poor workers for two days."

I bet she is tired. She will also be sorry. "Thank you, Livia."

"Are you sure you don't want to eat? Ms. Saar has

barely eaten, and there are so many meals in the fridge."

"Take them home, Livia. Why don't you take the rest of the afternoon off?" *That way I can kill my fiancée without witnesses.*

"Thank you, Mr. Quinn. I'll be back in the morning then. Could you ask Ms. Saar to let me know if there are workers coming tomorrow?"

"No," I bark, startling her. "The redecoration project is over." I tame my voice. This is not Livia's fault.

"Thank God," she mutters, and starts gathering her things.

I pour myself a glass of whiskey, hoping to find composure. Damn woman. She oozes style even when she wears a simple pair of jeans, so this is clearly an attempt to piss me off.

I down the whiskey and take a few breaths. No. Nothing. I need one more. I down two more glasses before I rush upstairs.

Soft music floats through the corridor as I approach Saar's room.

I knock. I may be on a mission to strangle her, but I'm not a savage.

No answer. She's in there, listening to some esoteric music. Is she ignoring me deliberately?

I knock again, this time with more urgency.

Nothing.

"Saar," I billow.

Silence. Bar the music.

"I'm coming in." I push the door open. "Saar." I blink a few times, adjusting to the darkness.

The blinds are drawn, the only light coming from a few flickering candles. The air is infused with vomit-inducing incense.

"What?" Saar pulls up her eye mask. "I was trying to sleep."

"At three in the afternoon?" I turn the switch on, and the light floods the room.

Saar groans and swings her legs to sit at the edge of her bed, rubbing her eyes. "I'm still adjusting."

"You can't have jetlag anymore."

And why am I even arguing this point? She can do whatever she wants. Aside from making my house look like a junkyard.

"What do you want?" She sighs.

She looks exhausted. Shadows of fatigue frame her eyes. She is pale, and is she thinner than she was?

My cock immediately remembers the feel of her against me when I crowded her in my office. I made that move out of exasperation. She really seems to push all my buttons. Regardless of my original—not very smart—intention, the power move ended up in an internal war between want and reason.

Thank God for Larissa's interruption, and for my business trip. Putting the distance between us was essential.

"Livia tells me you didn't eat much." That's none of your business, asshole. That's not why you came here. Fuck, she doesn't look good though.

"And you care why?" She throws the eye mask on the nightstand.

"You're right, I don't. What the fuck have you done downstairs?"

She gives me a feigned smile. "I thought you wouldn't mind if I made the place a little bit mine."

I open my mouth, wanting to bark something, but that's what she wants, isn't it? To rile me up so she has a false sense of control over the situation. "I have nothing against redesigning. But it looks like a yard sale downstairs."

Her eyes bulge out. "That was the look I went for. I'm glad you approve. Can I go back to trying to sleep now?"

"The magazine is coming in an hour."

"What magazine?"

"I don't remember every detail. They are coming to take engagement pictures."

"That's tomorrow." She reaches for her phone and finally stops the church music. "Shit."

"Yes, it's today. The only thing you have to do is keep on top of the schedule."

She flinches. Fuck, I'm such an asshole to her. But fuck, it's not like she's an angel.

"Well then, get out of here so I can get ready." She stands up and stumbles.

I rush to her side and snake my arm around her waist. Her body is so light, I almost lift her off the floor with that one move. The lavender attacks me through the thick air of incense.

It's like we're back in my office; the want surges through my veins right into my cock. Fuck.

She blinks a few times and turns her large eyes to me. Even exhausted, she is a vision. Truly beautiful. The shadow of vulnerability softens her edges.

"What's going on?" This time, my tone resembles a normal person, not the raging asshole she usually turns me into.

"Nothing. I just stood up too fast." She pushes away and bumps into the nightstand.

What am I doing worrying about her? She's a grown woman. "Okay." I step away, confused by my feelings.

It's like she stumbled, and my hatred for her softened. What the fuck?

Conflicted.

That's how I feel, and I hate the feeling. I march to

the door. The sooner I get out of here, the sooner I can reestablish the boundaries. Strengthen them. It must be the fucking incense that confused me.

"I hope you know how to cook." I turn before I leave.

She frowns. "You have a chef."

I groan. "Did you even read Betsy's brief?"

"Of course I did. But isn't the cooking together just staged?"

"We're trying to fucking sell a story. We're not going to do that with a plastic cauliflower. I'll cook. Make sure you look pretty. That's something you're good at."

Chapter 11

Saar

I hate my fiancé.

CORA

What's new?

LILY

Isn't he away?

He's back (crying emoji)

CELESTE

Just don't kill him.

But if you do, I'll help you hide the body.

You're such a good friend.

LILY

Let's start Corm Quinn fan club (laughing evil emoji).

CORA

To join you have to make him smile.

Or live with him instead of me.

CORA

We can all live in that mansion without him knowing.

CELESTE

I'm staying in my loft.

Why did I get the dates wrong? I go to all the trouble to redesign his downstairs to score a point, and he erases it immediately, catching me unprepared.

Shit. I can't even blame him. As much fun as I had making his living and dining room as tacky as possible, it wasn't worth it.

What point was I after, anyway? That I'm an immature, bored, soon-to-be housewife with no style?

It seems like I'm the only one in this competition anyway. It's annoying how he has everything under control while I float through my days aimlessly.

It's like the Universe sent me Cormac Quinn to contrast with the current idle phase of my life. Well, thank you very much, dear Universe; perhaps send me a mentor, or a more inspiring example.

And he can cook? Like seriously, the man must be perfect at everything? I could have cooked, but... I groan.

I need to grow up, get out of his way, and only

show up for the events. Maybe I can speed up the wedding prep and get this over with sooner. Yes, that's what I need to do.

I'll deliver on all the events beyond his expectations. Perform my part and push for the earliest wedding.

I twist my hair into a messy bun on top of my head. Betsy's instructions stated a casual but classy look. I touch my cheeks with a bit of blush. I wouldn't have bothered with makeup, but I look like a zombie by now, so I cover the circles below my eyes.

I review the schedule again. I need to find out more about that deal Corm is trying to close. Without that deal, I don't get my divorce. I must get some information from Cal.

The doorbell snaps me into a frenzy of preparation. Why are they here already? I glance at my watch. Because, of course, they're punctual.

Dashing to the closet, I put on an off-shoulder blue cashmere sweater and a pair of beige ankle-length slacks. A quick check in the mirror makes me pause. I actually look quite good. Funny how being away from the spotlight made me not care for myself at all.

But I do feel less shitty when I'm not wearing leggings or jeans and any old T-shirt. Maybe I should start my self-discovery with a bit of self-care.

I give myself a soft smile and take a selfie. As I exit

my room, I quickly post it with a simple caption: showtime.

My gaze lands on the pic I took downstairs a few days ago. I forgot about that moment of radical honesty. I almost click on the delete button, but a female giggle from downstairs reminds me I have duties to perform.

Putting my phone into my pocket, I force a smile. Not that anyone can see me yet, but I need to fake it now. I might make it believable by the time I descend.

"Sorry I'm late," I chirp while still mid-staircase, smiling as if my life depended on it. In some ways, it kind of does. Unfortunately for me.

Corm and a woman beside him with dark hair and orange lipstick—why, I ask?—turn their heads.

The woman returns my smile, and Corm... I swear he startles at seeing me.

He rakes his eyes down my body—the asshole is probably making sure I look presentable enough for his precious image—and then gives me a slow, sexy smile.

It's shocking. And blinding. And—God save me—genuine. That can't be.

He's wearing jeans and a V-neck long-sleeve T-shirt. This dressed-down version of him is a new level of sexy. So unfair.

"Here you are, darling." He walks toward me, offering his hand to aid my descent. "This is Diane, and she will be grilling us today."

I giggle, a bit too enthusiastically, and Corm tilts his head, frowning.

"I thought you were the one grilling tonight, sweetheart." The honey in my tone is nauseating.

With his back to Diane, he rolls his eyes. "I'm making a chicken pie; did you forget, darling?"

Putting his hand on the small of my back, he leads me gently toward the reporter. The touch is featherlike and firm at the same time. It burns through the cashmere.

For the three steps between the staircase and Diane, I force myself to ignore the tingling that innocent connection sends through my body. But it's impossible.

And what is worse, it's not only the visceral reaction of my treacherous body. As sad as it is, his touch makes me feel safe.

How fucked up am I after years of being objectified, that my nemesis puts his hand on my back and it's like a veil of protection.

"Nice to meet you." Diane offers me her hand.

"The pleasure is all mine. Again, pardon my tardiness, and welcome." I step to the side. I need a moment to recover from that touch.

What is wrong with me? I've always been immune to shit like that.

"We're ready," a male voice hollers from the direction of the kitchen.

"Great, let's start." Diane moves like this is her house, but I guess if her team is already in the kitchen, she knows her way. "It's a shame you're remodeling, but I think we can get good shots in your beautiful kitchen."

I spy the large, black plastic sheets covering the entrance to the dining and living rooms. When did he manage to cover my handiwork?

"I want to make sure Saar feels at home here, so of course, she needs to add her touch to the decor."

He throws my earlier words back at me while he follows Diane, without giving me a look. I trudge behind them, conflicted. A part of me wants his attention and affection to be real. It must be my sleep deprivation playing tricks.

Beam lights and two large portable reflectors make the kitchen less grand, more cramped. A way too familiar setup that should make me feel comfortable. Instead, sweat covers my skin, my stomach revolting.

Didn't I want to escape this?

Corm leans in and snakes his arm around my waist. He lowers his mouth to my ear. "You look like you want to vomit," he bites out a warning.

"It must be your company," I hiss. "What can I

help with, sweetie?" I ask louder and put my hand on his chest, playing my role.

His muscles tense under my palm. I swear it's like any physical connection has a direct line to my core.

And why am I imagining how that chest looks naked?

"Why don't you sit and look pretty while I cook?" He kisses my forehead and slaps my ass, sending me to a high stool by the island.

Asshole. "Diane, a confession, I can't do shit in the kitchen." I plop on the chair, and she climbs beside me, laughing.

"You and me, you and me." She fishes a notebook and pen from her bag. "Where is your ring, Saar?"

Oh, fuck, I forgot about it. "Diane, I'll show you the ring later, but I can't possibly wear it at home. It's ridiculously extravagant." I think I manage to pretend how pleased I am.

"Only the best for my fiancée." Corm winks.

Diane looks like she is going to melt. Like he was talking about her. "So, what was the first meal Cormac ever cooked for you?"

A humiliation pie. An asshole corn dog. A frustration soup.

"Well, I don't know if that's not too private, but it was breakfast." I smile coyly.

Corm looks at me and smirks. I think that's his way of showing approval. Not that I need it.

He slices chicken expertly, like he really knows what he is doing. His long fingers wrapped around the knife's handle draw my attention with their precise, almost mesmerizing moves.

An image of those hands moving around my body flashes through my mind. Jesus. What's wrong with me? Am I worshiping his hands now?

"Did he bring it to your bed?" Diane asks, shimmying her shoulders.

What?

"Come on, Diane, now behave; some things need to remain private." Corm points the knife at her playfully.

"Okay, okay." She giggles again. "I mean, this is off the record, but it's not a secret that Corm has been partying hard in recent months. Doesn't it bother you?"

Off the record, my ass. In the periphery of my sight, I more sense than see how Corm's knife falters.

"I'm not the jealous type, Diane. I know what we have is special, and I trust him. Corm has a demanding job, and he needs to decompress. Unfortunately, I couldn't be here with him, but I wouldn't want him to give up living."

I add a gentle smile to my performance.

My gaze meets his, and I blink. He's staring at me

with... admiration? That can't be. Is he pleased with my lies?

I may lie through my teeth, but the words stir an unknown longing. I want to have a person in my life I can trust.

"That's a solid base for a lasting relationship. Not that I would know." Diane laughs. "Is it true that you gave up your career for him, Saar?"

Definitely not. "I was planning to retire, and maintaining a long-distance relationship isn't ideal. Especially after Corm's father passed. He needed me, so I came."

"So romantic," Diane gushes.

Corm takes a towel and wipes his hands, moving to me, his gaze glued to mine. What is he thinking?

He leans to kiss my hair. "It's nice to have someone by my side."

It's like a wish. And maybe it's my own baggage, but I almost feel the loneliness behind his words. His lips linger in my hair for a beat longer than necessary.

I know we're both spitting lies, performing for the audience, but why do I feel we just had a strange bonding moment?

A shutter click startles me, and I blink a few times as the camera flashes. I swallow a gasp, my stomach shrinking in a nervous vise.

Do I have photo-related PTSD? I want to laugh at

the thought, but after another few shutter clicks, I have to excuse myself.

I stumble out of the kitchen and rush to the powder room in the foyer. I grip the edge of the sink and bow my head, trying to catch my breath while my chest seems to have collapsed. Shit.

It's like I've been tortured for years under the lens's aim, and now, after I experienced a few weeks of freedom, the clicks and the flashes reopened the wounds. Wounds I didn't even know I had.

Is this burnout? Or am I completely mental? Scared of a camera. What the actual fuck?

On the street after my lunch with Nora, I thought it was a reaction to being accosted with the engagement-ring questions. But maybe it's deeper than that.

I breathe in and out for a few rounds, and then flush the toilet and run the water to cover my little freak-out.

When I open the door, I collide with a solid body. I brace for his condescending words, reminding me I should entertain the media. Instead, two strong arms wrap around me, and my fiancé holds me without a word.

What is happening? Besides my heart rate spiking and butterflies flapping around my stomach? Has Cormac Quinn just exhibited a rare show of affection and compassion?

How did he even pick up on my distress?

His heart beats against me as his chest rises and falls. The comfort of his embrace does the exact opposite of his intention. It brings tears to my eyes, painful hotness searing my throat. I can't trust this, though.

I don't deserve his kindness. It's fake, anyway. And how am I going to hate him after this? I blink the tears away, hoping he won't see them. But also hoping he will.

How would a man like him—a powerful business tycoon who has no kind bone in his body—react to me crumbling down under the burden of my current misfortune? And my newly discovered anxiety? I can't even unwrap that one.

Will he laugh at me? Will he use it against me? Or will he hold me, like he has been for the last minute?

"We should return," I whisper into the fabric of his shirt.

He doesn't let go but leans back. Not entirely sure I've blinked away my tears, I lift my gaze. His jaw is clenched, and a line splits his forehead. His eyes glow dark.

At that moment, we belong together. Two strangers stranded on an island. No longer lonely. No longer facing the world, each by themselves. It's comforting, and oddly peaceful.

The silence stretches like neither of us is ready to move past this tender connection.

He's blocking the door, and I have no way to disentangle from our stance. A part of me doesn't want to, if I'm honest. I know this is just some outlandish moment of truce between us, but fuck, my tired mind wants to revel in it.

He drops his arms, but doesn't move. I feel the loss of his touch immediately and mourn it. Mourn it! God help me.

We remain frozen, just looking at each other. It's almost like the other day in his office, but also different. Like the hatred level is slightly less, replaced by heightened desire, but also some deeper connection. Even though it makes no sense.

But he did look at me like this at the restaurant on our first official date. In fact, every time I drop my walls and give him a glimpse of honesty, he reacts... well, almost humanely.

Is there a chance we could play nice? The notion seems preposterous. But if someone asked me a few days ago, the idea of wanting to be kissed by this man would be equally absurd.

Yet here I am, thinking about it. His gaze is intense, all-consuming, forcing me to hold my breath and not dare to look away.

There is a battle behind his stormy look, but I'm

not sure if he's fighting with me or for me. Or against me.

His tongue darts out, and he licks his bottom lip. I can't look away, no matter how much I want to. He shakes his head and starts turning, and a part of me deflates. But then he shocks me when he swears and grabs my face.

His palms are warm, his fingers rough against my skin. He leans down, his eyes not leaving mine.

"I asked them to refrain from documenting, and promised we will pose for a few pics during and after the dinner. Is that okay?"

I blink. Once. Twice. Who is this man?

I nod. "Thank you," I breathe.

"Are you okay?"

Three simple words.

A short question, but it unravels all my insecurities and my stupid need for validation, for affection from those around me.

The girl who was deprived of love all her childhood begs for attention. The woman who lived by herself since she was a teenager wants to rebel against that need, but it's a lost battle.

I'm not okay, but I'm so grateful for his genuine inquiry, I nod.

He keeps holding my face in his hands. I don't

know if he wants to say something else or kiss the hell out of me.

I don't know if I want him to talk or to kiss me.

Talk perhaps. Verbal sparring has been our safe place.

No, kiss, definitely a kiss. Because if this pent-up tension and attraction doesn't get released, we might kill each other.

"Fuck it," he mumbles.

I gasp as he captures my mouth. Snaking one hand farther to cup my neck, he uses the other one to angle my head for better access.

He doesn't waste time and thrusts his tongue, and I don't waste time and give him immediate access.

My body ignites. I feel his kiss all the way to my toes. It's gentle and rough. Discovering and certain at the same time. Wonderful and scary.

All the conflicting feelings rake through my body, which quivers with every swipe of his tongue.

One thing is for sure, Cormac Quinn kisses like he does everything else. With perfection, he controls the pace, while delivering an experience that has my heart racing, my stomach tickling with butterfly wings, and my core clenching.

This is the best kiss of my life. The thought pops up from nowhere, and I want to discard it, but I lied enough tonight already. Even if this is my last kiss from him, the damage is done.

I won't forget it. I won't be able to erase the memory of this delicious pain. Not now, not tomorrow, not after we divorce.

Shit. This is a disaster. We're to live together for what... at least two months? I need to save myself.

I push him away, both of us panting. He stares at me bewildered, like he can't believe it happened.

Or he's equally shocked by the intensity of the connection. Surely not. He must have kissed hundreds of women.

"What was that?" I step away, as if that could save me from reliving this impulsive moment for the rest of my days.

The venom in my voice is such a stark contrast to the warmth of that kiss, I almost recoil at my question.

He flinches and then gives me his unimpressed smirk. I guess we're both very capable of turning our internal thermostat on and off.

"That was a moment of insanity. Forget it; let's get this dinner over with." He turns on his heels and leaves me standing there.

Chapter 12

Corm

Saar's eyes widen as she grabs a napkin and spits into it. We're seated around the kitchen island since my dining room is out of commission.

As much as I'm pissed about a fucking diner replacing my dining room, this setup seems better for the purposes of the cozy, natural experience we're trying to sell. Better for my image.

"This is delicious, Corm," Diane exclaims. "The best chicken pie I've ever had."

Saar blinks a few times and looks at Diane like she's just grown a horn. I guess my beautiful fiancée doesn't like the extra spoon of Tabasco I doctored her portion with.

Not my proudest moment. In my defense, I had planned it to punish her for desecrating my house.

I briefly abandoned the childish idea when she flinched under the flash of the camera. She should be used to the dog-and-pony show, but clearly something in the whole setup triggered her. It was obvious the minute she stepped into the kitchen.

Her struggle awakened something primal in me. Like it's my job to protect this woman.

And then she answered Diane's questions, professionally and with a believable conviction.

The way she fucks around with the wedding planning, trying to rile me up all the time, the way she destroyed my house for fun, I was getting worried she might make me look worse, not better in the public eye.

But this woman is eloquent, well-mannered, and quite delightful company. And, apparently, a proficient liar.

And the absolute mind-fuck is that for a moment, I believed the ruse.

For a beat of insanity, I almost wished it was real. That she truly was my partner. There to support me. To trust. I didn't even know I needed someone like that in my life.

And why the fuck did I kiss her?

She was looking at me with those doe eyes and I... I couldn't resist her pull. It was a mistake. I returned to the kitchen so pissed that despite my better judgment, I poured hot sauce into her meal.

With her stupid antics—bouncy castle, carnival meal, and the trailer decor in my house—she turned me into a teenager. At least mentally. Not only because I return her pranks, but because my cock dictates my actions.

I should have known living under one roof with a supermodel would impact me. I'm only a man, after all. *Yeah, keep telling yourself that it's about her looks.*

"Saar, I envy you. To have such a wonderful cook at your disposal." Diane continues making noises like I was eating her pussy, not feeding her a simple dish.

"And that's not even his best asset." Saar glares at me with that fake smile plastered on her blushing face.

"So when is the wedding?" Diane takes a sip from her wine.

"We're not in a hurry," I say.

"The sooner, the better," Saar says at the same time.

Diane's eyes dart between me and my fiancée. "Oh, you haven't set the date yet?"

This has been too long of a night. Fuck. "Diane, I have an early morning tomorrow. I don't mean to rush you, but we should get the pictures done."

"Of course." She beckons the photographer with her eyes, and he drops his fork and picks up his camera.

Saar slides from the stool. "Where do you want us?"

Diane discusses a few ideas with her one-man crew, and then we follow their instructions, moving around the kitchen and playing the happy couple.

We pose for what feels like another two hours, but my watch confirms it's only been twenty minutes.

Saar seems to have relaxed a bit, leaning into her expertise, but she looks tired, and every time I touch her—at the photographer's bidding—she tenses.

I hate that I'm noticing it. She can't wait to get away from me, and yet here I am, making it my responsibility to make her life somehow better. As if she cared. Or extended the same courtesy to me.

"I think we got it all." Diane claps, and they start packing up. Thank fucking God.

It takes another forty minutes before they are out the door, and I rush to my living room to pour myself a glass of whiskey. Only to stop at the stupid plastic sheet I used to support the remodeling story.

Over my dead body would I have pics of that circus in a magazine.

"Fuck," I mumble.

I find Saar in the kitchen, tidying up. I retrieve a bottle of vodka from the pantry and pour myself half a tumbler.

"Leave that for the housekeeper," I growl, ready to retire to my bedroom and finish this hellish day.

"It's nothing. If we leave it, Livia would have more

work. It's not a big deal to load the dishwasher and soak the pan."

She moves around my kitchen like she's done it many times. Elegant and efficient. She's been living here for a minute and half and seems to know this space better than me.

I watch her with my glass halfway to my lips, kind of intrigued by the idea of sharing the space with someone. By the effortless domesticity of the moment.

The thought shocks me, so asshole that I am, I smirk. "I didn't expect you to have a housewife in you."

She sighs and looks at me with resignation. "You know nothing about me."

The truth of that statement surprises me. And reminds me of the files Mathison sent me earlier.

"Not yet." I shrug.

She snorts. "Not ever."

She kicks the dishwasher door up and closes it with her hip. My cock twitches. This is the worst night ever.

She wipes the counter and moves a few things around. I should go to my room, but something keeps me here.

Like I've been stuck in a dark tunnel, and Saar van den Linden is the first flicker of light I've seen in ages. I know her flame will burn me, turn me to ash, but I'm still drawn to its warmth. Its glow. Its fleeting fragility.

Saar busies herself, not really doing much

anymore. It's like she is stalling. I hope to God she doesn't want to talk about that kiss.

It was electric, and dangerously satisfying, but as I said, it was a moment of insanity. Though I probably didn't need to be such an asshole about it.

She finally stops fidgeting and takes a deep breath. She clears her throat. "We should set the date."

"I don't feel too eager." I down the vodka and glare at her.

Her eyes flare. "Are you for real? I'm not playing house with you, so you get everything and I get nothing. The sooner we marry, the sooner we can divorce."

"That's true. But given the shit you keep stirring..." I march across the room and yank at the plastic sheet covering the double door frame that leads to the dining room. "Case in point. I don't feel very motivated to get you what you want from this arrangement."

She rolls her eyes. She opens her mouth, closes it, and sighs. "Okay, you got back at me with the fucking inedible volcano pie—"

"Are you fucking kidding me? My prank doesn't compare to this. Or to the cost of the wedding planner whose time you're wasting." I advance toward her, and she steps back, her back hitting the fridge. "I told you already, The Morrigan, play nice or you will regret it."

Her breath hitches as she holds my gaze. "I promise

to stop." She swallows, and her throat moving sends shivers down my spine.

The woman fucking swallows and I'm aroused. Goddammit. While this thought travels through my useless mind, my brain gives up control or reason, and I grind my hips against her.

Her breath hitches. She fists my sweater, and for a moment I believe she'll pull me closer. I can almost pinpoint the moment she decides against it, her expression smug.

"Momentary insanity again?" she taunts.

Fuck. I step away, and she dashes to the door. "The date, Corm."

I run my hand through my hair. "Your promise is worth shit to me. Follow the script for a week, and we'll set the date."

"Asshole," she mumbles, and turns, stumbling. She grips the edge of the counter and closes her eyes.

Before I know it, I'm by her side. "Are you dizzy again?"

"I'm okay." But she doesn't move.

"What is wrong with you?"

"Nothing." But her answer is weak, and she slams against the stool, lowering her head to her palms. "I just need a moment."

The pale skin, the shadows under her eyes... the lack of food. Fuck, and I kept her hungry tonight.

"I'm calling a doctor."

"Don't be ridiculous. I haven't been sleeping well, and I'm anemic."

"Why?" I ask like an idiot, the feeling of helplessness foreign and unwelcome, but so very present.

"Obviously I had a career that fucked with my hormones, and the only thing I have to show for that is getting married to you." She climbs on to the stool.

I sigh. "I'm calling a doctor."

"Don't be so dramatic. Can you just get me some apple juice from the fridge?"

I pour her a glass. She downs it. Fuck, she looks so tired.

"Let me heat up a meal for you." I turn to pull something from the fridge. Damn it, Livia took it all. "I'll make you a sandwich."

"No hot sauce, please."

* * *

"You don't have to—" Saar yelps when I pick her up bridal-style.

"Shut up." I carry her upstairs. "I'm not risking you fainting on the stairs and cracking your skull. Media would have a field day with that. I don't need to be labeled an abuser."

"That wouldn't be that far-fetched." She smirks.

"Again, shut up." I scowl.

She weighs nothing, her hands are cold around my shoulders, her hip is protruding into my pecs, and yet... it's like carrying precious cargo.

Like regardless of how much she hates me, or what stunts she orchestrates to piss me off, she's my burden now, whether I like it or not.

I don't like it, obviously, but there is a gentleman buried somewhere deep inside me, and that fucker decided to awaken. The worst timing ever.

The cavalier sentiment is about as welcome as the erection pressing against the zipper of my jeans. What the actual fuck is she doing to me?

It's like her mere presence messes with my lifestyle, my values, and my general screw-you-all attitude. I fucking honed those all my life, and reinforced them after the old man surprised me from behind his grave. Only to lose them as soon as The Morrigan landed in my life.

Her defiance mingles with insecurity. Her sharp tongue is refreshing, but all the secrets and things she doesn't say are even more intriguing. The walls she's built around herself are thicker than mine.

And for the life of me, I don't know why I want to break them. Like breaking them, breaking her, is the only interesting, invigorating thing in my life. Was I really that bored?

I kick the door to her room open and sit her down on the bed. "What do you sleep in?"

She frowns, smirking. "Really? I can get changed. I was a bit dizzy, not paralyzed."

"I told you to behave if you want the wedding date. Lift your arms. I'll help you get changed." What am I doing?

"What if I sleep naked?"

Little tease. I grip her jaw, not too rough but firm enough to force her to look at me. "You keep running that pretty mouth of yours, and I will stuff it with my cock."

She glares at me with heat and shock. Ha, so a bit of dirty talk does the trick to finally shut her up. Or did the innuendo—and again, what the fuck am I doing—fluster her?

Is Saar van den Linden a prude? Or is she inexperienced? Fuck, I need to get out of here before I investigate.

"Good night." I drop her chin and practically run out of her room into mine.

I really should have given her a room that wasn't in my immediate proximity. Is she really sleeping naked? What if she faints again and hits her head? Should I leave her alone?

I pull my sweater over my head, annoyed by everything and anything. I'm too tired to have a shower at this point, but I need to take care of the painful strain in my pants.

Dropping my jeans, I collapse into the armchair in the corner of my bedroom. My cock springs out heavy as soon as I lower the waistband of my briefs. I fist it and give it a tug.

Fuck, what are you doing to me, The Morrigan?

I close my eyes, fatigue and need fogging my brain. Briefly, I consider getting the lube from my nightstand, but I can't be bothered. Spitting into my hand, I jerk off like I'm a teenager again.

Images of dark blue eyes—pleading, hiding, taunting, confronting—flash through my mind.

You know nothing about me.

You would love to win, wouldn't you?

Because they saw me for the first time...

"Fuck," I groan.

I practically smell the lavender. As I tug almost violently, my head covered with precum already, I swear I can even hear her gasp.

I lift my eyelids and... Fuck.

She is only a shadow in the opening of my door.

But she is there nevertheless. Watching me. A vision. So close, and so far at the same time. I open my mouth to tease her, but then I think better of it.

I didn't think my cock can swell harder or my hand move faster, but the surge of need spreads through me.

I don't want to spook her, because the only thing better than having her eyes on my cock while I chase my release would be to have her sit in my lap and chase it with me. At least in my mind.

The familiar tingling at the base of my spine makes me want to close my eyes, but I want to see her face when I come.

And fuck, I come. I grunt as white ropes paint my stomach. The orgasm crushes through me with such intensity, I almost black out.

My gaze collides with Saar's. I don't know if I searched for her eyes, or if she simply lifted her gaze, but she gasps and freezes for a brief moment before she runs away.

"Next time, feel free to join in, The Morrigan."

Chapter 13

Saar

I think I'm attracted to him.

LILY

To whom?

CELESTE

Cormac the devil Quinn?

CORA

Who isn't? Have you seen the man?

Have you met him? His personality negates everything else about him.

CORA

(laughing emoji) ...and yet.

CELESTE

How does he feel about it?

Who cares? I despise him.

LILY

Aren't you attracted to him?

That's the problem. But none of you are helping.

CORA

(laughing emoji)

I shower, blow-dry my hair, and sit on my bed, waiting for Corm to leave for work. I don't know his schedule yet, but a busy man like him must be gone by nine o'clock. Sooner for sure. But I don't want to risk it, so I'm idling around my room.

I can't face him. I don't know what I was thinking. I don't even know why I went to talk to him last night.

His abrupt departure from my room unsettled me, and if I want him to set the date, I want to make sure that... Argh, hell if I know.

His door was ajar. Or did he leave it open on purpose? I didn't expect to interrupt *that*. And I didn't even interrupt. He continued.

Why? Why am I never on a level playing field with him?

I thought he didn't see me. But something about seeing him naked—God, the man is gorgeous—making himself come, paralyzed me.

Just seeing him all-powerful and vulnerable was mesmerizing. It made him look human. That is, if a man with the body of God can be human. I couldn't take my eyes off him. I almost fucking came myself from just seeing him come undone.

But it wasn't just *me* seeing *him*. He saw me. How long did he know I was standing there? He probably got off on my spying. Disgusting. Or hot. I'm so confused.

As if my existential crisis isn't enough, now I have to tango around this unfortunate situation. Plus my weird hateful attraction to him.

I sigh. Facing Corm today isn't even the biggest of my issues. It's my inability to unsee what I witnessed last night.

My libido has been so low, I haven't used my vibrator in months. Until last night. I was wet when I returned to my room, arousal trickling between my thighs. That rarely happens.

Shit. I'm physically attracted to the man I hate. One that has been playing a power game I keep losing.

Now I have to play the dutiful fiancée if I want him to move forward with the stupid wedding. Can my life be more fucked up?

On top of everything, Vito hasn't returned my calls in two days. Poor man probably wants to spare me more devastating details of my dire situation.

Okay, no more wallowing. I'm going to rock the shit out of this arrangement. I'm going to buy all the books about burnout, set up as many networking meetings as possible, and find my purpose by the end of this month.

And hopefully, by the end of the month, I'll have my money and can have my freedom back. Life looks better after a few self-inflicted orgasms that made me fall asleep.

Nora's offer flickers through my mind, but I dismiss it. It feels like too big of a venture in my current state. I need to find myself before I can do something so big.

My improved mood goes down the drain the minute I enter the kitchen.

With his back to me, my fiancé stands by the bay window, talking on the phone. He's wearing a navy button-down with the sleeves rolled up, and black slacks that hug his ass to perfection.

His muscles bulk up as he raises a cup to his lips. He stands with his legs apart, owning the room without even trying.

I know he technically owns this room, this house, but it's the energy of power that simply washes off him so naturally, and consumes everyone and everything in his vicinity.

I stay rooted in the entrance, momentarily startled by his physique. He truly is gorgeous. Like male-underwear-commercial quality.

Why isn't he in a suit? Or at work already?

"Thank you." He disconnects the call and turns.

Our gazes collide. If he is surprised to see me, he doesn't let up. He studies me with an aloof coolness, and a shiver rakes down my body.

Cut. It. Out.

"What are you doing here?" I accuse, because apparently, fight or flight is my default setting. And my stubbornness doesn't allow me to flee, so here I am, confronting him as if I had the right. Or as if it was in my interest. No fucking filter.

"I live here." He smirks, taking a sip of his coffee. "Making a habit of spying on me?"

Heat rises to my cheeks, and I swallow a retort. Getting married is the goal here.

"I didn't expect you to still be home."

He puts the cup down and slides his hands into his pockets, observing me with an expression somewhere between annoyance and curiosity. "Let me make you breakfast."

"What? Why?" My heart rate spikes, and now I am somewhere between annoyed and curious. What is happening?

He moves around, shaking cereal from a box, adding nuts and milk into a bowl. He puts it on the counter for me, ignoring my question.

I don't move. "Why are you not at work?"

"I'm working from home."

"Why?"

What's with the twenty questions? Just eat and leave. Or better, take the bowl to your room and get away from him.

Here is my problem. After the kiss last night and my unplanned voyeur session, something shifted, and my hatred for him softened. Which makes no sense at all. He's the same asshole.

It's probably just my good mood due to a better sleep, and he will piss me off soon enough, and everything will be balanced again.

"Eat," he barks, ignoring my question.

Ah, here it is, his charm. I cross my arms over my chest. "Or what?"

This man draws the worst out of me. I don't even know anymore why I am fighting it. I'm not very hungry, but having a healthy breakfast is the first step in resetting my internal clock, and finding a better, more regular lifestyle.

So what's my problem?

That the man who regards me like an annoying insect is here instead of yelling at people on the phone and serving me breakfast cereal. Why?

"Isn't that an iron-fortified cereal?" I beckon to the box behind him.

"So?"

So? With nuts and everything else, it's like he

googled breakfast for iron-deficient people and served it to me. Why? Too many whys for this morning if you ask me.

He eats the distance between us and picks me up.

"What are you doing?" I gasp.

He sits me on the stool gently and lowers his head to my ear. For a moment, we are frozen like this. His breath on my skin sinfully warm. His closeness dangerously tempting.

"Fucking eat, or I'll feed you," he growls.

His breath fans my face, and along with the timbre of his voice vibrating through me, I can feel him in my core. This should not make me giddy or excited. It. Should. Not.

"Why are you so concerned about my diet?" I mumble, desperately searching for my sanity.

He grumbles something I don't catch, picks up the bowl, digs in, and moves the full spoon to my lips. "Open."

It's not even a command. It's kind of a plea, I think. Maybe I don't need a well-rested mind, because that fucker offers wild interpretations of reality.

And it ignores me. Because I didn't decide to obey, and here I am, glaring but opening my mouth.

"I'm concerned with the health and wellbeing of my fiancée. As should she be."

I chew. Yum, this is really good. Not too sweet. Not too bland. "Stop patronizing me."

He uses the opportunity to stuff another spoonful into my mouth. "Stop acting like a brat."

Fair point. *Stop acting like an asshole.*

He gives me another spoonful.

"You don't have to feed me."

He raises his eyebrow, deadpan.

I snatch the spoon from him and resume eating. "I thought you were working from home? Since when is feeding your fiancée in your job description?"

"Since she keeps almost fainting near me."

"It happened once."

"Twice."

His phone rings, and he taps the earbud in his ear. "Yes." He doesn't move from me, just mouths 'eat'.

I roll my eyes and finish my breakfast, with him standing so close that my body shivers while my heart gallops.

He barks at someone on the phone. And a completely surprising feeling grabs me. I envy him.

I'm jealous that he has a job, a purpose, an agenda... a life that is put together. I finish eating and slide from the stool, taking my dishes to the dishwasher.

Corm listens to the person on the other side, but

his gaze is firmly on me. It's unnerving and comforting at the same time.

I pour myself a coffee and head for the entrance to sneak out.

"Lunch is in three hours."

I stop. Did he say that to me? Or is he still on the phone?

Turning, I collide with him. Is he a panther now? How did he creep up behind me? And again, I'm against his solid body which, as history taught me, robs me of my resolution or free will.

"What?"

"We'll eat here, since the dining room is... nausea-inducing." He towers over me.

I don't understand what is going on this morning. He's his usual aloof asshole, but exhibits intentions of care.

"Have you stayed home to babysit me?"

His jaw tenses as he studies me through hooded eyes. We stand there in yet another silent duel.

And again, my vital functions go haywire—I can't get enough oxygen, my stomach is fluttering and churning at the same time, my heart is thumping in my temples, and goose bumps and sweat dust my skin.

A full-blown arousal mingled with anxiety. The worst possible combination. Corm Quinn elicits the weirdest cocktail of emotions in me.

"I have a conference call to prepare for."

He pushes past me and storms toward his office, leaving me there, staring into the empty space for I don't know how long.

* * *

"Let's go." Corm pokes his head through the opening in the sliding door.

I have been enjoying the silence on the outdoor patio. A fire-pit coffee table surrounded by lounge chairs softens the large, cold, tiled rectangle. Several large potted plants lining the corners augment the cozy feel.

It's only five in the morning, but I couldn't sleep, and this place is my favorite part of the house.

Sitting here always calms me.

Perhaps it's because this part of the house's exterior is the first peaceful place in my life. I haven't had a space like this before. Definitely not at home growing up.

Not in the student home at my Swiss school, and never while I was working, despite owning two apartments in Europe.

I can't possibly imagine Corm spending time here. It's filled with fresh air and harmony, unlike his stifling mercurial personality.

"Go where?" Why is he even up this early?

"Just come." He sighs like he's annoyed with my non-compliance.

Fuck him, but I'm too tired to argue, so I stand up and follow him. On my best behavior for a few more days, and we set the date, I remind myself.

He turns to the kitchen and then along the pantry to the garage.

I didn't venture here during my house exploration, mostly because I have no interest in cars.

"Wow, are all these yours?"

Five different cars are parked under his house, but I've only ever seen him in his Escalade with a driver.

Lined up here are a Porsche, a Ferrari, a Lamborghini, and a car I don't recognize. Its lights blink after a beeping sound, and both doors lift like wings.

"Who else would they belong to?" The annoyance in his voice is now more pronounced.

"Why do you wake up this early if it makes you grumpy?" I roll my eyes.

"Get in."

Sighing, I climb into the seat. He slides beside me, and the doors close. The car purrs, and the front gate hums before it rolls up.

"Where are we going?"

"For a ride."

"Really?" I exaggerate my fake shock.

We drive out of the garage, and he stops, turning to me. "She needs to go for a spin. There is no traffic at this hour."

I want to ask why I have to join him for his joy ride, but he leans over, and all words evaporate.

His masculine scent hits my nostrils, and my breath catches. I'm not going to lie, I've been reliving that kiss from the other day. But is this a good idea?

His eyes pierce through me, probably reaching into my soul. Fuck, his gaze is intense. Heat spreads around my cheeks, and... well, all over my body.

His nose is just an inch from my face, and his warm breath elicits goose bumps all over my skin. He moves his arm, and I hold my breath.

The tension is thick with unspoken words and heavy with desire. Until he reaches for the seat belt and moves back to his side, buckling me up.

I look away, gluing my eyes to the passenger window, my heart hammering in my temples. This man will drive me to a loony bin.

We drive in silence, and the monotony of the movement falls heavy on my eyelids. I close my eyes and find it hard to open them again.

When I do, I'm slouched in the seat, my cheek wet from my saliva. The sun is up, the streets full of life. I blink a few times and stretch. I recognize we just turned into our street.

"Good morning," Corm says.

"What time is it?"

He pulls into the driveway and kills the engine. The door rises again.

"A few minutes past nine." He gets out of the car.

What? I scramble off my seat while he rounds the car and gives me his hand. Fuck, these low cars are hard to get out from.

"We drove for four hours?" My hand lands on his chest as he yanks me up. Burn. But also, can I please keep it there?

"I didn't want to wake you up."

He strolls away, his words cracking something in the hard shell around my heart.

Chapter 14

Saar

"Your parents didn't mind you leaving the home at fifteen?"

I snort and shove a spoonful of my now-favorite cereal into my mouth.

"My parents were the ones who sent me to Europe. My father only cares about himself. I wasn't shaping into the socialite my mother hoped for, so I became a nuisance to her."

The man has an uncanny ability to make me talk. Or maybe I'm so starved for attention, I blabber away happily.

For four days, Corm has been doting on me. If making sure I eat, growling and glaring at me, and borderline threatening me can be defined as doting.

He ignores me most of the time, but he shares meals with me, and it's the weirdest thing, because most of those occasions are fairly civil. Like we became roommates, but we also make an effort to get to know each other.

Somehow it just happened, because I couldn't eat in silence while he glared at me. And somehow, I tired him with my attempts at conversation, and he conceded.

To a certain extent because he avoids most of my questions, but inquires about my life. And actually listens to everything I say.

"Is that why you're estranged?" He takes a sip of his coffee, not looking at his watch or his phone. It's strange when you don't trust someone, and he's one of the few people who listens when you talk.

"No, no, I still would go home and try my hardest to gain their... I don't know, approval, love, or at least kindness. When Finn and Cal pulled father's company from under him, I didn't have to think twice about whose side to take. My parents tried to guilt me into becoming a dutiful daughter. But by then I recognized who they were, and I knew their interest in me was more to demonstrate to the world they were the wronged party."

"How?"

"Mother didn't ask me how I am, didn't try to find out anything about my life, but she demanded I accompany her to an event. It was a PR op for her. Having one child turn against you publicly is one thing, but having all three of them... I haven't spoken to them since then."

"From what you're telling me, you're better off without them. But I'm sure it wasn't easy when you were a teenager."

"Luckily, Vito found me, and he became my proxy father. Or I made him into one. And the catwalk became my home. Strangely, having all those eyes on me somehow subbed for the attention I hadn't gotten at home."

"Do you miss it?"

I chuckle. "God no. It was demanding, like a real relationship, and yet all fake, superficial. I'm lost at the moment, but I don't ever want to go back."

"You will figure it out in no time."

"It's easy for you to say. You have money, a job, purpose."

"It's easy for you to have those things as well."

"I wish I had your confidence." I push the empty bowl away, a bit uncomfortable with spilling my anxieties over breakfast with him. Especially with him.

"Did you have those things once?" he asks.

"Yes."

He shrugs and puts his cup down. "That's all the proof you need to know it's possible."

"I don't know where to start." I sigh.

Perhaps it's easier to be vulnerable with him. He's just a stranger, and he'll be gone from my life in a few months, so I don't care what he thinks about me.

He's a transient fixture in my life, so even if he judges me, I don't have to live with that judgment for the rest of my life.

"You'll figure it out. Don't push it. You had a highly demanding career; allow yourself to unwind."

"That's what Nora Flemming told me."

He frowns. "The model?"

I nod. "Former model. I met with her to get advice on the transition from the job."

"That's smart. I'm sure there are other women like that you can talk to."

"She offered me a job," I blurt out.

He raises his eyebrows. "What job?"

I tell him about the opportunity.

"You'd be good at that," he says simply, like there is no doubt in his mind. It's an endorsement I didn't expect.

"I'm not sure if I'm ready to take it on." I look away because I don't want to disappoint him—the story of my life.

"You will know when you're ready. Nothing good transpires when we push too hard."

"You work hard."

"That's different. I don't chase. I allow things to

happen, and I'm building a company, and I invest my time where it matters the most. Working hard because something fulfills you and pushing hard to busy yourself are not the same thing."

"I hardly busy myself." I snort.

I'm moping around like a lost puppy most days. Tidying up my clothes, organizing my pictures, knitting, browsing, or reading about burnout.

He cocks his head, challenging me.

"Okay, I've been busying myself to stop the thoughts."

"Why don't you let the thoughts flow instead of quieting them? I know it's scary to start something new, but avoiding it won't make you happy."

"How would you know?" I scoff, mostly because I need to shield myself from his truth. It's safer.

"Merged is my something new. Before, I only invested in ventures as a silent partner. If something went south, I'd lose money, but nobody would know. Merged is the first company with my name openly attached to it."

The formidable Cormac Quinn was hiding behind silent investments? It's not the actual fact that shocks me, but his willingness to share that tidbit with me. Have I worn him down enough so he opens up?

"What made you take the leap, and why would you jeopardize it with your reckless partying?" I probably shouldn't ask, because talking about himself isn't ever on the table, but the question slips out before I can stop it.

He looks away, and when his eyes return to me, there is a storm behind them. "My point is, I know something about starting something. You need the idea to come to you, and that won't happen if you're distracted by self-pity or noise you create to protect yourself. You might miss what matters if desperation rules you."

I'm not getting more answers about him. I lost him already, I know. At least for now. But that doesn't matter, because talking to him has been the best part of my day.

I don't have to be alone with my own thoughts. I can assess them through his eyes. And as much as I hate to admit it, I'm grateful for these unexpected chats.

"I have to go to the office today. I'll see you at the fundraiser." He stands up abruptly and marches out of the kitchen. "Eat your lunch before you leave."

I roll my eyes. "Yes, Daddy."

He pokes his head back in, scowling. "Careful."

His warning is wrapped in desire.

The ginger Persian kitten is super tiny in my hand, curled up, purring softly. I'm almost worried to breathe so I don't disturb or break it.

I gather it closer to my chest, her warmth spreading through me with an unexpected sense of calm.

"It's so tiny," I tell Ethel, the animal shelter's manager. "How did she end up here?"

"Someone found the whole litter in a box in a back alley. Two of them didn't make it. Coco here is too small still, but she's a survivor."

A survivor. "It must be heartbreaking to see so much suffering."

"It's painful to know how cruel people can be, but I love my job. I get enough love from these innocent creatures to mend the heartbreak. Would you like to see the entire facility?"

"We should wait for Cormac. He'll be here any minute." I lean down to inhale the kitten, smiling to myself. There is something therapeutic about holding the furry ball.

"He should be here by now," Betsy grumbles from the corner, where she's been on the phone ever since she arrived.

"So what's the plan here? You give us a check and we pose for pictures?" Ethel asks, and something tells me she's been through this rodeo many times.

"Pretty much." Betsy joins us, eyeing Coco with suspicion.

"Are you more of a dog person, Betsy?" I ask, and Corm's handler looks at me with horror.

"Let me find out where Cormac is." She turns on her heels and puts the phone to her ear.

"More like a snake person. Preferably as a skin on her boots," Ethel murmurs beside me, and I swallow a snicker.

"I'm assuming our donation is helpful, but probably not enough. What will it cover?" I keep petting Coco with my finger, her fluffy coat soft on my skin.

I don't know how Betsy organized this. Corporate sponsorships are common, and so are private donations like ours, but this photo op? It's like Corm is running for office.

"Actually, your donation will cover food and rent for the entire year. We're very grateful."

"What else do you need?" I ask, as if I had any money to offer.

"Space is an issue. We're often overcrowded, pressed to call for adoptions. But often it feels that every time a pet gets adopted, two or three more find their way here. And then staff. We can't afford enough qualified people, so we rely on our volunteers."

"Here he is," Betsy exclaims behind me. "What the—"

I turn and swallow a laugh. Cormac crowds the entrance, looking like he's just walked out of a magazine cover page. The man is edible, I swear. His hair is mussed to perfection. He's sporting stubble that frames his square jaw.

Said jaw is clenched, but that's normal. The most significant feature on his beautiful face today is a scowl.

Shit. That's my fault. While he looks like a movie star, he's also dressed to the nines. In a tuxedo.

"I'm Ethel Keely, the manager here." Ethel recovers first. "Welcome. Thank you for coming."

Corm gives me a look that makes me want to squirm, but I won't give him the satisfaction, so I glare back at him with my chin high.

In my defense, I completely forgot about those stupid labels in his closet.

And why should this be on me? The man is an adult, running a successful business. Can't he check his agenda and dress appropriately?

"What are you wearing?" Betsy hisses louder than she probably intended.

Corm looks at her like she's polluting the air he owns, and then he smiles—like actually smiles. "I'm sorry I'm late. I'm coming from a luncheon, and I didn't want to keep you waiting any longer, so hence the attire." He takes off his dinner jacket, drops it into Betsy's arms. "Why don't we walk around, Ethel?"

Ethel giggles. The woman giggles. "Let's do it then."

Corm undoes his collar, rips off the bow tie, puts it in his pocket, and proceeds to roll up his sleeves. Pure arm porn, if you ask me. But nobody is asking me. Or even looking at me anymore.

Ethel probably forgot I'm even here. My fiancé ignores me as he follows the manager. I snuggle Coco closer to me.

The whole excursion lasts about twenty minutes.

Twenty minutes of cuteness and sadness. Hopelessness and helplessness.

The entire time, Coco sleeps in my arms. Corm asks questions, pets animals, appears to be interested. It's a pose, I know. He's playing a part, and he's doing a pretty good job of it.

I wonder if his care for me and his listening are also a pose. Has he had me fooled?

Ethel and her volunteers are all in awe of him. And some of them openly ogle him like I'm not even here.

On one hand, I'm enjoying the shadow. After years of living in the spotlight, this is a pleasant reprieve and freedom. I'm not the principal attraction. That role belongs to Corm, and he embraces it.

He doesn't seem concerned about doing anything

wrong, or making a wrong move. He flourishes in the limelight.

On the other hand, come on! I don't deserve to be ignored. Being in the shadows by choice is one thing, but this?

Invisible. Insignificant. Alone.

I can step out. I should step out. I need to claim my spot beside him. But he doesn't want me beside him.

If he did, I would have been there already. If only as a part of the charade, but still by his side.

I wander around the place, balancing Coco in one arm while I pet and stroke puppies, injured dogs, and cats. I get lost in the moment. These animals are the kindest creatures I've met recently.

Collective ooh and aah sighs of adoration draw my attention. I crane my neck to get a better view above the shoulders of the volunteers. What's going on?

Jesus. If I thought Corm rolling up his sleeves was porn, I wasn't prepared for this. Nestled in the crook of his elbow, sleeping on his brawny forearm, is a tiny kitten. White, and a little bigger than Coco, it stretches its paw and mews.

The camera keeps clicking, and I'm mesmerized by the sight. Arguably, a sexy man holding a kitten is a sight for sore eyes. But it's Corm's expression that steals my breath.

He's looking down at the kitten, his eyes kind and

adoring. There is a ghost of a smile—a genuine one—on his softened face.

And then he looks up, and his gaze finds mine. For a brief moment, he gives me the same look, and fuck, I want to bathe in it. I've been in a shadow for half an hour, and now, the sun turns to me, and it's the warmest feeling.

It's a fleeting moment, though, and Corm's jaw sets rigidly immediately, and he puts the kitten down.

"Your job is to pose with him," Betsy mutters beside me, startling me.

"He doesn't need my help; the room is eating from the palm—"

"Saar, you're not in this to express your opinions. This whole circus was planned to showcase you as a couple contributing to the community. You have a role to play."

Her words dig deep into an already festering wound. It's like working all over again. Just a prop.

"Here you are, sweetheart." Corm's voice stops me from telling Betsy to fuck off. His arm snakes around my waist, and I want to recoil and lean in at the same time. "Who do we have here?"

He strokes Coco with the pad of his thumb while the camera clicks around us.

"It's Coco. Isn't she adorable?" I push the words out, playing the fucking role and smiling for the camera. What doesn't kill you makes you stronger and all that.

"As adorable as you," Corm says loudly. "You'll pay for the tux," he whispers into my ear, and before I have a chance to react, he steps away and talks to Ethel.

His phone buzzes. "Ethel, thank you so much for your time and for this wonderful visit. Saar and I are so happy we could help a little."

He turns and walks out into the front room.

"I'll miss you," I whisper to the ginger kitten. "I got quite attached to you, Coco."

A volunteer takes her from me and puts her back with her siblings.

"She's too little to be adopted, but maybe in a few weeks," Ethel says beside me. "I can save her for you."

I wish I was free to adopt her in a few weeks. "Well —" I try to think of a response that doesn't give away my current situation.

"I understand, you're planning a wedding and are surely busy, but if you change your mind." Ethel smiles at me.

"Thank you." I give Coco one last glimpse and rush out of there, my heart heavy.

"I don't know when you came to the conclusion that I care about your opinion, Betsy," Corm's voice stops me before I cross the threshold. "I'm having her followed, and you should be grateful I don't have you fired."

Who is he talking about?

"I've done a background check on her," Betsy's voice shakes with indignation.

"Not thorough enough apparently," Corm hisses.

What the hell? Are they talking about me?

I step into the room. The glass front gives a view of a gray, rainy street. Corm is now wearing his suit jacket, glaring at Betsy, and looking like an attractive action-movie hero. Or rather a villain.

Both of them stand in the middle of the linoleum floor, the fluorescent light casting a harsh glow on their skin.

Betsy notices me and clears her throat. "Good, I think we got nice pictures to continue with the positive story. Have a nice day." She yanks the door open and marches out.

Corm looks at me, his eyes void of emotion. He opens the front door. "After you, darling." His smile could freeze Hell.

I step outside, trying not to roll my eyes. It's like any tender connection we established over the last few days has disappeared. Like outside the confines of his house, our relationship is back to hatred and pretense.

"We agreed no more childish stunts, and then I

fucking come dressed up here like an idiot." The rain drizzling is warmer than his tone.

"What are you talking about? Everyone in there loved the James Bond look." Come on, he must see it was funny.

"I thought you wanted to set the date ASAP."

I sigh. "I'm sorry. I played with those labels before we agreed. And I never assumed you wouldn't check where you were going."

"I was on a conference call while getting changed, believing I can trust my system and not be bothered by trivial things. I'm fucking busy. A concept unfamiliar to you, obviously."

His words are like a slap. "Fuck you. I said I'm sorry. Nothing bad happened, so cut the drama."

He scoffs. "I was looking for a fiancée, not a fucking child." His car stops at the curb, and he yanks the door open. "Get in."

"No."

"Suit yourself. Don't wait up, darling, I'm going to The Velvet Room."

My stomach sinks—and has no right to do so. "That's a—"

"Sex club. Yes, I have needs." He gets into the car and leaves.

A fucking sex club? Asshole. I wipe the wet hair from my forehead and dash to a coffee shop I spot.

Shaking off the water as I enter, I order a latte and sit in the corner. Was he talking about me with Betsy? Is he having me followed? Why? What did she miss in her background check?

A man enters and takes a seat. He doesn't look my way, but I'm still wondering if he's my tail.

Corm has me followed.

And he went to a sex club, not even trying to hide it. I should call some gossip column and tip them off.

I pull out my phone to call Cora, and the screen draws a smile on my face. I have my camera on with a few selfies I took in the shelter with Coco.

I sit for a moment, scrolling through the pictures. A beautiful memory of a few carefree, loving moments, and a painful reminder of my lack of freedom.

Let's spread some Coco cuteness to the world. I open my feed, ready to upload the pic, when I notice my draft post.

Perhaps the world—or at least me—needs an unfiltered truth more. I can post the kitten later.

Chapter 15

Corm

"I talked to Donovan." Xander saunters into my office without knocking.

Dressed in black shorts and a sweaty T-shirt, he plops down on my white sofa. He reaches into the bowl in the middle of the coffee table and helps himself to a handful of nuts.

Since when do I offer snacks in my office? Fucking Larissa and her efforts to humanize me.

"Ever heard of showering after a workout? Get your sweaty ass off my sofa."

He chuckles but doesn't move. "You're a ray of sunshine, as usual."

He doesn't know the least of it. I've been in the worst mood since yesterday. First, I opened the file on Saar I got from Mathison. I thought I'd started to get to know her.

I don't know what possessed me to work from home for almost a week, but having every meal with her was more pleasant than I anticipated.

Her metabolism is fucked up after years of irregular schedules, and probably some crazy diets. I took unwarranted pleasure in seeing her eating regularly. That, by itself, should—is—concerning me.

I took her for a ride in my Bugatti, because cars seem to be the only place where she falls asleep. I drove around for hours, just so she got some rest. I told her I didn't need a child instead of a fiancée, but I took to the babysitting duties pretty fast. Fuck.

And then there were the conversations. Some of them trivial, all of them interesting. It probably was a much-needed distraction from my daily grind, because I found myself looking forward to the next meal.

Saar is smart and well-read. She is strong, perhaps a bit too cynical at times, but I suspect that's another result of her career. She grew a thick skin to survive the demands, the toxicity.

She's kind of lost at the moment, but instead of crumbling, she's searching for answers. Not that she gives herself any credit.

And she is hot as sin. I've been walking around with a semi, lusting after that body of hers. A very unfortunate development.

But then I read the file on her, and fuck, if that

wasn't the biggest disappointment. I couldn't even look at her when I saw her at the shelter.

And still, I was stealing glances at her with the kitten. The woman is a siren. I need her out of sight, and hopefully soon out of my life.

She thought I was pissed about the tux. Fuck, I was upset about that, but it was kind of funny. It's not like I can't afford to throw it out after walking through the kennels.

I wanted to confront her then and there, but I have a business deal to think about. Screw her.

And yet she's been on my mind every freaking minute of the day. Perhaps because she played me so well.

Never did I suspect Saar van den Linden was so deceitful, but what is worse, my bullshit radar failed me around her.

Now I have the evidence that the woman is not only bad news, but that I can't read her at all. And it still didn't help me stop thinking about her.

I even went to the fucking sex club to get rid of that need she sparked. But nobody got the job done. The manager was pulling his hair, sending one girl after another to my booth in the VIP section.

I sent them all away. Why? I tried to come up with lies, but to be honest, I sent them away because they were not Saar.

The Morrigan bewitched me. Her smiles, her quips, her body, her wit. All of it is wrapped around my cock.

But there is no way I can succumb to that temptation after what I found out. And like an idiot, I have her followed now. Because the best guy for the job, Mathison, uncovers something, and I still need more proof. Or hope for her redemption. Goddammit.

I shouldn't have kissed her. But that's a minor mistake, and I won't deepen it.

"What the fuck do you want, Xander? I'm busy."

"And as pleasant as ever. Hopefully, this news will cheer you up..."

"Impossible." Declan walks in.

Where the fuck is Larissa? I don't have an open-door policy. Quite the contrary.

"You're probably right." Xander snorts. "Anyway, Donovan complained AetherTech is not taking their calls. I guess Vlad is keeping his promise to stall for two months."

Declan nods. "That's why I'm here. How much do you want to send to Vlad's charity?"

"Let's wait for that. Betsy finally got me the invitation to his fundraiser—it got lost in the mail." I clasp my hands behind my head, leaning back. Lost, my ass. But if Vladislav expected to be rid of me, he was mistaken.

"I guess it's smart to wait. We'll adjust the donation to his expectations once you see what others throw his way."

"Yeah, the event is in two weeks. Hopefully, by then, he will be mollified enough by my recovered image."

Xander snorts again. "So how is the wedding planning?"

"Let's focus on business. Vlad said he doesn't like how long it's taking to sign the deal, and then he suggested he'd stall to ensure our involvement." I tap my fingers on the table.

"Motherfucker." Xander immediately picks up on my line of thinking. "You think he's talking to another firm?"

"I think you should shower." I glare at him. "And then find out who might be courting AetherTech."

"Excuse me." Larissa pops her head in. "Betsy Ham is on the phone, claiming it's urgent."

I sigh. "Put her through."

Declan sits beside Xander like this is a fucking theater. "Do you mind?" I snap.

"Unless you start paying her from your own pocket, put her on speaker," Declan says. He raises his eyebrow, daring me.

"The vote of confidence is duly noted." I press the

answer button. "Betsy, Xander and Declan are here with me. What's so urgent?"

"Things have been going so well, and you can't keep your fiancée on the leash, Corm?"

"Careful there, Betsy." I have had enough of this woman's patronizing attitude. How dare she talk about Saar like this?

"We have a crisis on our hands," she snaps. "Your fiancée—"

"Watch your tone, Ham. You found her, not me." I'm not sure why I bother reminding her.

It's like my mind wants to avoid whatever she wants to say. Because as much as I want to stay away from Saar, I don't want more reasons to do so.

"Have you seen Saar's social media?"

Why would I? "No."

Xander pulls out his phone and whistles.

"I suggest you read her last post. It went viral. I don't know what she was thinking, but I suggest you ask her to pull it down immediately."

What the fuck? I gesture to Xander, who comes over and turns his phone to me.

The image rams into me like a freight train. Fuck, she's beautiful. Sitting on the bench in the window of my house, she looks small and lost but also like she belongs.

Seeing her in my space like that squeezes at something in my chest. Like she's mine.

Her dark blue eyes stare at me with such raw honesty, almost pleading to be seen. The photo captures her looking fragile and strong at the same time.

Okay, well, based on Betsy's fussing, I thought Saar posted nudes.

"What's wrong with the picture?"

Betsy huffs. "Not the picture, the caption below it. Look, we're coming up with a mitigation strategy, but try to motivate her to take it down. She's not answering my phone."

"What makes you think she'd answer mine?" I rumble.

"I'm adding a pain-in-my-ass markup to your next bill. Find her; talk to her. I'll call you in an hour with an idea on how to spin this, or at least make sure it doesn't derail your deal."

I hang up and snatch Xander's phone and read the post.

My new home... And it's a lie... I have never felt more out of place than I do right now... I'm exhausted... And pretty damn lonely... Just me, sitting in a huge mansion, wondering what the hell I'm supposed to do next.

"Wow, she has over a quarter of a mil likes already.

She spent a week with you, and she's suicidal." Xander grabs his phone and leaves, laughing. Fucker.

I pinch the bridge of my nose. *I'm pretty damn lonely*. You and me, The Morrigan, you and me.

That woman will be the death of me. Because not only did she make me look like an asshole, but she made me feel responsible for her wellbeing.

And her honest cry in the form of a social media post makes me want to strangle her and embrace her at the same time.

"You can cajole huge corporations to do your bidding, and you can't control your fiancée? Seriously, Corm, get your shit together, finally. Dad is dead. It's been almost a year. He wouldn't want you to derail your life like this." Declan sighs.

"What the fuck do you know about what he wanted, or who he even was?" I grab a stapler and hurl it at the window.

Declan shakes his head. "He's gone, Corm. You're giving him way too much power."

"This has nothing to do with him."

"This has everything to do with him. Otherwise you wouldn't get arrested, drunk, high, fuck strippers, and jeopardize your business. What was in that fucking letter he left you?"

"It doesn't matter." I stand up, yanking my suit jacket from the backrest. "It doesn't fucking matter."

"If you say so." He opens the door. "Go to talk to her, and try to leave your charming personality behind. If you want to spiral down, so be it; just don't drag us all with you."

* * *

"Saar, Saar," I holler before I even close the front door. Livia comes from the kitchen, blinking. "Where the fuck is she?"

"Mr. Quinn, Ms. Saar is on the patio. It's such a lovely day finally. We didn't expect you to—"

"Take the afternoon off, Livia," I snarl, rushing through the long hallway to the glass wall with the double door.

I stop at the threshold and take a deep breath to calm myself, but also to take in the vision in front of me.

Saar is wrapped in a thick, long, woolen dress that hugs her slender form, hiding and seducing. With her legs stretched out on a lounge bed, she's wearing sunglasses, looking like the model she used to be.

With her side to me, she doesn't know I'm there yet. My anger—irrationally—dissipates a notch just from the pure beauty of her. Her presence has an air of serenity that calms me.

It makes no sense, because most of the time she

gives me her sass, and yet having her around has given me a sense of… what?

I can't name it. Fuck, I don't want to name it. These unchartered feelings are unwelcome.

For a moment, I wish I could just join her, sit beside her, and close my eyes. Let her breath wash over me. Make me feel whole and not so… lonely. Fuck, no wonder her post went viral; it even relates to me.

But that's not what I'm here for. That's not what would get me my deal.

I clear my throat, and she turns to me. "You're home early. Or at all." A sarcastic smile tugs at her lips.

The sunglasses are huge, covering half of her face, and it's still the most beautiful face I've ever seen.

"Enjoying yourself?" I growl, clenching my fists because if I'm honest, I want to fuck her and kill her too.

"Yes." She turns her face to the sun to demonstrate I can't spoil her fun.

"Enjoying your minute of fame? I thought you were over the attention." I sit on the lounge chair beside her, bracing my arms on my knees.

She raises her glasses, pushing them into her messy hair, and frowns at me.

"What were you thinking, Saar?"

"You need to be more specific, darling. I've been thinking about a lot of things. All the ways I could rid of your body. What I will do with my life once I'm free of you. What to wear to the theater on Friday—"

I snap, pouncing. With my knee beside her, I grip her jaw and lower my face to her. Her breath hitches, and I immediately regret my impulse because her gasp goes directly to my groin.

"I thought you understood the deal, The Morrigan. We're supposed to be presenting an image of stability, not broadcasting that you're lost and isolated. You're making me look like I don't even know how to make my fiancée happy."

She glares at me, but the hatred mingles with something else, something more primal, raw. Carnal?

And then I remember: I can't read her. That Mathison's file confirmed she showed me only a tiny part of herself. And even that might be a lie.

"It's true, though. You can't make me happy."

My hand shakes on her jaw, and despite my anger, I'm acutely aware of the softness of her skin, the lushness of her lips, the fire in her eyes. The need to kiss her.

"We're not in an actual relationship; the truth is irrelevant here. I've regretted this arrangement a thousand times over, and every time I think we might just cohabit decently, you have to act out."

"If you want to get rid of me so badly, just set the date finally. The sooner we get married, the sooner I'm gone, and you can replace me with one of your sex-club trophies."

"Are you jealous?" More importantly, why do I want her to be? And why am I derailing the conversation?

"You wish."

Yes, I do. Fuck. "Delete the post."

Against my will—that's the story I'm sticking to, because I've become proficient at lying to myself—my hand moves, caressing her chin, down her throat, her skin like smooth velvet under my touch. I dip my fingers into the neckline of her sweater.

We stare at each other, tension and lust mixing, morphing the moment into something it shouldn't be, filling it with agonizing temptation.

I want to move away, but I can't. Fuck, I don't want to.

She breaks first, cups my nape, and pulls me to her, her lips fusing with mine. It's not a sweet kiss or a claiming one. It's a desperate one—full of pent-up tension, frustration, and all our animosity.

Our teeth clash, our tongues fight as we suck, lick, bite, full of frenzy. I forget where we are, who we are, my entire being craving more of this woman. Craving a release from this fucked-up situation.

I scoop her and flip us around. She straddles me

without breaking the contact, gripping my hair in a rage and fervor and pure need.

"This means nothing." She pants.

"Agreed."

"I mean it, Corm." She looks at me, the fire in her eyes pouring lava into my veins.

"This means nothing," I say, wishing for it to be true.

She grinds her hips against me, and fuck, I'm going to come in my pants. What is she doing to me?

Her dress rode up, exposing her lean legs clad in thick, black tights. "Fuck, there is too much fabric between us."

She smirks against my lips. "What are you going to do about it?"

I slide my hands up her thighs, the feel of her under my hands electrifying. It's like our bodies held on by a thread for weeks, and now all the bets are off.

No inhibition. No control. No reason.

She whimpers when I bite her bottom lip, and the sound reverberates through me with maddening intensity.

I want all her whimpers, all her gasps, her moans, her cries. All her sounds.

Even for this one time. One time. The thought stops me, and my hands sliding into her waistband from behind freeze.

She senses my hesitation and cups my erection. "What is it, Corm, you think you can't handle me?"

"You I can handle, The Morrigan. Are you sure you can handle me? And the aftermath."

I cup the back of her neck and seize her lips in a punishing kiss. Like I don't want her to answer. We are past the point of return.

"This means nothing, remember?" she grits out against my lips, her hand holding me in a tight grip.

Like she knows what I like. Like she needs what I need. Like this has happened many times before, and we know the choreography by heart.

We know shit, but for this one time, I can surrender to the illusion. Because, fuck, I need her wrapped around my cock, and damn the consequences.

I've been reckless many times over. As a teenager. In recent months. And now, again. But never have I been reckless with such dedication.

My hands glide down the globes of her ass, squeezing it. She straightens up and pushes her pelvis forward, seeking friction. Greedy little nymph.

The shy spring sun shimmers through her tresses, creating a halo around her.

Her slender body in the black, knitted dress is gorgeous, and I can't wait to see the beauty underneath.

We shouldn't be doing this, but the forbidden fruit always tastes the best. She starts working on my belt, but I put my hand over hers. I need her nice and ready for all the ways I wish to devour her.

She looks at me, frowning, uttering a frustrated huff. God, she's adorable. Fuck, I shouldn't be noticing this.

"What?" she grumbles.

"Greedy much?" I chuckle.

"Asshole much?" She glares.

"Always." I pull down her tights and her underwear. "Lift."

She obeys, and they come down to her mid-thighs. This won't do. I grip the front and rip them off.

"What the fuck, Corm?"

"They were in my way." I pull the lever to recline the lounger's backrest. Saar yelps as I jerk her with me, her body sprawling over me in the new horizontal position.

I find her lips again, my cock twitching painfully. She tastes like sin and innocence. Like storm and sunshine. Like mine and definitely not mine.

She pushes my jacket down my shoulders, but I don't budge, so she yanks my tie.

"Come sit on my face, sweetheart."

I take in her swollen lips, wild hair, and flushed

face. And that strange sense of serenity grabs me again. I stare at her, mesmerized. Spellbound. Taken.

Screwed.

Fuck. My. Life.

She stills. "What?"

"Be a good girl and listen for once, The Morrigan." I grab her hips, prompting her forward.

"I don't think that's a good idea." She tries to distract me and goes for my belt again, flustered. I like this version of her. Fuck, I like every version of her.

"As you wish." I flip us again, hovering over her. "You don't have to sit on my face for me to thoroughly eat your pussy."

She cringes like the idea isn't appetizing.

"I'm going to eat your pussy, because it's been the only meal on my mind for the past few weeks. And you're not going to deny me, The Morrigan. For once, stop fighting." I slide my hand up her leg and cup her between her thighs.

She is staring at me, a mixture of apprehension and need. And like she wants to surrender. Or maybe that's just my wishful thinking.

I spread her with two fingers and flick my thumb through her folds. She inhales sharply, arching her back. I remove my hand and put the thumb to my mouth.

"Delicious," I hum.

Her eyes widen. What kind of ultra-vanilla idiots was she with before? My other hand grips her hair, white-knuckled, the thought of other men making me completely unhinged.

I crush my lips against her and then move down to her neck. My hands explore her wool-clad body, and I briefly consider moving to the house so I can explore every inch of her flesh. But there will be time for that.

Right now, I'm a man starved. I lean back on my haunches and bunch up her dress. I roll down the remnants of her stockings, her skin silky under my fingers.

"Open," I growl.

She scoots higher and spreads her legs a bit, her eyes glued on me with scorching heat and something else. Something soft and confident. Like she believes she is safe with me. Like she's decided to trust me.

It should scare me. It really should make me pause and reconsider, but instead it instills responsibility and desire. I don't want to let her down.

I can see the moment when the intimacy of our silent exchange spooks her.

She licks her lips. "Are you just going to stare at me?"

"Here she is, The Morrigan. Spread wider," I order.

She slides her feet on the lounger closer to her ass and then she drops them to the side, opening wide.

"This is the prettiest pussy I've ever seen. You should see yourself like this. So ripe for me, already dripping."

Her cheeks turn pink, and she lifts her head like she wants to make sure I'm not lying.

I chuckle. "Relax, sweetheart."

With my hands on her thighs, I lower my head and dive in. Flattening my tongue, I lick her from her ass crack to her clit and back first, and then I take her sensitive bud between my lips, sucking.

She gasps and bucks her hips, her hands gripping my hair almost painfully. I look up, and fuck, if that's not a picture to keep me on my knees.

Saar's head is back, her beautiful long neck straining and bobbing as she moans and sighs with delight.

That one look, along with her sounds, spurs me to action. Okay, and my painful cock that wants in on some action. "You taste better than I imagined."

"You thought about this?" She almost snorts, but her pants turn it into a moan. Even getting unraveled, the woman sasses me. Fuck, I love it.

"Every minute of my days since I saw you in that restaurant. Perhaps even before."

I add a finger, sliding it deep inside her. "Fuck,

you're tight." My cock twitches again, straining against my zipper. I really might blow in my pants. Jesus.

Saar gasps and arches her back as I add another finger and another; I curl them while assaulting her clit with my tongue, and she cries out.

Her walls close around my fingers, and she comes undone. "Oh my God, Corm. Oh, my God."

I pump my fingers in and out while she's coming, hoping to prolong her pleasure. She's beautiful even when exhausted and scowling at me.

But Saar in the glow of her orgasm is alluring. I don't think one hit of her could ever be enough.

I stand up, ignoring my painful erection, and scoop her up. "I need you naked. And we need a condom."

She sighs contentedly. "And lube."

I step inside the house and stop. What? "You want me to fuck your ass?"

"No," she cries and slaps me.

Chapter 16

Saar

Corm lowers me to the floor. "What the fuck?"

He holds my elbow, so I can find my balance. The man is a walking contradiction. He yells at me while making sure I don't fall?

I grew up being ignored and overlooked. I worked in the spotlight to find attention, only to realize that was even lonelier.

And now this? This gentle care and annoying control morphed into one.

"Why would you think I would give you something so intimate? Our first time, no less." I snatch my arm away from him as if he burned me.

"And the only time, The Morrigan," he warns. "You're dripping wet; you just came all over my face; why would we need lube?"

Fuck. Heat rises to my cheeks. "Because that's not usual for me. I'm not normally wet; it's not easy for me to... to..." I don't know how to say it, my eyes darting around the floor, hoping it will swallow me. "With my lifestyle, my sinuses are drier than normal, so are the tissues of my—"

He steps toward me, cupping my cheeks in his palms. "Sweetheart, I'm not going to hurt you. I'll make sure you're ready for me. I'll slide in like my cock belongs to your pussy."

I feel like an idiot. After the best orgasm of my life, I'm humiliating myself again in front of him. It must be the orgasm-induced fog.

As if he feels my hesitation—frankly, the mood is kind of gone—Corm pulls me closer and lowers his lips to mine. The kiss is different this time. Almost sweet.

And just like outside, for some incomprehensible reason, I feel safe. I feel safe in the arms of a man who can't stand me most of the time, but who makes sure I eat well. Who doesn't ridicule my endless mind spiraling while trying to figure out what I want. He simply listens, and calms down the storm in my head.

Before the wardrobe incident, in those few days, he might have believed in me more than I believe in myself.

And now he's kissing me. Not with want or need—even though his cock is hard between us—but rather with reverence. It's like every time I show him some broken piece of me, he rewards me.

A part of me knows it's a false sense of safety. I can't trust him, but I don't want to be alone. I don't want him to leave again and be with other women.

It's like I need to prove to myself I can keep him here. If only for a brief moment. That I'm interesting enough for him to stay.

Fuck. I need therapy.

I moan as he deepens the kiss, his fingers sliding into my hair. His cock jerks between us, and my body ignites with a desire so strong, I stop thinking.

I twist my leg around his, and he cups my ass and lifts me up. As I wrap both legs around his waist, my core is now deliciously exposed to his length. I tilt my pelvis back and forth, and he groans into my mouth.

He carries me down the hall and stops at a console table in the foyer. He pulls out a condom from the drawer.

"I don't even want to know why you would have them there."

"That's where I keep my wallet and keys. These are refills."

I giggle, but then I cover my mouth. "Put me down," I whisper.

He frowns, but places me gently on the first step. My pussy weeps at the loss of friction.

"What now?" he growls.

"Livia."

Jesus, I won't be able to look the housekeeper in her eyes. And I like her. She's my only company in this huge house.

"I sent her home." He snakes his arms around my waist and jerks me to him.

"You planned this?"

"I was planning to kill you." He captures my mouth this time with urgency.

I woke up this morning to all the messages and likes of my post. It was unexpected. It was scary and empowering at the same time.

The confidence that all the reactions gave me didn't serve me well. It made me feel like I matter. It made me feel like I have choices. It made me kiss Cormac on the patio.

Not only to shut him up. Not only because he is so fucking hot. But because I didn't want to be the girl who waits for instructions, for approval, for agreement. I wanted to be the girl who takes what she wants.

Even if what she wants is the insufferable man kissing me currently, whom I have no business to crave.

My body strongly disagrees with that notion. I don't want to buy into that reasonable stance anymore.

I'll deal with the aftermath later, after at least one

more orgasm. Pretty please. The last one clearly wiped out my brain.

I tug at his belt, and this time he doesn't stop me. I fumble while he doesn't stop kissing me, devouring me with his mouth, but finally, I trace the waistband of his briefs.

I pull away from him and gently peel his underwear down. His cock springs out, glistening with pre-cum. It's huge and stiff. I stare at it for a moment. Mesmerized. And a bit scared.

"Wow," I breathe, and he chuckles.

"Okay, sweetheart, this is not show and tell." He tugs at my dress, pulling it over my head. "Beautiful," he drawls.

His gaze roams down my bra-less chest. Oh my, I've been paid handsomely for my looks. People around the world have admired my pictures. I've been named one of the most beautiful people in the world at one point.

And never, ever have I felt like one. Until this man uttered the word, said it with his mouth and his intense eyes, I've never felt truly beautiful.

He's not touching me, just admiring, and yet I feel it everywhere. Butterflies tickle around my stomach. Goose bumps and sweat pepper my skin. My entire body is ablaze.

It's too much, so I quickly divert the attention. I sit

down on a step behind me. Corm frowns at me, and I smile.

"Let me taste you." I reach for him.

He steps closer, standing in front of me one step below. It's not the best alignment, but something about having him between my spread legs while I sit instead of kneel makes me feel empowered.

I lean forward and grip his girth, my tongue darting out. I've never particularly enjoyed giving head. But I wrap my lips around his cock like it was the most delicious ice-cream.

His sharp intake of breath tingles through my body, and I feel it everywhere. It's encouraging and rewarding. I take him as far as I can, helping myself with my hand, and he hisses again, his hands finding my hair.

His grip is almost painful, but not as agonizing as the need coiling in my center. Jesus, I might come just from sucking him off.

I don't know if it's all that pent-up tension, or simply an unprecedented chemistry between us, but my body is on fire. My heart is thumping, drunk on hormones. My core is clenching of its own accord.

"Fuck," Corm groans, and pulls away from me. With no effort, he flips me around, and I'm on all fours, with my ass propped up.

He rips the wrapper and kneels behind me, nudging my entrance with his cock. I bow my head to deal with the sensation but also to look at what's happening between my legs.

"Touch yourself," he demands.

What? "You're right there. I want your cock."

A slap echoes through the cavernous room, and my ass turns ablaze. "What the fuck?" I protest, but fuck if my pussy doesn't contract with pleasure.

"Touch yourself." Corm grips my hips, probably bruising me. The only consolation is the strain in his voice. He's barely hanging onto his control.

I reach between my legs and swipe my fingers through my folds. Jesus. Can I be already close to coming? Everything with this man is more.

More infuriating. More intense. More alive.

"Show me your hand."

Part of me doesn't want to lose the contact, but it seems if I want him to give me what I really crave, I'd better surrender to his whims.

I remove my hand and snake it around my opposite shoulder so he can see it. Corm leans forward, his body covering mine.

The soft fabric of his jacket slides around my torso as the heat of his body envelops me through his shirt. How is he still fully dressed?

He takes my fingers into his mouth and sucks. Oh, my God. I can't. I can't anymore. I push my hips back, desperate for him.

He chuckles. "I told you we won't need the lube. Look at these fingers..." He kisses each of them. "Covered in your need for me. Such a good girl, Saar."

Good girl.

I want to retort something at him, just out of principle. But this is such an honest transaction between us, I just accept what his words do to me.

Turns out, I hate his controlling ways outside the bedroom—well, staircase—but I welcome it when his cock is out.

He lets go of my hand, and I collapse to my elbows. Corm pushes just his tip in, and I stop breathing. He is too big. I close my eyes to deal with the burning sensation.

"You're so tight, sweetheart." He hovers above me and takes both my breasts into his palms, finding my nipples and rolling them achingly between his fingers. "Relax, Saar; let me in, baby."

I don't know why 'sweetheart' had no emotional charge for me, but his calling me 'baby' spreads through me like a sweet liquor, warming me inside and making my legs weak.

He pushes farther, and I gasp, adjusting to the onslaught of pleasure and pain. The latter subsides quickly as Corm finds my clit with his hand. He massages it, and I melt, letting him fully in.

He fills me to the hilt and stills. "Are you okay?"

I always knew Cormac Quinn would fuck like God, but reconciling this with the fact that he's a considerate God overwhelms me. Instead of answering, I roll my hips.

He kisses me between my shoulder blades. It's a tender kiss that surprises me, sprouting goose bumps all over my skin.

But that's the last gentle gesture from him, because after that kiss he withdraws and rams back into me with such force, I almost fall flat on my face.

"Hold on for the ride, The Morrigan," he growls.

He pumps in and out like this was an athletic competition. And of course, he is the winner. And thank God for that, because as he repeatedly hits the right spot like he had some secret compass to my body, I'm ready to build a shrine to his prowess and worship at it in my free time.

The echo of our bodies slapping and my moans hit the high ceiling and bounce off the walls. He fucks me like he hates me—probably true—but couldn't help himself.

I'm on my knees and completely at his mercy, and yet somehow I'm an equal partner in this. Unlike in our real lives.

"I'm coming," I whimper.

"Thank God." His voice is strained as he pinches my nipple.

My walls clench, my toes curl as my body completely takes over, convulsing with the most intense orgasm I've ever had. He continues to thrust, but I'm lost, the reality blurred out into one amazing euphoria.

"Fuck, Saar," he roars, and I feel him jerk inside me.

I drop my forehead, the coolness of the marble slowly bringing me back to reality. The metallic sound of his zipper snaps me out of my stupor. Is he going to walk away? Not if I do that first.

Not very elegantly, I scramble to crawl away from him.

He grips my ankle. "Where do you think you're going?"

He scoops me up and carries me upstairs.

Still dazed, I consider how to get away from him. I'm up for more orgasms, but let's be realistic here. The aftermath—as he rightfully warned me—is going to be awkward.

But it's hard to think about retreating when his muscles envelop me, his scent deepening the hazy feeling.

And his gaze... it has always been intense. But the post-orgasm Corm is looking at me like I'm a goddess.

There is still a dash of disdain, like he doesn't know what to do with me, but it wars with something softer, and very contradictory to that contempt.

He enters his bedroom and drops me onto his bed before he walks away.

"Where are you going?" Fuck, I hate the need in my voice.

"The condom is still on my cock." He disappears into his bathroom.

He has large windows on two sides of his room, meeting in the corner. The drapes are open, and the dusk colors the sky in a multitude of hues. It's beautiful and peaceful. Unlike my hammering heart and my wandering mind.

What have we done? Frankly, if he left me on the stairs I would be less concerned, because it would follow our hateful pattern.

But he brought me to his bed. Is it for round two, or is it a new dynamic? Count me in for the former.

The latter? I don't think I can survive that. I may be all feisty with him, but is my sass enough to protect me from him?

The bathroom door clicks, and I turn my head. And all the thoughts and conundrums leave my mind immediately.

Completely naked, Corm prowls toward me.

"Stop." I stretch my arm, sitting up.

He does, his eyebrows drawing together.

I swallow and stare. So I knew the man was a hunk. That his forearms are works of art. That his face is gorgeous.

But seeing every bulking muscle, every delicious ridge, every hard sinew of his torso? The broad shoulders and trimmed waist. His athletic legs. How much does this man work out?

I used to spend my time around beautiful people. Around very attractive men who model underwear, but I don't think I've ever seen a better-defined chest or pecs. This is not even a six-pack. This is...

Shit. I rake my eyes to his face quickly. What am I doing? Ogling him. Based on the smirk on his face, he not only caught me—obviously he's not blind—but he enjoys my gaping.

"Like what you see?"

"Mm-hm." I nod, not even trying to cover it.

He walks over and gently pushes me on to my back. Only then do I notice a white hand towel in his hand. He spreads my legs and cleans me.

A lot of things that happened today shocked me, but even after the two best orgasms of my life, this may take the cake.

I blink and look away, covering my face, feeling strangely exposed. More than I was when he went down on me, or fucked me on the stairs.

My heart hammers in my chest, looking for ways to

escape. When he's satisfied, something rattles, and I hear liquid sloshing. I lift my arm, peeking.

"This will sting a bit." His voice is almost apologetic.

He sprays something on my knee and, fuck, it smarts. He uses the towel to gently dab around my knee. I sit up, and shit, my skin is chafed.

"How did you even notice?" I lean forward and blow on it. I didn't even know I was scratched.

"I see you." He shrugs, throws the towel to the floor, and dives into the mattress.

Wrapping his arms around me, he arranges me by his side and takes my lips. Oh my.

I see you.

I don't know what to do with that simple statement, so I channel my shock into the kiss. Corm's hands roam up my rib cage, and I moan into his mouth as he cups my breast. I have small breasts, and his hand is huge, but somehow, it's a perfect fit.

He dips his head and takes my nipple into his mouth. And while he ravishes my breasts, taking his time, I let my hands discover his body, his sculpted back, his brawny biceps, his firm ass.

This man is perfection. There is a lot to hate about him, but his body is a thing to admire.

"Oh," I moan as he bites me playfully.

"Are you sore, The Morrigan?"

Jesus, that Irish accent. "Not enough yet." I smile at him.

"Well then, let's correct that."

* * *

"I miss Coco," I murmur into his chest. We've fucked so many times, I've lost count already. I'm thoroughly dazed and relaxed.

"Who is Coco?"

"The kitten."

"You held her for half an hour and you miss her?" And there we go with his tone again.

"I had your cock inside me five minutes ago, and I miss that already."

He slaps me playfully. "You can have my cock anytime."

"Can I have the kitten?"

"No." The answer is so resolute, I push away from him.

"Why not?" I lie on my back, folding my arms across my chest.

"Ethel said she is too young." He turns to his side, propping his head on his hand.

"How do you know? You were out with Betsy when she said that."

"I asked her during the tour." He bites my shoulder.

"Why did you ask her?" I turn to him, all excited.

"Do you really want a kitten? We need to ask Livia if she is okay with that."

"I will take care of her, not Livia." I rake my fingers through his hair above his ear, rubbing his cheek with my thumb.

"Soon enough, you'll have a job."

"What job?"

"The one Nora offered you. Or something else. And who would take care of her when you move?"

My hand in his hair stops moving, the mention of the transiency of my stay here hanging heavily between us. It shouldn't, but it does. Here I am feeling all clingy, and I hate it.

Corm sighs and runs his hand over his face, but he doesn't say anything. He doesn't placate me. And I'm grateful. There may be no love lost between us, but at least we're honest with each other.

My disillusion is only temporary anyway, post-multiple-orgasms-induced. I will snap out of it tomorrow.

"I'll take the kitten with me." I roll away from him, and he doesn't follow.

The silence doesn't get a chance to thicken because Corm's phone pierces the air.

"Fuck," he mumbles, and rushes to the bathroom where he left his clothes. "What?" he barks.

I roll my eyes, but there is a smile on my face. I kind of like that he is consistent in his assholeness. As I said, the hormones.

"I was busy." He walks over and sits on the bed, his gaze scanning every inch of me.

I don't know what the person on the other end of the line is saying, but despite his tensed jaw, his eyes are hungry and his cock twitches, already hardening.

"I don't know, Betsy, I'll think about it."

I blow out air through pursed lips. Betsy Ham only means yet another public engagement.

"As I said, I'll think about it." He hangs up and pinches the bridge of his nose.

And I feel it in my bones that the fleeting peace between us has just reached its limit.

"You need to delete the post." He walks to the bathroom like he's just asked me to wear a different dress or something equally trivial.

I sprint out of the bed so quickly, I lose balance and fall to my knees.

"Jesus, Saar." He rushes to me and lifts me up.

"Don't touch me." I jerk away from him.

He rolls his eyes and returns to the bathroom.

"I'm not deleting it." I stand on the threshold, and he stops on the way to the shower. "Have you seen the comments? Many people related to my message. I gave them courage, or just encouragement. This is not about you and me anymore."

He eats the space between us and backs me up to the door frame. "Isn't it?" He breathes into my face, his nostrils flaring. "You're in your new home, all fucking lonely? That's your message? All the while you're supposed to show the world I'm settling down."

I push him away, but the man is a wall of muscles and doesn't budge. "You care about the surface only. Media spin, your reputation. My post might have been sparked by my current situation, but it grew beyond that."

Somehow, I slide under his arm and rush into the room, far away from him. "If I can inspire someone..." I try to control my volume—failing. "If I can speak up for people who feel isolated, trapped under the weight of expectations, or just sad, I will do it. I'm not deleting the post."

"If you want to have a voice, stop being a chicken and take the job with Nora's network."

His words are like a slap. How dare he use my insecurity against me now?

I look around his room to wear something, but my dress is on the stairs. Shit, I don't want to argue while naked.

I rush back to the bathroom while he follows me. I

snatch his shirt from the heap on the floor. Sliding my arms into the sleeves, I wrap it around me.

He watches me, shocked. That's a first.

"Saar." He sighs. "I care about my business. You agreed to a deal; don't you have an ounce of integrity in you?"

"I'm not your puppet. You don't get to dictate how I feel or what I share. You wanted a perfect image, but I'm not going to pretend I'm something I'm not just to fit into your stupid narrative. Don't you dare talk about integrity. Part of our deal was that you won't control me."

He throws his arms up in exasperation. "Here we go again. No control over your life, but that doesn't give you a free card to jeopardize our deal."

He marches to his closet and puts on underwear.

How did things go south so fast? "The post has nothing to do with you."

He pulls a T-shirt over his head. "You claiming you're lonely a week after our engagement has nothing to do with me?"

Okay, he may have a point. "That's not what I meant. I was talking about the need to be someone else, to always perform. I just showed them the real me, and yes, that day I felt particularly lonely. But it had nothing to do with you."

He balances on one foot, putting on his jeans. "You posted it after our argument in front of the shelter."

"That's not when... You know what?" I yank his shirt off my shoulders. "This was a mistake." I rush to the door.

Away from this bedroom. Away from him. Away from this stupid arrangement.

"What did you expect, a happily-ever-after?" He follows me, pulling a T-shirt over his head.

I stop at my door. "Oh please, you're incapable of happiness, and I don't believe in ever-after."

He snorts. "Of course not, with your daddy issues and inability to cut the cord from your brothers."

The nerve of him. "Fuck you."

"You just did." He walks away, but turns before he reaches the stairs. "You can forget about setting a date now."

"Are you for real?" My heart hammers in my temples, almost deafening me. I hug my torso, trying to cover myself, to protect myself.

"Yes, The Morrigan, as I said before, I'm not the one who needs the marriage certificate." He jogs downstairs.

I run to the banister. "But you can't afford a breakup either."

"Don't worry, I'll take care of the situation." He grabs his keys and wallet.

"How?" Sudden worry sneaks into my voice.

"Betsy has a brilliant plan, actually." He taps his forehead with his hand, saluting me on his way to the front door.

"What plan?"

"I would share that—"

"But?"

He opens the door and looks up. There is no warmth to his gaze anymore. No heat. No desire. No care. Just a stone-cold expression. "But I don't fucking trust you."

Chapter 17

Saar

CELESTE

I'm bored, Caleb doesn't let me go to work anymore.

I like it better when he's on your case rather than mine.

LILY

Why can't you work?

CELESTE

I'm officially a beached whale. I can't reach my toes.

CORA

Why do you need to reach your toes?

I agree with @Cora. I don't touch my toes. (laughing emoji)

LILY

You're beautiful @Celeste.

That's true.

CELESTE

And bored out of my mind.

CORA

Fresh croissants in the morning, anyone?

CELESTE

I'll try to sneak out. (eye-roll emoji)

Sleep.

Sleep.

Sleep.

No matter how much I repeat it, it eludes me. I stare at the ceiling, because every time I close my eyes my mind spirals, and it's not upward.

I don't trust you.

Why did it hit me so hard? It's not like I trust him. Do I? There are glimpses in our existence—in this unlikely forced partnership—when I feel like he's the only person in my court.

My brothers are well-meant but overbearing. My friends always have my back, but they have been busy, and I'm not good at this opening-up spiel.

Somehow, Corm draws the truth and honesty out of me—its ugly face, its vulnerable certainty. It's like his perception of me is so damaged, I don't mind pretending.

He does, however, pull the worst out of me as well. I've never yelled as much as I have with him. But then, it's not like I've ever spoken up.

'Keep your head down' used to be my jam. That was the way to deal with my life. I had fun, of course, but I didn't think much about what I truly wanted or needed.

Now I have all this free time to think only about that. It's an all-consuming, dark place to be in.

I don't trust you.

I don't trust myself. Lately. Or have I ever? I went from under my father's thumb to Vito's care. It was such a lovely change, I never thought twice about actually standing up on my own two feet. For myself.

In the absence of any real direction in my life, I'd welcome having something going well. It could have been my sex life, but even that went south before it even started.

Maybe it's for the better. Sleeping with Cormac Quinn would lead to heartbreak only. Or another confidence crisis.

Groaning, I reach for my phone. Six o'clock. I don't think I slept at all. I drag myself out of my bed and put on sweatpants and an old T-shirt.

Trudging out of my room, I find Corm's bedroom door open. His bed is empty. I guess he had his fun at The Velvet Room. Asshole.

Why does it bother me? Why would I even be jealous?

The hard-to-swallow truth is that being in his shadow in public is a comfortable place. But having his attention in private is ecstatic. Wonderful. Orgasmic.

I pick up my dress from the stairs, ignoring the dull ache coiling inside me. I'm hollow again. Well, I was hollow, and then I was filled for a moment, and it was addictive.

While I make my coffee, I scroll through my contacts and dial Vito. I haven't heard from him, and frankly, I'm getting worried.

I get his voice mail again, but then I remember a big fashion event in Asia at this time of the year. I should just let him work. I should go to Italy and find out firsthand what the status is.

Yes, that's a good idea.

"Good morning." Livia comes in. "Do you want me to wash this?" She picks up my dress from the stool where I must have dropped it without thinking.

"Good morning, Livia." I take a sip of my coffee. "No, I'll take it to the cleaners."

"I can do that for you. It's a beautiful dress."

"I made it."

Her eyebrows shoot up and then she smiles. "You knitted this dress? My, my, you're quite talented."

Even with the lingering heaviness pressing on my chest and stomach, I manage a smile. God, I'm a glutton for praise. "I can make something for your grandchildren."

"Really? That would be nice."

"Okay, I'll start with scarves, and then, after I meet them, I can make them sweaters."

She stares at me, blinking. "You want to meet my grandchildren?"

I shrug. Shit, I'm probably crossing boundaries here. It's not like I would be around long enough to meet her family. "Or you can take their measurement, so I get it right."

She nods, a ghost of a smile tugging at her lips. "Maybe I'll bring them around when Mr. Quinn isn't here."

I snort. "That would be for the best."

"Things have changed since you arrived." She walks to the pantry and comes back with a bottle of vinegar. She pours it into a bucket she filled with water. "I don't like those fancy cleaning concoctions. Good old vinegar is the best."

"What do you mean, things have changed? Besides me destroying the living and dining room, I mean." I bite my lip, and she laughs.

"Yes, you keep him on his toes for sure. But at least he seems alive now."

Alive? If devils were alive, perhaps. "He seemed plenty alive based on his media coverage."

I lean against the counter and sip my coffee, hoping she will share more. I should not care. I should stay away from anything Cormac-related. Especially pulling information from his trusted employee.

Livia clearly knows a side of him not available to the rest of the world. I'm perversely invested in learning more from her.

"After his father passed, he was a shell of a man. Before that, he was living life like it was nobody's business, but he was never reckless. After that, something changed. His mother doesn't come by anymore."

"Since I arrived?"

"No, no, since the funeral. And those two were close. She's a lovely woman, and despite his grim personality, you know a man is a good apple if they treat their mother well."

I shouldn't be having this conversation. What is it good for? Last night was a mistake, and forming any attachment to him would be a disaster. I should just leave it. "Did they have a falling out?"

And, apparently, my mouth doesn't follow my mind.

"I don't know what happened. I hear him on the phone with her from time to time, but usually just making excuses. Do you want me to make you breakfast?"

"No, that's okay. I think I'm going to go out."

"Mr. Quinn said to make sure you eat well." She raises her eyebrow, pursing her lips with kind reproach. I imagine that's what it would be like to have a caring mother or grandmother.

"He did, did he?" I shake my head, smiling.

"Yes, he texted me last night and said you need to eat breakfast."

My hand stops on the way to my mouth, the coffee wafting to my nostrils. "He texted you last night about my breakfast?"

"But of course. He reminds me all the time when he can't be here. You're not a model anymore, my dear; you should indulge a bit." She winks and raises her finger to stop me. She opens the cabinet and puts a large plastic bottle in front of me. "And you should take these."

I glance at the iron supplement, and my heart echoes in my temples. "I've got to go, Livia, but I promise to grab some breakfast outside."

"Well, take these." She shakes two pills into her hand.

I take the supplement and leave her in the kitchen. Overwhelmed. Confused. Touched.

I grab a sweatshirt and head outside, my soul

soaring and hurting at the same time. He doesn't trust me, but he makes sure I eat, and buys me supplements. Two weeks ago, I'd have concluded this was his ultimate power trip at controlling me.

But having spent some time with him, I wonder if it's more a genuine care than anything else. God, the man is confusing.

Fresh air lifts my spirits as I walk aimlessly for almost an hour. People rush around, jogging, dropping kids at daycare, on their way to work. Everyone moves with purpose while I just roam the streets.

But I don't feel as lost as I did last week. Just moving, engaging in people-watching gives me some sense of routine. Maybe that's what I need. To get out of the house, to lay order over the chaos.

Without making a conscious decision, I find myself in front of the shelter. Through the front window, I glimpse Ethel behind the counter, typing away.

I push the door open. "Good morning."

"Saar." She takes off her glasses, standing up. "What brings you here? And this early."

"I don't know. Can I visit Coco?" I shrug, feeling stupid all of a sudden. I should have called ahead and made an appointment. I don't want to slow these busy people down.

"But of course. Go right in; you know where to find her." She sits and returns to her paperwork.

And just like that, I have something to do.

Half an hour later, Coco wakes up in my arms and stretches her paws, letting out a loud mew.

"She's hungry." Ethel enters the room.

I put the little one into her box. "Thank you for letting me sit with her." My eyes land on a small, white fluffy dog eyeing me from his cage.

"Anytime. She's yours already."

I wish. I crouch by the white dog. "What's your name, cutie?" He scoots farther into his corner.

"He was abused and doesn't yet trust anyone." Ethel sighs. "His name is Rolfie."

"Someone names their dog Rolfie and then they hurt him?" My heart constricts as I swallow around the lump in my throat.

"Human cruelty has no boundaries."

I push to stand, and Ethel gestures for me to stay still. "Look, he crawled closer."

Carefully, I lower myself to the floor, and sure enough, Rolfie did move. "What should I do?"

"Nothing. Just stay with him if you want. He usually cowers, so him moving toward you is a great step forward. But I understand if you're busy."

"I can stay a bit."

This may not be my life's purpose, but it's a purpose that warms my soul. Perhaps Rolfie is helping me more than I'm helping him.

* * *

"Wow, not making much effort." Cora waves her hand in front of me.

I look down at my hoodie covered in cat hair and some other stains. "What? I combed my hair today." I shrug, grinning, and make my way to our table where Celeste munches happily on a croissant.

She kisses my cheek as I sit beside her. "I think Cora makes the best pastries in the world."

"These are from a supermarket," Cora whispers, and Celeste's eyes widen.

I bite my lip, trying not to smile. "You'll give her a heart attack."

Cora laughs, and I join in while Celeste scowls at us. "Don't do that to me. I can't have my blood pressure spiking."

"Does Cal have a monitor attached to you so he knows everything about your bodily functions?" I try to keep a straight face.

"Merde. That hasn't occurred to him yet. Don't tease him about it, because he just might..." She takes another huge bite, flakes of the soft dough falling to the plate.

"Never have I pictured my brothers settled with families. They were such players." I shake my head.

"Don't remind me he slept with other women." Celeste pokes my ribs.

"But all that practice, and now you're reaping the benefits." Cora laughs, sitting across from us, and I shudder at the idea of my brother having sex.

"Are you reaping the benefits yet?" Celeste turns to me.

Shit. "I reaped one, and then we had the worst argument."

They both stare at me. "You slept with Quinn?" Celeste shuffles her chair to face me.

I shrug. "It's not a big deal."

"Are you okay? Why did you argue?" Cora asks.

"I'm okay. It was just a hookup. But then he asked me to delete my last post."

"What?" Cora shakes her head and stands up as the door opens. When she realizes it's Lily, not a random customer, she plops back down.

"That post is gold. You can't remove it. It's public service," Celeste says.

Lily slides into the empty seat. "I'm sorry I'm late. Are you telling them about the wedding?"

I look at her, deadpan. "Hardly. Corm doesn't even want to set the date until I remove the post."

"What do you mean?" Lily looks at me, frowning.

"What a controlling bastard." Celeste pushes the empty plate away.

"But—" Lily pulls her phone and scrolls. "What about this? It's trending even better than your last one." She turns the screen to me.

I blink, my jaw slacking.

"What is this?" Celeste turns the phone to her.

My heart pounds in my temple as I pull out my phone and open my feed. My most recent post is a photo of Corm kissing my hair.

It's a fake candid shot in his kitchen, and we look like a real fucking couple. Based on my clothes, I recognize it from the magazine photoshoot.

And while I recognize the origin of the shot, I don't understand how it ended up in my feed.

Fucking Betsy. Have they hacked my account? My stomach churns. I fist my hand and read the caption.

"I don't want you to feel lonely ever again. Let's be real together." That's what Corm said to me, and I can't be happier to share the big news with you: We eloped.

Three red hearts follow the short caption.

"Motherfucker," I bite out.

A woman in a sharp suit regards me, scrunching her nose, and steps to the farthest corner of the elevator. The mirror in the back gives me pause.

I rushed to the Merged offices from Cora's. I should have probably dressed up for this battle, but it was fury driving me here.

The door opens on my floor, and I step out. Roxy waits for me.

"Saar, wow, I love your take on casual. Corm is in a meeting."

She has her dreadlocks in a high bun on top of her head. Wearing a black pencil skirt combined with a black T-shirt with a leather jacket, she looks like the rebel she is. Dressing up while saying fuck-you to the dress code.

"I love your style too." I smile.

"Do you plan to wait for him? Maybe I can find a boardroom for you."

I'm not sure if she wants to remove me from the reception area to avoid altercation, or to save everyone else from seeing me looking like I... well, like I spent my morning sitting on the floor of an animal shelter.

I need to play this smart. He's always been a step ahead of me. "Actually, Roxy, is Cal here?"

"Yes, you can wait in his office." She perks up. "Follow me."

People turn their heads as I walk through the

swanky offices. I wonder how I smell, because Coco peed on me, and I forgot about it while I sat with Rolfie. Okay, I should have gotten changed, because these clothes are crippling my authority. Goddammit.

"Your sis is here." Roxie doesn't bother to knock and practically pushes me inside Cal's office before she closes the door.

Cal looks up from his computer. "What's wrong?" He stands up, rushing to me.

"Nothing is wrong," I lie. I don't want him to problem-solve my way out of this.

He kisses me on both cheeks. "Why do you look and smell like you fell into a dumpster?"

"I spent the morning at an animal shelter," I bite out.

"You're volunteering? That's great." He gestures to a sofa in the corner. "What's up? I have a meeting in ten minutes."

Instead of sitting, I walk to the wall of windows. "You have a nice view."

"I know." A tinge of impatience laces his tone.

"I need you to get me on the list at The Velvet Room." Only once I blurt out my request do I feel strong enough to face him.

I swallow a chuckle when I meet his gaze. I don't think I've ever seen my brother shocked. He studies me for a moment, and then he laughs. "Are you out of your mind?"

"You used to be a member. Why is it okay for you and not for me?" I fold my arms over my chest.

At Corm's house, I saw the membership card on the console table, and I remembered seeing the logo before. I'm bluffing, but I'm pretty confident Cal has connections there.

He rakes his fingers through his hair. "Why do you want to go to a sex club?"

"To have sex." I raise my chin, smirking.

He shudders. "I don't want to know about my little sister's sex life. What the fuck, Saar?" He walks around his desk and sits, turning toward his monitor. Is he dismissing me?

"Since when are you such a prude? Cal, please, I need to go to that club."

He shakes his head and turns to me. "I don't know why I'm asking, but why to that particular club?"

"Corm is cheating." I lean against his desk beside him and pick a folder, flipping through it mindlessly.

He snorts and snatches the folder from me. "You're not in a real relationship."

"He's an asshole. Come on, Cal, I want to catch him there, so I have something to hold over him. He can't afford a messy breakup, fake or not."

"I can't afford your messy breakup. Merged's

biggest deal hangs on his reputation, unfortunately. I need Corm's image fixed as much as he does."

"Then get me on the list." I insert a threat into my tone, surprising myself perhaps more than him.

"Why can't you just wait for a divorce?"

"Because I'm not married."

He frowns. "What do you mean? The latest post was a genius PR step. People are dubbing you Sarmac already."

"Yes, the problem is, my fucking fake fiancé hacked my feed and planted that post. I need a marriage certificate, otherwise father's lawyer won't even take a meeting with me. Corm is not setting a date to control me."

Cal stands, his chair rolling across the room. "I'll fucking break his jaw."

"Stop it." I grab his shoulder. "Stop fucking treating me like a little girl. I can take care of myself. I can fight my battles. Just get me on the list."

He glares at me, a war brewing behind his eyes. "You know what kind of men go there?"

"Men like you and Finn?" I tilt my head.

He grinds his teeth. "How do you even know he would be there?"

"He's been there more than he's been at home," I quip.

I don't tell him he probably has me followed, and if

I go to The Velvet Room he will know, and probably show up. God, I hope he will show up.

"What an asshole. What if someone finds out? It's like he's bent on fucking up the deal."

"My point exactly. Let me catch him there and hold it over him, so he finally behaves."

Cal grinds his teeth a bit longer, contemplating. "I'll make some calls."

"Thank you." I kiss his cheek.

"Don't fucking tell Finn about it." He shakes his head. "I have a feeling I'm going to regret it."

"I love you, Cal." I open the door and collide with a wall of muscle.

The familiar scent of a lover that fucked me six ways to Sunday swallows me. I look up and meet Corm's stormy gaze.

The feel of his chest under my palms as I try to find my balance throws me off. It's like I hate him with everything in me, and the minute his cologne hits me and his touch wraps around me, it's all out the window.

He narrows his eyes and sniffs. "Why do you smell like piss?"

I groan. "I went to visit Coco."

"Is that a code for something?" Cal groans from behind me.

Corm doesn't move, and for some outlandish

reason, I don't move either. I should. I definitely should.

It's like his body has magnetic properties, and we're both charged to attract. I can't move. We stare at each other for several beats, the air between us filled with something carnal and frustrating.

With every breath my nipples brush his chest, and those traitors remember him.

"Do you mind?" I finally grit out.

"Let me walk you out, darling." He gives me the most dazzling fake smile.

"I can find my way."

"I insist." He steps to the side and takes my hand. He fucking takes my hand.

"Are you worried I'll run?" I spit, trying to reconcile the cocktail of feelings that range from how-normal-it-is-to-hold-hands to don't-fucking-touch-me.

His touch is electrifying, setting tiny but potent explosions in my stomach, my chest, my core. Everywhere. His hand burns mine.

"I'm pretty sure you would. Why are you leaving already?" He raises my hand to his lips and kisses my knuckles.

I look around, bewildered. The few people working in the glass-walled offices don't seem to notice us, so what's with the performance? And again, my body remembers his lips. His hands. Him.

"Do you want me to stay?"

"Didn't you come to yell at me?" He stops, forcing me to look at him. His thumb moves up and down my hand.

I hate how he thinks he can play my body like a violin. It doesn't matter if he can. He totally can, but that doesn't give him the right to toy with me like this.

The source of my confusion lies elsewhere though. His gentle stroke of my hand isn't sexual. It's not the touch of a hungry man. Or a man who wants to declare his claim.

It's just a mindless touch, familiar, comfortable. Does he even know he's doing it?

I snatch my hand away from him. "Elopement was the brilliant Betsy's idea of how to shut me up?"

He shrugs and calls the elevator. "You wanted a fast wedding."

I glance at the receptionist and grit out quietly, "But we're not married. I need the marriage certificate."

"Yes, you do." He smirks.

He leans down, snakes his arm around my waist, and lowers his lips to my ear.

The man has done this on multiple occasions, and my body revels in it like it's the first time. Jesus.

"As soon as I can be sure you'll deliver on your side of the bargain, we'll elope for real." He drags his cheek against mine, inhaling and probably consuming all the oxygen because I can't draw air into my lungs.

Taking advantage of my hesitation, he captures my lips. Taking no prisoners, his tongue dives in. I part for him, hungrily joining in the dance.

For a beat.

Before I realize what I'm doing, I jerk my head back. I would step away, but he holds me in a vise-like hold.

"Fuck you." I glare at him.

He smirks. "Maybe I'll come home for that tonight."

Chapter 18

Saar

"Saar." Livia's voice penetrates my drifting mind.

Shit, I was finally falling asleep. "Yes," I croak.

I don't open my eyes, letting the sun warm my skin for a beat longer. Let me sleep, Livia.

I came out to enjoy an afternoon on this huge stone deck. It's bathed in sunshine today. I can only imagine how lovely it would be in summer.

I'll miss this place once I'm gone. Which should be very soon.

It took Cal two days, but tonight I can finally catch Corm in the club, and then I can blackmail him to get me the freaking marriage certificate.

It was childish of me to think I could sway him with my demands. But I learned from him. Blindsiding and playing dirty is his language, so now I'll speak in a way he relates to.

"Mrs. Quinn is here," Livia whispers.

Now that gets me to open my eyes. I blink a few times behind my dark sunglasses. "Mrs. Quinn, as in...?" Okay, I'm sleep-deprived and kind of slow.

"Mr. Quinn's mother," Livia says with urgency, and I scramble to sit up.

"Did you tell her he's at work?"

"She came to see you. She's standing in the foyer." Livia glances back like she could see her. "I have to bring her out here."

"Okay...?"

"You want her in the living room?" Livia raises her eyebrows.

"Oh no. Why don't I go greet her while you make us tea?" I stand and grab a backrest, my head swimming. "Do we have some biscuits?"

Livia shoos me forward with her arms. "Don't keep her waiting."

"Okay, okay." Jesus. Livia said Mrs. Quinn is a lovely woman, so what's with the anxiety?

I wrap myself in my wide shawl and make my way to the foyer. "What a pleasant surprise."

A tall, slender woman turns to me with a smile. "Here you are. Nice to finally meet you, Saar. I'm Dorothy Quinn, Corm's mother."

"Dorothy." I extend my hand, but she pulls me in for a kiss on my cheek, wrapping her arms around me.

Okay, she's a hugger. But her honest embrace isn't as uncomfortable as I'd imagined.

She lets go, eyeing me with the kindest smile. I swallow and clear my throat, suddenly self-conscious.

People have stared at me all my life, but her scrutiny flusters me. Her gaze is warmer than her son's, but the intensity is similar.

"Do you mind if we sit on the patio?" I croak.

"It's such lovely weather, let's take advantage of it. I see you're redecorating." She waves her hand toward the plastic sheets covering my handy redesign.

My cheeks warm up. "It's a work in progress."

I sit on the lounge chair, and she takes a seat on the other side of the fire-pit table. Closing her eyes, she turns her face to the sun.

Her silver highlighted hair is shoulder-length and wavy, styled but not overdone like my mom used to wear. The woman is beautiful, with her high cheekbones and Corm's eyes. She's wearing a pant suit that is chic but casual.

"Livia will make us tea," I say when she doesn't speak.

"That's lovely. Thank you. I know we don't know each other, but could I ask you to keep my visit between us?"

And the plot thickens. Can I trust this woman?

Livia appears with a tray and sets it between us. Along with a teapot and two cups, there is a selection of mini-cakes, scones, and clotted cream. What the fuck? How did she...? When?

Livia pours us both a cup. "If you need anything else, you know where to find me."

"Oh, Livia, you're wonderful. All my favorites." Dorothy smiles and Livia shuffles away, beaming.

"I wanted to meet you. I'm so glad Corm has you in his life. I was hoping to meet you before the wedding." She takes her cup. "But I guess the two of you couldn't wait anymore."

"Well..." I don't know what to do here. But I guess this is one of those moments where Corm wants me to deliver on my side of the bargain.

"I was a bit hurt hearing about the elopement," she continues. "But Corm has been very impulsive lately, so I shouldn't be surprised. I've been so worried about him." She takes a small plate and sloshes a scone with a thick layer of cream.

My mother would rather die than be caught eating with such abandon.

"Worried?" I avoid her eyes, busying myself with my plate. If she's assuming I know about her quarrel with Corm, I need to tread carefully.

"He always looked up to his father." She sighs and takes a huge bite.

Such a hungry move from such an elegant creature is shocking, and kind of human. In fact, very human. Something tells me this woman lives unapologetically.

"He took his death hard," I parrot the narrative, not that Corm confided in me.

She sighs. "Yes, we all did. And Corm is grappling with the letter his father left him. I was worried when he went off on a bender, but now he has you."

She talks and eats. Is it her way to deal with stress? She looks so composed.

And what letter?

"Perhaps focusing on his future family, becoming a father himself—sorry I don't mean to assume... just the elopement. Anyway, I'm sure you, this, will give him better focus."

"I'm not pregnant."

She pauses and looks at me, wiping crumbs from the corner of her mouth. "Oh."

I can't help but feel bad about disappointing her, which makes no sense. "I'm sorry."

"Oh, silly me, *I* am sorry. I shouldn't have assumed. It's just, I miss him so much. And he says he's not angry with me, but I know he is. He's been avoiding me since he read that stupid letter. I don't know what Connor was thinking."

What is she telling me? I sip my tea, hoping she'll continue.

"You know, Corm grew up not knowing, and what good did it do for him to find out now? It feels like Connor forgave me but needed to punish me again after all those years. And the way Corm deals with it is not healthy. He hates Connor and me now. Oh, Saar, I'm so glad he has you. When I read your engagement announcement where he openly admitted he's been struggling with Connor's death… I was so relieved."

I smile at her, trying to understand what the hell she is saying. And also feeling like shit for deceiving her. I didn't draft the engagement announcement, or the post about the elopement, but I'm playing a role in Corm's PR story, and she believes the lie.

She is even happy about the lie. Many times in my life have I felt like a fake. But this moment right here feels real. I might have been selling a pretense in front of the cameras, but this up-close and personal?

My stomach drops, and I put the plate down.

"He's a complicated man," I say, in the absence of anything real or substantial to say.

"Men just seem that way because most of them don't know what they want. Corm has been hiding it well, but he's been lonely, and I guess that gap in his heart grew bigger after Connor passed. Is he looking for his real father?"

What?

It takes all my D-list acting skills to hide my shock, and I doubt I manage, but she seems busy with the mini cakes.

I swallow and rack my brain for something to say. I can't digest the revelation. I also know nothing about Corm's search for his real father. Or that his father wasn't his father.

"Dorothy, Corm is a very private man." *And he certainly doesn't open up in front of me.*

"He is, very much, but I'd hoped..." She wipes the corners of her mouth. "So what are you planning to do now you've retired?"

Whiplash anyone? Let's talk about Corm's father or Corm some more. Did she come to find out about Corm, and when she got nothing from me she's just moving on to the next topic?

And yet, I don't think my mother has ever spent this much time alone with me, or asked about my plans.

"I-I don't quite know yet."

"It doesn't matter; take your time to figure it out. I always thought that staying home with kids was the way to go. And it was for a while, but something was missing. So I took classes and started playing the markets. It's rewarding, not only financially, and I can still play housewife." She laughs.

"Wow, how did you choose the class? Did you want to trade before you got married?"

"No, I went to university to find a husband. What I found was trouble in the form of Connor Quinn. He was a daredevil, and I was so impressionable." She looks beyond me, her eyes glistening. Her entire countenance softens as she talks about her late husband. So much love. "I miss him." She sighs.

"He was a great husband and a wonderful father." She shakes her head. "Where were we? Yes, my classes. I just went to the local college and signed up for several classes, from art to finance. Turns out I'm not artistically gifted." She winks.

"Maybe I should look at colleges. I feel kind of lost." What is it with the Quinns and my need for honesty? Goddammit.

My cheeks go aflame. I close my eyes, and this time I turn my face to the sun.

"But of course you do. You started working when you were too young. I don't know you, Saar, but I can imagine you had to take care of yourself way before it was normal for your peers. I'm sure taking a bit of a time now to figure things out is exactly what you need. Enjoy it. Lean into it."

We continue chatting for another two hours. The words and laughs flow effortlessly with this woman, and as I walk her to the front door, I regret that she isn't my real mother-in-law.

"Can I invite you for a proper high tea? I'm organizing one at the end of the month. It's a blind charity date?"

"A blind charity date?"

"Something I came up with. I host a tea, each lady suggests a charity of her choice, and at the end of the event, we draw the winner and pull out our checkbooks."

"I'd like that. I'll be happy to come." If I'm still faking it with Corm. The thought depresses me.

"Don't tell Corm I came. He likes to do things on his own timeline. I'm sure he'll bring you over and introduce you soon."

I force my lips to stretch into a smile. "It's going to be our secret. No matter what, I'm so happy I met you, Dorothy."

"What do you mean no matter what?" She frowns.

Oh, shit. "I meant no matter when he introduces us..." I'm becoming quite proficient at lying.

"Hopefully soon. In the meantime, we stay in touch." She pulls me into a hug.

God, I only just met her, and I'm going to miss her.

"I don't think it's a good idea, babe." Celeste shrugs on the screen of my phone.

I look at the two dresses on my bed. The sequined black one would hug my body like a second skin. It's a glittery variation on the little black dress, classic with a bit of flare.

The deep red one is more daring, exuding sophistication and sensuality. Its sleek, halter neckline elegantly wraps around the neck, leaving the shoulders bare. The bodice is fitted and the skirt flows to the ground. A thigh-high slit on one side reveals a glimpse of my leg, adding a bold touch to the classic design.

"Did Cal tell you to talk me out of it?" I sigh.

"Maybe." She sits on the sofa in their penthouse, the light from the windows behind her creating a halo around her. "On the other hand, at least he's so absorbed by your plans he isn't on my case all the time."

"What case?" I prop the phone on my nightstand and sit on the bed.

"You know all his smothering care, like do I eat regularly, do I sleep enough, did I take my prenatal vitamins? His love is overbearing sometimes. But the pregnancy sex is really good." She takes a bite of a banana.

"Stop it. How many times do I need to tell you I don't want an image of my brother having sex?"

But I'm far from thinking about their sex life. My mind wanders to the man who makes sure I eat regularly and take my iron supplement. It didn't feel that overbearing. And it certainly wasn't out of love. And yet, he cares. He cares?

"You know how your niece or nephew were made, don't you?" She laughs.

"I'm hanging up." I reach for the phone.

"No, wait, I'm bored. Let me help you choose your outfit," she whines.

"I thought you didn't think it was a good idea."

"I delivered *our* concern, so I don't have to lie to my husband. But I can't wait to hear all the juicy details. If I wasn't pregnant, I would be coming with you." She shimmies her shoulders.

I laugh. "That would have been nice. Maybe after you give birth, we can both go."

"Do you want Caleb to go to jail?"

"Over our sex club visit?"

"Over killing any man who looked at us while there."

"Yeah, fair point. Ask him to take you," I tease, but she doesn't laugh it off.

"Maybe I will. Or I'll take him for his birthday. Okay, scout it out for me. What are you wearing?"

God, I love her. Not only does she make my

brother ridiculously happy, she has this easy-going flare about her that is contagious.

I pick up the black dress and pose for her. "This one is simple, but not boring." I switch the dresses and hold the red one in front of me.

"Hm, both are a huge upgrade from your current hobo style." She takes another bite of her banana.

Celeste is a walking-talking, ultimate classic-elegance personified. The woman missed her time by a few decades, because she would have been a perfect Golden Age movie star.

"Hobo? Again, I went to an animal shelter," I protest, even though I ended up in the shelter by accident.

"Every day since you returned from Europe?" She raises her eyebrows. "When you were stopping by in between your jobs for a few days here and there, wearing comfy clothes and no makeup seemed like a reasonable choice. But you're pushing that comfy style a bit too far now."

"I hate wearing makeup," I mumble.

"Do you hate plucking your eyebrows?" she deadpans.

"It's just a phase. I like being comfortable." Why am I defending myself? I can wear what I want. If I knew what I wanted. "Which dress should I wear?" I snap.

"Babe, all I'm saying is that it feels like you're getting a bit too comfortable. Challenge yourself a bit."

"In my closet?" I quip, but I know she's no longer just talking about my wardrobe.

She sighs. "Wear the red one if you want to draw attention to yourself."

"Do you think I'm making a mistake?"

"I think Corm had no right demanding you remove that post and then announcing the elopement. He's breaking the deal, and I think he deserves to sweat a little. Is catching him in the sex club the best way to deal with the situation?" She shrugs.

"So you think it's a mistake?"

"Not necessarily. But escalating the war between the two of you might not lead you to your trust fund."

I sag on to the mattress. "This is such a fucked-up situation."

"The sooner it's over, the better. You need to get away from him and finally focus on yourself."

"Yeah." I smile sadly. "I better go get ready. Love you."

"Love you, too. Good luck tonight, and don't spare any details tomorrow morning."

You need to get away from him and finally focus on yourself.

The irony is Corm has been encouraging me to

focus on myself. He's been caring for me in his own roundabout way. Plus we had mind-blowing sex.

And yet... we still end up on opposite sides of the barricade. Life was easier when I hated him.

Now?

A part of me wants another glimpse of the man who cares and encourages me—and delivers the best orgasms—but a part of me can't even look at him because of his games.

The man is utterly infuriating. But more infuriating is that I don't hate him as much as I used to. Goddammit.

And don't get me started on the bomb his mom dropped. Yes, there is curiosity cruising through my veins, but there is also a stupid—and quite selfish—sense of dejection. I shared my fears with him, and he never even eluded to the turmoil of his situation.

I take a shower, blow-dry my hair into loose waves, and apply minimal makeup. The whole routine takes less than forty minutes, but the task itself gives me some sense of purpose.

Maybe taking care of myself is the first step in self-discovery. On a whim, I pick the red dress and call an Uber.

As soon as the car pulls up in front of the club, my stomach constricts with both excitement and dread.

I've never been to a sex club, and my curiosity is

piqued. Corm hasn't come home for a few nights now, so I assume he's here.

But there is a part of me that hopes I won't find him. It makes no sense, because if I don't find him here, then I have no ammunition to fight for the stupid marriage.

He'd better be here, because I fucking have had enough of this dependency on other men. In any case, I hope his people will report to him where I am. Shit. What if he doesn't come even then?

I shed the thought and get out of the car in front of an unassuming residential building. It's a brownstone like so many others in Chelsea. What the hell? Did I get the address wrong?

The soft glow of the streetlamps reflects off the wet pavement while a light drizzle kisses my face. New York is having fun with the April weather.

Okay, showtime, before I look like a wet puppy. I square my shoulders and take the few steps to the front door, half disappointed I'm probably at the wrong address.

The door swings open. "Good evening, ma'am. Isn't the street quiet today?" a man in a tuxedo greets me.

"I prefer it a bit more crowdy," I respond with the code Cal gave me.

He steps to the side and lets me in. My heart beats

so fast and loud, I wonder if he can hear it as I step into a tiny, dark reception area.

"Welcome to The Velvet Room." A young hostess dressed in a red corset and dark flared pants smiles from behind a sleek black counter. "May I have your phone?"

"My phone?"

She draws her eyebrows together, still smiling. "No phones are allowed here. Is this your first time?"

How am I going to take pics of him? Goddammit. "Yes, my first time."

I breathe in and out, calming my nerves. Not that the intake of oxygen does anything. I hand her my phone.

"Would you like a tour?" She puts my phone into a small compartment in a cabinet behind her. She locks the small door and gives me the keys.

"No, I think I'll just get a feel tonight."

"Good. Do you need a mask, or do you have your own?"

"A mask?"

She smiles at me. "Everyone wears them in the common areas. We pride ourselves on discretion." She hands me an intricate black lace mask. "If you need anything, my colleagues inside will help you." She turns to the black door behind her and swipes a card in the reader. The door clicks open. "Enjoy your evening, ma'am."

"Thank you." I tie the sash around my head and cover my upper face.

Behind the door, a large lounge opens up. It's like they gutted all the walls in this place and opened up the floor.

To my side is a bar, and the floor is mostly filled with haphazardly spread comfortable sofas, lounge beds, or armchairs.

The light is dimmed, but the place is inviting. I don't know what I was expecting, but this place is like a modern version of a high-end speakeasy.

Luckily the bar is just along the back wall near the entrance, so I don't have to walk through the room to find a seat.

I was prepared to look for Corm; but I didn't quite appreciate how it feels to be a lonely woman in this environment.

The majority of the patrons are men, most of them having women by their side, but those women are probably working here. The music is demure; the conversations are hushed.

Some people are kissing. I spy a woman on her knees, her partner panting with his head thrown back. He has silver hair, and relief floods me. Okay, I guess I'm not as ready to confront Corm as I thought.

What do I care who he is with? Because if I'm completely honest, I want him to be with me. I don't have a claim on him. And yet…

I find a stool at the bar and sit, scanning the room. Will I recognize him in his mask? If Cal wasn't such a pain in my ass, I would have asked him more questions and come better prepared. Well, too late for that.

"What can I offer you?" A young woman dressed in the same outfit as the receptionist leans over the counter.

"I'll have whiskey." I always liked the smoky taste and the warm feeling.

Her face stretches in a wide smile. "Great choice. Macallan?"

I nod. I'm paying for this with Corm's credit card for household expenses, so I may as well indulge.

My eyes dart around the room, but I don't think I see him anywhere. Two men stand and go up a winding staircase. I should have gotten that tour. But I guess I would have to explore myself.

"Here you go." The bartender places a crystal tumbler on a velvet coaster beside me.

"Thank you. What's up there?" I take a sip, reveling in the smooth taste.

"Private rooms of all sorts, for all kinds of kinks. Is this your first time?"

I nod.

"Good for you. I love it when we have female customers. I hope you'll have fun."

I don't think I will, but well, I might enjoy a glass of good whiskey. I sip on my drink, strategizing about my next move.

The music changes, and the room gets darker with spotlights illuminating a stage across the room. I didn't even notice it was there.

A woman in a satin robe saunters to the middle of the stage, and a swing lowers down from the ceiling. A sex swing. I should look for Cormac, but instead, I'm drawn to what's happening on the stage.

I'm not the only one. The murmur in the room quiets down as everyone turns their attention to the stage.

My heart hammers in my chest. I should go up and look for him, but if he's in one of the private rooms, I won't be able to find him.

That's what I tell myself as my attention stays glued to the beautiful woman who now sheds her robe. She is wearing a lacy lingerie top that exposes her breasts, and a matching garter with stockings, no panties.

Two men join her and lift her to the swing. It's almost like a dance performance, just a bit salacious. They tie her wrists and ankles, and before they leave the stage, they give the swing a little push.

"Well, gentlemen, are you ready for the show?" Her voice fills the room. She must have a mic I didn't notice.

Her voice is melodic, with a tone of jest and a lot of confidence. Like she's the one ready for the show and enjoying it.

Her presence on the stage is all-consuming. She is exposed, swaying gently, but somehow also powerful. Despite being trapped, she exudes a similar confidence to my brothers, my father, or Corm.

A man in a suit in a mask walks on the stage. He's well built, his muscles bulging under his clothes. I don't see his face, but I imagine he's handsome. Besides that thought, he looks like any other man in the audience.

He approaches the swing and traces his hand between the woman's breasts down to her pussy. He cups her roughly, and her gasp echoes around.

I hold my breath, a tingling sensation swarming in my core. What is this? Like a live porn performance?

The man on the stage unzips his pants and his cock springs out. It *is* live porn, only somehow better.

I grab my glass and gulp two long sips. On the stage he pulls at some ropes, and the woman is now tilted with her head facing down, and her core aligned perfectly to his height. Two projections light up on the wall behind them, showing the couple from different angles.

It's official: this is the first porn that has ever aroused me. Jesus. I'm panting, a hot ache spreading inside me, and they haven't even started. The man gives himself a tug and pushes inside her aggressively.

The room fills with appreciative sounds, and other sounds that suggest the audience is inspired. I'm so out of place, and yet strangely grounded.

"Is this your first time here?" A thrilling, chilling drawl shatters the world around me.

Chapter 19

Corm

"Do you ever leave?" Roxy leans against the door frame.

She's in a smart dress with a jean jacket over it. I long ago gave up on reminding her of our business dress code. The woman wears her mismatched clothes with more style and elegance than anyone else I know.

Besides Saar, if she was willing to dress at all.

"What do you want, Roxy?" I growl and push my chair from my desk.

I'm getting claustrophobic in my large office because she's right, I have been stuck here for days.

And nights. Not that I'd admit that. I made Saar believe I'm in The Velvet Room, but instead I'm here, pretending I'm a workaholic.

"Just making sure you turn off the lights when you leave." She snickers.

"Go home."

"I will after you tell me why you are sleeping in the office." She takes off her heels and saunters to my desk where she plops into a chair opposite me.

"I don't sleep here," I lie.

She raises an eyebrow. "You know, a man is only powerful if he can be vulnerable. I know that society teaches you boys not to cry, but it's fucking bullshit."

"Thank you for your insight into the problems of modern men. Not sure why you feel I'm interested in this conversation."

She rolls her eyes. "Look, you're extra nasty with the staff, and I'm frankly tired of the constant flow of resignation letters because people fear you—"

"If they did their jobs and used their brains, they would have nothing to fear."

I stand, walk to my shelves, and pour myself an inch of whiskey. I take a sip, but when I turn, Roxy is still sitting there.

I sigh and pour her one as well. "Look, Roxy, this deal with Atlas is stressful, but I'll try not to bark at people if you try to hire more competent staff."

"The Atlas deal is the reason you don't sleep at your own house?" She swirls the liquid in her glass.

"Roxy—" I warn.

"I'm just saying, if you've developed feelings for Caleb's sister and now you sleep in your office to avoid her, it's pretty immature, but it's your choice. If you fucked her and are now avoiding her, then you're a coward. In any case, may I book you into a hotel?"

"I can't go to a hotel and risk someone taking pictures." I pinch the bridge of my nose.

"So it is because of Saar and your feelings for her?" She takes a sip, looking at me through her lashes.

I fell into that one. "If the feelings are exasperation, frustration, and a mild case of anxiety, then yes."

"And attraction, perhaps?"

"I found out why she needed this arrangement, and her attraction plummeted. I'm avoiding her because if I confront her, we might kill each other."

"I thought her reason is her trust fund."

"But why would a woman who worked since she was a teenager need money so urgently?"

Roxy frowns. "What did you find out?"

"I offered you a nightcap, not a sharing session."

She rolls her eyes. "It's my bonus that is at stake here."

I chuckle. "Don't worry, your bonus is safe. I will fucking get this deal done. Next week is the fundraiser, and Vladislav will see what a perfect couple we are and how I have settled down."

"And then?"

"We helped him merge with Atlas, and my fake marriage is over."

"So you'll just let her go like that?"

And there lies my problem, and the real reason I'm avoiding Saar. Just before I opened the files from Mathison, I was sure I wanted to keep her around for longer. Forever perhaps?

I love my house, but I realized after I moved in how lonely it feels. And she filled the space effortlessly.

She destroyed a part of it, but besides the decor disaster, I enjoyed sharing my space with her.

Ironically, her post about loneliness and pretense hit me straight in my solar plexus. Because I could feel her. I could feel her pain, because I live what she talked about.

That constant pressure of expectations that isolate you in the game of pretense, when you no longer know who you truly are.

When I came home that day, I didn't plan on sleeping with her. Knowing what I already knew about her, it was a tactical mistake.

A mistake that led to this. I can't pretend this is a simple case of attraction. I fucking want her.

But she's a walking red flag. I hoped that having her tailed would give me more tangible proof, and that would finally ease my mind into forgetting about her.

But she's been spending days at home, in the shelter, or at her friend's bistro. Her behavior doesn't match what Mathison found out. She might hide it well, so she gets her stupid trust fund. Fuck.

"You men are such idiots." Roxy sighs when I don't answer.

"Maybe your bonus is not safe after all." I glare, sagging back into my chair.

She laughs. "Okay, boss, I'll finish my nightcap and let you sleep... I mean, work." Her grin is as annoying as my current situation.

My phone screen lights up on my desk. I check the message, and my blood pressure spikes immediately.

"What the fuck?" I grab my jacket, rushing to the door.

"What happened?" Roxy stands.

"Saar is in a fucking sex club." *I'm going to kill her.*

Roxy belts out a laugh. "God, I love that woman."

I text my driver before I reach the elevator. Fuck. Fuck. Fuck.

What was she thinking? Is she there looking for me? The thought spreads some weird, not completely negative, feeling in my chest. Is she jealous?

It's more like she has some other plan to rile me up. The idea of her there among all those horny bastards churns in my stomach.

It takes ten minutes for my driver to come, and another half an hour to reach the club. By then I'm ready to break into the stupid place and kill every man who's laid eyes on her. And then take her home and fucking chain her to her bed until the deal is signed.

I bang at the door, and it opens immediately. "Good evening, sir—"

I push past him.

"You can't." He steps in front of me, and immediately, two bulky security guards appear from somewhere.

I raise my arms in surrender. "I prefer the streets fucking crowdy."

The two guards exchange looks, probably thinking I'm so horny it killed all my brain cells.

I drop the phone on the counter, and the hostess gives me a mask, saying something I don't register because I see red, but I smile at her in an effort to reassure them I'm not a lunatic. Though the jury is out on that one.

Finally, she slides her card through the reader, and I walk in. A show is happening on the stage, and I squint under my mask, adjusting to the low light. Fuck, how will I find her here?

But before I even take another step, I spot her. In a red dress exposing her long, beautiful leg, she sits at the bar, her attention on the performance. Her hair falls down around her shoulders, her face hidden behind the lace of her mask.

But there is no doubt it's her. Something wild and untamed spreads around my chest, and my legs move before I even think, beckoning me to her.

The mask gives her an air of sensual intrigue and mysterious elegance. She sits in the shadows and still manages to shine.

I stop a couple of feet from her, but she doesn't notice me, completely enthralled by what's happening on the stage.

Is she enjoying the show? I smile to myself. I hate that she came here, but at the same time I admire her guts.

She's been acting out and hiding mostly, lost in her self-discovery. That damn post was the first glimpse of the real woman behind the broken facade. And now this.

I don't know if it's the fact that she sits alone, or her alluring presence that calms me down, but instead of dragging her out of here, I stay behind and watch her.

The moans and grunts on the stage allude to what is happening, but I don't look there; I'm completely absorbed by the woman in front of me.

She is perfectly still. Like she's posing for a painting or a statue. She is a true piece of art.

She occasionally licks her lips, her chest heaving delicately. I get a vision of her coming, and my cock presses against my zipper.

I approach her slowly, taking in her glowing skin, her shiny hair, her parted lips, her torso wrapped in that sinful dress.

When I'm beside her, I lean in, the lavender scent making me even harder. "Is this your first time here?" I drawl.

She tenses, her spine straightening as she parts her lips. The lipstick she wears is subtle, and yet I can't look away from the shimmering fullness of her mouth.

The quick movement in her throat reveals a moment of hesitation before she croaks. "Maybe."

It's just a whisper, but after not speaking to her for a few days, I'm like a deprived junkie who needs a hit.

"May I get you another drink?" I glimpse the almost-empty tumbler beside her. Does she drink whiskey? Or is this just part of the persona she came here to play?

Suddenly, I'm irrationally upset that I don't know that. That I don't know her favorite drink? Or that she didn't come here for me?

Based on her apparent enjoyment of the show, she came here to piss me off, not to find me.

"No." She turns to look at me. The mask's lace softly clings to her skin, highlighting her eyes. "Thank you." She returns to watching the debauchery on the stage.

"Then maybe you want to play," I hear myself

saying as I step closer, my body pressed against her side.

She swallows again but doesn't say anything. My fingers dust her exposed leg, and her eyes flutter as she gasps silently.

I should require her consent, but I'm riddled with rage and want—no, need—so I take her silence as permission.

I trace her delicate skin up her thigh. The feel of her spreads through me, and while the contact is at my fingertips, it reverberates into my heels. And my cock. That fucker is painfully hard.

Saar's eyes are glued to the stage, but the rest of her is very much here, reacting to my touch. Her throat bobs, her chest stutters, goose bumps cover her skin.

I love what my touch does to her. That she welcomes it. For a moment I allow myself to forget who we are, and where we are.

Dipping my head to hers, I rest my forehead beside her temple like I'm going to say something, but I don't. I just inhale her, feeling her essence, wanting more of her. From her. With her.

My fingers slide under the hem around the daring slit, and I reach between her thighs.

With my thumb, I press against her clit, and she sucks in air. I massage her gently, just teasing her really, and she shifts in her seat, chasing my hand.

I chuckle. "Look at you, all wet and ready. Is it the performance or my hand that arouses you?"

I'm barely touching her, but her breath becomes labored. God, I wish I didn't know what I know. That I didn't have all the questions.

I have no right to demand the truth from her. She didn't lie to me. She just hides her secrets carefully. And I'm irrationally upset about it. As if I shared mine with her.

I hook my fingers into the hem of her panties and tug. "Go to the bathroom and take these off."

Chapter 20

Saar

Dizzy.

Dazzled.

Disoriented.

I slide from the seat and stumble, my legs like jello. I move, or I think I move. Mostly I'm just wondering if I lost my mind.

I don't even know where I'm going.

Away from him? To do his bidding? To hide? To run away?

My eyes dart around frantically. Where the fuck are the bathrooms here?

The woman on the stage climaxes with abandon, and several men move to the stairs. The whole depravity of the situation is arousing and mortifying. Wrong, and somehow normal. Primal.

And the primal need is what moves my legs.

Finally, I see a discreet sign for the bathroom. I practically run there and push the door open.

Does he know it's me? Or is he playing with a stranger?

I shouldn't play along. *But shut up, brain. I want to play.*

He must know it's me. I knew it was him the minute he spoke. I probably registered him even before. His voice, his musk, his presence—so unmistakably him.

Even while I deliberate, I slide my panties down and slip them into my small purse.

I stare at the woman in the mirror's reflection. The woman who vowed to free herself from all the people controlling her life.

I've craved that freedom for years. Could this be the first step? To do something I want instead of something I should? Will that be liberating, or just plain reckless?

My cheeks are flushed and my hands are trembling. Anticipation. Desire. Vengeance?

When I return to the main floor, the music has changed. So has the mood. Three dancers gyrate around poles on the stage. A woman moans, folded over the backrest of a sofa, with a man thrusting behind her.

The room isn't as full as before; most of the guests

probably moved upstairs. But I don't really look around; I'm on a mission.

But I stop when I realize he's no longer at the bar where I left him. My heart races like it wants to vacate my chest.

Did he change his mind? Did he find someone else to play with?

I look around, and my mind spins into overdrive. Do I go upstairs? Do I leave? Maybe the bartender would know. Not my best option, but in the absence of any other idea, I move in her direction.

"Hello, sweetheart, you seem lost." A stocky man with a sheen of perspiration around his mask grabs my arm. "Maybe you're looking for me?"

He is in a suit, his belt undone. His pudgy hand on my skin turns my stomach. "Let go of me."

"Oh, come on." He yanks me closer. "I can show you a good time."

I stumble, my body slamming against his belly. I gag as his repulsive musk hits my nostrils.

His fingers dig into my arm, and I try to yank away, but the fucker is strong. "I said let go of me."

My pulse hammers in my temples, but suddenly my mind clears completely. I've had it with men ruling me. I propel my leg forward, driving my knee up.

He groans. "Fucking bitch. Security!"

I don't know if I hit the intended target, but his grip loosens. The impact sends me backward, staggering.

And I hit something firm and warm. Someone firm and warm.

"She told you to let go of her." Corm's voice floods me with relief.

"She fucking kicked me," my attacker sputters.

"Good." Cormac wraps his arm around my waist.

Home.

He turns to me. "Are you okay?"

I nod.

"I will break every single bone in your body if you as much as look at my wife again."

He beckons me forward with his hand on the small of my back, leaving the asshole behind. A shudder rakes through my body—part solace, part yearning.

My wife.

"I can take care of myself," I argue, just to regain some sort of control.

"I know." It's a terse statement, said with the same unwavering confidence he usually oozes.

My poor heart.

"I'm not your wife." I desperately cling to... what? An upper hand? A winning point? Our usual bickering mode?

"Technicality." He shrugs and swirls me toward the staircase.

"Where are we going?"

"Upstairs."

Asshole. "Why?"

"I got us a room."

Butterflies set off in my stomach. "Why?"

He doesn't answer. Fuck, the man is infuriating. I glance over the banister and see my assailant talking to security.

I rub my arm; his touch is still repulsive even after it's gone.

Corm stops, takes my hand into his, and turns my arm slightly, glowering. I follow his gaze to the red handprint on my upper arm. Shit, that will leave a bruise.

Corm's nostrils flare. "Wait here." He turns and jogs back downstairs.

What the hell?

He reaches one of the security guys engaged with the asshole and exchanges a few sentences with him. The guy nods slightly.

Corm taps the stocky asshole on his shoulder and before the other can fully turn, Corm draws his arm back and delivers a punch. Two. Three.

The man doubles down, swearing, and falls to his knees, blood staining his face.

Corm shakes his hand, cracks his neck, and adjusts

his cuffs. He saunters toward the stairs while security drags the other guy outside.

I swallow.

I blink.

I take a deep breath.

My heart is still beating like a spooked horse. But a smile ghosts my face as well. I shouldn't condone violence, I really shouldn't, but fuck, that punch was satisfying.

Almost as much as my kick was. Almost.

Corm takes two steps at a time and joins me. He seizes my hand and steers me down the hallway, flanked by doors on either side.

At the end, he taps a card against a pad on the door and opens it.

"After you." He bows his head quickly, the energy from the altercation still seeping from him.

I step inside a dark room, my palms sweating and my heart fluttering. Jesus.

Corm flips the switch and steps behind me. I gasp as he snakes his arm around my waist, yanking me to his chest. I fight not to lean my back into his firm body.

It's always like this with us. Push and pull—neither of us willing to give in.

He lowers his head to the crook of my neck, his whiskey-infused breath tickling my skin. It's intoxicating.

His arm clamps around me, unyielding. It's firmer than the unwelcome grip from the asshole downstairs. It's more possessive. Almost more aggressive.

And yet... it feels a thousand times safer. Familiar. Essential.

I definitely need to find a therapist.

Right or wrong, I don't think I can ignore this weird, confusing desire.

This unexpected challenge to my value system. This unlimited feeling of not giving a shit and claiming what I want.

And based on the hard outline of his length against my ass, what he wants.

He kneads my breast with one hand and shoves the other inside the slit of my dress. The intrusion is rougher, more urgent than the feather-like exploration in the bar earlier.

He cups my bare pussy, and I whimper. It's like he knows, he feels, he somehow senses I don't want gentle and caring at the moment.

I've just kicked a guy; I want to be fucking equal for once.

"Where are your panties, The Morrigan?"

His voice skims my skin, erupting goose bumps in its wake. I hold my purse up, and he snatches it. With his arms still around me, he opens the clasp and pulls out my underwear.

He drops the purse to the floor and brings the fabric to his nose. His head dips beside mine as he holds my body against his. He inhales and hums with indulgence.

Oh my God.

My mind shuts down, and my body takes over. My core throbbing, I try to turn. To face him? To kiss him? To look into his eyes?

But to my dismay, he steps away. It's so sudden, I have to find a purchase with my arm against the wall.

My entire being mourns his loss immediately, despite the energy shifting somehow. And for once, I don't have words to spit, threats to render, challenges to extend. It's like I've exhausted all the fight in me.

Like this man won, because let's face it, I've never had a chance. I fought long and hard, but this man owned me before I gave any conscious consent. Before I probably allowed myself near him.

He puts my panties into his pocket and saunters to the loveseat by the window.

I blink, disoriented. What the fuck?

The room looks like a luxurious hotel room with a large four-poster bed against the wall. In the opposite corner is a sex chaise and two love seats, where Corm sits now, and a glass coffee table.

His legs spread, his eyes hooded, he drapes his arm

over the backrest and studies me. He shed the mask, and I reach for the sash on mine.

"Keep it," he orders.

Fuck, he is hot. And infuriating. And gorgeous. He has the whole big-dick energy down, and as I had a chance to find out—which was the beginning of my fall—substantiated.

"What?" I choke out, not sure why there is a lump in my throat.

It's like the heat plummeted completely, and I'm now trapped in some game, but I'm not sure what the rules are. Something has shifted, and I'm the prey here.

As usual.

Fuck him. I turn to reach for the doorknob.

"Don't," he warns.

"What do you want? Why are we here?" I snap.

He reaches into his inner pocket and drops a small box on the table. "Sit down, Saar." He doesn't say please, but the tone is pleading. Tired. Like he has had enough of our dynamic.

Was I wrong? This is not a game but perhaps a peace offering?

And the obedient girl in me—I guess some habits aren't as easy to break—crosses the room and sits opposite from him on the other loveseat.

"Let's play." He gestures to the table.

It's a deck of cards he retrieved from his pocket. "You carry cards around?"

"This club provides anything."

"And you want to play cards?"

He raises his eyebrow. "Or you can suck my cock."

"Fuck you, Cormac." I stand.

He chuckles. "Come on, one game. If you win, I'll get the marriage certificate in the morning."

That stops me. "Why should I believe you?"

He gestures to the seat and pushes the deck toward me. "You just have to take the leap."

I came here to blackmail him into marrying me. But this may be easier. I sit, my eyes glued to him.

His gaze holds mine hostage, and I wish I could know what he is thinking, but the man is unreadable.

"Can I choose the game?" I ask.

"Sure."

"Blackjack?"

I need skills, not luck with this card game, and blackjack is probably my safest bet. But I need something else. I hug myself, rubbing my upper arms.

He nods and then frowns. "Are you cold?"

"A bit." I shrug.

Corm takes off his jacket and comes to wrap it round my shoulders. I slip my arms into his long sleeves. Not ideal, but it will do.

His warmth envelopes me through the fabric he's

just shed, and I revel in it for a moment. His scent is now strong and distracting.

I shuffle the cards, the familiar motion calming my nerves. His gaze on me remains sharp and unyielding. This feels like a test. Why cards?

Focusing on my breathing, I will my hands to stop trembling. I cut the deck and deal the cards. "What if I lose?"

"You will have to find another way to get your trust fund." He shrugs and loosens his tie.

"Can't wait to get rid of me, darling?"

He picks his cards but doesn't look at them, piercing me with his eyes. His tongue darts out to wet his bottom lip, and I fidget in my chair. The air between us fills with tension—the good and the bad kind.

I can't rip my gaze away from his lips. He smirks and looks at his cards. I pick up my hand. A five and a six. Not even close to winning, but I don't need luck. I have skills.

"Hit or stay?" I keep my voice calm while my heart thrums in my temples.

I enjoy playing cards, but only when I know the stakes. Something tells me the damn marriage certificate isn't it. Or, at least, it's not the endgame.

"Hit," he says, his tone steady.

I deal him another card—a four. He's probably close to 20 now.

Now, it's my turn. I slide my fingers over my cards, and in one swift, practiced motion, I swap them.

"I'll stay," I say, leaning back, the fabric of my dress falling to the side, exposing my legs.

Corm's gaze lowers to my skin, then he flips over his cards—a six and a nine. Not bad, but not good enough.

His eyes flick to my hand. Slowly, deliberately, I reveal my cards—first the ten, then the ace. Twenty-one.

For a moment, Corm's expression doesn't change. He just stares at the cards, his eyes narrowing slightly.

"Impressive," he says, his voice smooth but with a hint of something else beneath it—something darker, more calculated. "How come you are so good at this?"

"I cheat." I smile at him.

"Is cheating in cards another pastime like knitting?" He stands and walks to a cabinet beside us and retrieves a bottle of whiskey and two tumblers.

"How do you know I knit?" Where is this conversation going?

"Observation skills." He pours two inches into each glass.

"You've never seen me knitting." I take a tumbler from him and wet my lips in the amber liquid.

"True, but there are yarns and needles in the kitchen."

"How do you know they are not Livia's?"

Why am I engaging in this idle conversation? He forced me to play cards, and now we are talking about my hobbies? And the fact he knows mine is unnerving. I won a game, and I still feel like he has the upper hand.

Because he fucking has. He can still stall on his side of the bargain.

"She wouldn't dare to sit around while at work. Where did you learn to cheat at cards, Saar?"

The question hits me with its coldness and directness, his tone not leaving any room to deflect. Not that I need to. What is going on?

"Jesus, you're a sore loser. I learned some tricks from a girl in school. I palmed my cards while I was shuffling. That's why I needed your jacket. The challenge is timing, but I've done this enough times to know when I can get away with it." I straighten and shake the garment from my shoulders, letting it drop behind me.

He takes a sip. "And how did you perfect the skills?"

I frown. "Why are you being weird?"

He moves with the speed of a predator and leans down, propping his hands on the armrests, caging me.

The alcohol in his hand sloshes around, staining my dress.

"Answer the fucking question, Saar."

His nose is an inch from my face. There is room behind me on my seat, but I'm not sliding back. I'm not scared of him. His jaw ticks, and he shakes, barely hanging onto his control.

"Every summer, Finn and Cal would come to Europe to take me on vacation, and we played a game to choose the destination. Two years in a row I lost, and we went to Ibiza, the horny players they were. So I picked up a few tricks to finally choose where we'd go."

He stands up suddenly and paces to the window and back. He takes a sip of his whiskey and then chugs the glass across the room. It hits the wall and shatters into pieces behind me.

"What the hell is wrong with you?" I jump up, rushing to the door.

He reaches me before I manage two steps and whips me around, one arm around my waist, his other hand pinching my chin, forcing me to look at him.

I pant.

He pants.

I tremble, and so does he.

The tension stretches around us, while I feel strangely threatened and safe at the same time.

How fucked up is it that I crave his wrath the same

way I crave his care? I'm definitely calling a therapist in the morning.

He closes his eyes briefly and takes a deep breath. "When did you start gambling, Saar?"

What?

I push at his chest and stumble as he lets me go, glaring at me.

"Gambling? That summer was the last time I played, if you don't count a few friendly games while waiting around at a modeling gig."

"Don't lie to me," he bellows.

I rip the mask off. "Fuck you, Corm."

"So you don't bet on races? No high-roller online poker or blackjack?"

I laugh bitterly. "You've lost your mind. I'm. Not. A. Gambler."

"Why are you broke then? Where is all your money, Saar?"

Heat rises to my cheeks as I fight to get more oxygen into my lungs. Stupid tears threaten to come.

No, no, no. Don't cry. Not in front of him.

I don't want him to laugh at my lack of financial acumen, but I definitely don't want him to see me crying.

"That's none of your business," I snap.

"It is my fucking business. You entered into a deal with me to improve my reputation, and conveniently forgot to mention that you owe taxes, are completely bankrupt, and owe money to people who collect without finesse."

I frown, shaking my head. "What are you talking about? My accountant embezzled from me. I will pay the taxes as soon as I have my trust fund. The authorities in Italy are investigating. Ask Vito."

He glares at me for what feels like an entire lifetime. In that snapshot of time my mind races, trying to comprehend what he is saying. Why is he saying it?

"There are debts in your name with all the major bookmakers in Europe. Care to explain?"

"That's impossible. I-I..." As I rack my brain for something to say, an eerie feeling wraps around my shoulders.

Did Maria place bets in my name? This makes no sense. But while I don't understand what is happening, somehow I know—or rather feel—he's telling the truth.

My shoulders slump as fatigued resignation washes over me. I wrap my arms around my midriff, but it doesn't protect me. It only makes me feel more isolated.

He steps closer, the energy shifting between us again, no longer threatening. Like he feels my struggle with the realization.

Like the moment I started believing him, he immediately trusted me.

He wraps his arms around me and pulls me to him. "We'll find out who is behind it."

I let myself revel in his support for a beat or two, enough to let the thoughts settle. But even then, they make little sense.

"How do you know?" I murmur into his chest. I want to be mad at him for his accusations, but I'm so tired of fighting this battle alone.

"That doesn't matter, but the information is reliable."

"Is it, though?" I look at him, and I startle at the change in his countenance.

Gone is the indifferent, latent hatred. His features are softer now. Is he pitying me? Or is he just relieved his information is incorrect?

"Yes." He nods.

I step away. I need to think, and I can't do that when he holds me, regardless of how lulling it is.

"Your informant led you to believe I'm a gambler, so forgive me if I doubt the source."

"My source didn't dig deep enough because they had no reason to assume someone exploited you."

"Why did you even look into it?"

"Why didn't you tell me?"

"You treated me like a nuisance already. I didn't need to give you more reasons."

He lowers his head, nodding slightly. "Fair enough. I'm not very good at trusting people."

The rare moment of honesty shocks me. I blink a few times, unsure how to take it. His admission hangs between us, a deepening intimacy that scares me and appeals to me.

"But do you trust me now?" I want to specify that I'm talking about this instance, but I don't. I'm surprised at how much I want him to say yes.

"I do." He doesn't think about it, and the finality of it is clear. Indisputable. Rewarding.

"Why?"

"I don't know why?" He shakes his head. "Goddammit, Saar, perhaps I just really fucking want your words to be true, because I'm tired of our constant fights, of trying to one-up each other. I trust you, not because you gave me any reasons to trust you, but because somewhere, deep down, I feel like you're the answer." He searches my face, bewildered, like he can't believe his own words.

"The answer?" I rasp, the lump in my throat swelling.

"The answer to everything that's missing from my life."

An entire kaleidoscope of butterflies flutters in my stomach. I'm cold and hot at the same time—just purely overwhelmed.

I'm his answer?

"You're refreshing. You're beautiful, brave, and smart." He steps closer.

"Okay, I'll give you beautiful." I try to lighten the mood, but it's flat even to my ears. His honesty scares me more than his wrath.

He flaps his arms in exasperation and starts pacing. I don't want him away from me. But can I allow him closer?

"Stop constantly questioning yourself, The Morrigan. You started taking care of yourself when you were a teenager. You stand up to me daily. I saw you interact with Livia and people at the shelter and many others... You care, you listen, you encourage. You spread compassion, and you stand up for yourself. Point in case, the fucker downstairs. Just because you're a bit lost right now, it doesn't mean you're less."

Oh, my poor heart.

"You're a survivor, and I admire the shit out of you for that. That fucking post? It wasn't a cry for help; it was your new beginning. To inspire. To shake. To provoke."

I don't know what to say. My lungs constrict; my heart races. I open my mouth, but he cuts me off.

"You bewitched me. You fucking stripped me of my control. You infiltrated my life, and despite my best efforts, my mind wanders to you all the time."

He crowds me again. The intensity of his declaration moves my legs backward, even though, on some very deep level, I want his closeness more than anything. My back hits the wall.

"I'm done fighting, Saar. Tomorrow, you get your fucking marriage certificate, but we're done pretending, and we're giving this thing between us a real try."

Again, my poor heart.

"Do I have a say in it?"

"No."

Chapter 21

Corm

Control.

Fucking control. I've been hanging onto it by a thread. But when I cup her cheeks and seize her lips, and she whimpers into my mouth, it snaps.

I push my hand into her hair, fisting the silky strands with more force than I should. I can't help myself.

I want to punish her for stripping me of common sense.

I want to hold her closer, because somehow, this woman became my oxygen.

I want to—need to—own her. Possess her. Protect her. Praise her.

I hike her up, the skirt falling around her legs as she

wraps them around me, her hands frantically working the buttons of my shirt.

I grind my hips, hating all the fabric between us, but lost in the frenzy of kissing and groping and feeling her against me.

I told her I trust her, and fuck if I knew when that happened. She's not a gambler. She has many issues, but gambling addiction isn't one of them.

Perhaps it's the relief that after days of wondering what snake I had allowed into my life, I now know my impression of her wasn't a lie.

She's the person I got to know. The infuriating, annoying woman who makes me feel alive.

Who makes me believe I can get past my fucked-up issues and focus on something else. A woman who keeps me on my toes.

And whose pussy is rubbing against my cock in a desperate cry for friction. For attention. And attention I give.

Finally she's done with the buttons, and she pushes the shirt off my shoulders. Her touch on my skin burns, and I fucking want to go down in flames if it's at her hand.

I pull away, staring at her, needing that one last confirmation that this is us. The genuine us. No more games.

She looks at me wide-eyed, bewildered, and so

fucking beautifully broken, it's like a punch in the guts. I let her slide down and step back.

Her chest heaves with shallow breaths. "What?"

"Your dress. Off," I growl.

She pulls the zipper on the side down and shimmies out of her dress. No bra. Naked, and real. Fucking mine, even if she doesn't know it. Or doesn't want to yet. She's fucking mine.

Roaming my eyes over her skin, I make quick work of my pants while I kick off my shoes. I take off my socks, not once moving my eyes away from her.

The unrestrained desire in her eyes.

The wanton curve of her lips.

The confidence of her posture.

I'm getting a more authentic version of her than what everyone knows from her photos. And this show is for me only.

It's private, and after studying the facade she offers to the world—yes, I've been perusing her work—I'm pretty sure it's genuinely true.

As raw as my desire for her.

I pull down my briefs, my cock springing out, the head glistening with pre-cum.

I walk to the dresser and get a condom from a black glass bowl and give it to her.

"Let's see if you need the lube." I smirk and hoist her up.

Her legs come back around my waist as I push her against the wall. Her body hot—literally and figuratively—against mine feels like too much and not enough at the same time.

She rips the wrapper with her teeth and almost drops it in her frenzy to cover my cock. God, what her eagerness does to me. I really am a simple man.

"Arms over your head."

Resilience flashes through her eyes, but she raises her arms. I grip both her wrists in one hand and reach between us with the other.

I have always been an over-confident asshole, and I hate how this woman makes me doubt myself. But having her now at my mercy is intoxicating. Magical. Empowering.

Feeling her body against me is so arousing, I may just blow from this contact.

"Look at that, baby; I still need proof that you usually depend on lube." I swipe through her folds and bring my glistening fingers to her mouth.

Smearing her arousal on her lips, I kiss her roughly and then dip my head to the crook of her neck. Just inhaling her.

She whimpers, grinding her pelvis against me. I grip my cock and line it at her entrance. In one violent thrust, I push in, and I'm home, sheathed in her tantalizing pussy.

Saar screams at the sudden intrusion. "Corm."

"That's right, scream my name, The Morrigan. This is going to be fast." I glance at her face, seeking consent, and meet a challenge in her eyes. Fucking vixen.

I set a punishing tempo, releasing her arms, so I can use both hands to hold her ass. The room fills with her moans, my grunts, our perspiration-covered bodies slapping.

"I'm going to come," she pants.

"Not yet," I growl, pull out, and drop her to her feet.

She whimpers something unintelligible that sounds like a string of profanities. I laugh as I whip her around.

"Hands on the wall, baby."

She obeys immediately, and I drive into her like a man possessed, bruising her hips in my grip.

It takes only a few thrusts before she whimpers again. "I'm close." She pushes her ass to me.

I stop moving, and she groans. "I fucking said not yet."

"You don't control my orgasm," she snaps with frustration.

Fisting her hair, I pull her to me. Her back warm against my chest now, I take her earlobe into my mouth, biting gently. "This is where you're wrong, baby. In the bedroom, I'm in charge. Understood."

She tenses, but I cup her breast and roll her nipple between my fingers. The shudder that ripples through her is a good enough answer, and she nods.

I smirk. "Use your words."

"Understood," she grits out.

"Do you want to come, The Morrigan?" I skim her rib cage, enjoying the goose bumps sprouting under my fingertips.

"Yes," she growls, almost stomping her foot.

"Then beg for it, baby." I bite her shoulder gently.

Now she actually stomps my foot, but it's like a tickle given how light she is in my arms, and I chuckle.

"Fuck, Corm, I want to come. Now." She pants and tries to bend.

I let go of her hair, so she can reach the wall again, her ass jutting out. The movement almost makes me come.

"We'll work on your attitude later." I ram into her once. Twice. Three times. "Touch yourself."

She slides her hand between her legs. I snake my arm around her and pinch her nipple.

"Oh my God," she cries out, and her body stiffens, her walls closing around my cock as she explodes around me.

I continue moving in and out, her skin slipping

from my grip as she slackens, completely taken by her orgasm.

It's a beautiful thing to see her come undone.

It's a beautiful thing to let her come.

It's a beautiful thing that pushes me over the edge, and I spill myself inside her.

She slams against the wall, and I cover her with my body, finding purchase with my forearm. Holding her light frame upright is almost impossible as I try to find my ground.

What is this woman doing to me?

Breaking my walls.

Redefining my beliefs.

Uprooting my priorities.

And the biggest problem: I don't mind. I don't mind at all.

I pick her up and carry her to the bed where I collapse beside her.

Pulling her into my arms, I hold her so tight she probably can't breathe. I'm unbearably in need of contact. Of having her in my arms in the aftermath of our climax.

I may be an asshole, but I'm no stranger to aftercare. Yet this is the first time I'm holding a woman because I need it probably as much as her.

The connection. The calm after the storm. The care.

Again, what is this woman doing to me?

* * *

"Where did you go?" I lace my fingers behind my head.

Saar is in the bathroom, but she kept the door open. It's a little thing, yet it wraps around me, grounding me.

In lieu of her verbal declaration of trust or any commitment, I take her peeing with open doors like a just replacement. For now.

She laughs. "I'm in the bathroom."

In the mirror on the wall, I see her as she hovers above the toilet, wiping herself. The image spreads honey around my chest, tugging at the corners of my mouth. When was the last time I felt this content?

"When you cheated your brothers in cards." I roll on to my side, propping my head in my palm, my gaze on the mirror.

She saunters to the sink and washes her hands. God, her ass is a masterpiece. She dries her hands and messes her hair a little before returning.

"We went to a cooking school in Tuscany." She grins, the mischief dancing in her eyes.

"So you know how to cook?"

She lied that night the magazine came. She didn't want to share pieces of her then. She does now. And it makes me swell with something primal. Like it's my achievement. Like I earned her trust.

It's fucking cooking, you idiot.

"Hmmm." She picks up my shirt from the floor and slides her arms through it. Fuck. I don't ever want her wearing anything else.

"Cal bailed after two days, but Finn stuck around, and it might have won him his wife." She angles her head sideways, studying the abstract artwork on the dark wall.

"You said you played them one year only..."

She turns and smiles at me, but it doesn't reach her eyes. "The following year, my face was in such demand, I didn't get to go on another vacation."

Fuck. I've half the mind to have my jet fueled and take her to every destination in the world.

She leans against the chest of drawers, biting her lip while she studies me. Her long, bare legs crossed at the ankle, she looks comfortable in my shirt.

Or maybe it's the lighting in the room. She still has the shadows under her eyes from the lack of sleep, but there is a fresh glow on her face. Like she isn't expecting to be attacked or threatened anymore, so she's finally relaxed.

"Every time we talk, it's me talking and you avoiding," she says, tucking a strand behind her ear. "Tell me about your father."

Fuck. I scoot to sit up, my back against the headboard. "He died."

She sighs. "You said you trust me."

"You need to improve your pillow talk."

"You see... avoiding."

I close my eyes. I do trust her. I think I want to tell her. I just don't quite know what to tell. How to share the mangle of thoughts and emotions that the mere mention of Connor Quinn stirs in me.

The mattress dips at the foot of the bed. When I open my eyes, I find her mirroring my position, leaning against the footboard, her long legs stretched alongside mine.

She isn't pushing the topic, nagging me to share. It's like she senses my turmoil, so she came closer, creating space for me to share.

I wish she would push, though, because I can retort her words, but her silent support is hard to rebut.

I sigh. Maybe it's time to share. "He is not my father."

She doesn't flinch. She doesn't react; she simply holds my gaze. But her composure is telling.

"How did you know?" I have to restrain myself from moving away from her. How could she know?

She quirks her eyebrow up. "You know an awful lot about me."

"Touché."

Silence, filled with my lack of will to talk and her abundant patience to listen, stretches for what feels like a lifetime. I have never shared anything personal with anyone, other than my immediate family.

The concept is foreign, foul-tasting, and yet not completely outlandish with Saar. As she pointed out, she shared, and, most of the time, honestly.

Perhaps it's her upbringing, starved for attention, and then later sharing spaces with so many people all the time. Maybe talking is not a big deal for her.

But what good can come from sharing my thoughts, my disappointments?

"You said you trusted me," she repeats softly.

"I grew up admiring him. He was my mentor, my hero, my example. But he wasn't my father."

"What you just described sounds like a pretty damn good father to me."

Compared to the old van den Linden, it feels laughable and privileged to complain about a father figure in my life. "Yes, I guess he was a good father. I was always a cocky bastard, and everything came to me with ease. I didn't want to apply myself too much—only interested in fun and breathing through life just below the surface.

"But he saw more in me, and he challenged me to start something that was mine. Merged is the result. His illness was progressing quickly, and I just wanted to make him proud. And he was. But for some reason, he decided to leave me a letter in his will. Telling me how proud he was to be my father, even though he didn't sire me."

I close my eyes again, as if the truth was easier in the darkness.

"Maybe he just felt like he lied to you all his life. It may feel like a selfish act of atonement. But perhaps it's simpler. Maybe he believed you deserved the truth."

"But what good is the truth for? I'm just so fucking mad at him. With the fucking letter, he robbed me of the opportunity to grieve. And I'm mad at her. Along with Declan, they were my people. And now..." I shake my head.

"They are still your people. That letter doesn't erase all the memories you have with him. Your mom misses you. She doesn't deserve this either. And whatever his intention was, I'm sure he didn't plan for you to abandon your mom. To break your family."

"Well, that's exactly what he did."

"Don't let him."

I snap my gaze to her, and her peaceful beauty hits me right in my chest. I want to argue her point, but she's right. Also, how am I going to argue—with a woman whose parents abandoned her—that my loving parents don't deserve my company or affection? Fuck.

"Okay, let's move away from this heavy portion of the night," I grumble.

She chuckles and stands up again. I was hoping the next point on the agenda would be in this bed.

When I suggested—okay, demanded—we explore this thing between us, I wasn't expecting digging into wounds. Or helping them heal. Fuck. I'm really out of my depth here.

In a cowardly effort to move the attention away from me, I switch the topic. "When are you going to take Nora Flemming's offer?"

"The question is *if*, not *when*. And the answer is, I don't know yet."

"For what it's worth, I think you should explore the opportunity. She knows what she sees in you. I agree with her. The only person to embrace your own potential is you."

She saunters to the bar cart and pops open a bag of nuts, ignoring the conversation. I guess she isn't ready. "Do you want anything?"

Shit. "When was the last time you ate?"

She chuckles. "I'm okay." She peruses the room again, my shirt hiding and showing parts of her, taunting me.

She opens a drawer, and since I know what's there, my cock springs to applaud her immediately.

"Oh." She utters a curious sound and retrieves a pair of handcuffs, turning to me with heat in her eyes.

I crook my finger and beckon her to me, the arousal replacing all the heaviness of our previous conversation.

Ironically, the intimacy is the same—just its expression is different. This time more carnal. I'm all for that, way more eager than I was with sharing words.

She lets the handcuffs dangle from her raised hand, her eyes darting between them and me.

"Saar," I warn. "Come here."

She wets her lips in slow motion, the little tease. "Make me."

Fucking brat. Within seconds I'm on my feet, and before she even decides where to run, I pounce.

I whip her around and twist her arm against her back. Both my arms imprison her against my chest. She makes a sound that is a groan and a laugh while pushing her ass against me. My cock twitches, but I don't let her distract me.

In one quick move, I grip her other hand and click the cuffs locked, binding her wrists behind her back.

"Hey," she protests, wriggling and thrashing as if that would make me stop. It only makes me want her more. To tease her more. Torment her more.

I yank her close to me and thrust my hips forward,

so she feels the effect she has on me. Holding her tight, I lower my head to her ear.

Her usual lavender scent is mixed with my after-shave and, well... me. It makes her feel mine. And suddenly, that becomes my only mission... to make her truly mine.

"Didn't I tell you who is in charge in the bedroom, The Morrigan?" I growl into her ear, and appreciate the shudder that rakes through her. "I think I need to punish you."

Her breath hitches, and it may just be my imagination, but she leans into me, gyrating her ass.

"Use your words." I suck on the soft skin in the crook of her neck, suddenly very dedicated to marking her. Fuck, I have never felt this unrelenting need to claim someone.

"What was the question?" The words are a breeze only, but they are laced with frustration.

"Who is in charge?"

"You."

"How should I punish you for being a little brat?"

"That wasn't the question." She elbows me, but the jab is a tickle.

"It is now," I growl.

She stills for a moment, but then shocks me. "What are my options?"

I laugh. Fuck, she's amazing.

I reach for the drawer and pull out a multi-tail whip. With one hand closing around her throat—not too hard, just to gauge her reactions—I trail the tip of the handle around her clavicle.

She swallows, and her pulse quickens against my palm. I continue to softly trace her skin with the whip.

"Look at these nipples begging for attention." I circle each hardened bud, and she moans, throwing her head against my shoulder.

Her eyes are hooded, her lips parted, with my hand around her neck, and I almost abandon the game to bend her over and fuck her.

My cock would certainly be happy. But I don't want to rush things.

I graze her torso farther down until I reach between her thighs. I stop while another shudder rakes through her body. I want to edge her, draw this out, but I also need another hit of her like a junkie.

I settle on capturing her lips. She welcomes me eagerly, dueling with my tongue, sucking, biting, moaning into my mouth.

No kiss ever felt more desperate and more rewarding at the same time. She tastes like anything and everything I ever needed in my life.

And she definitely doesn't taste fake. No longer a convenience, she became the reason. The purpose. The answer.

"Is this the punishment?" she says against my lips.

"Not yet, The Morrigan; this is my reward." I kiss her, squeezing her throat a little more, her heart thumping wildly against my palm.

She bites my bottom lip hard enough to draw blood. "Whatever should you be rewarded for?"

I smirk, my face only half an inch from her, our noses touching. "For all the orgasms I gave you."

"As if you didn't come, as well," she teases, her voice heavy with lust while sassing me.

"I think I need to put that mouth of yours to better use." I whip her around, fisting her hair and pulling gently, so she looks at me.

She meets my eyes with a challenge in hers. With heat and unabashed desire. "Is that my punishment?"

Fuck, the things I want to do to her. "You would like to suck my cock, baby?"

She nods, licking her lips, and I summon every ounce of control not to succumb. "Not just yet." I kiss her roughly. "First the punishment." I swat her gently with the whip, just brushing the skin of her ass.

We stare at each other for several long beats. Our mutual need swirls around us while the moment of stillness sharpens it. I've never felt such burning desire. Such essential longing. Such an all-consuming craving.

And it's not just her body I want at this moment. Or probably long before this moment.

"Okay," she rasps her consent, trepidation and longing lacing her tone.

I smile and kiss her again. "Good girl." I graze her ass with the whip again. "Where?"

She blinks. "What?"

"Where do you want the whip? Your pussy or your ass?"

Chapter 22

Saar

G*ood girl.*

I stare at him, my heartbeat drumming in my head and air slipping from my lungs. An insatiable ache flows through my veins, spreading fiery lust. "I have never had my pussy spanked."

I had a healthy sex life before. Or so I thought. With Corm, in this moment, I'm self-conscious about my lack of experience. Judging by the flash of desire in his eyes, my answer pleases him.

"It would be my honor to be your first." He winks, but there is no jest in his tone. It's grave with need. Jesus, this man is intense.

Still, I find comfort behind his lighthearted comment. I bite my bottom lip, my heart and mind racing. I want this so much, but at the same time it feels like I'm giving up something.

"Stop overthinking, baby. It's a simple question: Do you want to have your pussy spanked?"

Fuck, the timbre of his voice quivers through my body, adding to the languid lava already bubbling inside me. "I think so?"

I have never shied away from a good time, so what am I considering?

Because something shifted tonight, and having casual fun is no longer on the table. And that is way more than I bargained for when I agreed to this arrangement.

With his thumb, he traces my lip, my jaw, my cheek. The admiration in his eyes is almost too much. I don't deserve it, but he still rewards me with it, and it feels so genuine it's unbearable.

Now, I'm standing in front of this man who decided to give us a try—whatever that means—and... well, careful what you wish for.

His adoration is so intimate, so honest, so unconditional, I want to look away to shield myself.

But I don't, because as scary as this connection is, it also makes me feel alive for the first time in I don't know how long.

"I will need a more definite answer, baby." He kisses my forehead.

It's gentle, and in such contrast to the topic of our

conversation that I close my eyes to cope with the overwhelming feeling.

"Will it hurt?" I wrinkle my nose, heat rising to my cheeks as I try to hold on to my confidence.

"Obviously." I could hear the smirk even with my closed eyes.

I huff, but I'm grateful he brings playfulness into this. Or his assholeness, I don't know which.

"Look at me, Saar."

It's a demand, but there is softness behind it. I pry my eyes open.

"The border between pain and pleasure is very thin. The hurt will be fleeting compared to pleasure, but we don't have to go there."

"I thought I have no say in the bedroom."

He shakes his head. "You have all the say, baby. I may be writing the script, but you're directing the play. Do you trust me to offer the best scenario?"

I nod, swallowing.

"Is that a yes?"

He runs the whip up my thigh, its leather tassels erupting small explosions all over my skin and across my center. I'm clenching and shaking and gasping, and having so many visceral reactions I want to bolt and stay at the same time.

"Yes," I say, with such resolution I surprise us both.

"Good girl," he growls.

And again, the words do things to me I would never admit. It's just a phrase. But fuck if I don't want to be his good girl.

He reaches behind me and unclasps the handcuffs, only to secure them again with my hands in front of me.

The whole time, his cock twitches. His engorged length is an encouraging reminder I'm not the only one affected here.

The anticipation builds up between my thighs as he drags the tassels up my ass and spine, across my shoulders, and between my breasts. I think I'm going to black out.

He kisses me roughly, and then swats with the whip, again only grazing the skin of my hip. "On the bed."

I try to walk across the room with some grace and dignity, but twelve fucking years of promenading myself on runways around the world and I almost trip over the few feet.

Sitting on the mattress, I look at Corm. He really is gorgeous. I didn't get a chance to admire him before, but the man is flawless. Sublime. Arresting.

"On your back, your hands above your head." He prowls around the bed, tapping the whip on his other palm.

I obey, scooting farther and lying across the

mattress, trepidation and arousal cruising through my body.

He comes to my feet and traces my skin with the leather in his hands. I buckle, so oversensitive to any contact by now I may just climax from his gaze.

"Spread those beautiful legs for me," he drawls.

I open for him, because I no longer question anything. I only want this to move on and get to the main program. He pushes my knees farther apart and kneels between them at the edge of the bed.

"You keep your arms above your head. I'm going to start with five for your sass earlier, and then I'm going to eat that delicious pussy of yours, but if you move your arms, I'll punish you again. Understood."

I nod eagerly, and the bastard chuckles. He picks up my leg and puts it on his shoulder, peppering my ankle with gentle kisses. I get so distracted and confused by his tender routine that the first slap catches me by surprise.

"What the fuck?" I cry out, but he whips without mercy until he lands all five.

The sensation is blazing, but it ignites a decadent need I've never felt before. Fuck, this hurts, and I want more.

Corm drops the whip beside us and leans in, kissing me gently between my legs. "Look at you, baby, dripping for me. Are you okay?"

"Yes, yes, I need..." I can't talk.

He flattens his tongue and runs it through my throbbing folds. "What do you need?"

"I need to come," I whimper.

He leaves the task, glowering at me from between my thighs.

What the fuck? Why did he stop? He raises his eyebrow, challenging me, and I scramble to figure out what's going on, and then it hits me.

Fucker.

"Please," I practically wail.

Oh my. He thrusts his tongue into my channel with such dedication, I almost black out. Pushing my thighs apart, he digs his palms into my skin, holding me in place while I thrash and squirm, trying to buck.

"You taste so good." He spreads me with his fingers and blows.

The cold air on my pulsating pussy elevates the sensation to a new, unbearable level. And why did he change the pace? I can't stand it.

I bring my arms down and grip his hair. He jerks away, and before I realize what's happening, the whip comes down five more times.

I cry, or moan, or roar; I'm not sure what the sound that comes out of me is. "I can't; I can't anymore..." I whine.

"Arms," he growls.

Shit. "Corm, I swear to God—"

He puts the whip's handle across my lips, and I shut up and move my arms back above my head. He smirks and dives back in. Thank fucking God.

He builds me up with his talented tongue, and then he lifts to his knees and starts grazing my skin gently with the whip. Up my leg, around my belly, over my breasts.

"What are you doing?" I'm practically mad with desire by now.

"What does it look like?" He leans down and takes one nipple into his mouth while moving the whip around my throat, down my arm.

"Corm, I begged," I cry with frustration. "What else do you want?"

He smiles at me with the most devilish grin known to mankind. I swear, I can feel it between my legs.

He pulls up higher, bracketing my face with his forearms and covering my body with his.

"I want you to have the best orgasm of your life, baby." His nose is just inches from mine, his breath warm on my skin.

His mouth fuses with mine, and I taste myself and him and... us. It makes me wild, filled with urgency, with so much hunger for him I don't think I'll ever be satisfied.

This kiss is different from any before. I don't know

if it's the result of the edging and my currently oversensitive nerves, but he owns me with this kiss.

It's possessive and worshiping.

It's blinding and enlightening.

It's everything and not enough.

It's a kiss that makes me forget about my needy pussy. Almost. I'm still quivering with the need.

"Corm, please." I'm ready to get on my knees and beg. I'm not above anything anymore, my mind wiped out by yearning.

He pushes to his knees; somehow he produces a condom. Throwing my legs over his shoulder, he yanks me closer and fills me with one aggressive thrust.

I cry out with pleasure and pain and relief and everything in between, just completely overcome with the most potent cocktail of sensations.

He sets a punishing tempo, but I'm not complaining, finally getting closer to my release. I want to move my hands to touch him, but somehow that obstacle heightens the thrill.

"Eyes on me, Saar."

His words register through the fog of bliss. "What?"

"I want you to watch what you do to me," he pushes through his teeth, barely hanging onto his control.

I lock my eyes on him. It's a beautiful thing to see

this man surrender. So beautiful that it pushes me over the edge.

A freight train of an orgasm rams through me, breaking me into pieces and putting me together at the same time.

I'm still in a haze, high on my release, when Corm tenses deep inside. He roars something, throwing his head back before he collapses on top of me.

I wrap my arms and legs around him, surprised I have any energy left to move. He lifts his head and kisses me.

"What kind of losers have you been with if you ever thought you couldn't get wet without lube?"

I chuckle. "You really want to talk about my former lovers?"

"Fuck," he grumbles. "Forget I said anything."

I laugh, feeling lighter and happier than I have in months. "Running the risk your ego will suffocate me, that was the best orgasm of my life."

He looks at me with a passion that spreads a warm feeling through me. I'm probably drunk on hormones, but his look feels like a commitment.

Definitely drunk on hormones.

"Can I have my hands back?"

He unclasps the cuffs, kissing my wrists with such reverence I want to slap him. Because really, this thing between us was so much safer when we hated each other.

"Are you sore?"

"A bit."

He frowns. "Sorry."

"I loved every minute of it."

He raises his eyebrow. "You were quite whiny for a moment there."

I poke his ribs. "Asshole."

"As always." He kisses me. "Let's shower, and then I need to fuck you against that vanity there."

He jumps up and scoops me up bridal-style.

I grin. "You're insatiable."

I stare at the ceiling, Corm's soft breathing a rhythmic soundtrack to my sleeplessness.

We're giving this thing between us a real try.

Several orgasms later, in the shower, against the mirror, and back in this bed, I think giving it a real try is fucking amazing.

But he didn't mean sex only. His gaze on me when he fucked me had the intensity of a commitment.

Let's face it, I've been in a committed relationship with my work only. I'm not against it, but it wasn't on my radar. I had no time, and my hookups were there for the ride, mostly because they knew I didn't have room for anything serious.

I was kind of hoping to be by myself for a bit. To truly find myself. Can I do that in Corm's all-consuming presence?

Especially in my current desolate financial state. Someone has stolen my identity? Betting under my name? Was it Marie? Or maybe someone in her family?

I was grateful for yesterday's diversion from the topic. It was not like I could do anything before we understand what happened, but now, staring at the ceiling, without Corm's talented hands, tongue, and cock distracting me, anxiety slips in.

How am I even going to defend myself against it all? Owing people I don't know? Turning my head, I look at the man beside me. His peaceful face gives me a bit of a confidence. At least I don't have to face this alone.

But my money is truly, really gone. Even if Maria is convicted of embezzling, I'll not be able to recover any of it.

Dad's trust fund is my only option for financial independence. And then what?

What did Corm mean by *a real try*? Do we stay married? Do I want to be married?

I roll on to my side and watch him. His broad chest

is rising and falling, the movement spreading peace through me.

Propping myself on my elbow, I let my gaze kiss his face. Without the frown or the scowl, it's even more beautiful.

The sheets are tangled over us haphazardly, and I lift the cover slightly to look at his impressive cock. I never considered the appendage visually attractive, but that was before I saw and experienced Cormac Quinn.

And a sample of his goods is not enough. I move to my knees, careful not to disturb him, and I peel the sheets away.

He makes a sound and throws his forearm over his face. His knee bends on the mattress. Giving me better access?

Is he up? I glance at his covered face, his lips slightly parted, his breathing still regular. And like a starved woman, I curl between his legs and without touching him, I lower my head and lick him from the base to the crown.

A rumble makes its way from deep in his throat, and his cock twitches. I wrap my hand around him and swipe my tongue around his tip. He tastes clean and sinful, and a bit like me. It's an intoxicating palate.

I take him into my mouth and suck gently. I don't rush things, just enjoying. The harder he grows, the more wet I get. It's a heady feeling as the ache builds up in my core.

I glance up and startle when my eyes meet his hooded gaze. I smile around his girth, not letting his piercing eyes distract me. But they are.

They spur me forward and make me want to pause at the same time. And as if he could hear my thoughts, he cups my cheek gently and rasps, "Go on, baby. This is quite the beginning of the day."

Fuck, his just-woken-up voice is sexy. And his encouragement does the trick, and I bob my head, sucking like this is my favorite ice cream.

My saliva is coating his skin, drooling down my chin. I never understood how this visual is appealing to men, but based on Corm's deep humming, my state of choked up and messy doesn't deter him.

He bucks his hips, getting his tip farther than I anticipated, and I fight my gag reflex. What I also fight is the growing need in my pussy. Corm grips my hair and takes over the rhythm.

I can't breathe, I can't see through my tears, and yet the only thing that reigns over me is my growing ache.

Greedily, I shove two of my fingers inside me, but I whimper around him because it's not enough.

"Do you want to come, baby?"

I can't talk, so I nod eagerly, half prepared for him to bully me into begging, or deciding it's his turn or some other frustrating bullshit—that in hindsight always ends up being about me more than him—but he surprises me.

I yelp as he sits up, grabs me under my arms and before I blink, I'm on all fours with him behind me.

"Grab the headboard. This won't be gentle."

Fuck, his manhandling with his threat... No, no, his promise... has my center clenching.

He pushes his tip inside me, and I tense, not sure why. Like after barely fitting him into my mouth, I'm worried about his size. It makes no sense, since he stretched me deliciously several times tonight.

He snakes his hand to reach my nipple and tweaks it. "Relax, baby, let me in."

Let me in.

I don't know if it's his words or his hands, but my pussy responds. I guess he was talking to her, anyway.

He fills me, and stills for a moment. My body tries to adjust to his intrusion, but I'm sore after the night we had.

Any thoughts of discomfort disappear when he moves in a frenzy. Good that he told me to grab the headboard, because I would have cracked my skull.

The bed bangs against the wall in the background of my hazy mind as an immense pleasure takes over, and I come, wave after wave of pleasure washing over me.

Corm follows immediately with a roar, but he doesn't stop pounding me, prolonging my bliss into oblivion. I think I'm going to die. But then I've already been to heaven.

He collapses onto his back and pulls me to him. We pant, sweaty and spent.

As the fog slowly dissipates, so does my euphoria. "Fuck, Corm." I sit up and almost collapse, my head swirling from the sudden movement. "Condom."

He looks at me with a lazy smile and shrugs.

What the hell? I raise my hand to slap him, but he catches my wrist and pulls me to him.

I struggle to wriggle away, so he rolls us over and covers me with his huge body, holding my wrists above my head.

I thrash, trying to get away from him, but it's a lost battle. "You knew! You did it on purpose. I don't fucking want your STDs."

He chuckles and lets his body sink a bit, practically suffocating me. If I wasn't so mad, I would actually enjoy his warmth and, as much as I hate to admit to myself, the show of power.

"Calm down. I didn't plan it. I realized once I was in. I don't have STDs."

"What if I have any?" I spit the stupid argument.

"Then I have them too now." His expression is completely nonchalant, no smirk, no mocking.

"Are you out of your mind? That was irresponsible."

"It was. From both of us," he says calmly. That shuts me up for a beat, because yes, it's not just his responsibility.

"But you were the one who remembered, and you decided for both of us that it was okay?"

Fuck, his scent is distracting. And his warmth. His breath so close to my face.

He kisses my forehead. "Pretty much."

I growl in frustration. "What if I get pregnant?"

"Wouldn't be the worst thing."

I writhe, or attempt to, but it's impossible to move under him. "Let me go, Corm. What, do you have some breeding kink?"

He pinches my chin between his thumb and finger. "I have a you kink, The Morrigan."

Chapter 23

Corm

She glares at me with a venom that might truly poison a weaker person. I should apologize, or admit I was wrong. But fuck if it didn't feel right.

"You're crazy." She tries to yank her hands from my hold, but I'm not ready to let go.

I need her to understand she's mine, even if it currently requires my brute force. And I don't want her to kill me, which certainly looks the case at the moment.

"I'm crazy, Saar. And the source of my madness is the woman who waltzed into my room two years ago. She was completely out of her depth, but felt such an inspiring loyalty to her asshole brother that she dared to demand I get rid of a lucrative property. That was the day I decided you were mine."

I expect her to roll her eyes, to scoff, to fight, but she just stares at me. And not that I would ever admit that to anyone, but this may be the first time in my life my confidence falters.

I'm holding her trapped, her chest moving with effort, her breath on my face, her heart beating against me. I know I should give her space, but I can't. I fear she may run.

I can't let her slip, so I'm abusing my strength and forcing her to give me something. Anything.

Whatever it is she is willing to give. I don't know how much time, or lifetimes, pass while she just stares at me, but as each moment slides by, I feel my prison sentence is getting worse.

Or better, if the prison is shared with Saar. She's holding my heart in her hand, and based on our past few weeks, she's probably considering how to squash it.

She licks her lips. She swallows. She takes a breath. Everything amplified. Everything in slow motion.

"I wanted you to take me to the high school dance."

Her words are the last thing I expected her to say.

Have I deprived her brain of too much oxygen? I lift, shifting my weight onto my elbows more.

"I'm sorry I didn't take you, but if you want to dance...?" Fuck, I'm confused.

"I'm just saying, I decided to be yours way before you."

This time, her words hit me right in my fucking heart.

I fuse my mouth with hers, and finally allowing her some room, she wraps her legs around me. I kiss her with a frenzy spurred by the confession, trying to absorb the magnitude while at the same time hoping to escape more words.

The intimacy they forged. The implication they cast. The warmth they spread. It's all overwhelming.

Her stomach growls, and she giggles against my lips. And while my cock has opinions about what should happen next, I need to put my wife first.

My wife.

Fuck. That needs to happen, too.

"Let's get out of here and get some breakfast." Reluctantly, I pull away from her.

"I'm still mad at you." She sits up, and I'm distracted by her naked beauty.

"Fair enough. But I swear, I wasn't planning it. In the heat of the moment, I didn't evaluate the situation correctly." I stand and saunter to the bathroom.

"You being in control in the bedroom doesn't give you the right to knock me up." She follows me.

Now, I'm annoyed. "Don't act like it would be such a horrible thing."

She groans. "You're infuriating. We just started...

to tolerate each other, and you think having a child is okay?"

The pause before she defined our relationship as *tolerating each other* hurts like a punch in my gut. But I'm not a man who gets deterred easily.

I get her, I truly get her, but the cocky bastard in me doesn't care much. While her argument is valid, it's not like we can change what happened fifteen minutes ago.

I sigh. "Are you on birth control?"

She throws her arms up in exasperation. "Oh please, I haven't had a period for months."

Fuck, the toll her body paid for her career makes me see red, but that's a topic for later. Soon, but not right now. "So you're fighting me on principle?"

"An important principle."

"Good, let's do that over breakfast."

"It's not even that cold," Saar complains as we walk across the busy street to a bistro where they serve the best Eggs Benedict.

As soon as we got ready—her mostly glaring at me —I threw my jacket over her shoulders. And, of course, she had to add it to all the things she hates about me this morning.

We reach the entrance. "I'm not fucking having you traipsing around in that dress."

"So much for not controlling me." She rolls her eyes and pushes the door open.

We find seats in a booth in the corner and order breakfast.

"You need to see a doctor," I start before we even get our coffees.

She scoffs. "Anything else?"

"Our future kids aside, you're too young to have so many health issues."

Her glare intensifies while she taps her fingers on the table. "I don't have many health issues—"

"You can't sleep, you have iron deficiency, and you don't have your periods."

The waitress chooses that moment to appear with our coffees, her eyes darting between us.

Saar groans and hides her face in her palms. When the coast is clear, she peeks at me. "How do you know I can't sleep?"

I raise my eyebrow. Really? She should know by now that very little escapes me.

She sighs. "Of course, you know everything. I'm not discussing my period with you."

"You don't have to, but you will discuss it with a doctor."

"Or what?" She lifts her chin.

One other thing I came to understand about this infuriating, beautiful woman is that she fights me more on principle than on merit.

I take a sip of my coffee, not biting this time.

She huffs, folding her arms across her chest. "Whatever. I have an appointment for next week already, anyway."

"Good girl," I tease her, and she rolls her eyes again.

"And stop talking about our future kids. You haven't even taken me on a first date."

I open my mouth to remind her about our dinner, but she raises her hand.

"A real one, you asshole."

"Where would you like to go?" I weave my fingers and place my joined hands under my chin.

"To the courthouse to get my marriage certificate."

"Why, baby, you're such a romantic."

The waitress approaches carefully with our plates, and a smile tugs the corners of Saar's mouth.

My phone dings several times with incoming messages. Fuck, not now. Barely a minute passes and it rings.

"It might be important," Saar says, and stuffs a forkful of hash browns into her mouth.

I pull my phone out to see Mathison's number.

"Eat," I mouth at Saar, who rolls her eyes yet again but takes a bite of her toast.

"What is it?" I answer the phone.

"Manners," Art growls, like he has ever followed any social conduct rules.

"Good morning, Art. How are you?" I mock.

He grunts. "Check your emails. Your wife may not like what I found." He hangs up. *Manners*.

I open the first message he sent and click on the attached video.

"Is everything okay?" Saar's concern rolls through the rage the footage sparks.

"Give me a moment." I open the other file and then scan the summary report.

Motherfucker.

I reach over to take her hand in mine. Bringing it to my lips, I kiss her knuckles.

"Okay?" She angles her head to the side and narrows her eyebrows.

I pass her my phone. "I'm so sorry, baby."

She frowns and clicks on the video. "That's Vito. What is he doing? Where is this?"

There is a part of me that wants to somehow shield her from this. Protect her. Give her all the money and let her move on.

But that wouldn't be fair to her. As painful as this discovery is, I can't fix it for her. Not immediately.

The feeling of helplessness coils around my stomach, and fuck, I want to get on the plane right now and kill that bastard.

"Baby, Vito has been placing bets in your name. He's the person who not only embezzled your money, but he also put you in jeopardy when he pretended to act on your behalf."

She shakes her head left and right vigorously. Tears pool around the crevices of her eyes, not yet spilling.

How have I just gotten a reluctant commitment from her and I'm already failing her? I stand and round the table to sit beside her, pulling her chair between my legs. "Talk to me, baby."

"That can't be." She wipes a stranded tear and snatches the phone again. I let her watch one of the security videos showing Vito at a high-end bookie shop. "This proves nothing."

Leaving the phone in her hands, I click out of the video and open Mathison's summary.

"There is footage at several locations where you owe money. And sure, that might be a coincidence, but the online bets are traced to his computer. All his online aliases are linked to your bank accounts. He's been doing it for years, but only got more reckless recently when he bet and lost a substantial sum. He borrowed to cover the debt. From the wrong people, and the ball started rolling."

She drops my phone and aims her gaze at the empty space in front of her. I rub her back and sit there like an idiot, wanting to do something, anything to take her pain away.

Having her money and identity stolen is shitty, but fixable. Having it done by a person who she trusted and loved like her own father, that's traumatizing. Unforgivable. Terminal.

"We'll get him," I offer, uselessly.

I can have him arrested and convicted easily. I may be able to make sure he returns every single penny to her and fucking dies a slow death.

But none of it would be enough, because it doesn't even scratch the surface of the betrayal.

She continues staring in front of her, and while she is motionless, still sitting beside me, I feel her retreating, erecting the walls, and leaving me on the other side.

It's the subtle shift in her energy that makes me hope she's just composing herself to stand up against the challenge. But that hope is feeble, just in my head.

When she looks at me after what feels like an agonizing eternity in the worst purgatory, I know she has made up her mind. That I'm no longer in her plans.

That after being abandoned by her parents, and now betrayed by the only proxy she's ever known, I'm slowly but surely becoming yet another person—man—in her life she can't trust.

"You promised me that marriage certificate," she says.

Her tone is impersonal, and her detached words fall like stones into my stomach. And for the first time in my life, I'm scared shitless. And I choose not to bully someone to my will. Also a first.

She needs time to digest it.

I'll fight for us from afar for the time being.

I kiss her forehead, and she flinches.

Fuck. One punch after another, but I take them all. From her and for her.

"Let me get the bill."

I ease my arm and wrap it around Saar. Her head falls onto my shoulder, and I hold her gently not to wake her up.

This may be the only time I get to hold her for now. We barely spoke on the way to the courthouse where I picked up the marriage certificate while she waited in the car.

I had everything arranged up front already, so this was just a pit stop. As soon as the car started moving, the exhaustion claimed her, and she fell asleep.

We have been driving for three hours, and I told the driver that if he stops and wakes her up, he's fired.

She needs all the sleep she can get, and if the motion is helping her get there, we'll keep driving.

I itch to talk to Mathison, to my lawyer, to my security council, to anyone who can help us determine the next steps.

But I don't want to disturb her, so I just sit with all my frustration and anger. And fucking fear. Fear that she will shut down completely. She barely started trusting me, so the odds are against me.

But I guess, over the past few weeks, I became the man who hopes. A sentiment I always considered useless.

Saar's head slides forward, and I help her settle in my lap. I pull out my phone, turn off the sound, and start shooting texts to everyone who can help us get Vito fucking Conti.

The confirmation of our marriage license filing glares at me from my email. Somehow, it feels wrong. Fake.

More fake than it really is. Because we're no longer fake. I almost regret not giving her the stupid large wedding. Like that would have made this more permanent.

I regret a lot of things when it comes to her. That I ever made her feel like she needs to be guarded around me. That she can't trust me. That I didn't introduce her to my mother.

Now, I'm stuck with the consequences. I regret keeping things from her. I regret we didn't meet under different circumstances. So much fucking regret, I want to roar, punch someone, or get drunk.

Or get lost in the woman sleeping in my lap. If she lets me.

"Sir, we're running out of gas," the driver speaks softly into the intercom.

Saar stirs, mumbles something but doesn't wake up. Thank fucking God.

"How far are we from home?"

"We'll make it. I've been circling in the neighborhood."

"Okay."

When we arrive, I slide out of the car and gently scoop her up bridal-style. I carry her over the threshold, the irony not lost on me. My bride.

Her head settles against my chest as I take the stairs up. Briefly, I stop in front of her room, but no fucking way I'm leaving her alone.

She belongs in my bed, anyway. Our bed.

I kick the door open and lower her down. Grabbing a blanket from an armchair in the corner, I cover her. After closing all the blinds, darkness swallows the room, and I slide in to lie beside her.

Her breathing is even, her face serene, and I'm grateful she found some peace this morning. So she could face the reality rested.

Checking my emails, I confirm my security firm hired a PI in Italy who will bring the evidence to the authorities. Vito Conti should get arrested any minute now.

The information should give me some relief, but it's only a ticked-off item on my to-do list. It may give Saar some solace, but it won't heal the betrayal wound. Or her financial situation.

The latter is inconsequential, but I'm afraid that's not the way she sees it. I almost wake her up so we can talk, so I can get out of my head, but suffering in this limbo of helplessness is a small burden at the moment.

I glance over at my liquor cabinet. Yeah, whiskey is in order, my companion for the past few months. But then I look at the sleeping woman beside me and decide to stay put. She needs me sober.

The humming sound infiltrates my mind, and I fight the darkness. What is it? A vacuum cleaner? Fuck, it will wake up Saar.

I sit up so suddenly, I get dizzy. Have I fallen asleep?

I blink a few times, trying to adjust to the darkness, but even with fuzzy vision, I know… I feel that I'm alone.

One look around me confirms the dread coiling around my stomach. I bolt out of the room and almost topple over the cleaning lady.

She startles and jumps to the corner, the vacuum hose flipping around, tripping me.

"Fuck," I swear, probably losing my employee in the process. I barrel into Saar's room, but she isn't there. "Where is she?"

The woman shakes her head, backing up, clearly scared of me. Fuck. "Never mind." I try to smile at her and rush downstairs.

In the kitchen, I find a whistling Livia. My housekeeper is actually whistling cheerfully. What the fuck? "Where is Saar?"

"Good afternoon, Mr. Quinn. She said she's going to see a lawyer. Are you hungry?"

I close my eyes and breathe through my flared nostrils, fisting my hands. "No, I'm not hungry. Thank you." I pivot to leave. "Oh, the cleaning lady upstairs…"

Livia frowns. "What about her?"

"Give her a raise." I don't wait for Livia's response and rush to my office.

ME

Where are you?

A lawyer? What lawyer? Is she getting the divorce already? Why the fuck did I fall asleep?

I pace my office, pulling my hair, waiting for her response. When the message pings, I swipe the screen so violently the phone almost flies across the room.

SAAR

At my father's lawyer.

Her father's lawyer. She went to get her trust fund released. And now I know with certainty, I'm the third man who betrayed her.

Chapter 24

Saar

I need emergency coffee.

CELESTE

That tired?

LILY

I think she means a coffee meeting.

CELESTE

Merde. The pregnancy brain.

LILY

I have a day off. Can be at Cora's in 30 mins.

Great. Thank you.

CELESTE

Are you okay? We're going out with Cal. I'll cancel.

Don't. It's okay. I'll just talk Lily's ears off.

"You look better. Glowing? If married life is this good, I may give it a try," Cora greets me with a smile and throws her apron behind the counter. "Sanjay, I'm clocking off."

Her employee, busy at the coffee machine, nods.

"I slept for more hours than I have in weeks, but I'm certainly not fucking glowing," I groan and march to our table.

"What's wrong?" Cora plops down beside me, her smile gone.

"Let's wait for Lily." I sigh.

"I'm here."

I turn, and sure enough, our petite friend is barreling around the tables to reach us.

"What's the emergency?" She sits down, wiping a strand from her face and adjusting her oversized, ill-fitting glasses. "You look good."

I groan. "Yeah, my skin is all refreshed." I can't help the sarcasm in my tone. And feel like shit about it. These women don't deserve my bitterness.

And they are right, several hours of good sleep, and I lost the deep shadows under my eyes. Several hours of mind-blowing sex with Corm and I gained a new glow.

Fuck. If only it wasn't all so complicated.

The hollow feeling inside me keeps spreading despite my outside appearance.

"What happened?" Cora asks.

My eyes move from her to Lily and back. Over the course of the last few hours, I've been stunned, in denial, upset, in denial, frustrated. But mostly in denial.

And that was when I thought that Vito's betrayal was my only problem.

Now, I'm just hollow.

I tell them what Corm found out about my manager, the man I trusted. The man I considered my friend and mentor.

I don't tell them about another man in my life who confessed his commitment to our relationship, and casually threw around the notion of having babies with me.

That particular issue makes me feel all sorts of feelings, ranging from livid to strangely excited. He must have fucked my brains out.

But there is too much drama happening in my life at the moment to even unpack that baggage.

Well, I can be telling myself that, but that would be yet another denial. If I'm honest with myself, I don't appreciate his bullying manner of professing his intention, but I find myself strangely intrigued by the idea.

It's preposterous really, because there are so many red flags when it comes to me and Corm as a couple, let alone as parents. And yet... what trips me is that he is the first man I could imagine a long-term relationship with.

But that's another problem. Right now, I'm trying to unpack the Vito bomb.

And based on Cora and Lily's shocked faces, the explosion is palpable.

"I'm so sorry, Saar. That level of betrayal from someone you trust..." Lily reaches for my hand. "It's heartbreaking and violating, and so fucking damaging."

Cora glimpses her way, with her eyebrows raised. "Agreed, a great summary, but no comfort."

Lily shakes her head. "I mean, I can't possibly imagine."

Something tells me that her words were closer to home than she lets on. That she can imagine from experience.

"Yeah, I walked from the grasps of my father right into that one. The only difference is that my father at least didn't pretend he cared."

When I woke up this afternoon, Corm's body beside me was comforting. It felt like home.

But if I want to find my figurative home with yet another man—another person—I need to first take control of my life. Come to a new relationship with my feet firm on the ground.

For a moment, the intimacy I felt in his bed scared me. If I accepted him and gave us a shot, wouldn't I be just moving to yet another person to control me, to betray me?

As I watched him there, sleeping peacefully, his chest moving, his face so serene, I decided I won't let my fear and my past come in the way of my happiness.

There is a lot the two of us have to figure out, but that doesn't diminish the support and care Corm gave me.

Realizing that, I decided to act fast and get my fucking trust fund. Gain my financial independence, so I can be an equal partner.

"Saar, you didn't deserve this," Lily says.

For the first time since I was fifteen, a tear rolls down my cheek. "Don't I, though? It seems to be the pattern of my life. A pretty face who can't take care of herself."

"You were fifteen when Vito gave you the opportunity. Promised the world to you. After your shitty parents, you were in no position to recognize he was a predator," Cora says.

"Or in a position to take care of your finances," Lily adds. "Is there anything we can do?"

I shake my head. "Thank you. Right now, I don't even know what to do."

"Kill fucking Vito," Cora mumbles. And I love her

for being so indignant on my behalf.

"I'm in." Lily doesn't miss a beat.

I chuckle. "You're both good friends. But I'm not letting you rot in jail for that weasel."

"I'm so mad." Cora stands up abruptly. "Who wants something stronger? I have vodka in the back."

"I've never drunk vodka," Lily says.

I look at her in shock. "Seriously? You're not that young."

Sometimes, I think Lily ran away from some commune or alternate universe. Her appearance aside, she's polished and well-spoken to a point that doesn't fit with her dire financial situation.

But who am I to judge? I have no money and no education. She probably has at least the latter.

"I'm just not a big drinker, I guess." Lily looks away.

Cora brings a large teapot and three cups.

"What is this?" I frown.

She sits down and pours us each an inch into the cups. The scent of alcohol hits my nostrils.

"I don't have a liquor license. We can't do this openly here," Cora whispers, looking around like she could be caught any minute.

"I feel like a criminal." Lily giggles and brings the cup to her lips. "Ew, I don't think—"

"It's not about the taste, Lils. It's about the feeling

and the buzz. Just down it," I instruct, and do just that, closing my eyes as the burn hits.

Cora follows and immediately refills our cups.

Lily scrunches her face but then joins in. "I hope the buzz comes quickly."

I giggle, and it feels so good, but then I remember... everything... and I quickly down another shot. "So to put a nice red bow on all my problems, I went to see my father's lawyer."

"About your trust fund?" Lily downs the second glass and grimaces.

I nod and pick up the teapot, refilling our cups. The scent of the spirit lingers around us. "Turns out my father dissolved my trust fund and forgot to inform me."

"What a prick." Cora salutes with her cup and drinks. We follow.

"Your father stole your money?" Lily slurs her words a bit.

I snort. "It doesn't even surprise me. The level of shit my father did to me, and even more to my brothers, already conditioned me to expect the worst from him."

"What did Corm say about that? That kind of voids your agreement with him." Cora pours us another round.

"I came right here after I found out."

"Wait, if you went to see the lawyer..." Lily speaks

with a bit of an effort. Or maybe it's me who follows with slight difficulty. "Is your marriage legit now?"

"Yeah, the irony... Corm finally relented and got me the marriage certificate, and it turns out I never needed it."

"So your deal with him is over?" Cora asks.

That gives me pause. On paper, there is no reason for me to stick around anymore.

After last night, I feel our deal is over anyway. Or rather, he wants me to stay for him. not for another benefit.

The thought thrills me. Intrigues me. Scares the shit out of me.

It was easy to succumb to his vows last night when I was dazed from my need for him, and then later from all the orgasms.

It was harder to believe them when I woke up. No longer hormone-influenced, I panicked a bit.

Now, with some space and distance between us, I don't know what I feel.

Confused. Excited. Terrified. Belonging.

The last one is a mixed feeling, though. The man made it clear how much he wants me. He cared for me even before he declared his intent to give us a real try.

If I'm honest, I want him too. The idea of putting aside our hatred and leaning into this undiscovered territory is appealing.

And it's the only area where I don't feel lost. With him by my side, I feel like something is going well in my life.

But can I find my other parts, rediscover myself, if I'm with him? If I'm his?

"He still hasn't signed the deal that was dependent on his image lift," I say.

"And you care about his needs since...?" Cora asks.

"That!" Lily clings her cup against Cora's. "Have you developed feelings for the hot devil?"

I giggle. "We might have entered into a new phase of our relationship." I bite my lip.

"Like beyond the bed-rrrooo..." Lily shakes her head. "Bedroom?"

I want to say yes, but we have experienced little beyond the bedroom since we decided—or rather Corm ordered—that we are trying this for real. I chuckle. "He *is* smoking hot."

"True." Cora sighs.

Shit, did I say that out loud? "We're exploring."

Cora chuckles. "They are exploring, Lily. Lily?"

Our friend is snoring softly, her head lolling.

"Shit, you got her drunk," I tell Cora, and for some strange reason it makes me giggle again.

"Me?" Cora looks offended. "I'm pretty sure I only poured the first two." She sways in her seat.

"Shit. I should go home."

"Because your honey is waiting."

"Hell will freeze before Corm Quinn can be called honey."

Cora snorts. "Yeah, no honeys in Hell."

"Hey." I punch... the air since I miss her arm. "You're right. He's a devil. My devil."

"Ma'am, are you okay?"

"What?" I jump, meeting the driver's eyes in the rearview mirror.

Disoriented, I look around. I'm in front of Corm's house. Shit, did I fall asleep in the cab?

I wipe the drool from my face and get out, grateful the ground isn't moving. Not too much, anyway.

The early evening's fresh air hits my skin with cool relief. I'm still tipsy—that was a quick death—but the snooze in the car helped me a bit.

It didn't help with my situation, but I'm not as drunk as I was when I left Cora to deal with Lily. Poor thing. We should have been more responsible with her.

I stumble up the few steps, leaning on the balustrade. I push the door open and trip over the stupid threshold.

"Ouch," I yelp as my knees hit the tiles.

And finally, my life pushes me down to my knees,

ladies and gentlemen. Quite literally. But for whatever reason, my current unflattering position breaks something inside me, and the angst of the last few weeks releases through a snort... or a giggle... or I don't know what the sound is.

It starts a chain reaction, and I tremble on the floor with a half-laugh and half-cry. The tears are of an alcohol-induced irrational joy, and of desperation.

"Saar." Corm's voice comes from somewhere in the house.

My soul melts a little. It *is* like honey.

"What happened? Are you okay?" He squats beside me.

I wipe the hair from my face and look at him. Holy shit. His facial muscles are full of tension, a line creasing across his forehead. His face is full of worry.

And blindingly beautiful. It's like he got even better looking while I was gone. I reach to trace my fingers around the scruff of his rigid jaw. "You're so beautiful."

He tilts his head and swears under his breath. "You're drunk."

He cups my elbow and tries to help me up. Unfortunately, the floor exudes a super potent gravitational field today. I slip or stumble or something, but the result is that I'm still more horizontal than upright. And hilarious.

God, it's good to laugh. "I'm not that drunk anymore. I slept in the taxi. Wait... not a taxi—in an Uber. You don't call it... like when you use the app; do you still call it a taxi? Is taxi a service or the actual yellow car?"

"For fuck's sake." He scoops me up bridal-style. "Let me get you to bed."

"I don't want to sleep. Let's sit together on the patio. Maybe you can start the fire." I grin at him. "I like when you carry me."

He sighs, but he heads toward the patio. "Did you eat?"

"Hm, don't be mad. I have been really trying to eat regu... re-gura-ri-ly. Fuck, that's a hard word, but I didn't get a chance today."

My answer changes his trajectory, and he now heads to the kitchen where he sits me on the stool.

"You're mad." I pout.

He wraps his arms around me and smothers me in a hug. It's comforting and worshiping, and kind of worrying.

"What's wrong, Corm?"

He kisses the crown of my head. "Nothing, The Morrigan; I was worried."

"Why?" I hiccup. "Oops."

"Let me make you something to eat." He saunters to the fridge, and my gaze lands on his ass. He's wearing a pair of dark gray sweats, and he's positively edible.

"You should cook naked." I slide from the stool.

He chuckles, shaking his head. "Should I now?" The heat in his eyes sobers me up. A little.

My pussy awakens, full of memories from last night, and even more full of yearning. "Yes, I'll join you."

Shaking his head again, he puts a dish into the oven. "Well, at least you're an adorable drunk."

He opens the fridge and hands me an electrolyte drink. "Chug it."

While there is a ghost of a smile playing on his lips, I can now see how exhausted he looks. I unscrew the cup. "Is everything okay?"

"You mean besides all the shit that is not okay currently?"

Another dose of sober pills. "Well, yes, but you look more worried. What's going on, Corm? Do you regret marrying me already?" I keep grinning for some reason.

His eyes bore into me, his expression fierce. "The only thing I regret is that it took this long to get here."

He leaves to get something in the pantry, and I drink because it's easier than to look for the appropriate response to his admission.

It's also probably helpful to sober me up a little more, so I can have a proper conversation with him.

I should tell him about my trust fund. But I fear he'd go into a full-blown Corm-to-the-rescue mode, and it will only piss me off.

He returns with a tray as the oven dings. The scent of thyme and tomatoes permeates the space between us as he scoops some pasta into a plate.

"You ate already?" I ask, trying to ignore the eerie feeling sneaking inside me. Something is off, but I don't quite know what.

"I'm not hungry. Let's go." He picks up the tray now laden with my plate, cutlery, and a large glass of water.

"Where?"

"Your favorite place in the house." He walks to the large glass patio entrance.

"How do you know it's my favorite part of the house?" But of course he does. He notices things about me, sometimes before I do.

"It's where I went down on you the first time." He pushes at the door handle with his elbows.

I roll my eyes and follow him, the stupid grin still tugging at my lips.

While I finish the most delicious pasta I've ever had, Corm makes the fire. Sitting beside me, he takes my empty plate from me and hands me the water.

The food and the liquid have sobered me up, and I sigh as he wraps his arm around me. We haven't kissed since before the Vito-geddon. I should just turn and press my lips against his.

Though kissing feels very intimate right now, and something feels off.

We watch the dancing flames in silence, and I try not to project, but Corm emanates tension even as he pulls me closer to him.

What a beautiful setup for a romantic evening—not that I'm into romance—but I'm consumed with insecurities.

Does he regret last night? Our conversation? Or rather, his declaration? Did he change his mind? Is he upset I didn't wake him up before I left?

Fuck this. If we're trying this for real, I'm not going to construct and guess. "What is wrong?" I ask.

"What did the lawyer say?" he asks at the same time.

I shift around on the seat, so I'm facing him, cross-legged. "My father dissolved my trust fund."

I never wanted my father's money in the first place. I went after it out of sheer necessity. In fact, only because Vito encouraged it.

He made me believe I deserved the hand-down from people who should have been there for me many times in my life, but they never were.

And still, my father's decision stinks. It hurts while it shouldn't. It spreads misery it doesn't warrant. It burns inside me like acid, spreading through my organs slowly and painfully.

"How do you feel about it?" Corm takes my hand in his large warm one, but his gaze remains on the fire.

For a man who glares and stares, he's avoiding eye contact a lot tonight.

"I mean, I was broke before, so that's not a new feeling. I don't know, getting drunk probably wasn't the best way to assess or address the feelings, but it was a good way to delay my real reaction."

"I'm sorry." He bows his head, sighing.

This is not a sorry about the discovery. This sorry feels more significant. He's not telling me something—

"You knew?" I search his face, hoping for his denial, but it isn't there.

He finally meets my eyes and nods. "Yes."

"How?" That is really not a question that matters at the moment, but my mind is misfiring in too many directions.

He looks at me deadpan. "The same way I knew you were at the club last night. Or what happened with your money."

I push off the seat and slide farther from him. "How long have you known?"

He pinches the bridge of his nose. "For a while."

"So you knew I don't need this deal, and you didn't tell me?"

I spring up and round the fire-pit table, creating a distance between us. I'm hurt, disappointed, outraged, confused. All at once.

In the absence of being able to yell at Vito or my father, Corm becomes a very satisfying target.

He stands up, our gazes colliding. I glare, and he pleads.

Standing above the flames, the yellow flickers of the fire dance across his beautiful face. And just looking at him is devastating.

I was shell-shocked when I found out about Vito's betrayal—this—Jesus, was it only this morning?

I was deflated and hurt when I found out my father had disinherited me.

But neither of those revelations—however negative —gutted me as much as Corm's admission.

The man across from me has been in my life for the shortest time, and yet it's agonizing to realize I'm just a puppet in his show.

Just like I've been all my life.

"So you trapped me in this arrangement, even though you knew my only reason was no longer valid?"

"Saar." He sighs, closing his eyes briefly.

I chuckle humorlessly. "Don't Saar me. Let's do this for real?" I mock. "It's just a deal for you, after all."

"That's not true," he roars. His nostrils inflate. He clenches his fists.

"So what, you kept that tidbit from me because you just fucking have to control everything?"

"I'm not trying to control you. I was trying to protect you. Protect us."

"Protect us? There is no us, Corm. There was your illusion of wanting to own me. Demanding to own me. Well, fuck you. I'm leaving. I've been controlled by my father and then by Vito all my fucking life, I'm not staying with another asshole." I rush toward the house, away from him.

"Don't you fucking dare compare me to them." He follows.

I whip around, glaring at him. "Then tell me, where is the difference?"

"I fucking didn't tell you because I knew you'd leave."

"And then you wouldn't get your fucking deal."

He grabs my upper arms and pulls me to him like he wants to shake me. "Because I wanted you to stay."

"So you fucking wanted to manipulate me into a relationship?"

He sighs and closes his eyes again. His grip loosens, and I should run up to pack, but I don't move.

I don't move because there is hurt in his normally

calculating expression. Or I'm wishing for it to be there.

"It was a mistake," he says finally, and lets go of my arms. "I didn't want to lose you."

There is so much fucking honesty in that statement, it takes my breath away. This is so fucked-up. "So instead of asking me to stay, you tricked me into it?"

"You wouldn't have stayed." The finality of his conviction startles me. He truly believes I wouldn't.

"Is this the reason you were delaying the marriage certificate?"

He flinches. "I was delaying it because I wanted to see how serious your gambling issue was... and I guess I was hoping you would *want* to marry me eventually."

I blink. "You're an idiot."

"That's clear now. Damn it, Saar, I fucked up. I was going to tell you after last night, but with everything about fucking Vito, and then you just left before I had a chance."

Never have I thought I would hear desperation in Corm's voice, or see it in his face. But it's there, and it's mingled with remorse.

The problem is, I want to stay. I want to forget and be with him. I hadn't even realized how quickly this house became my home.

As fucked up as it is, I never truly had one, so I

guess the little girl in me was just too eager to accept this situation as her home.

And as controlling as he is, Corm is caring and smart. Lonely like me, and a bit lost like me. He's been encouraging and patient with me.

But I need to stand on my own two feet; otherwise, I can never trust again, to truly lean into a relationship.

I need to focus on my relationship with me, my body. I need to find myself, so I have something to offer in a relationship.

"I can't stay." My words squeeze at my stomach, spreading a nauseating pain. "Even if I forgave your manipulation, I would be completely dependent on you, jumping into the same fucked-up dynamic I've lived all my life."

I turn and enter the house. Trudging toward the staircase, I try to swallow the stupid tears.

"No." Corm's voice halts me as I put a foot on the first step.

I don't turn, but I don't move forward. His footsteps approach, but he stops before coming too close.

Still, his scent hits me like the most potent drug, weakening my resolution.

"Don't go anywhere. Stay here. I'll go."

Sighing, I turn to look at him. "That makes no sense."

"Humor me." He steps toward me. "It's late; all

your things are here. It makes no sense for you to leave now. Let me help you, please. Stay here. I won't bother you. You take your time, hating me, thinking about things. Whatever you need."

I want to back away, and at the same time lean closer. "I can't take away your house from you, even for a short time. I don't want to owe you and—"

"Then take that job finally, so money is not an issue in your head."

Jesus, it's easy for him to say. "It's not an issue in my head only."

"As far as I'm concerned, it is. I will take care of you, whether you like it or not."

It's strange when, after years of being lonely, I have someone forcing their attention on me so fiercely. It's wrong, and yet intoxicating.

"Why?"

I should go upstairs, pack, and leave, and yet, deep down in my heart, I know his intentions are noble, not scheming. Are about me, not about that stupid deal.

His execution is all fucked-up, but despite being betrayed brutally in the last few weeks, months, years, I still trust this man. Or for some stupid reason, I really, truly want to.

I trust you, not because you gave me any reasons to trust you, but because somewhere deep down, I feel like you're the answer.

Just like he confessed his feelings last night.

So I seek his confirmation for my insanity.

Because there is another thing I know deep down. If I leave now, we would be over, and I would be even more lost than I am now.

He takes my hand and kisses my knuckles. "Haven't I made myself clear yet? I love you, Saar."

This should not make me want to stay, but it does. It does. Perhaps I'm a person who needs an audience to shine.

Who needs someone to support her and remind her who she is when she is lost. And maybe I always chose the wrong person before.

Maybe I can find myself while I feel safe and cared for. Even if I have to fight for my independence every step of the way.

Especially since the fight with this stubborn bastard ignites me more than anything else currently.

"Can you try to understand how hard this is for me? I gave you control in the bedroom, but in real life you can't bully your way into my life. I need to think about everything."

All my trust issues bubble to the surface and fight an ugly, bloody fight with my need to be loved. Loved by this controlling, demanding man who makes sure I eat regularly.

Will I give up on myself if I stay? Or will I give

myself a better chance to find myself?

He nods and kisses my forehead. "I understand, baby. Get a job, so you can gain your independence and stand up on your own two feet. Because you're capable, and there is no doubt in my mind you will succeed."

Oh, what his praise does to me. And what it means to have someone believing in me. More than I believe in myself.

"Thank you," I say simply, overwhelmed by his sincerity and by the unwarranted hope blooming inside me.

This man loves me.

He cups my face and kisses me gently. It's just a peck, but the tremor it triggers is unreal, silencing the faint voice that is telling me I'm giving up too quickly. But perhaps this is just surrendering instead of fighting the inevitable.

"Find your ground, The Morrigan, but you're fucking doing it from this house, and while I'm by your side."

I open my mouth, but he captures my lips in an arresting kiss. And perhaps, sometimes, you need a controlling person in your life so you can fight harder for yourself.

And fight I start. "That's—"

He puts a finger on my lips. "Non-negotiable."

Chapter 25

Corm

She pulls away. "This is what I'm talking about—"

"You're talking about leaving me. And I can give you all the autonomy, but I can't let you do that."

"But you can't order me to stay here."

"Unfortunately."

"Corm—"

"No, let me talk now. I'm the person who betrayed you, just like Vito or your father. I take full responsibility for it. I kept things from you for my personal gain, but that gain had nothing to do with my ego, or a need to get richer, or just simply getting off on manipulating you."

God, the humble pie tastes like shit.

"I shouldn't have done it. I should have told you

about the trust fund and hoped. Hoped that you would still stay. But I've never tried to hope. Hope terrifies me. And you, Saar van den Linden, expose me to that futile emotion daily. I operate with facts and certainty. I balance risk and profit. And I make a decision. Selfish decisions."

She studies me, and it's like she sees me for the first time. Like despite her reluctance to trust me, she does.

"You really love me?" she asks, and I hate the doubt in her voice.

I hate that the people in her life, who should have protected her, damaged her so badly that she won't ever trust anyone.

I hate that my own needs and desires drew us into this standstill.

"I really, truly, deeply do. But I understand you see my words as another attempt to manipulate you."

She sighs and sinks down, taking a seat on the stairs. "I don't think I feel much at the moment. I'm torn between us and me. Between trust and leap. Between past and future. Between giving up and trying."

"I'll go and sleep somewhere else. For as long as you need. I'll give you space. It might kill me, but I will step aside, so you can step forward."

I take her hand, and she lets me. A win.

I look at her, and the corners of her mouth curl up slightly. Another win.

I hold my breath, and finally, she nods. A home run.

"Stay. It's your house. And I'm going to stay here as well. In the guest room. Not because you deserve it, or because I really fucking have nowhere to go. I'm going to stay here to give us a chance."

I vividly remember many exhilarating moments in my life. When my father got me my first Ferrari when I was a stupid teenager. When I made my first million. When I closed the first deal at Merged. And many fleeting blissful moments in between.

But the freight train of emotions that destroys me at her reluctant but genuine commitment is so overwhelming that I want to run away just to deal with them.

Instead, I pull her to me and hold her tight. "I'll take that, The Morrigan; I'll take that."

"You're still on probation," she mumbles into my chest.

"Good girl," I whisper into her hair. "Don't let anyone take your power away from you."

"I hate my father." She sags into me.

"He deserves that."

"I hate Vito."

"Me too."

We sit in silence, the enormity of everything slowly seeping through.

"My father had muscular dystrophy." I'm not even sure why I am bringing this up now. "Declan got tested and he isn't a carrier. I didn't want to know. I didn't want to deal with the implications of positive genetic test results.

"Instead, I lived my life like nothing matters, chasing my mortality, not really applying myself anywhere. Because, here is the twist, I thought not knowing would spare me, but it did the exact opposite. Without realizing, I acted like my life didn't matter. As we all know, it only got worse after Dad passed."

She squeezes my hand, and while I stare into the foyer where a large vase of fresh flowers creates more home than this house ever did, I still can sense her eyes on me. And I know they are full of compassion. Because that's who this woman is.

Love and compassion.

I swallow around the lump in my throat. "I think he left me that letter to tell me I'm not a carrier. That I can open up to a commitment. And I'll deny ever admitting this, but it scares the shit out of me. And yet not committing to us is scarier."

I turn to look at her. She moves my hand to her lap and just holds it there in silence. It's like she is holding my heart, though. When she lifts her gaze, finally, there is a new level of softness on her face.

"I'm scared to trust you."

"I know, baby. I'll prove you can, and in the meantime, kick me every time I make decisions for you."

A gleam of mischief flickers through her sad eyes. "Can I aim for your crotch?"

"That wouldn't be good for your other needs." I smirk.

She chuckles humorlessly.

I pull her to my lap, and she doesn't really cooperate but doesn't fight me either. It's like we reached this tentative truce, but it's so fragile, it can shatter at any moment.

Our lives are still filled with unresolved issues. Our relationship is still undefined. But at least she is here.

"I will gladly take any pain, all the hurt, if that makes you feel better, Saar."

"Still sleeping in the office?" Declan takes a seat on my sofa without invitation.

Fucking Roxy. Does everyone know about that?

"Since when do I have an open-door policy?" I growl.

I'm tired, and frankly I'm annoyed by the amount

of work. For the first time since we opened these offices, I don't want to be here.

I want to be with Saar. Or I just... Well, I want to be with her, but I'm fucking scared like a little boy that she won't be home when I return.

We agreed last night she'd stay, but I still fear she may have been overwhelmed in the moment. That with me gone, at work, she has enough time and space to realize she doesn't need me.

I should have worked from home. I would have concentrated better without constantly thinking about her. Just being closer to her.

And I wouldn't have to deal with unwanted visitors. I glare at Declan.

"I'm here as your brother, not for work." He glares right back.

I don't know what it is with the Quinn men and scowling, but if there is someone who rivals my non-verbal threats, it's definitely my sibling.

"I will go visit Mom. I'm bringing Saar to meet her this weekend." I assume the reason for his visit.

"Good for you. Mom will be happy." He pulls his phone from his inside breast pocket.

I guess my assumption was wrong. "What's going on?"

He taps a few times on his screen and turns it to me. Reluctantly—there are still projections to plow through and Saar waiting, hopefully—I round my desk and sit across from him.

"What am I looking at?"

"Kendra is getting married."

Fuck. I read the announcement, and sure enough, Declan's ex-wife is getting hitched with some oil heir in Texas. "So? Good for her."

In three short years, the woman was married twice after Declan granted her divorce. Both times to some loser, costing Declan money. I guess she upgraded her lifestyle.

"She reached out. She wants shared custody."

"No fucking way. She can't abandon the babies and then waltz back into their life." I put his phone down.

"I agree with that. Every reasonable judge would probably agree with that. The problem is, now she has money to fight me on that."

I pinch the bridge of my nose. "Fuck. I'm sorry."

"Yeah. I'd even consider the arrangement, because they need a mother. But she abandoned them twice before."

He's been blaming himself for this way more than he should. The credit goes to that heartless woman. "At least they don't remember it."

"But they will this time."

"Fuck, bro, can I help somehow?"

"I would ask you to be my character witness, but I'm not sure your notoriety would work in my favor." He smirks. "You can distract me with a glass of your Macallan."

"Only one. I want to get home." I drop his phone to the table and walk to my liquor cabinet.

"So you're not sleeping in the office?"

"It's complicated." I pour us both an inch.

"Of course it is. Nothing is ever easy with you."

I twist the cork and re-shelve the bottle. "What do you mean?"

"You're a stubborn bastard. When you set your mind to something, there is no reasoning with you."

I'm a reasonable man. If the other party is reasonable.

I return to the table. "You don't mind when my focus makes you money."

"Fair enough, but even with my poor record, I don't think your power-tripping tendencies are good for a relationship. You're like Dad." He takes the glass from me.

I take a sip. I hate when Declan is right. The man doesn't speak much, but when he does, he hits the bull's-eye every single time.

"He wasn't my biological father."

I ignore his power-tripping-tendencies comment and their implication on my relationships.

But as soon as I throw the juicy tidbit out there, something inside me dislodges.

Saar was right, keeping that rage inside me only made things worse. Confessing to Declan didn't lift the level of betrayal, but it still felt good. Like the first step on the road to acceptance.

"Bullshit—" His eyes widen as he connects the dots. "Is that what was in his letter?"

I nod, raising my glass in a mock toast. "I've been so mad at him... Well, never mind. You know how I reacted."

"Is that why you don't visit Mom? Fuck, who is your father?"

"I don't care. He was a sperm donor as far as I'm concerned. Dad was my father, even if I'm so fucking angry with him. With both of them."

"Fuck."

"You know what is the most pathetic thing? I'm mad at them, not for not telling me sooner, but for telling me at all."

"I'm sorry. This is fucked up. Why would he do it?"

"I guess after I refused to get tested for MD, he decided to let me know I can't be a carrier."

"As I said, you're just like him. He wanted something, and he forced you to accept it. For your own good, but it still sucks, doesn't it?" Now it is his turn to raise his glass. "Like father, like son."

Several of my interactions with Saar flicker through my mind. Fuck, did I make her feel the same way my father's last deed made me feel?

The situation is different, but the means are very similar. I've been manipulating our arrangement, trapping her.

Limiting her choice because I know I'm her best option. Because I want her to realize I'm the only option for her.

That I'm her answer.

I know she can't trust me because of the other men in her life, but what if that is just an excuse to distance herself from my… well, my bullying?

Fuck. Fuck. Fuck.

"I need to go home." I put my unfinished glass down and snatch my jacket from the back of my chair. "Let me know if there is anything I can do about the Kendra bullshit."

Of course, the fucking traffic concentrates on all the roads I need to take to get home. I should have used my helicopter.

It takes me a good hour before I reach my house. The lights are on in the dining room. What? We haven't used that room since Saar turned it into a fucking burger joint.

I rush inside, not even sure what I'm trying to achieve. Like if I'm beside her faster, she can forget how I've been treating her?

After dropping my keys and wallet on the console table, I cross the foyer and pause at the entrance to my living room.

My furniture is back. The room is put together like it was before Saar moved in. A blanket of panic cloaks me.

Is she gone? Did she leave the house in its previous condition? Like a good tenant?

I want to call her name, but fuck, I'm scared. What if I call her name and there is no answer?

I rush to check on the dining room, because in some fucked-up logic I hope it's still a diner, and that would prove that... I don't fucking know what.

I glimpse a new flower arrangement in the foyer. Not my statue. Is that her farewell gift?

When I spy my fucking Italian table, my heart sinks. But then my eyes land on its corner. It's set for two, with flowers and a candlestick and two place settings.

A new painting hangs on the wall that actually fits here really well. New items adorn the buffet table. It's my old dining room, but with new touches. Saar's touches.

The panic lifts, followed by trepidation. Jesus, the range of emotions this relationship wrangles out of me is becoming health-threatening. And now I'm apparently a drama queen. Fuck.

With the bout of anxiety subsided, I now notice that a delicious smell of garlic and curry permeates the air. I don't find Saar in the kitchen, so I head outside.

Sure enough, bundled in one of her knitted shawls, she is staring into the flames, her legs curled under her.

She's a fucking vision. I'm rooted to the ground for a beat before I can breathe finally. "You're here," I rasp.

She turns and smiles. "You're back."

I rush to her and pull her close, seizing her lips. She tenses at first, but then wraps her arms around me and yields to me.

"Hi." She smiles when we pull apart.

"Hi yourself."

"I cooked you dinner." Dark shadows line her eyes. She probably hasn't slept much again. Fuck.

"And you redesigned again."

She smiles. "Yeah, I realized I didn't give you much reason to believe you can be reasonable with me."

"Baby, if you really want to have a tacky, over-cluttered living room, we will have that."

"God, no, we wouldn't be able to entertain." She

wraps her arms around my waist, and I want to stay here like this forever.

"What's for dinner?"

"Curry chicken with roasted baby potatoes."

"Fuck. Those cooking classes in Tuscany paid off."

She laughs, and it hits me straight in my chest.

I'm going to stay here to give us a chance.

I guess she truly meant it.

"I spoke with Nora Flemming today." Saar blows her tea, holding it close to herself.

My wife can cook. Like she's a fucking goddess in the kitchen. After we ate, we came back out here.

I haven't used this patio much before. Once, maybe twice, since I've moved here. It's slowly but surely becoming my favorite place in the house. But I guess any place is my favorite if she is there with me.

"Did you take the job?" I draw lazy circles on her shoulder.

"I did. I'm officially a podcast host. I'm recording my first show on Monday." She bites her lip.

"You're going to be great."

She beams at me now. "Thank you for believing in me."

"Always." I take her tea from her and put it on the

table. Cupping her face, I dust her lips with mine. "I missed you."

"I want a divorce."

The warmth of the fire ceases. The tentatively lighter atmosphere between us shatters. My heart stops and restarts in a new distorted rhythm.

"No."

I don't think your power-tripping tendencies are good for a relationship.

"Why?" I add begrudgingly, because no amount of talking about it will make me ever agree to that.

She sighs. "I realized today that if I'm to give this thing between us a chance, I don't want the fake marriage to be a part of that. I want us to date."

"Why would you lead with the divorce part, woman?" I cup her neck and pull her in for another kiss. "I love you, Saar. And if it's wining and dining and dating you need from me, then that's what you're getting."

"Thank you."

"But do we really need to divorce?"

"I don't know. I just think we need a clean slate."

"This is our clean slate, baby. You choosing us and staying, even though you can't trust me yet. You staying while choosing you and taking the job. You cooking me dinner when I come home. You making me want to be a better man."

"I'm failing miserably on the last one," she teases.

"But you're not giving up, and that's what counts."

She stifles a yawn. I want to bring her upstairs and cherish her in all the ways imaginable, but she needs to sleep more.

"Let's go for a ride."

"What? You're sexy enough; you don't need to dazzle me with your flashy cars."

My cock twitches. Fuck, I'm a goner.

Definitely a goner, because I drag her with me so I can drive her around; otherwise, she doesn't get any sleep.

And as she dozes off in the passenger seat later while I drive aimlessly, I plan all the dates I will take her on. And all the vacations I will give her to compensate for the years she didn't take any.

We drive for hours. My wife sleeping, and me blissfully unaware that I won't be able to take her on any of those dates.

Chapter 26

Saar

CORA

I listened to your first episode. Loved it.

LILY

Me too. You're so relatable and the topic was interesting.

CELESTE

So proud of you, babe.

Thank you. I'm having so much fun with it.

CORA

When are you all coming here? It's been ages.

LILY

I met a guy.

CORA

OMG, now you have to come.

LILY

(Heart emoji)

What about the mystery voice at work?

LILY

He is just a fantasy. It's not like I can tell my client his voice is hot.

CELESTE

You have to tell us everything.

CELESTE

Coffee today?

Adoration.

Full, uncensored, slightly salacious adoration.

That's what I find in Corm's gaze when I descend the stairs.

"Fuck, you're breathtaking," he drawls.

I'm wearing a stunning, deep navy satin gown. It's a one-shoulder, floor-length fitted piece that clings to my waist and hips, before it flows down in a straight, streamlined shape.

The dress would be simple if it wasn't for the bold detail—a large sculptural bow on the shoulder. It's big enough that I don't need a necklace.

And the dress is too long to show my heels fully, so I paired it with large, statement earrings.

I've worn a gazillion dresses in my life, and I've

been adored by thousands when wearing them. But never, ever have I felt as beautiful as today. It's partly the beautiful dress, but it's mostly the raw admiration in Corm's eyes.

"Thank you." I finally reach the ground floor, beaming at him. "You cleaned up nicely, too."

A major understatement. This man can fucking rock a tux better than James Bond. Seriously, I think tuxedos were invented for him only. All the other men are riding the wave, but not coming even a close second to my husband.

My husband.

It's been two weeks since I asked him to grant me a divorce. In that time, he has made my life a fairy tale. Not that I ever realized I needed one. Or wanted one.

But this man excels at everything, so what did I expect? I must say that dating my husband is an unexpected delight.

To the point—not that I told him yet—that I'm not interested in that divorce anymore. I guess the man gets what he wants after all, and I'm defenseless against him.

We're good together. While I'm still waiting for him to betray me—that's some hard shit to break—I choose to trust him one day at a time. And what days we've had.

I've been happy these past two weeks. Besides

dating Corm, I started recording the podcast and streamed the first episode, with almost a million downloads. Now, I know the success is due to Nora Flemming's marketing genius, but I didn't disappoint.

We uploaded the second episode two days ago, and it surpassed the first one. What's more important, I'm having fun.

I started seeing a therapist twice a week to work through my parental issues and Vito's betrayal. It's a long journey, but just taking charge and owning the issue gave me a much-needed self-confidence boost.

"Now you just want to get into my pants," Corm teases.

He is not wrong. It's been two weeks since we stayed in the sex club, and I've been staying in the guest room.

I think he's waiting for me to initiate, truly giving me space. And our date nights end up in this awkward dance in the hallway by our bedrooms when Corm gives me a peck on my forehead, wishes me a good night, and leaves quickly.

Probably to take care of his raging erection. And every night, I hope I can just drag him into my bed or drop to my knees right there in the hall.

But something stops me. It's like if we went back to being intimate, I would be exposed again. Vulnerable. Prone to get hurt.

I know I can still get hurt. I know abstinence is not going to prevent it. It makes no sense, and yet… it's like my last line of defense.

But it's getting harder every single night. And seeing him in that stupid tux, desire pools between my legs. There is no way to put it more delicately. I'm horny as a teenager.

"Am I succeeding?" I wipe a piece of lint from his lapel and keep my hands on his chest, the fabric soft under my palm.

"Don't," he warns.

"This dress is tight, but if we're careful, I might drop to my knees for you in the car."

He groans. "If you drop to your knees, this dress won't survive it. Nothing about the things I would do to you could be described as careful."

His gaze is dangerous. Dangerously tempting.

I swallow.

I lick my lips.

I'm pretty sure I stop breathing.

Fuck the dress. But the thought is erased as soon as he grabs my hand and drags me out.

"Oh," is all I manage.

"Come on, Saar. I have a deal to close, and I'm in a hurry."

"Apparently," I grumble, disappointed.

He opens the door of his Escalade. "In a hurry to come back and fuck my wife."

Corm makes that displeased sound he does when something doesn't go his way. It's somewhere between a sigh and a growl. It's so distinctively his that despite its undertone, I find it sexy.

I guess living with a sex god and not taking advantage of it can drive a girl crazy.

"What's wrong?" I put my hand on his thigh.

He puts his phone away. "They still can't find him. I'm sorry."

He doesn't have to say who *he* is. Vito disappeared, and the authorities can't find him.

"Don't be sorry. It's not your fault. Frankly, I don't really care. It's not like he can return my money, or like finding him would lessen the damage."

"The good news is that my people made quite some progress in disentangling your name from his debts."

Corm has dedicated a lot of resources to making sure the debts, especially those from dangerous people, are not in my name. I don't know what it's costing him or how he does it, but I'm grateful I don't have to deal with it.

It's the only part of my financial past and present that I let him handle. I'm in charge of everything else. To Corm's dismay, I forced Cal and Finn to give me a loan. Well, to their dismay as well.

All three of them would just hand me the money, which I guess may be perceived as chivalrous, but it wouldn't allow me to learn how to take care of myself.

Cal was probably the only one who got it—Celeste's influence, no doubt —and agreed to a market value interest on his loan.

Corm is still sour about that, but he'll live.

"Thank you," I whisper, and stifle a yawn.

He looks at me with that intense, hooded gaze. "You'll thank me in about ninety minutes."

I chuckle. "That's awfully specific."

"It's an estimate, but I think between the traffic to the venue and the necessary time of schmoozing Vladislav, we should be right on time."

"Right on time?" I bite my lips, my pussy singing with need.

"For you to drop to your knees, and since it will be a post-evening occasion, we won't need to be careful about the dress."

"But I like the dress."

He looks at me like I've lost my mind, and then leans in, his breath fanning my ear. "I'm fucking my wife on the way home from the venue. If you want to save the dress, you could take it off before getting in."

"Oh, I thought we were trying to keep your image intact. I wear nothing under this dress, so taking it off will cause a scandal."

I shiver as the most satisfying growl reverberates through his body. "I'm already pissed about all the assholes seeing you in this dress. But alas, we'll have to rip it apart later."

"Will we now?" I tease, but I can't wait.

But Corm doesn't react. He's leaning forward, trying to see something through the window on my side.

"What the fuck, Saar?"

I follow his gaze but see only the pedestrians. Confused, I tilt my head sideways, and I see it.

"Oh, I forgot about that campaign. Jesus, I did that shoot like eight months ago."

Corm hits the button to open the window and take a better look, clenching his fists.

The billboard is a jewelry campaign, showing only my cleavage with a large necklace.

My hair tied back, I look like I've just come out of the shower, droplets of water scattered around my skin. I remember wearing a bikini, but I guess they went with my neckline only.

"You look naked," he growls.

"Maybe I was," I tease, but by the death glare he gives me, he may not be in the mood for jokes.

"I'm not having the entire city jerking off to this."

I try to stifle a chuckle. "You know, they have probably been jerking off to my pictures for years now."

His nostrils flare, and I'm worried the vein in his temple might pop. At the same time, I'm trying hard not to laugh.

"Are you jealous?" I bite the inside of my cheek, but I can't help it and grin.

His overreaction is kind of adorable. Stupid and possessive, but who knew I'm into that?

He takes a picture and starts typing furiously.

"What are you doing?" I ask, but his phone rings.

He picks up without a greeting, and I hear a woman talking on the other side.

"Just get it done, Roxy. Find out where else they feature the campaign and buy those spots as well. Outbid, bribe, kill someone if you must, but get those pictures down." He listens for a moment. "I don't fucking care—replace them with your nephew's drawings." He hangs up.

"I don't think it can be done." I shake my head, the warmth spreading inside me.

"Watch me," he snaps.

I fight my laugh, barely succeeding. "Well, even if

you somehow manage to cancel their campaign, it's going to cost you way more than it's worth."

"I'm not putting a price on your safety. Thank fucking God you're a podcaster now." He leans back, pinching the bridge of his nose.

"My safety? As much as I appreciate this abandoned display of jealousy, Corm, you're being ridiculous."

"My money. My wife. My decision."

When did I come to love his growls?

The blinking flashlights interrupt the ridiculous conversation. I flinch, bile rising in my stomach. Shit, I forgot the media would be here, snatching pics of the crème de la crème of Manhattan society.

The mood in the car shifts. As if Corm drops his brooding the minute he senses my discomfort. He wraps his arm around me and kisses my temple.

Without confirming with me, he knows. He hits the intercom. "How many cars in front of us?"

"About four, sir."

"Can you get us to the back entrance, please?"

"Sure. It will take us another fifteen to twenty minutes to outmaneuver the traffic and road closures."

"That's fine."

He smiles at me, and my chest explodes with fluttering wings and warmth. "We'll be late, and Betsy won't be happy we don't get photographed."

"Fuck Betsy. We'll arrive together, and that's what Vladislav needs to see."

"Thank you."

He lowers his lips to mine in a slow, languid kiss, and I moan into his mouth, leaning for more, for deeper, for longer.

But he pulls away, adjusting his pants. "Sorry, we can't. We'd never be able to get in."

I smile and lean my head against his shoulder, closing my eyes. *Home.*

Corm's lips touch my forehead, and I stir. His scent provides an intense sense of safety. I fidget a bit, still unwilling to open my eyes.

Waking up beside this man makes me almost not want to get up. I wish we didn't have to. Ever. Wait a minute? Am I in his bed?

I startle and sit up. "Oh my God, I fell asleep?"

The bow of my gown is all wrinkled and squashed. The car is moving, but we're crossing a bridge. I look from one window to the other. Brooklyn Bridge?

"Where are we?"

"I don't know." He glances out of the window. "You needed to sleep, so we drove around."

"What time is it?"

"Past midnight." He reaches to tuck a strand behind my ear. "You're beautiful."

"Did you go to the gala without me?"

He shakes his head.

I must be still dazed and slow from my sleep. "What do you mean? We missed it?"

He nods and takes my hand, kissing my knuckles. "The dress can come off now." He traces my skin around the rumpled bow.

While my pussy is totally on the same page as him, how can he think about that right now? "Corm, that deal was important to you. You've been waiting for that event for weeks."

"I know." He tugs at the bow, and the strap comes off my shoulder. He leans in, peppering my neckline with kisses.

My mind is now hazy from my sleep *and* from his gentle assault. I try to push him away. "You missed an important meeting, so I can sleep. That deal—"

"No deal is as important as your well-being. You needed to sleep."

Oh my poor heart. Jesus, I love this man.

I love him. The emotion sneaks up on me, unbidden. I need to tell him.

"Would you focus on getting that dress off, finally, The Morrigan?" He yanks at the hem of the neckline and my breasts spring out, the nipples already hard and yearning for his touch.

"Wait. I need to tell you something."

It would be the first time, and I don't want it to sound like an in-the-heat-of-the-moment statement.

He wraps his lips around my nipple, kneading the other one in his hand. God, I missed this. I missed his touch. My body is immediately aflame. It's not even heat I'm feeling. It's an inferno.

"Corm," I moan. I don't know if I'm moaning to stop him or to urge him to continue.

He pulls at the hem of the skirt, but it's too tight. "We agreed we don't care about this dress, didn't we?"

Not really, but I don't get to protest, because he doesn't wait and rips the skirt apart.

Everything else happens in the frenzy of touch and feel. Give and take. Control and surrender.

He sheds his jacket, and I undo his pants. He tears off the bodice of the dress, and it ends up discarded on the car's floor.

"Fuck, I missed this pussy, baby."

He spreads my legs so wide, I fear he might dislocate my hip joint. He blows air between my thighs where I'm already embarrassingly soaked. It triggers a series of shivers, my back arching away from the leather seat.

"This pussy is mine." He kisses me there, and then continues kissing me up my torso.

"All parts of me are yours." This will have to do for now instead of the L word.

He looks at me and abandons the languid assault, capturing my lips. "Sorry, baby, but I have to fuck you rough and fast first. It's been too long."

"Then stop talking," I tease, but it comes out with the same desperation that he oozes.

He arches his eyebrow, like I should be careful what I wish for, lines his cock at my entrance, and drives in.

We growl, and for a beat we still.

"The most tantalizing pussy in the world, Saar," he grunts. "Gripping my cock so well, baby."

And then he moves, and fuck, rough and fast doesn't even cover the intensity.

His belt is scratching my thigh. Our moans fill the car. The leather beneath me is sticky. Nothing about this feels sensual or attractive.

It's animalistic. It's wild. It's savage.

Exactly what I need. I'm weightless and floating. Completely at his mercy, surrendering and cruising so high, I don't even know if I'm still in this dimension.

Somehow we climax at the same time, which only prolongs the ride, squeezing every last drop of bliss from us.

"Are you okay?" Corm rasps into the crook of my neck, trying to shift his weight a bit.

Sprawled on the seat horizontally, somehow he fits on top of me, and I didn't even realize he was cutting off my oxygen supply.

But that his first thought goes to my wellbeing again makes my eyes water. "I'm better than okay." My voice trembles, and Corm looks at me, his eyes filled with adoration.

"I—"

I don't get to say the words.

"Shit." He looks up. "Why are we not moving?"

We both scramble to sit, only to realize we're home. Home? When did that happen? It's been Corm's house until... until it wasn't.

Corm picks up his jacket and wraps it around me. "Put this on."

I slide my arms into his sleeves while he zips up. Opening the door, he helps me out.

My legs shaking from the earth-shattering orgasm, I lean into him, but he pulls away, studying me with a heated gaze.

"Fuck, I might need you to dress like this all the time. So sexy." His eyes roam over my body, lost in his jacket, down my naked legs to my heels. "You feel so mine right now."

The driver leaves to park in the garage, but we

don't move and just stare at each other, heat and adoration swirling between us.

The air is thick with a storm about to break. My own heartbeat feels louder in my head than it should be.

I step closer, and open my mouth to finally tell him.

"Saar." A familiar voice cuts through the air.

I whip toward the gate where it came from and my stomach sinks, confirming my fear.

Vito.

Corm moves, but before he can step in front of me, my body tenses before my brain catches up.

The sound.

I've only ever heard it in movies. Sharp and final, it shatters the air.

"No," Corm screams.

For a beat I don't feel anything, my mind stuck in that moment of disbelief, not processing what is happening.

White-hot, searing pain explodes in my head. I think. I feel it kind of everywhere. My body seizes, and the ground tilts. Before I hit it, Corm's arms are there.

The scent of him envelopes me. *Home.*

"Saar, baby," he yells. Or whispers, I'm not sure.

My vision swims, darkening at the edges. I open my mouth and try to focus on the task. I need to tell him.

Why am I drowning? There is no water around me, but I feel like I'm submerged. The pain is fading, but the numbness that follows is even more terrifying.

Focus, Saar. He's so beautiful. His lips keep moving, but I can't make out the words. His face blurs, frantic and scared.

Don't be scared, love. I love you. I open my mouth, but I can't speak.

I love you.

The thought flickers through my mind, the words so clear, so final.

I open my mouth again, but the world is slipping away.

I love you.

Chapter 27

Corm

The double door springs open, and I glimpse familiar faces and stop my pacing.

Cal and his wife barrel in. Their shoes squeak obscenely on the linoleum floor, adding another atrocity to the disinfectant-infused air and my overall agony.

The harsh fluorescent light casts a menacing look on my business partner's face, but as he gets closer, the look remains.

It's full of fury, worry, and helplessness. It mirrors the turmoil swirling inside me.

Cal's expression hardens as he takes in my blood-stained shirt. His nostrils flare, and he clenches his fists. It does shit for his composure, because he still launches at me.

Gripping my collar, he pushes me against the wall.

"You fucking use my sister, and then you can't protect her?"

I push him off, but secretly, I want him to punch me. Not to give me an excuse to return the hit, but to finally feel some other pain. Physical pain is so much easier to deal with.

"Really?" I smirk. "She was shot by a man who had been taking advantage of her for years. Where the fuck were you all that time?"

"Merde." Cal's wife puts her hand on his shoulder. It's a tender touch followed by stern words. "Stop it right now, you idiots." She looks at me. "Where is she? What's the status?"

Her hand on his shoulder has an immediate effect. He's still vibrating with anger and worry, but he exhales heavily.

Something I haven't been able to do for the past two hours. I fucking hate him for having that level of comfort. For having his person beside him.

Accusing Cal of anything is a shitty thing to do, but I want to do shitty things right now.

I want to kill someone—Vito, in the first place—and punish someone for what happened to Saar tonight. And all the years before tonight.

I want to take my anger out on someone because I'm a coward. Because it's easier to throw punches than to look in the mirror and accept that it's all my fault.

I should have prevented that.

If only I had stepped in front of her faster. If only I had increased the security after Vito disappeared. If only we had come home earlier. The *if onlys* have been eating me alive.

"She is in surgery. One bullet grazed her head. The other one ended in her arm. They are taking it out right now."

Cal rakes his hair and swears. Celeste takes a fortifying breath, tears pooling in her eyes as she rubs her pregnant belly.

"Okay," she says. "Cal, send someone to get a clean shirt for him. I'm going to call Lily and Cora." She goes into action mode, like that can make the situation better. She turns to me. "Is your brother on his way?"

I stare at her blankly, and she rolls her eyes.

"Cal," she snaps, and he pulls his phone out.

On some level, I guess doing something, any nonsensical thing, keeps the mind occupied. But I can't deal with people right now.

I resume my pacing. In the next half hour, Roxy arrives with clean clothes for me. Someone shoves a coffee into my hand. Saar's other brother, Finn, and his wife show up.

And then the friends, Cora and Lily, I think. I remember them from Cal's vows renewal last Christmas.

I'm glad she has them in her life. I'm kind of grateful they are here, I think. At the same time, they grind on my nerves.

All the silent gazes, whispered words, unspoken accusations, and the fucking behemoth of worry they bring with them are unbearable.

When the double doors open again, I groan. Dorothy Quinn walks into the hallway, dressed in a simple wrap dress and without makeup, and yet looking very put-together.

And while I am still not ready to face her, her presence somehow makes the harsh light softer, the cold room warmer, the bleak situation slightly more bearable.

"Declan had to stay with the children." She wraps me in her arms, and I somehow get lost in her embrace, even though she is at least a foot shorter than me.

Her hug is... it's all it used to be when I was a little boy, and just like a little boy, a sob escapes me.

I tame the fucker, and don't let everyone see me broken, but, fuck, it's hard to pretend I'm whole.

Mom pats my back and ushers me away from the group as if she knows me. Because she fucking does.

She opens some door and pushes me inside an exam room, where I'm pretty sure we shouldn't be. She pulls me into another hug. "Let it out, son."

And fuck, if this woman doesn't know how to kill

me with her love and compassion. I let go and sob. "I should have—"

"No should-haves. Cry because you're sorry. Cry because you're sad. It's okay. Let go. But I'm not letting you blame yourself for anything that happened tonight. Unless it was you who pulled the trigger." She pushes me to a chair, hands me a handkerchief, and holds my shoulder.

I lower my head to my palms. The pain, spreading like acid, burns my throat, chars my chest cavity, singes my stomach.

"I love her." Not sure why I'm clarifying that.

"She's a great woman. I'm happy for you."

I wipe the stupid tears. "You met her?"

Mom shrugs, a coy smile on her face.

"I'm sorry I ignored you for so long." I lower my head.

"Well, you owe me some quality mother/son time, but let's focus on your wife now."

My wife.

She felt so mine just a few hours ago, but it's so easy to fall into that illusion when I'm around Saar.

"According to the latest update, the injuries are not life-threatening. Let's go back in case there is more news." Mom swipes her hands over my shoulders, adjusting my now-clean shirt, like looking presentable is what matters now.

"How do you know?"

"I'm on the board here, didn't you know?" She shakes her head and gives me a peck on my cheek.

"Thank you, Mom." I stand, my legs shaking, and reach for the door handle.

"Corm, this might not be the right time, but I guess..." She trails off, and then takes a deep breath and continues, "Your father was never home. After Declan was born, Connor dived into work. I lost a baby girl a year later, and we grew apart. I was alone with my grief. He was working in the office to deal with his.

"I met a man, and he was there, listening, available, charming. But being with him made me realize how much I loved your father, and it made me fight harder for him. He forgave me, he accepted his role in my affair, and he accepted you with love. You became the reason we healed."

I bow my head, shaking it. "If you're trying to distract me, it's not working. I don't have the capacity to deal with this."

"What I'm trying to say is that you deserve love. I'm glad you stopped pushing it away, but it's in times like these when we need to embrace love rather than anger and fear."

I swallow around the lump in my throat. I want to retort that *that's easier said than done*, but Saar deserves better. Saar deserves all my affection.

She's had enough of my bullying and power-tripping. She deserves better. I might not be the best she deserves, but fuck, I'll try to be that for her.

And hopefully, she will learn to trust me.

But that hope dies before I can allow it to fully blossom.

Chapter 28

Corm

Helpless.

When we join the others, an administrator is waiting for us. I guess Mom being on the board got many people an early wake-up call.

"Mrs. Quinn, I'm sorry to have kept you here. We have a waiting room set up for you. From what I understand, they will be transferring Ms. van den Linden to the post-op soon, and the doctor will come to give you an update," he informs us.

I want to remind him that Saar is no longer Ms. van den Linden, but I refrain, because with the other Mrs. Quinn present, it would only cause confusion. And it would not help Saar anyway.

Helpless.

We're all corralled into a boardroom, where trays

with fruit, bagels, and fresh coffee are waiting like this was a business meeting.

"This is the best we could do," the administrator apologizes, but I tune him out and walk over to the window, ignoring the others.

But my need for solitude is interrupted immediately. I more sense than see a small figure beside me. In the window's reflection, I recognize Saar's friend with the weird amateur pixie haircut.

Is it Cora or Lily? I should know that. I should have cared about her life more. Fuck, I'm going to have these women over at my house regularly from now on.

Lily or Cora doesn't say anything, and I don't quite know how to react, so I grumble. "If you say everything is going to be okay—"

"I wasn't. Not because I don't think everything will be okay. It will. But I'm sure you're probably sick of hearing that."

Something tells me she speaks from experience. "Then—"

"I didn't come to say anything. Words are meaningless in these kinds of situations. I came to stand here because I know Saar wouldn't want you to be alone."

I whip my head to her, stunned. Well, she may think words are meaningless, but her words just tilted my world on its axis.

"I thought I made her life miserable." I shamelessly

fish for some confirmation that Saar told her friend... I don't know what. Something she didn't tell me.

"Well, you both rode that hate train with honor." She giggles. "But in the last few weeks, you made her happy. I think she makes you happy, too."

"She does."

We turn to stare at the awakening city in silence. Behind us, chairs squeak, coffee is poured, things are moved, but nobody talks.

Helpless.

Everything is happening in a silent choreography, where everyone is exhausted by the waiting and uncertainty. On the background of that soundtrack of worry, I'm grateful for my current company.

"I'm Lily, by the way," she offers.

Shit. "How did you know?"

"You might make my friend happy, but you're still an asshole." She giggles.

I chuckle humorlessly, and want to vow to her I will protect her friend better from now on, but the door opens and I whip around.

"Oh." A man in scrubs with a mask pulled down to his chin looks around the room, probably taken aback by the number of people.

"Dr. Freedman, you can speak freely," my mother says gently, like she is in charge here. "It's just the immediate family." She smiles confidently, as if she knows everyone in the room besides me. And the doctor, apparently.

"Mrs. Quinn?" he asks, and she nods.

I guess they didn't know each other, but someone warned him a board member was here. I wonder if that's a good thing.

I also wonder if my domineering tendencies don't come from my mom, but I file that thought to digest later and focus on the surgeon who looks too exhausted.

"Is she okay?" The words rasp my sore throat.

He steps in, the door closing behind him. My chest feels tight as he takes a cup of coffee from my mom.

Seriously, we're going to host a party now? What the fuck? He's been here for half a minute, and I feel like I lost several lifetimes.

"She sustained two injuries—one to her upper arm, which required surgery to repair the muscle and tendons, and a second, more superficial wound to the head."

Yes, fucker, I know that. I squeeze the back of the chair in front of me in a white-knuckle grip.

"The head wound?" I choke out, dreading and clinging to his every word, a cold weight settling in my stomach.

He glances at the chart he's been holding. "The bullet grazed her skull, causing laceration and concussion. Fortunately, it didn't penetrate her brain. She did, however, sustain some trauma to the scalp and skull. We're monitoring her closely for any signs of swelling or bleeding. As of now, she's stable."

I shake with pent-up anxiety, struggling to process his words. "As of now?" My voice comes out rough, barely controlled.

"Right now, the primary concern is physical recovery. She will require physiotherapy to regain full mobility of her arm. The head injury is more unpredictable. We'll need to monitor her for neurological function once she regains consciousness."

The knot in my chest that has been depriving me of oxygen since the first gunshot tightens. Panic rises, but I try to breathe through it.

"What does that mean?" Celeste asks.

"Emotional trauma is not uncommon in victims of violent incidents," Freedman says. "She could develop symptoms of PTSD, flashbacks, anxiety, difficulty to process what happened."

The words hit me right in the solar plexus, cold sweat trickling down my back. My beautiful Saar—so strong, so fierce—might wake up with her body shattered, and her mind locked in a nightmare.

Never in my life have I felt this powerless.

"What does she need now? What do we do?" Finn steps forward, his voice shaking with anger.

"She needs rest," the doctor replies, his voice steady. "We'll keep her sedated for the next several hours to give her body and brain time to heal."

"When can I see her?" I start toward the door before he gets a chance to answer, grinding my jaw so tightly it aches.

"I will have to insist that only one or two of you stay with her." He looks around the room again, his gaze stern, ready to throw the group out if we protest.

"I'm her husband," I growl.

"For fuck's sake. It's not a real marriage," Finn snaps.

Somewhere behind me, my mom gasps.

Freedman's eyes widen. "I'll send a nurse here while you choose who is staying with Ms. van den Linden."

"Mrs. Quinn. She's my wife," I roar at the doctor who rushes out.

"Cal and Celeste should stay with her," Finn says. "Celeste is her best friend."

"I'm her fucking husband, and I'm staying with her."

Celeste groans, standing up. "I'll stay with her, but I'm sure she would want Corm by her side."

Finn and Cal glare at her, and then at me.

"Jesus, the three of you." The other friend—this must be Cora—stands between us. "Their marriage is not so fake anymore. So lay off, the two of you. We'll stay here, and Celeste will text us updates."

Cal huffs. "The marriage is real?"

"What the fuck?" Finn glowers at me.

"Finn van den Linden, sit fucking down right now," his wife orders. I like her instantly.

The nurse comes in, and with no further altercation, Celeste and I follow her.

Saar's chests moves evenly. I've been staring at that even, peaceful movement for twenty-four hours.

I've been clinging to it like it's the only thread that connects me to my sanity. To some sort of solace.

Celeste left to catch some shuteye, but I refuse to move from her bedside. Livia sent meals that are left uneaten on the windowsill. Everyone kept texting me, so I turned off the phone.

Time stretches and collapses at the same time, while I sit here suspended in a vacuum of fear, doubt, and anxiety.

Never have I felt this broken.

Never have I felt this insignificant.

Never have I felt this hopeful.

Never have I wanted to switch places with anyone this much.

When we're out of here, I'm taking her on vacation. I'm taking her on all the dates she deserves.

I've been making plans for us to pass the time and focus on the good, the future, on us instead of the uncertainty.

Fuck, I hate uncertainty.

The door opens quietly, and Celeste comes in. She is worried, but looks rested, wearing a different dress.

She takes a chair on the other side of the bed and lifts her eyebrows in question. I shake my head, and she understands.

"No change is good, too," she murmurs, rubbing her belly.

"I'm going crazy here," I admit.

"Go outside for a moment—"

"No." I would rather go through Hell and back than leave her side. "They lowered the sedatives; she could wake up any minute."

We sit in silence while I continue staring at Saar's breathing chest like it's my lifeline. It is.

"I never liked you," Celeste says.

"I don't particularly care."

She snorts. "But you cracked her veneer, so I guess I will have to accept you."

Again, like with Lily, I'm a man starved for validation. "Her shell is thick; the hairline fracture I might have caused is not enough yet."

"Her shell is, but her skin is thicker, so that may be to your advantage."

I frown, momentarily moving my gaze from Saar.

"She knows how to deal with assholes." Celeste shrugs, a ghost of a grin on her face.

"Thank you for your vote of confidence." I miss the silence before she returned.

She chuckles now. "What I'm saying is that she is tough, toughened by people in her life and by her career. A weaker man would never get through her walls, so I guess I do approve."

I never wanted her approval, but fuck, I didn't realize how much I needed it. "Thank you for telling me."

"You better treat her like the fucking queen she is."

I smile; these women will be the death of me. But Celeste's words quicken my pulse, regardless.

Returning my gaze to Saar, I tense. Am I imagining it? Her breathing is more labored. Her hand is twitching.

Celeste perks up, noticing the change as well.

"Fuck, my head hurts," Saar rasps, and I gasp, a mixture of relief and a different level of worry lodging inside my chest.

"Saar," Celeste whispers. "Let me call the doctor." Celeste stands to reach for the call button.

I grab Saar's hand, taming my need to squeeze it too tight.

Her eyelids flutter like she is trying but failing to open her eyes.

"Baby." I swallow a sob and kiss her forehead.

Saar frowns and finally pries her eyes open. The dark blue of her eyes is the most mesmerizing sight I've ever seen—even though her pupils are dark, still dilated from the medication.

She blinks a few times and then looks around, probably not sure where she is. Her eyes land on Celeste, and the panic on her face subsides slightly.

Mine, on the other hand, reaches a new high when she rasps, "What the fuck is he doing here?"

Chapter 29

Saar

I'm married?

I'm fucking married.

To Cormac Quinn, no less.

What a nightmare.

The confusion that settled in the moment I opened my eyes hasn't left in the past forty-eight hours.

And being married to that jerk is not even the biggest revelation. Vito Conti stole all my money and shot me?

And my father stole my trust fund. I'm broke and married.

What a nightmare.

And I'm a podcaster. Apparently being shot increased the number of downloads of the two episodes I released so far.

I listened to them both, hoping the missing pieces

would come together. It was my voice, my ideas, but I don't remember saying those words.

Lost.

That's how I feel. At least everyone left now. After I threw them out because I need to think. I need to remember.

Retrograde amnesia caused by trauma. Fuck. It's confusing.

Unable to recall events leading to the incident. In my case, the last memory I have is waiting for Vito at the coffee shop in Milan. I was going to tell him I'm done with modeling.

Corm's hurt face keeps flickering through my mind.

What a nightmare.

Someone knocks softly, and while I don't answer, the door opens anyway.

"Hey." I smile at Lily.

"Sorry I couldn't come sooner; I was working." She tiptoes into the room like she was doing something wrong.

"It's okay. I'm glad you're here."

I sent everyone away because they were too concerned, too worried, too overbearing, but Lily's company has never been over-anything.

She pulls a chair closer and sits, adjusting her glasses. "So you remember me?"

I chuckle. "You're unforgettable."

A smile tugs at the corners of her mouth. "Because of my horrible haircut?"

"Promise me I can give you a makeover when I'm out of here."

She rolls her eyes. "When are you out of here?"

It's a simple question, but it brings the temporarily lighter mood down immediately. "They want to discharge me tomorrow."

"That's great." She toes off her sneakers and lifts her leg on to the chair, resting her chin on it.

"I don't know where to go, Lils." My words hit me with a new intensity, like I haven't been spinning them in my head for hours.

"You don't want to go to Corm?"

"I don't remember his house, or that it was my home. I remember hating the man, which doesn't make me feel particularly keen on going there."

"Your things are there, so maybe go and pack, and you will see how it feels. Maybe returning there will trigger your memories."

"Celeste said the same. She offered I stay with them, but she thinks I should give Corm a chance."

"He loves you, Saar."

"The Cormac Quinn I know only loves himself," I quip, but Lily's words ram through me like a wrecking ball.

His hurt face flickers through my mind. Again.

"He was so devastated the whole time. If I've ever seen a man who wanted to take a bullet for his wife, Corm was it."

I bite my lip, my heart beating wildly, my stomach a knot. "Everything feels so surreal. So many things happened in such a brief span of time, and I don't remember any of them."

"Many significant things happened during that time. You lost yourself, and you kind of found yourself, started to reinvent yourself. In the last two weeks, you were happier than I've ever seen you before."

"Maybe it was the job. That podcast is good."

Lily snorts. "She said humbly."

I close my eyes for a moment. Every time I do that, I hope for a flashback, for anything that confirms I belong by Corm's side.

But it's all just darkness.

"Saar, nobody would blame you if you decide to start anew away from him. But I think it would always bother you. It would always hang above you as this unresolved part of your life. What is the worst outcome, anyway?"

"That I won't remember, and I will be staying with a stranger. A stranger who is clearly suffering from my memory loss the most."

"Or you will remember, and this nightmare will be over. Or you fall in love with him again."

"Was I in love with him?"

She sighs, the sadness rolling off her, seeping into all corners of this room. To all dark corners of my heart. "I don't know."

"Isn't that something I should feel rather than remember?"

She looks at me, her eyes full of compassion, glistening. "Fuck, Saar, I don't know. Do you feel unsafe returning there?"

Unsafe? The question gives me pause.

Weird. Full of doubt. Confused.

But when I close my eyes, what I remember is that fleeting touch of his lips on my forehead when I regained consciousness. It burned my skin in the most familiar way. It warmed my heart, like being home.

Before my mind registered who he was, and I squashed the feeling. But its imprint is there, inside me, vibrating with something I don't understand.

"I don't worry about my safety."

"So what do you worry about?"

I don't really have an answer. "You're right. The worst-case scenario is that I won't remember. He was hurt when I sent him away."

"He must have had something to say about that. That man is a bully."

I stare at her. A bully? That sounds more like the Cormac I know. But he just left, his head down. "He looked broken. I don't want to hurt him again if I don't remember and leave."

"Does he want you to return to his place?"

"I don't know. We didn't really talk."

"Then let him decide if he wants to risk it."

I stare at the ceiling, the sleep evading me. The monotonous humming of the heart monitors should act as white noise, but I'm nowhere close to tired.

Perhaps it's the pain. My arm throbs, but I lied to the doctor to lower the dose of the drugs. I don't want to be sedated. The painkillers make my head foggy, keeping me further from accessing those lost memories.

Maybe I should just call the nurse and confess, so I can get some sleep. Five more minutes and I'll request medication.

I check my phone again. I texted Corm after Lily left, but he hasn't responded. He must be sleeping.

And yet, I'm strangely disappointed. And relieved.

He has a role in my accessible memories. And that role is not a pleasant one. I can't wrap my head around that animosity ever changing. And yet, apparently it did.

I check the phone yet again and then drop it to the nightstand, reaching for the nurse call button.

A soft knock on the door spikes my heart rate.

The cone of light stretches on the floor, and when I look up, my breath hitches. God, the man is breathtakingly beautiful.

He's in jeans and a navy V-neck, his hair messy like he's been running his hand through it. I have seen a lot of models in my life, but God, he rivals them all.

"Hi," he rasps.

I swallow, my mouth a desert. "Hi."

"May I?" He shifts his weight.

I nod, suddenly tongue-tied. That's a new one for me. Well, for the me I remember.

"Sorry it took me so long, I was... Never mind." He shakes his head. "How are you feeling?"

Something in his tone strikes me like lightning. It's the genuine care. He came because I texted him that we should talk. Frankly, I expected him to call back, not to show up.

But it's the caring attitude that throws me off. I used to think my parents cared in their own weird way. That Vito cared—God, was I stupid.

But having Corm's full attention is a very different level of adoration. I don't know what to do with that.

It completely throws me off, and my eyes water.

"What's wrong?" He rushes to my side.

I wipe a tear. Apparently, I lost pieces of my memory and became a crier. "You do care about me, don't you?"

He hangs his head, sighing. When he looks up, he locks me in his gaze, and I'm powerless. My chest constricts, fairy wings fluttering in my stomach.

What is happening? I'm scared to look away. It's like something is passing between us that I don't understand, but which is familiar.

It's fleeting at the same time, just grazing the edges of my mind, teasing me. I try to grasp it, to catch it, to keep it, but I can't. Goddammit.

He opens his mouth and closes it. Then he tries to start again.

Please don't say you love me, because I don't know who we are to each other, but I don't want to hurt you.

"Of course I care." His tone is aloof, like he gripped the reins of control and governs his reactions and words now.

It's strangely disappointing, and freeing at the same time.

"They want to discharge me tomorrow." I shift and wince. I should have taken the stupid drugs.

His entire body moves, and then stills. Like he wanted to reach out, but he caught himself. "I'm calling the..." He shakes his head. "Should I call the doctor?"

"No, it's okay." We stare at each other, awkwardness stretching between us. "Thank you," I add, and his shoulders relax a bit.

"So, you're out of here tomorrow..." He licks his lips, looking at me with hooded eyes.

He doesn't look like the Corm I remember—larger than life, owning the air around him, ego spread through several zip codes.

He looks like a man grieving.

"Is it okay if I stay at your house?"

His eyes widen. "Of course." He steps closer, his arm rising.

"For the time being," I add, to protect myself and to stop him from touching me.

He drops his hand to the side-railing of my bed, squeezing it in a white-knuckled grip.

"Anything you need, The Morrigan," he rasps, his eyes searching mine.

"The Morrigan?"

"Never mind." He shakes his head. "You should get some sleep."

I nod. "Yeah, I guess." I fidget.

"Are you sure you don't need the doctor?"

I chuckle. "Chill. I'll call the nurse to help me."

"Anything I can do?"

I sigh. "No. I need to go to the toilet. I hate that

stupid bedpan, but they don't want me to walk alone at night yet."

"I'll help you."

The authority in his voice startles me. On impulse, I want to refuse just to make a point... Not sure what point exactly, but I really need to pee.

Also, having him here isn't as weird as I feared. It actually is comforting.

"Okay." I nod reluctantly.

I pull the heart monitor clip from my finger and shift to one side, so I can apply my weight on my healthy arm to sit.

I grunt. "Give me a moment."

He practically vibrates with pent-up energy beside me as I attempt to push off the mattress again.

"Fuck it," he growls, and scoops me up bridal-style. Carefully.

"You're not a patient man, I take it."

It was meant to be a reprimand, to assert my independence, but it comes out like a tease. Maybe because being in his arms distracts me, and not in the unwanted way.

His scent envelopes me with the same familiarity his presence does. It's confusing, but I decide not to fight it.

I'll be living with him—in his house—so I may as well lean into all the complicated emotions.

Running away from them won't help me sort things out.

"I'm learning," he grumbles.

He puts me down gently by the toilet in a small hospital bathroom, but doesn't move.

"Are you going to watch me?"

"Yes."

He doesn't even flinch, just leans in the doorway looking like a god of sin. My pussy clenches with appreciation. Really?

Sighing, I sit down and pee, hoping the gown is covering me enough to retain some modesty.

"Have you watched me in the bathroom before?"

"Yes." A playful smirk ghosts his worry-stricken face, and God, I want to see more of it.

"Do you have some strange peeing kink?"

The question wipes out his grin, and I regret bringing awkwardness into this.

But when I look up, his gaze meets mine, full of heat and something else I can't decipher.

"I have a you kink," he drawls, and I swear his words have a direct line to my core.

I'm in the most un-sexy position, and yet I feel like a goddess under his dangerous scrutiny. I might not remember being his wife, but my body hums with... Is it recognition? Or is it just chemistry?

We stare at each other, suspended in a strange

vacuum where this man I think I hate feels more like a kindred soul than anyone ever did.

Perhaps the heart does remember. And if not my heart, my lady parts do. Or she is just one greedy pussy.

“This is so strange.” I swallow.

He licks his bottom lip, and the simple notion wipes out any thoughts.

“Do you want some privacy?” He breaks the silence that stretched for a lifetime.

I nod, and he averts his eyes away from me. He doesn’t move, doesn’t turn, doesn’t step out. He stays rooted in the doorway like a sentry.

And for some outlandish reason, I miss his confining gaze immediately.

After I clean myself, I stand up and shuffle to the sink. Our gazes lock once again in the mirror.

His eyes tell a tale of hurt and love.

My eyes try to understand his silent story.

But my mind is blank. It doesn’t catch up with the freight train of emotions and the raw need swirling through me.

“Can I stay tonight?”

Warmth floods my cheeks, and my heart races.

Corm chuckles. “Relax, I will just sit by your bed.”

* * *

If I thought having Corm helping me pee and then watching me sleep was awkward, I didn't fully appreciate how useless my arm is when getting dressed.

While I sit on the bed, he slides my panties up my legs. His fingers graze my skin as he pulls them up my ankles to above my knees.

I'm indignant and aroused at the same time. More embarrassed. I think. By my helplessness, and by my reaction to his touch.

While he can't push my panties any farther, his hands continue up my thighs. His touch sears through the flimsy fabric, and I stifle a moan.

He swallows, his gaze burning my skin.

I need to look away. I should stop him, but I don't want to. I want him to trigger something in me, anything that would bring the memories back.

It's not only about the two of us. It's about my own identity. I didn't know how two-plus months of a blackout could almost undo the rest of my life that I still remember.

I keep waiting for some revelation, and none is coming. The therapist told me to be patient, and I want to be, but as Corm slides his hands up my torso, I want him to do something to remind me.

To remind me of him.

Of me.

Of us.

Instead, he scoops me under my arms and lifts me to stand.

"You okay?" He checks, his voice rough as he squats and pulls my panties up.

I nod when he straightens as if I am okay. I'm not. I'm in pain. I'm confused. And I'm fucking horny.

"Did I love you?" I don't know why I ask. What would either of the answers resolve?

He tenses for a beat, grinding his jaw. He takes my hands in his, not really holding it, just grazing my palms with his fingers.

"I can only hope." There is pain in his voice. I might not know him as my husband, but I know agony. Not sure how, but I see it all over his face.

"Hope?"

"You never told me."

Suddenly, I wish I could tell him now; his regret is so palpable, it coils around my insides, spreading pain.

We stand there, so close yet so far from each other. I take a breath, my nipples grazing his chest. His cock hardens between us.

He tucks a strand behind my ear and his hand lingers, his touch feather-like. Cupping my face, he leans forward but stops an inch from me.

His breath fans my face. I shake all over with anticipation, but it seems like he is waiting for my consent.

Can I give it? Will kissing him be a good thing? Or

will it confuse me further? What if I don't feel anything?

And why the fuck am I in my head right now? It's not like my mind has been useful as of late.

As if he senses the turmoil, he takes the leap and closes the distance, his lips grazing mine.

The jolt of electricity shudders through me at the tender touch. I part my lips, inviting him.

"Ready to get out of here?" Celeste's voice fills the room, and we jump away from each other like she caught us doing something forbidden.

Her hands on her belly, her lips freeze in an unspoken O, her eyes darting between me and Corm.

Cal stops, surprised his wife didn't move, and raises his arm, a coffee sloshing around. "What the fuck are you doing here?"

Shit, I forgot to let them know I'm returning to Corm's.

Corm walks to the window, probably hiding his erection behind the bed.

"The therapist recommended that returning to familiar places might trigger my memory." I clutch my arm, trying to ignore the throbbing—around my wound, in my temples, and in my pussy. Jesus. What timing.

"His house isn't familiar since you don't remember it," Cal rumbles.

"What's your problem?" I yank the sling from the bed, struggling to pull it over my head.

"He should have—"

"Stop it now," Celeste orders and comes to help me, hanging the sling over my head. "Let me help you get dressed."

For some reason, I search for Corm, meeting his eyes and feeling somehow grounded immediately. The intensity of his gaze hits me with a dose of something intimate. Sensual. Raw.

Celeste collects my clothes where Corm laid them out earlier. "Be nice, boys," she warns.

Reluctantly, I break the eye contact and follow her to the small bathroom.

"How did you trick her again?" Cal whispers, his words infused with fury.

"Maybe you should give your sister more credit. She can make her own choices."

Corm's defense brings a smile to my face.

"If something happens to her—"

"Nothing will happen to her," Corm snaps, his tone now laced with anger.

Celeste rolls her eyes before she pulls a crew neck over my head.

"Really? Wasn't it in front of your fucking house she got shot?" Cal retorts.

I pull my good arm through the sleeve, and Celeste

carefully navigates the other sleeve around my wounded arm. She pulls my hair out of the neckline and points to the toilet, so she can help me with the jeans.

I strain my ears, but the room behind the door remains silent. Corm is not rebutting. Why? Is he blaming himself for what happened to me? That's preposterous.

He must feel so alone with that guilt. Losing me and blaming himself.

But I can't take on the responsibility for that. I don't have room to deal with his baggage. And yet a part of me wants to own it, wants to lead him out of his misery.

I barely let Celeste button up my jeans, and I burst out of the small bathroom. The walls were closing in on me already.

"It wasn't your fault!" I glare at Corm. "It wasn't his fault," I tell Cal, and turn back to Cormac. "Don't you dare blame yourself. We can't change what happened. You didn't pull the trigger. You didn't invite Vito into my life. Both of you stop this right now. I have enough chaos in my head at the moment; I don't need either of you adding to it."

The silence that follows is filled with raging testosterone, animosity, and remorse, but at least neither of them dares to protest.

"Is there anything else we need to pack? Are we waiting for the doctor?" Celeste redirects our attention.

I'm about to tell her I have my discharge papers already when the door bursts open again.

When I see the two people who decided to join the party, I step back and hate myself for it.

Corm appears at my side. "What the fuck do you want here?"

My father flinches. "Who the fuck are you?"

He asks as if he doesn't know Cormac Quinn. He might not know my connection to him, but they must have met at functions. Or he must have read about him.

This is just Dad's typical way of showing people how insignificant they are.

"I'm Saar's husband, and I respectfully ask you to get the fuck out of here." Corm's words seem to slap my father. I never knew how satisfying it would be to see my old man taken aback.

My husband.

My married status terrified me after I woke up without my memories, but right now, right here... I step closer to my husband.

"Oh my, you really got married?" My mother clutches her pearls.

"My daughter got shot; I think I have the right to be here, young man." Dad regains his composure, glaring at Corm.

Cal moves to stand by Celeste, like she needs physical protection against our father. Or maybe he needs to be protected from her.

"You mean the daughter you disinherited? The daughter you shipped to Europe when she was a teenager? Get the fuck out of here before—"

I put my hand on Corm's back, and he stops, whipping his head to me. "There is no point," I whisper.

"Charles, will you let them throw us out?" Mother huffs.

"Of course not. I have the right to be here. And I never disinherited my daughter; she chose to abandon the family and betray me."

"Well, if I'm such a disappointment, I fail to see why you bothered coming," I say, getting tired of all the drama this morning keeps bringing.

"It's time you step up and behave like a van den Linden," my father retorts.

"What does that even mean?"

"People are still talking about our fallout, and we don't look good. It's not the image the name van den Linden deserves." Mother pretend-sobs, now clutching her necklace with both hands.

"I will give you your trust fund if you help us fix the optics," my father says.

I blink, almost laughing. My parents want to bribe me to become a dutiful daughter?

Stunned by their lack of compassion or affection, by their negligence and absence of any parenting skills, I rack my brain for words to say.

I don't get to say anything, because my husband's fist lands in my father's face. Charles van den Linden stumbles, patting his bleeding lip as he leans against a door frame.

"You'll regret it," Dad warns. "I have witnesses."

Cal chuckles. "No witnesses here, Dad. Just get the fuck out."

Corm shakes his hand, his knuckles red, and turns to me. "I'm sorry. I shouldn't have—"

"You shouldn't, but I'm glad you did." I smile.

And for the first time in a very long time, I feel like I truly have someone in my corner. Which is confusing as fuck since that someone means nothing to me.

Chapter 30

Corm

The car stops in front of Mom's apartment building. I get out and hold out my hand for Saar. I haven't tried to kiss her since that almost-kiss in the hospital.

I can't have a taste. Not until she's fully on board. I can't give the stupid hope more power.

So I've been waiting.

I've been waiting patiently.

Okay, not so patiently.

But I do wait.

It's her call now.

Mundane tasks have filled the four weeks since Saar returned from the hospital. She's integrated back into life gradually. She's back in the studio recording the podcast, and her audience is soaring.

Her physiotherapy is progressing nicely; she

manages without the painkillers, and is regaining complete mobility in her arm.

The sick bastard in me almost regrets that development, because now she is less and less dependent on me, and it fucking sucks.

We coexist in some strange harmony. It's even more fake than our fake relationship was before. Because this time around, we don't pretend for the public; we avoid in private.

It's like being in love with a woman who lives behind a glass wall. She is here, within my grasp, but the wall is impenetrable.

Some days feel like a continuation of before. We eat together, we laugh, we talk. Other days, she retreats somewhere I can't reach her.

I fucking wish she didn't try so hard to remember. That she would just stay in the present. The present is painfully fragile, but at least it allows her to form new memories of us.

The whole situation between us is so tentative, it drives me crazy. But at the same time, it teaches me patience.

Fuck, if someone had ever told me my life would revolve around the needs of a woman, I would have laughed at them.

But here I am, putting someone else first, trying to let go of my inherent need to control her, to control the situation. Because at the end of the day, I can't fucking control her mind.

"You're here." My mom greets us with a smile that guts me. And reminds me I ignored her for way too long.

"Sorry we're late," Saar says, a bit startled by my mom's embrace.

"You're here, that's what matters. Come on in. I love your dress."

Saar runs her hand over the delicate knitted ridges of her sleeveless dress. "Thank you."

"Saar made it." The pride I feel surprises me.

I mean, my wife is a former top supermodel, and slowly but surely becoming one of the most influential podcasters, and I'm bragging about her knitting skills like I had any credit to take for them.

But when I meet her gaze, my stupid heart swells. She's smiling at me with something akin to adoration... I'm projecting, perhaps, but her smile reaches her eyes. It's not the polite thank-you smile.

It's filled with gratitude, like she feels about me the same way I feel about her.

"I would probably poke my eye with the needles. You should start selling these." Mom ushers us into the sitting room, breaking the moment.

On impulse, I slide my hand into Saar's. She tenses for a moment, but doesn't recoil. A win.

A few steps farther, and she squeezes a bit. Another one.

And when my mother sits us on the sofa, Saar puts my hand on her thigh, leaving her slender hand over mine. Home run.

That simple gesture makes me want to roar. To use all the billboard spaces I bought—okay, not my finest moment—the night before the incident and have my claim on her transmitted to the world.

"Sweetheart, could you go to the cellar for me? I have guests coming over tonight, and I need help with the wine. The menu is on the counter in the kitchen."

I don't want to move, but I'm a grown-ass man, and I can't tell my mother I want to hold hands with my wife. So begrudgingly I trudge away, knowing that this is probably just a ploy to get me out of the room.

After retrieving the menu, I cross the hallway toward the cellar, and I glance into the sitting room.

My mom moved to sit beside Saar, and both of them are laughing. The two most important women in my life are sharing a joyous moment together. I'm rooted to the floor.

Despite my relationship with Saar being in an agonizing limbo, this moment right here is worth waiting for as long as she needs.

She's my wife.

Though I'm a bit jealous of my mother. Saar seemed to have built a bond with her easily.

Is it just me whom she is guarded around?

I go to retrieve the wine, and when I'm back the two of them are standing by the window, their backs to me.

"I've never seen him so smitten. Don't tell him I said that, though," Mother says.

"I wish I knew what I'm feeling," Saar confesses.

I should let them have their conversation or announce my return, but I have never claimed to be noble.

My mom rubs Saar's back. "Feelings are to be felt, not to be known."

"I wish I remembered who we are together."

"But why? If there wasn't history between the two of you, if you met him in the hospital, and that's where your story started... would you be with him now?"

Saar turns her head to my mom. She swallows, but doesn't say anything. The sun seeps behind her, adding soft hues to her ethereal profile.

"That's the question you need to answer for yourself." My mom hugs her. "Take as much time as you need, darling Saar. But if this thing between you doesn't feel like a new beginning to you, please release him, so he can heal."

"I will." Saar nods, and my heart bleeds, spreading dull pain in my chest.

* * *

Things shift between us in the two weeks after our visit with my mom. We attend several functions together for my work, or for Saar's charity causes. It's like we're faking our marriage for the public again.

But we also continue to fake in private. We fake our patience. We pretend we're not frustrated. We feign we don't wonder how long we can go on like this.

I don't work from home as much as I did after her return from the hospital. She doesn't need my help anymore. She needs space.

And I fucking want to occupy all her time and all her space, but I'm learning to give her freedom.

It's fucking killing me. But at least she hasn't left.

"I'm out of here," I tell Larissa, who jumps from her desk like I caught her watching porn.

"It's three o'clock," she sputters.

"So?"

She gives me a puzzled look. "Can I leave too?"

I'm about to nod.

"No, you can't," Roxy warns behind me. "I'm sure you have enough work to fill your paid hours." She smiles, and Larissa rolls her eyes but sits back down.

"Xander needs to talk to you," Roxy says.

"What, are you his messenger now?"

I check my watch. The security camera showed Saar returning home, and I wanted to join her. We have no events to attend tonight, and I'm hoping a quiet night at home can... I don't know what.

"He's on the phone. He just texted me that it's urgent."

By the time we get to his corner, Cal and Declan are already opening his door.

Xander looks up, beaming. "They are all here for your good news, Don." He hits the mute button. "And a bit of groveling." He shimmies his hips like a fucking stripper.

I roll my eyes and hit the speaker. "Donovan."

"Cormac, long time no see. I'm sorry about your wife."

Everyone looks at me, because apparently a response is required when he throws fake compassion my way.

"She is doing well, but I'm assuming my marital bliss isn't the reason we are here."

"You're as pleasant as ever. I got the approval from the board to continue the negotiation with AetherTech, with Merged as the facilitator."

Approval, my ass. They know Vladislav wouldn't get to the table without us. He kept his word and dodged their calls. And after Saar got shot, he forgave my no-show at his pet project gala.

"That's great news, Don. We'll be sending you a draft contract by the end of this week," Xander says.

After we hang up, I make my way to the door.

"Where are you going?" Xander calls.

"Home. My wife is waiting."

"Who knew the marriage would actually sway them at the end," Declan mumbles.

"It was their greed that swayed them." I leave them there, glimpsing Xander pouring whiskey as I round the corner.

It was their greed, but fuck, I'm glad they made me jump through the hoops. The deal may have started it all, but it lost its importance a while ago.

I come home with the same pit in my stomach—part excitement and part dread. I find Saar on the patio. As always.

The days are warmer, the humidity slowly becoming an everyday toll of life in Manhattan, but she started the fire, anyway.

She is wearing an off-shoulder dress, and in the flickering flames, she looks so beautiful. My chest constricts. Fuck, I love this woman.

"Sometimes, I fear you'll remember." My voice is gruff.

She turns her head, half smiling, half frowning. "Why?"

I eat the distance between us and sit beside her. On the first breath, I get a hint of lavender and immediately feel better. "Because if you remembered, you might not choose me. Because then you'll find yourself and realize you deserve better."

She holds my gaze, and fuck, I want to take her into my arms. Take her away from here and start anew.

"Was I unhappy with you?" she asks, and reaches to play with my hair. Fuck, the amount of déjà-vus every day is messing with me.

I want to tell her a similar moment happened already, but what's the point? For her, this is a new moment, and I should cherish it.

Maybe it's me who is stuck in past memories. Maybe it's not her need to remember, but my need for her to remember.

Fuck.

"I hope you were happy."

She picks her phone from the seat beside her. "I was looking at my feed. This is very romantic." She clicks on a post and turns the phone to me. Our elopement announcement.

My stomach sinks.

My initial reaction is to redirect. To avoid. To obscure. That has been my go-to mode for years.

But I don't want to be that man with her. "It's fake."

She knows our match was arranged, but we never talked about the gory details. She turns to me, cross-legged.

Fucking déjà-vus.

"What do you mean it's fake? You don't want me to never feel lonely?"

I close my eyes briefly. "I do, Saar, I do want you to have everything that you need and desire. Even things you don't know you need or desire. You deserve the world and the stars."

She smiles.

"But this post... I hacked your feed, because your previous post competed with my interests. So I told the world we were married. To turn the narrative."

"So we're not married?"

"Yes, we are."

"But—"

I sigh. "We got married later. Or rather, I paid to have a marriage certificate issued."

"So you hacked my feed for your own gain, and I still stayed for the ride?" She leans back like she can't stay close to me.

Fuck. Fearing I'm going to lose her in this conversation, I lean into levity. "I have a magic cock."

I swear, her pupils dilate. Her chest rises and falls

faster. She wets her lips, and the glimpse of her tongue stirs my cock.

She looks at me, heat radiating from her gaze, from her entire body language. "Can I see it?"

"You want to see my cock?"

Said cock stiffens at the idea, all eager, pushing at the zipper of my pants.

My heart hammers in my chest like I'm about to lose my virginity. No, I was high for that event; I don't think I was this... I don't even know what.

"More like I want to feel it." She pushes to her knees beside me.

"Are you sure?"

She gives me a lazy, sexy smile. "Something tells me this is the first time you're denying sex to me... to any woman."

I stand up. "You're the only woman, and I'd never deny you anything."

I unbuckle my belt and lower the zipper, the energy around us zapping with chemistry and anticipation. I lower the waistband of my briefs, and my cock, already covered in pre-cum, springs out. I give it a rough tug, unreasonably pleased with her admiring reaction.

She shuffles closer on her knees and starts unbuttoning my shirt. With every inch of exposed skin, she takes her time discovering. With her lips. Her fingers. Her heated gaze.

Her touch is new and familiar at the same time. My cock is painfully hard, but I don't dare move. It's a strange feeling, letting someone lead.

It's heady as well.

Letting her take the lead and admire my body, decide the pace and the extent of her exploration should feel emasculating, but here, I'm learning from this woman—from my wife—how surrendering is equally powerful.

She pushes my jacket and my shirt off my shoulders. The fire is hot on my back, but it doesn't match the scorching sensation of her gaze.

"You're beautiful," she whispers.

I want to return the compliment, but I'm choked up.

She wraps her hand around my cock and looks at me through hooded eyes. "Can I?"

A shudder rakes through me at her touch. "It's yours, baby; it's always been yours."

I wrap my hand around hers, and her breath hitches.

"It's always been yours." I squeeze around my girth, her hand soft but firm under my palm. "As has been my heart, my soul, my every fucking thought."

She pulls her hand a bit like she wants to retreat, but I don't let her. I move our hands along my shaft.

"You really did love me?"

I'm not sure if it's a question or a statement, but I answer it anyway. "No, Saar, I didn't love you. I still very much do."

I continue giving myself a hand job with our joint hands, barely hanging to any remaining control. I don't want to blow yet.

"But I feel like I'm someone else." She puts her other hand on my heart, probably feeling how it beats like a spooked animal.

It's a simple move, and it may just be to maintain balance, but it feels like so much more.

I kiss her lips gently. Fuck, I miss her. "I would love any version of you. I probably loved the Morrigan's version of you without even knowing. And, baby, you might be a bit lost, but you're still you."

"I don't quite know who that is."

I don't know if it's her or me who starts moving faster, and my cock gets harder, if that's even possible.

"You will discover yourself again. And if you let me be a part of that journey, there is one part of your identity I can offer you." My words come out choppy, the release building up.

She tilts her head in question. "What identity?"

"Mine," I grit out and seize her lips. The kiss is

sloppy and quick as pressure builds at the base of my spine. "My wife."

The world stills as I spill ropes of white into our hands, on her dress, and my stomach. My knees shake, and I rest one on the seat beside her, finding support.

I wipe my hands quickly on my pants and capture her lips and finally kiss her properly.

Fin-fucking-ally.

It's like a first intake of air after being submerged under water.

She moans into my lips and starts tugging at her dress, desperate now. I grip the hem and have her out of it in no time.

Discovering she is naked under it, I groan, my cock immediately ready to go. "Fuck, you're beautiful." I kiss her again, grazing my teeth around her jaw, down her clavicle.

"Fuck me, Corm." She pulls me to her, lowering us both on the sofa and wrapping her legs around my waist.

I'm kissing her and touching her, and wondering if I can ever get enough. But then something makes me pause. Will sex confuse her more?

She groans, exasperated.

"Are you sure about this?" I'm not even sure why I'm asking, because if she hesitates, I don't think I'll be able to stop.

She tugs me to her. "Yes, yes, fuck me." And then she pauses. "But it means nothing."

It feels like an afterthought, a last sane thought to protect herself. And I wholeheartedly disagree, but I can't have her recoil.

"That's what you said the first time we had sex." I find her nipple with my lips, and she arches her back.

"Hm, I guess history repeats itself."

"Fuck, I hope you're right."

I thrust, her pussy stretching around me, and fuck if it doesn't feel like home. "You take me so well, Saar. Fuck, I need to fill all your holes. I missed you so much."

She bucks her hips, seeking friction.

"God, I love this greedy cunt of yours." I start moving. I've just come, but I feel like I'm going to blow again.

But she tenses, and I stop. "What's wrong?"

"Have we done this without condoms?" Her deep line splits her forehead.

I sigh, hoping this déjà vu will morph into a new memory quickly. "Yes, but I can get one," I offer, even though I would love nothing more than planting my baby in her womb.

She smiles. "No, it's okay. I want to feel you."

Perhaps there are memories we can overwrite.

Chapter 31

Saar

Corm roars and collapses beside me in his bed. We enjoyed several surfaces in his house, and I'm blissed out of my mind.

If I thought multiple orgasms would trigger my memory, I was wrong. What they triggered is much more tangible, though.

Connection.

Intimacy.

Tentative trust.

We revisited most of the places in the house. Well, Corm revisited, and I experienced anew. I learned my husband is dominant in the bedroom. Not shocking, knowing him.

More interesting is that I discovered I love it.

Surrendering to him. Belonging to him. Letting him draw pleasure from me, and for me.

"I guess I'm not going to divorce you yet." I roll on to my stomach, teasing him as I kiss his shoulder.

"As if that was an option." He slaps my ass.

The burn is delicious. "Of course, it's an option."

Silence filled with anticipation wraps around us. This time, it's not our bodies that crave release; it's our hearts and souls. Unsaid words, the need for commitment clings between us, stifling the air.

"I married you even after you hacked my feed. Even after I learned I don't need my trust fund?" I repeat my question from earlier.

One that got sidetracked by my need to connect with him physically. I wanted to have sex with him because I hoped my body would remember how it felt.

While the sensations were mind-blowing, I'm still unsure how I used to feel about this man.

He sighs. "You stayed because you wanted to give us a real try."

I lift my gaze to him. The torment in his eyes sucks oxygen from my lungs. I groan and turn on to my back, creating a distance I so desperately want to bridge. I don't want to be hurting this man.

He turns to me abruptly like he's going to pounce, but he stops himself, plopping back onto the mattress with another heavy sigh.

I wish he'd pounce. I wish he would cover my body

with his. Trap me so I can't escape into the void my mind has been.

At the same time, I'm grateful he didn't pounce. He's giving me space, but with more space, more doubts spring, and the endless cycle of uncertainty consumes me.

"And I didn't even deserve it." His voice is gruff. "You stayed, despite me being a bully who tried to control everything in our relationship. You wanted to give us a try. Maybe all of this happened because it was the wrong choice."

He sits up. "But at least you needed me then. And I still failed to protect you. I still failed..."

He draws his legs closer to himself and rests his arms over his knees, his head bowed.

My heart... my very confused heart squeezes, his words searing my throat like I was the one pushing them out. A tear rolls down my cheek.

"And now, you came out of that horrible night stronger than ever, and I'm fucking lost and consumed by hope and fear. I hate it. I hate it so much, and still... still, it's the only place I want to be."

I push to sit beside him. "You said you love me," I croak, and he looks at me bewildered. "It's not just hope and fear you feel then." I give him a small smile, my heart breaking.

Breaking with my inability to give him reassurance.

To console this strong man who was brought down to his knees. Who dared to bare himself, and whose confession opened wounds inside me. And in some strange way, I know that it started the healing process as well.

His arms drop to his sides.

On my next breath, I feel his pinkie touching mine.

It may just be an accidental brush, but as if it were a lifeline, I hook my finger with his.

Our heads turn in sync. Our eyes meet. Our bodies lean toward each other.

I don't think any of those movements are premeditated, but they just happen, like some invisible force draws us together.

"Maybe tonight was me giving us a real try?" The words barely make it out, my throat hurting with emotions.

He smiles and leans in to kiss me. The kiss grows languid and lazy, both of us exhausted from the sex marathon but unwilling to interrupt the tender sensual bond.

When I almost yawn into Corm's mouth, he chuckles and gets on his back, and pulls me to him, arranging me on top of him. "Good night, The Morrigan."

"I can't sleep like this." I slide to his side but wrap my leg over his. "That's better."

My head fits perfectly into the crook of his arm. It makes me unreasonably giddy. I guess my hormone-induced brain is playing tricks on me.

We lie in silence, spent but unable to sleep. At least, I'm not able. As I draw lazy circles on his chest, a realization dawns on me.

I'm wasting my time trying to remember. As if the lost memories could ground me. But it's the new ones that anchor me. In my life. In our lives.

"I lied." Corm's words are like a cold shower over my new discovery.

"About?" I ask, even though I don't want to know.

"Tonight… us… it wasn't nothing. It meant everything to me."

Something dislodges in my chest, freeing my heart. "It meant something to me, too."

He kisses the crown of my head. "Something is better than nothing. I'll take that."

"What is it, Livia?"

I'm at the kitchen island drinking my coffee while trying to jot down notes for today's podcast. I've been flying solo for my first few episodes, but today I have my first guests.

A famous artist, Andrea Cassinetti, with his wife,

Ivy, are coming to talk about their community art classes. Ivy is younger than me, and she's achieved so much in her life already. I can't help but feel a bit intimidated by her.

Hence, I'm trying to be as prepared as possible, but Livia is hovering around like she has nothing better to do.

"You're not going to eat your breakfast today?" the housekeeper asks.

"I'm too stressed. I'll eat later."

She huffs.

Sighing, I put the pen down. "What does it matter if I eat?"

"Mr. Quinn doesn't like it when you don't eat properly."

I snort. "I'm not a child."

"Well, but when you moved here, you were half fainting all the time, and he was worried about you and made sure you ate well." She wipes the polished counter.

I don't know what to say to that. Because I don't remember fainting, but also because I know my iron deficiency used to be a bigger problem when I was still working runways.

Why Livia is mad about it is beyond me, though. "Corm made sure I eat."

"Of course he did. He cares about you, poor man."

"Poor? What's your problem, Livia?"

She shrugs. "It's horrible what happened to you."

Instinctively, my hand rises to the scar on my upper arm. And what does that have to do with me not eating?

As if she realized she's making no sense, she continues, "Not just your injury and your memory, which is horrible. But understandably, the focus is on you. Because you could have... Better not think about it. But that man is hurting, too, and who takes care of him?"

"I do," I say defensively, and so quickly I surprise myself. That came out of nowhere. Or out of somewhere deep and real.

I do want to take care of him. Livia is right. Everything revolved around my recovery. Who was there for Corm?

If this thing between you doesn't feel like a new beginning to you, please release him, so he can heal.

Deep down, in the hidden dark crevices of my heart, I know I belong with my husband. But can I trust that feeling? It's like my mind requires evidence. But aren't the last few weeks evidence enough?

What if it's only been weeks? Clearly it took me only weeks to fall for him the first time. Or to at least have a real relationship amidst the fake marriage. At least that's what he says.

Why do I need more proof? What am I afraid of?

Livia smiles like a Cheshire cat. Like she tricked me into admitting something I wasn't willing to admit to myself yet. She probably did.

"I'm going to get ready. Would you please make me a sandwich for the road?"

"It will be my pleasure." She opens the fridge.

"Oh, Livia, I'll text you a list of ingredients for dinner. I'm cooking tonight." I take my notepad. In the doorway, I turn to her. "Have I ever cooked for him before?"

She beams. "Yes."

* * *

"Saar, so good to see you. What are you going to do with your first paycheck?" Nora, my very hands-off boss, asks when I walk into the studio.

"I didn't know you'd be here." My interview-related anxiety spikes.

She laughs. "Don't worry, I won't breathe down your neck. I only stopped by to say how grateful I am you decided to join the team."

We only spoke over the phone since the injury, and probably before, I guess.

"It's a wonderful opportunity. I love it."

Frankly, this was the most wonderful surprise of my memory loss. That somehow, somewhere, I found the courage to be heard. To be seen for what I have to say instead of how I look.

I'm still in awe that I took the leap, if I'm being honest.

"You took your time, but you made the best decision. Good luck today." She waves at our producer and leaves.

Before I think better of it, I call after her, "Nora, this may be a strange question. But I'm kind of surprised I took the opportunity. I just... I don't remember..."

Shit. I should focus on my interview, not bothering her with my insecurities and confusion.

"When we met the first time, you were lost. As was I when I quit modeling. I guess you were just trying to find yourself again. It took you several weeks, but you finally called me and told me Cormac made you realize you needed to take the leap. I don't know what that handsome husband of yours said or did, but the world is grateful."

I lean against the wall, trying to piece the puzzle together. Something I promised myself not to try anymore.

New memories are what matters, but fuck the darkness—when it comes to my recent life, it is so frustrating.

"Look, Saar, I can't imagine how you feel. But I

know that the only way to live is by moving forward. You more than proved yourself, so who cares how you got here?"

I nod, smiling. She is right.

"Just don't get shot again to improve your ratings." She winks, and I gasp soundlessly. "Shit. Too early for that joke. I'm sorry, darling. You better go; your guests are here."

I turn to find Andrea and Ivy Cassinetti walking down the long corridor. Fuck, they are a gorgeous couple.

He whispers something, and she rolls her eyes. He growls something I can't hear, but his gaze on her is full of adoration. She shakes her head and then notices me.

"Oh my God, Saar, I'm so happy to meet you. And so freaking nervous about this."

And just like that, I know this interview will go well.

And it does. We talk about their community art program, but also about Andrea's addiction and recovery, and Ivy's body image issues. They are both relatable and honest. And I fall in love with my new job a bit more.

"Thank you for being so authentic, and not shying away from issues."

"My antics were well documented in the media, so at least now I own the narrative and hopefully will inspire someone," Andrea says. His phone rings. "Excuse me, ladies."

"Thank you, Ivy. You're such an inspiration." I shake her hand.

Her gaze, filled with adoration, follows her husband. "They say there is a woman behind every man's success, but I think it works the other way. We're often so insecure that it takes a domineering asshole to force us out of our safe cocoon."

And suddenly, I know how to spend my first paycheck. Or some of it, anyway.

* * *

"Is everything okay?" Corm rounds his desk to meet me as I enter his office, rushing to me. He stops abruptly.

We're now sleeping together, but he's been very respectful to me outside the house. Like he's waiting for me to truly commit before he hugs or kisses me out in the open. Perhaps he's trying to protect himself. Or just being as confused as me.

I don't think I'm confused anymore.

I snake my arms around his waist. "Nothing is wrong."

He startles, but immediately responds to my touch and wraps me in a hug, kissing me. Just a peck on the mouth, but I dart my tongue out.

He doesn't need more of an invitation. A guttural sound rumbles through his chest before he dives into the kiss.

It's a perfect kiss. Full of need and relief. Filled with urgency, and an equal amount of peace. It's a kiss to remember.

To never forget.

It's like we came together after a long dance of hesitancy and darkness, and suddenly, the kiss brings the light. To our hearts and our souls.

"What a pleasant surprise." He cups my face and stares at me.

His gaze, as always, starts small explosions all over my body. I almost forget why I came here.

"I got my first paycheck, and I'm treating you to lunch. Larissa says you're available."

"You're taking me for lunch?"

"Yes."

"Is it my magical cock?"

"Definitely." I turn to leave, before we end up testing the magic of his cock.

"I should have fucked you the minute you woke up."

I snort, but my retort dies on my lips. "What is this?"

I'm not sure why I'm asking since it's obvious. A large black-and-white candid photograph by one of the most sought-after photographers hangs on the wall above the sofa. It fits the space perfectly.

I remember when it was taken. I remember why I was laughing. I remember signing the release form for it.

"It's a photograph I got at a charity auction." He turns to get his jacket, avoiding my eyes.

I bite my lips, a grin forming. "But that was like two or three years ago."

"Yes."

"Did you get any other pieces at that auction?"

The photographer donated a collection for that event and called me afterward to tell me that mine went for double the amount of any of the other pieces. I didn't think much of it. I was overbooked at that time, so I was happy my face got more money for a good cause.

"No."

I don't hide my grin anymore. "And you had it here for years?"

He groans. "It was in storage, but I like it here." He sighs, rolling his eyes. "I had it at home, but I took it down before you moved in."

"Why?" My lips tremble with a chuckle I try to stifle.

He looks at me, deadpan. "Like I needed you to think I stalked you."

"Didn't you?"

"Are we going or what?" he snaps, and I giggle.

"Well, I stalked you way before that." I point at the photograph. "I wanted you to take me to a high school dance." For the first time, I don't feel stupid mentioning my teenage crush.

He smiles—and fuck, he should do that more often—and pulls me in for a hug. "Sorry it took me so long to catch up." His lips graze my forehead.

"Did we have this conversation before?"

He lowers his forehead to mine. "Some of it."

"It's a bit unfair; you get to live this twice." I kiss him.

"It's better this time around."

"If I knew you were taking me for burritos..." Corm complains in the car.

"You're so spoiled. You had two of them. You loved them." I roll my eyes.

"I'm not spoiled. I like to enjoy life in style and luxury. To the fullest."

"Sometimes you find the best things at the market, not in a Michelin-starred restaurant. But living to the fullest is something I'm learning."

He smiles at me, with something in his eyes I can't discern. Pride?

"What's with the face?"

"I love seeing you reaching for the stars."

Oh, my poor heart. Having his support means more than I thought I needed.

The car comes to a stop while I still deal with an onslaught of emotions.

"Where are we?" I frown.

"Picking up something." He helps me out of the car and leads me to an animal shelter.

"So nice to see you, Saar. Rolfie missed you, and so did Coco. She grew so much." A woman greets us.

"This is Ethel, the manager here," Corm says.

Ethel startles, but then I guess she fills in the blanks. She then explains how we know each other.

She tells me about our photo op and my volunteering here. I wish I remember that.

But then, I'm here now. He brought me here, and that's what matters.

"Wow, she really grew up." Corm looks at the little ginger cat with caution like she's going to bite him.

I giggle and take her from Ethel. Coco settles against me, purring immediately. "Oh my God, she is adorable."

"Are you ready to take her home?" Ethel asks.

My eyes widen, and I look at Corm, who looks like

he's regretting this visit already. "I guess so," he grumbles.

I squeal, and Coco bares her claws in protest. "Hey, little one, you're coming home with us." I rub her head and she settles again. "We don't have anything at home. What do we even need?"

"I have some supplies you can take, and I'll email you some links to give you the list of essentials," Ethel says. "Or you can study up a bit, get things for her, and come back in a few days."

I bite my lip, the sense of responsibility fighting with the affection I already have for this kitten.

"We'll take her now." Corm sighs, not even trying to hide his annoyance.

"He'll fall in love in no time," Ethel whispers to me.

"And you mentioned Rolfie?"

"We're not getting a dog," Corm says, in that tone of his that doesn't leave room for negotiation.

I roll my eyes. "Yet," I murmur.

"Saar," he warns. I guess he heard me.

Ethel takes me to Rolfie's kennel. The small, white mutt is curled in the farthest corner, but when we approach, his tail wags and he lifts his ears.

"Wow, there is something between the two of you. He's been so apathetic, and now look at him."

Coco fidgets in my hands. "I'll come back tomorrow to spend time with him if that's okay, Ethel."

"That would be wonderful. Before your injury, it looked like he might allow you to take him for a walk."

"Let's try to build his trust again."

We join Corm, who is on his phone in the front office.

Ethel puts Coco in a carrier. "Let me prepare some food and litter for you."

"No need. I got everything organized while I was waiting. Everything should arrive in two hours." Corm puts his phone into his pocket.

"Oh my." Ethel gasps, probably shocked at what money can do.

We get into Corm's car, and I snuggle against him. "Thank you."

It was quite obvious he didn't care much about the visit or Coco, but he did this for me.

"You can thank me on your knees later."

I lick my lips, desire immediately swarming inside me. "I was planning to cook for you, and the cat will need supervision to adapt to new surroundings, so I'm not sure if—"

He grips the back of my neck and turns me to face him. "It's my cock that you will have down your throat tonight, even if I have to hire a fucking cat sitter."

It's the most delicious threat I've ever heard. "I don't know," I tease.

"Are you telling me your pussy isn't weeping right

now, begging to be mine?" he whispers into my ear, and said pussy clenches. Drenched, no less.

Based on the tent in Corm's pants, we're both affected, and I hope Livia is still home to take care of Coco.

The car stops in front of the house. Corm helps me out, and I lean in to pull out the carrier with sleeping Coco.

He moves to cover me like a bodyguard. He's been doing that every time we get out of the car together.

With the reinforced security, there is no chance someone would sneak in and shoot at us again, but I guess we both have post-traumatic responses that help us cope.

I practically feel the anxious energy radiating from him each time we stand here. It's kind of ironic how, among all the memories I don't have, this one is the most prevalent. I don't recall the events, but I have a memory of it. In my scar. In the black space in my mind.

A sense of resolution grips me as I realize I need to rewrite this particular memory. Otherwise, I would remain the victim. I'm not giving that to Vito. I deserve better.

"Corm." I put the carrier on the ground.

He puts his hand on the small of my back, trying to

usher me in as quickly as possible, as he's been doing whenever we are here.

I stop. "No, wait. I need to tell you something."

He opens his mouth, but then closes it. Like he wants to order me to go inside, but feels my urgency to stay here.

"I think I'm falling," I say.

He blinks a few times. Then looks down and scans my body, before he understands what I'm trying to say.

He steps closer and cups my face, his own lit up. "I'll catch you, The Morrigan. I'm right here. I'll always be here."

"Even if I don't remember us?"

"Always. I'll love you even if I have to introduce myself to you every single day. You don't need to remember the past, Saar, I'm only asking you to embrace the future. You're my future. I love you, baby."

Epilogue

Saar

LILY

Sorry, I'll be late.

CORA

Are you on another date?

LILY

I'm breaking up with him.

Ouch. Are you okay?

LILY

Sure. No worries.

@Celeste are you coming?

CELESTE

I can't wait to get out of the house.

Are you still pregnant? (laughing emoji)

CELESTE

(crying emoji)

If I had any doubts that I love this man, seeing him snuggled on the outdoor sofa with Coco in his arms just about melts my heart.

He complained about her for half a minute before they fell for each other. This was supposed to be my cat, but the two are inseparable.

I stand in the door, not wanting to interrupt the moment. And I'm not going to lie, but seeing a brawny man petting a tiny kitten is downright sexy.

He is still a growly, domineering asshole most of the time, but he lets his softer side come out more often. At least at home.

"This animal is therapeutic." The timbre of his voice washes over me like honey.

I guess I can't go undetected. My husband has some special sense knowing where I am all the time. "Did you work from home again?"

"Maybe."

"Because of Coco?"

"She calms me, everyone benefits."

I laugh, and Coco stirs and jumps down, rolling around on the ground before she saunters away.

"Sorry I interrupted your cuddling time," I tease.

"I prefer your cuddles." He looks at me with that devilish gaze and pats the seat beside him. "Come here." It's an order, and *cuddling* is not what he has in mind.

"We have guests arriving in two hours, and there are things to prepare."

"What things? The caterers will take care of everything, and they're here in one hour. Plenty of time to check how soaked your pussy is, and decide where you would like my cock."

"I need to shower and get my hair done—"

"I said come here, The Morrigan."

Shivers shudder through me at his command, and at that stupid name he says in that sexy Irish accent. It rolls off his tongue with such sensuality, I almost want him to use it more often.

I amble to him, taking my time, using my modeling training to sway my hips just the perfect way.

He eats me with his gaze, tapping his fingers on the backrest, slowly losing his patience. I'm going to get it if I continue teasing him, but fuck if that isn't half of the fun.

When I reach the sofa, I jut out my hip to the side, perching my hand on it, and strike a pose as if this was a catwalk.

He doesn't move, but the heat from his gaze

scorches me, regardless. It's a hot, sweltering day at the end of June, and there are fans running around the patio to manufacture the breeze that left Manhattan for the summer.

My hair is flowing, and the hem of my dress shimmies.

"Nice dress. Take it off."

I don't know why I am such a sucker for his aloof commands. I grab the hem of the dress and pull it over my head, dropping it to the ground.

Moving one knee to the seat between his legs, I rake my fingers through his hair. Corm grips my hips and leans in.

"Look at the mess you made of your panties. I was going to dirty you up, but I see you started already." He buries his nose between my legs and inhales indulgently.

The approving hum reverberates through me with heat and want and need, and just everything.

I moan audibly when he squeezes my ass.

He looks up, gazing up and down between my thighs with his chin and devouring me with his eyes.

I'm desperate for him. Every. Single. Time.

"What is it going to be? Where do you want my cock?"

"I have a choice?" I try to sound teasing, but I'm

just a choked-up mess. Not even two minutes in. Jesus. "Aren't you in charge?"

He chuckles, blowing air on my throbbing center. "I'm in charge, but that doesn't mean you have no choice. You always have choices. And I will always honor them."

* * *

Coco hisses and sprints across the hallway as I go to open the door. Where the hell is Livia? The doorbell rings again.

Zoya and Zach, Declan's twins, barrel along after Coco. Jesus, this place is chaos.

"I'm sorry I'm so late." Lily gives me a hug when I open the door.

"How was it?" I ask, my eyes following the twins. Coco dashes from under the console table and practically flies up the stairs.

"Thewe she is." Zoya runs to the staircase.

"Zach, Zoya." I pull Lily with me. "Why don't we go make your burgers? Uncle Corm has a special sauce for you."

"But we want to play with the kitten." Zoya frowns at me, already halfway up the stairs.

"*She* wants to play with her." Zach puts his hands in his pockets with a bored expression.

I don't know how a six-year-old can be so similar to his grown-up grumpy father, but even his stance is a mini copy of Declan.

"Zoya, it's Coco's bedtime," I lie.

Zoya looks up, and then shrugs and bounces down. "What secwet sauce?"

"It wouldn't be a secret if she told you." Zach shakes his head. "Let's go outside."

Zoya starts toward the patio, but then stops. "Auntie Saaw, I wish we had a kitten."

"Dad is allergic," Zach growls. Like father, like son —what can I say?

"Can I come and play with Coco tomowow?"

She looks at me with her huge pleading eyes, and I'm torn between protecting Coco—the very spoiled cat—and teaching this little girl how to be gentle. Shit.

"Maybe Aunty can take you to the shelter where she volunteers, and you can help her with kittens and puppies there," Lily offers, saving me.

"That is a wonderful idea. I'll talk to your dad about it." I ruffle Zoya's hair and mouth a thank you to Lily.

"Dope," Zoya cheers, and runs off.

"Those are Declan's kids?" Lily asks, watching the little girl disappear outside.

"How do you know Declan?" I frown, and Lily's cheeks turn pink.

"From Celeste's Christmas party." She fidgets like I caught her stealing, not remembering someone.

"Oh, I forgot about that. Come and get a drink. How was it?" I don't need to specify. She knows I'm asking about her breakup.

"It was okay." She looks away. "I'm more shaken about a fire alarm at work."

"Oh no. Are you okay?"

She sighs. "I need a drink."

I put my arm around her, and we walk outside.

"Lils," Cora calls as soon as she sees us. They hug and walk over to a small bar set up in the corner.

It's a beautiful evening, and I love being a hostess. I love having a true home for the first time.

Zoya is telling something to Declan, her arms flying around in exaggerated motions. Zach stands beside them, mirroring his father's stance—spread legs, hands in their pockets, bored expression. Or... actually, there is some softness in Declan's face as he listens to his little girl.

Zach's face lights up a bit when his grandma brings him a piece of cake. Corm mended his relationship with his mom, and I'm so grateful, because I found a mother figure in her.

And as I look around the patio, I realize I found a family with these people.

Xander is all flirt and fun, already schmoozing with

Cora and Lily at the bar. It's so nice to see Cora relaxed and outside of her work.

Not sure what Xander is saying, but Lily's cheeks are aflame. But when I look closer, her eyes are on Declan. Or is it on little Zoya? I didn't know my friend liked kids so much.

Cal is doting on Celeste, who plopped on to the lounge bed the minute she arrived, her swelling belly huge.

Roxy is turning the meat on the grill while the chef we hired talks to her. Interesting.

"Here you are." Corm snakes his arms around my waist from behind.

I lean into him. "It's fun having people over."

"I prefer having you for myself." He kisses my neck, and I shudder.

"Behave, Mr. Quinn; we have guests."

"Maybe we can sneak into the pantry for a quickie?"

I laugh and turn to him. "You're incorrigible."

"Guilty as charged." He kisses me. "I love you."

"So, is this a good time to ask if I can adopt Rolfie?"

He groans. "Not this again."

"Come on, Corm, that dog needs a home, and he won't get adopted. He's attached to me," I plead. This is not the first time we've had this conversation.

"I'm attached to you, and so is Coco. There is no room for a dog here."

I roll my eyes. "There is plenty of room. And he won't be your responsibility."

"Baby, you know I'd do anything for you, but this is a hard no. I don't want a dog."

I sigh, but I don't push it further. Though I'm sure he would take to that puppy as he did to Coco, despite his initial hesitation. "Let me get a drink."

He grabs my wrist and yanks me to him, seizing my lips. It's not a sweet peck; it's an X-rated, panty-melting assault.

It doesn't make me feel better about Rolfie, but it does make me feel all giddy about this man who loves me. I guess we can't always agree on everything.

The kiss also earns a lot of cat-calling from the other men here, and hooting from Cora and Roxy.

I'm breathless when he lets me go.

With his hot gaze still on me, he wipes the corners of his mouth with his thumb and then turns to our guests.

"I want to thank you all for coming tonight. When Saar was in the hospital, I vowed to bring her friends around as often as possible. To help her to never feel lonely."

He looks at me, winking. His reference to his fake

post on my feed isn't lost on me, but it doesn't impact me much. I guess some things I forgot are better staying there, lost in my mind. And I know his words are not fake anymore.

He takes my hand and kisses my knuckles. "I grew up in a loving family." He looks at his mom and then his brother. "And I owe my parents a lot for the man I became, and for what I achieved. Saar, on the other hand, became the amazing woman she is despite her upbringing, despite being forced to fend for herself since she was a teenager. Despite growing up under the scrutiny of the public. I admire the shit out of her for that."

My stomach constricts, and a blush rushes to my face. God, this man!

"As you know, our relationship started as a sham, because I needed to close a deal."

"So it's true?" Corm's mom gasps, and Declan snorts.

"Shit, I guess not everyone here knew. Sorry, Mom."

I laugh. "It's not fake anymore, Dorothy." I bite my lips.

"Details, please," Xander calls.

"No," several guests protest.

"Shut up, everyone. Where was I?" Corm takes

over. "It started all wrong, not the way Saar deserved. And I'm not talking about my need to close an important deal... I wanted her back then, but I believed that when I wanted something, I could just take it."

Everyone goes still at the rare moment of public honesty from this man.

"But I know better now. As I said, Saar deserved better then. And she deserves better now, but she seems to have chosen me, and I'm the luckiest bastard. I want to earn her trust, and I'll spend the rest of my life trying to deserve her."

My vision blurs, and my eyes widen when he gets down on one knee, a ring in his hand. "Saar, will you marry me?"

I plaster my hand over my mouth, as if that can help me contain the emotions.

"Dude, you're already married," Xander shouts.

"Is amnesia contagious?" Cal asks.

"For fuck's sake," Corm growls. "Let her answer."

I giggle through my tears. "We are already married."

He sighs. "I got an annulment."

Several people gasp, and someone whistles. My heart jumps to my throat. "You divorced me?"

"How else would I be able to propose?" He smirks. "You deserve better than a fake start."

I sniffle through a grin. "*We* deserve better than a fake start."

"Is that a yes?"

"Yes."

He pushes a beautiful ring—an understated rose-gold band with a sparkling diamond—to my finger, and jumps up to kiss me.

"How could you even divorce me without my consent?" I grin, completely drunk with love.

"The same way I got us married without saying the vows." He kisses me again. "We'll do it the right way this time. A big wedding with carnival food."

"Carnival food?" I frown. Has he lost his mind?

He laughs. "Or whatever you want."

I look at my finger. "It's beautiful. What am I going to do with the other one?"

"I was thinking we can give it to Ethel. It should help them expand and take care of many more animals."

I think my grin will split my face. "I love you, Cormac Quinn."

* * *

The doorbell rings once, twice, three times. I groan. "What time is it?"

"Too early," Corm grumbles, rolling over and covering me with his leg.

"Is Livia here already?"

"I hope so."

Voices and wailing fill the house, and I sit up. "Is that Coco?"

"Fuck, it's ten already?" Corm jumps out of the bed. "Get dressed and come down."

He pulls on sweatpants and a T-shirt and throws a bathrobe at me.

"What's going on?"

"Hurry up," he urges.

"Jesus. Let me brush my hair and my teeth at least. What's the rush?" I slide out from under the covers.

"No time for that." He puts the robe on me and ties the sash, adjusting the two sides so I'm as covered as possible.

"You're weird."

"The surprise downstairs will force you to revisit the adjectives you use when describing me." He ushers me out of the door.

"What are we going to do with you?" Livia speaks in a baby-like voice, and when I look down, my heart stops and restarts.

I run downstairs and then pause at the last minute, remembering I need to approach carefully.

"Rolfie," I whisper, and the mutt perks up. The

tears fall freely as I lean to pet him in his box. He wags his tail and comes to lick my hand.

"Oh my, this is going to be a lively house." Livia sniffles.

Sitting on the ground, I carefully lower one side of the box and wait to see if Rolfie ventures out. He doesn't, but he keeps pushing to the side where I sit, and that's a win.

Completely overcome with emotions, I find Corm standing at the base of the stairs with Coco in his hands.

My family.

"Thank you."

"You can thank me later." He winks, his eyes dark with desire and adoration.

Declan

Fucking hell. Lily is my new nanny.

Thank you for reading Saar and Corm's story. While you're waiting for Declan's single dad/nanny romance, I have another romance with a grumpy, aloof billionaire. ***Reckless Deal*** *is an enemies to lovers* *romance where the job is a dream, but the boss is a nightmare.*

READ RECKLESS DEAL NOW!

Can't get enough of Saar and Corm? He plans a surprise for her, but she surprises him first. Read all about it in the ***bonus scene*** *here: www.maxinehenri.com/afp or scan this code:*

Also by Maxine Henri

Reckless Billionaires Series

Reckless Fate (Massi and Gina's Second Chance Romance)

Reckless Deal (Gio and Mila's Grumpy/Sunshine Bosshole Romance)

Reckless Hunger (Andrea and Ivy's Age Gap Romance)

Reckless Bond (Paris and Finn's Accidental Pregnancy Romance)

Reckless Vow (Brook and Baldo's Marriage of Convenience Romance)

Reckless Desire (Sydney and Hunter's Single Dad Romance)

Reckless Dare (Lo and Dom's Fake Relationship Romance)

Untamed Billionaires Series

Fall in love with the morally grey heroes obsessed with their women

Chosen by The Billionaire (Art and Violet's Enemies

to Lovers Romance)

Chased by the Billionaire (Ness and Rocco's Age gap/Innocent Heroine Romance)

Stolen by the Billionaire (Phillip and Lena's Forbidden Love Romance)

Tempted by Charlie (A Fake Relationship Novella)

Merged Series (Billionaire Marriage of Convenience Stories)

A Temporary Forever (Cal and Celeste's story)

A Forgotten Promise (Saar and Corm's story)

Declan and Lily's story coming in 2025

Book 4 coming in 2025

If you loved this book, please spread the word and leave a review. One sentence is enough to help other readers and make me very happy.

Author's Note

When my son was eighteen months old I got a new lease on life. After being diagnosed with leukemia, I was lucky to be matched with a donor who selflessly gifted me his bone marrow.

The experience changed me, helped me grow, and inspired me to live my life to the fullest.

I couldn't go back to the corporate rat race anymore. I didn't know what was next for me, but I was sure I needed to find a new purpose.

Saar's journey—navigating vulnerability and the uncertainty of identity—is inspired by my own experiences. When we feel a bit lost and a lot exposed. When we have to face our fear of the unknown.

I've had a gorgeous man supporting me on that journey. Thank you, Mr. Henri, for always having my back and for not giving up on me even when you didn't understand what was going on in my head (because I didn't either).

The good thing that came from that period is that I rediscovered my love of writing. Today, I can't imagine doing anything else.

Saar and Corm's story is the longest I've ever written and I apologize for that. I hope you had as much fun reading it as I had writing it.

While writing is a solitary endeavor, bringing a book to your hands, dear reader, requires support from others.

I would like to thank my editor, Kathy. We worked together for the first time and her encouragement and feedback became invaluable in polishing this story.

As always, thank you, Jaycee, for another gorgeous cover. I also need to thank my proofreader, Dan, who has such a keen eye that I always feel confident the book is in as good a shape as possible.

Thank you to the Hambright PR team for helping me spread the word about this book. And of course, my deepest gratitude to all the content creators who read the book and shouted about it. Your support means the world to me.

And you, my dear reader, I appreciate you so much. It is you who motivates me to write more and improve. I hope I didn't disappoint.

Love,

Maxine

About the Author

Maxine Henri is a contemporary romance author who infuses her stories with steamy passion and complex characters. When she's not crafting stories that will have you swooning, she can usually be found sipping on a cup of black tea while reading a good book. Or traveling to new destinations.

Maxine believes that stories matter. They facilitate emotional journeys, inspire and entertain. And when it comes to books and fiction, stories are a great escape and probably the most beneficial addiction on this planet.

Her billionaire romances are the perfect escape, offering a taste of luxury and adventure. Maxine introduces heroes who may have a dark past, but are always balanced by a lighter side. And her leading ladies? They're strong, independent women who may be a little broken, but always find their way in life.

You can connect with her on any of these platforms:

facebook.com/maxinehenriromance
instagram.com/maxinehenriromance
bookbub.com/profile/maxine-henri
amazon.com/author/maxinehenri

Made in the USA
Monee, IL
02 June 2025